John Macken works as a scientist in a large windowless building. He is married with two children.

TRIAL BY BLOOD

Reuben Maitland has lost everything: his job, his marriage, his reputation. Fired from CID's elite forensic investigation unit, he is forced to turn to the other side of the law to find work. Michael Brawn is serving time at Pentonville maximum security prison. He is not who he claims to be. He has been placed there on forged genetic evidence — submitted to the court on Reuben's authority. But who is he, and why is he there? Reuben's only hope of clearing his name depends on him discovering Brawn's real identity and his reason for falsely entering prison. In order to do that though, Reuben must enter Pentonville. And as he is about to find out, prison is a very dangerous place for an ex-copper.

JOHN MACKEN

TRIAL BY BLOOD

Complete and Unabridged

CHARNWOOD
Leicester

First published in Great Britain in 2008 by
Bantam Press
an imprint of
Transworld Publishers, London

First Charnwood Edition
published 2009
by arrangement with
Transworld Publishers
The Random House Group Ltd., London

British Library CIP Data

Macken, John
   Trial by blood.—Large print ed.—
Charnwood library series
   1. Forensic scientist—England—London—Fiction
   2. Ex-police officers—England—London—Fiction
   3. DNA fingerprinting—Fiction 4. Undercover operations—Fiction 5. Suspense fiction 6. Large type books
   I. Title
   823.9'2 [F]

   ISBN 978–1–84782–578–0

Published by
F. A. Thorpe (Publishing)
Anstey, Leicestershire

Set by Words & Graphics Ltd.
Anstey, Leicestershire
Printed and bound in Great Britain by
T. J. International Ltd., Padstow, Cornwall

This book is printed on acid-free paper

For Alison, Joshua and Fraser

ONE

1

Detective Inspector Tamasine Ashcroft leaves the office block, her excitement swirling through the double doors after her. This is the once-in-a-career moment of breakthrough, the link that unites several separate pieces of evidence. After two years, she knows that all three children have been killed by the same man. More importantly, she knows exactly who the man is and where he lives.

Tamasine skips off the pavement and across the road, fresh and excited, despite the fact that it is almost two a.m. Tamasine has been working almost without pause for eight days. When it is as important as this, her reserves of energy are almost boundless. And then, as she knows all too well, she will crash, struggling to get out of bed, a cold coming on.

There is the sound of footsteps behind her. She looks back and sees the figure of a man in the half light. He is moving rapidly, a squeak of trainers on damp paving stones. She is suddenly awake and alert. The alleyway is high-sided, a gap between office blocks and shops, and easily two hundred metres long. Joggers don't take short-cuts to taxi ranks, she recognizes.

DI Ashcroft quickens her pace and risks another glance back. This is no runner. Something in the way he is leaning forward, heading towards her, smacks of hunger. Tamasine hesitates. It is probably

3

nothing, but she should be on her guard. She curses that she has no weapon, no stab jacket, no police radio. He is gaining, and quick. She considers how to tackle him if need be. Think like a copper, she tells herself, not like a frightened panicking female. Stay low, aim a kick to the crotch, that ought to do it.

She stops and turns round, pulling out her warrant card. He is twenty metres away, fifteen, ten.

'I'm a police officer,' DI Ashcroft says, cool and slow, just like she has been taught.

The man stops. Tamasine sees him clearly for the first time, a small light illuminating his features. He is big, wide, bony and unhinged. Dense black hair, thick eyebrows, burning eyes. Teeth bared, a real-life psycho. From his jacket pocket he pulls out a six-inch hunting knife and a clear plastic bag.

'I am a police officer,' she repeats. 'Put the knife down.'

The man stares at her. Tamasine stares back. Her heartbeat is frantic, everything else shut out. Classes on disarming assailants flash through her brain. He smiles at her. Tamasine slides her warrant card away. She knows that if she fails to disarm him, she is utterly alone and at his mercy. The plastic bag scares her. He has done this before. For an instant, she pictures the man she is going to arrest in the morning. Is this just coincidence? she asks herself. And then, an instant decision, an automatic response: she turns and runs.

Halfway down, the alley dog-legs to the left.

4

After that, the main road will be in full view. Tamasine sprints with all her might. Panic is good, she tells herself. Nothing else matters. Forget the child-killing creep. Forget the urgent need for sleep. Just get the hell out of this alley and on to the road. Now.

For as long as she can bear, she doesn't look back. There is a noise behind her, and she glances over her shoulder. He is flat out, twenty metres away, but gaining. There is something in his eyes, and she knows she has to escape. Tamasine puts her head down, the lights of the main road just eighty metres ahead.

Forty metres. She flails, knuckles scraping the bricks. A couple of taxis pass the end of the alley in quick succession. She can hear traffic. He is too far back. When she reaches the main road she will be safe. A night bus pulls up and stops opposite the mouth of the alley. There are people on board, witnesses, her protection. Tamasine risks a final look back in her last few paces. He is ten metres behind, and no longer gaining.

And then she stops dead. The buildings are looming over her. A strange feeling of reverse vertigo dizzies her mind. A flashing whiteness crashes behind her eyes. A bleeding numbness in her mouth. She is unable to move. It takes a second to register. Her brain tries to right itself. She is on the floor.

She tries to get up but can't. Something is weighing her down. The man who was chasing her comes to a halt. He keeps his distance, glancing down at his knife, and then slowly back up again. Tamasine attempts to right herself, but she is wedged firm. The reason floods into her, the last few seconds finally making sense. Something has smashed her clean in the mouth. And that something is now pinning her to the floor.

She cranes her neck round as far as she can. Another man. He is large and firm, an unshakeable bulk. Tamasine looks back at the psycho with the knife. He is bristling, the blade gripped so hard she can see his knuckles in the half light. His full attention has switched from her to the man holding her down. There is nothing but the sound of the psycho's breathing for a few long seconds. Tamasine watches his face gradually alter beneath his brush of black hair. He is boiling over, on edge, almost quivering with intent. But she can also see that he is conflicted. And what she detects in his eyes as she focuses more intently into them scares her more than anything so far.

He is afraid.

And then, pace by pace, he gradually backs away, swallowed by the shadows, never averting his eyes from the man above her.

Tamasine starts to thrash on the floor. A gloved hand reaches down and clamps itself over her mouth. She smells the rubber, her nose desperately sucking air in and out, the oxygen debt needing to be repaid. Another hand fixes itself across her windpipe. She sees the bus pull away from the stop, passengers oblivious, just metres away. Detective Inspector

Tamasine Ashcroft tries to scream but the air is blocked. As she fights and kicks for dear life, two burning questions fill her head.

What did the psycho see? And what was it that scared him?

2

Wide-open pupils stared hard into the fluorescent light, fixed and unblinking. Dr Reuben Maitland dragged a cottonwool earbud across the cold surface of one eyeball, feeling it judder, dry friction jerking its progress, shivering along with it. Up close, fibres of cotton stuck to the surface, while others grabbed at corneal cells and tore them off. He flipped the earbud round and drew it slowly across the other eyeball. Its frozen pupil continued to suck in the penetrating brightness. Surrounding it, burst capillaries oozed into the white, leaking a congealing redness.

Reuben frowned at the man standing over him. Kieran Hobbs half smiled, fascinated and appalled in equal measure. He straightened, scratching at his blond hair.

'Nice line of work,' he said.

'Yeah,' Reuben grunted, dipping each end of the stick into a different tube of blue fluid.

'What's next?'

'You enjoying this?'

'I'm just asking.'

'I've got cheek, hair, blood and eyeballs.'

'Sounds like you're starting a collection.'

'Belt and braces, Kieran.'

'And fucking cummerbund, by the looks of things. I mean, is there any bit of him you don't want?'

Reuben stared sadly down at the corpse on the floor. Or at least what was left of it. It had an amorphous quality, beaten literally to a pulp. The light shirt and trousers were seeping into redness. Reuben imagined for a second that the clothes were all that was holding it together, skin and bones mashed into an oozing paste that was straining to be free.

He lowered his voice. 'Look, if your boy had been a little less sadistic — '

'*Efficient.*'

'Then it might have been a bit easier. But as it is, the body will be contaminated with his fists, his boots and his iron bar.'

'Like I said, efficient.'

Reuben stared into the dead man's face. Efficient indeed. The nose was spread, the forehead collapsed, the mouth a gaping hole, the chin split open. His long black hair was tangled and matted, a burgundy sheen to it. Reuben tried and failed to imagine what he would have looked like before he made the mistake of trying to assassinate Kieran Hobbs. During his time running the élite GeneCrime unit of the Forensic Science Service, Reuben had seen a larger share of corpses than seemed fair. But rarely had he encountered one which had been so systematically ruined.

'I'll give him his due, though.' Kieran dabbed at a small stain on his tailored shirt. 'He didn't speak a word.'

Reuben glanced towards the rear of the disused factory. Leaning against a table was Valdek Kosonovski, one of Kieran's two full-time minders; on the tabletop lay a dark iron bar. Valdek was brooding and still, wearing a grey flannel sweatshirt flecked in red. His torso sustained an ugly musculature which yelled steroid abuse. He stared straight back at Reuben, his eyes lifeless, his face shiny with sweat. Suddenly nauseous, Reuben returned his attention to the ruined corpse on the floor.

'I mean, fair's fair. He came here to kill me. What does he expect?' Kieran asked. 'A cuff around the ear, and on your way, sonny? So my boys get a bit carried away from time to time. Well, tempers tend to fray when someone comes along trying to put a bullet in you.'

Reuben looked momentarily into the eyes of Kieran Hobbs. Thick knitted eyelashes blocked the light, pale blue irises prowling behind, lurking in the shadows. This was the law according to men like Kieran. Someone comes to get you, you get them first and you finish them off. The more brutal you are the better. Word gets around. Even psychopaths baulk at the idea of being beaten to death should it all go wrong.

Reuben glanced back at the mashed face beside Kieran's shoes. 'All the same . . . '

'Don't go soft on me now, Rube. You seen worse than this before.'

Reuben closed a small plastic box of tubes, and slipped it inside his case. 'Yes,' he said, 'I've seen worse than this. And I've also caught the people responsible.'

'What're you trying to say?'

'Keep your boys under control, Kieran. You

10

can't afford to have them killing people like this.'

Kieran glanced over at Valdek, who was now busy cleaning up, a stringy mop soaking up small patches of red and diluting them in a bucket of water. Kieran scratched his chin, his skin so pink and clean it almost shone, his fingernails leaving thin white tracks.

'Yeah, well,' he said, appearing to consider Reuben's words.

'Otherwise . . . '

'Otherwise what?'

Reuben removed his blue plastic shoe covers. He had helped Kieran on and off for almost a year, and still didn't feel comfortable around him. But Kieran had proved increasingly useful over the last twelve months, in ways that Reuben could never have imagined. There had been a time, at the beginning of their relationship, when events had almost come to a head. Like a couple who had rowed and made up, however, it had only brought them closer. But there were days like today when the whole thing stank. Now he found himself fighting every urge in his body to call for back-up, to have Valdek arrested, to have the factory isolated and searched. But he checked himself. He was no longer in the police, and no longer had any back-up to come and rescue him. As he screwed up the shoe covers and squeezed them tight in his fist, he reminded himself that he was an outsider, a civilian, an exile.

'Just keep them out of trouble.'

'OK,' Kieran answered quietly. 'So, when will you let me know?'

11

Reuben pulled his bloody gloves off and sealed them inside a small plastic bag, which he zipped into his case.

'Soon.'

'How soon?'

'Flat out? Forty-eight hours.'

'Great.'

And then Reuben asked the question he'd been trying to avoid. 'What will you do with the body?'

Kieran flashed him a comforting smile. 'You let me worry about that, sunshine.'

He placed his thick fingers on Reuben's shoulder and gave it a playful squeeze, and for a second, Reuben tried his hardest to stop his muscles from recoiling.

3

Reuben picked his way across the weed-strewn car park of a derelict block of flats in Mile End. The tarmac was sprinkled with chunky cubes of shattered windows. The burned-out vehicles had long since been towed away, but the glass lived on, a sparkling reminder of past damage, slowly being ground into the floor. Crunching towards an unpromising doorway, Reuben passed a metal sign proclaiming 'Quebec Towers', its black enamel paint cracked and peeling, its shiny steel supports browned with rust. He glanced around and pulled the main door open. 'Out of decay . . . ' he whispered to himself.

Inside, the cold footwell of the stairs clung on to a faint impression of piss. It was no longer intensely acrid, people now urinating elsewhere, but an acidic dampness had invaded the concrete and was reluctant to leave. Reuben ascended quickly, carrying his small leather case.

On the third floor, he entered a weed-infested corridor and stopped outside a flat. The window and door had been sealed with anti-squatter steel plating, grey and unyielding, perforated by an army of small regular holes. As Reuben ran his fingers over the perforations of the door, he imagined the flat breathing and sighing in the chilly afternoon air, redundant and retired, marking the days until its consignment to rubble.

He moved his hand to the top of the surface and fumbled for a second, until a quiet click released a hidden catch. Reuben pulled the heavy door open and closed it behind him, stepping into a gleaming white room. He glanced around at the grey equipment which lined the benches, at the series of fridges and freezers buzzing away in the corner, at the industrial light fittings bolted to the ceiling. Reuben hoped to God his two companions were home.

'Anyone in?' he called.

Almost immediately, two people shuffled out of the back room.

'You're late,' Judith Meadows announced. She was petite and dark, and, for Reuben's money, enigmatic sometimes to the point of frustration.

Reuben blinked in the brightness for a second, lights glaring off the antiseptic surfaces, the pulped man in the warehouse refusing to leave him.

'Blame the Reaper,' he said. 'He's not always as punctual as you might imagine.'

'So, what have we got?' she asked, squeezing herself into a stiff lab coat. Through the shapeless layer of protective clothing Reuben sensed she was putting on a little weight, her small frame not quite so lost in the garment.

'Eyeballs. Earbuds. Don't ask.'

'Nice. So then we'll find out who the hell he was?'

Reuben handed his leather case to Judith. 'That's the general idea.'

'What do you want doing with the samples exactly?' Judith smiled briefly, a light going on

14

and off in her face. 'I'm late for work.'

'I'll cut you a deal. If you get them dissolving, I'll finish up.'

'Done.'

Judith extracted the earbud from its bag, snipped it in two and manoeuvred each half into a separate tube. She pipetted some clear fluid and pulsed the tube in a small noisy centrifuge.

Over the metallic whine, Moray Carnock cleared his throat. 'What is it they say about the ends and the means?'

Reuben took in the compressed, shabby look of his business partner, glaringly out of place in the ordered laboratory. Even now, after everything, his sheer untidiness still made him smile.

'The less the better.'

'Look, I've got some more work for you.' Moray raised his Aberdonian burr a notch to be heard. 'A little bit borderline, if you catch my drift. But the money's good.'

The centrifuge slowed like a jet engine being turned off after landing. Glassware on a shelf vibrated, dull clinks as closely packed bottles rattled against one another. Judith extracted several more tubes from Reuben's case and slotted them into a hot-block.

Reuben drummed his fingers on a lab bench. 'Good enough for a new centrifuge?'

'Just about. And it's all fully legal and above board.'

'And morally?'

Moray licked his lips. 'Up to the usual high standards.'

Reuben hesitated for a second. 'If we don't do

15

the bad things . . . '

'We can't do the good things.'

Reuben frowned at Moray. Judith raised her dark eyebrows in conspiracy. Regardless of what had happened before, this was Reuben's team, the two people he trusted more than any other. Rights and wrongs were complex beasts. To hunt the truth often meant engaging in deception. But with Judith and Moray, there was an almost osmotic sense of what was just and what was not.

Reuben's thoughts were interrupted by a noise at the door.

'Either of you expecting visitors?' he asked.

Moray and Judith shook their heads, almost in time with each other.

He glanced round as the door swung wide open. In the doorway stood a uniformed police officer. She was late thirties and strikingly beautiful, pale blue eyes offsetting her blonde hair, which was pinned so tight it looked painful.

'So . . . ' she said, stepping inside.

'So indeed,' Reuben answered.

'The infamous Dr Reuben Maitland.'

'It's been a while.'

'I've been busy.'

'To what do we owe the pleasure, DCI Hirst?'

'Just being friendly.' Sarah Hirst flashed an icy smile around the flat. She flicked her eyes at the tubes Judith was holding. 'And this might be?'

'Probably not the sort of thing a detective chief inspector wants to know too much about.'

'Which goes for a lot of your activities, Dr Maitland.'

16

'Really though. What do you want?'

Sarah Hirst chewed her lower lip. 'Robert Abner requires a word with you.'

'*Requires?*'

'Big-boy Abner?' Moray asked. 'Is Dr Maitland in trouble?'

Sarah turned to face him. 'Ah, Moray Carnock. Long time no see. They say you should judge a man by the company he keeps.' Still staring at Moray, she said, 'Well, Dr Maitland, I'd say you were having problems.'

'Good one,' Moray answered dourly.

Behind them, Judith held a couple of tubes up in the air, pointed at them and said, 'Dissolving.' She wriggled out of her lab coat, picked up a pale blue motorcycle helmet, shouted goodbye, and left the flat in a rush.

'Seriously,' Reuben asked, 'what does he want?'

'No idea. Don't have anything to do with him these days. He just came into my office and asked how he could contact you.'

'Something going down at GeneCrime?'

'Just the usual. The odd murder. Maybe a serial rapist . . . '

'And?'

'And that's all I know.'

'If I say no?'

'I'll bring him round here.'

Reuben glanced at Moray, who grimaced a silent 'ouch'.

'What the hell,' Reuben said. 'Let's have a look at the mess you've made of my old department.'

* * *

Sarah Hirst's unmarked police Mondeo stuttered through the crowded streets and alleys of East London, heading towards Euston. A bitter easterly wind was getting up. It flapped at the coats and jackets of the people they passed, who walked quickly, their movements staccato and jerky, as if their whole bodies were shivering. At a set of traffic lights, and surrounded by waves of freezing shoppers, Sarah turned to face Reuben, both hands firmly on the wheel.

'So, how've you been keeping?' she asked, her voice softening.

'Fine.'

'Really?' Sarah glanced from the lights to Reuben and back again. 'You look like shit.'

Reuben smiled. 'It's all the fresh air and exercise. What have you been up to for the last few months?'

'This and that.'

'Anything I need to know about?'

'Certainly not.' Sarah risked another glance away from the lights. 'What's eating you up? You seem a little . . . '

'What?'

'Rough around the edges.'

'Thanks again.' Reuben rubbed his face. He was reluctant to talk. DCI Sarah Hirst wasn't the sort of person you opened yourself up to. But things were getting on top of him, and as long as he stuck to generalities, he couldn't see much harm in spilling his guts. 'Oh, I don't know, Sarah. Things are tough. I can't get access to my

18

son, who always seems to be ill anyway. Lucy is using all her legal skills to keep me away. I spend my days in unsavoury company — no offence — and my evenings, well . . . '

The lights turned green, and Sarah pulled off briskly, tyres squealing in complaint.

'Where, exactly?'

'Sorry, Sarah, you know the rules.'

'Oh come on. Just because you scare the pants off half the Met doesn't mean you have to hide all your life.'

'It's not just the police. I mean, you appreciate that an ex-copper digging into the affairs of an occasionally corrupt police force won't necessarily be welcomed with open arms. But there are others out there. The private investigations — '

'Which I should have you arrested for.'

'Involve some nasty punters.' Reuben reached over and flicked the heating up a notch, already regretting opening his mouth. 'Identifying killers can be taken personally.'

'You play with fire.'

'You're going to get burned by Abner.'

Sarah indicated and pulled over in one seamless movement, braking hard. Reuben pitched forwards, his seatbelt biting.

'I'll drop you here.'

'Do you have to drive so much — '

'What?'

'Like a copper?'

'Just trying to enjoy myself.'

Sarah turned to face him. Reuben noted the concern in her face, a slightly pinched brow, her mouth tight. But Sarah had made a career out of hiding her motives deep below the surface of her expressions.

'Reuben?'

'Yes?'

'A piece of advice. Be nice to him. He's got a lot on his plate.'

Reuben winked at DCI Hirst and left the car. He crossed the road and walked towards a blank and unmarked building. Around the corner, and hidden from direct view from the street, was a security checkpoint manned by an officious-looking guard. As Reuben approached, the guard straightened and took a step forwards.

'Well, well. The long-departed Dr Maitland.'

'Hello, Amit,' Reuben answered, holding his hand out.

Amit gripped it and shook it vigorously. 'Good to see you,' he said, 'after what happened.'

'Likewise, my friend. How's things?'

'Quiet since you left.' Amit picked up a security clearance badge, and waved it under a scanner. 'So, what brings you back to GeneCrime, doc?'

Reuben shrugged. 'Your guess is as good as mine.'

Amit passed the security badge through his window. 'Who are you meeting?'

'Commander Abner.'

'The great man himself. You are indeed honoured.'

'We shall see.'

Reuben raised his eyebrows and opened the door marked 'Forensic Science Service, GeneCrime Unit'. It had been a long time. The antiseptic hum of its corridors rushed to meet him. He paused, breathing deep, the inhalation sucking in a wave of unpleasant memories. Then he stepped forwards, and was slowly swallowed by the building.

4

Reuben took in the sheen of the furniture and the size of the ornaments. Things had changed. The carpet was thicker, his shoes silent across the floor. On the walls hung a number of wooden plaques embossed with obscure mottoes and interlocked pistols. The glass desk was large and round and seemed designed to concentrate attention on its occupant like a lens.

Commander Robert Abner, thick-set, angular and greying, looked up from his paperwork, brown eyes sparkling as he flashed a smile. He gestured for Reuben to sit down.

'Miss your old office?' he asked.

Reuben pushed his pupils around the room. 'You should see the one I have now.'

'What's it been? Nine months?'

'Ten.'

'Still angry?'

'I've moved on. But the personal stuff still gets to me.'

'Nature of the beast. You spend all day hunting the truth at work, there's a danger it'll follow you home.'

'Yeah, well. And now I'm paying for it.'

Reuben looked up from the desk and into Commander Abner's face. He appeared tired and haunted, and Reuben understood that this was an occupational hazard of running GeneCrime.

Similar pressures had driven Reuben deep into amphetamine dependency.

'But you know what still bothers me, Robert, a year on?'

'What?'

'How easily it leaked into the public domain.'

'Once things were in the papers . . . It's no consolation, but letting someone as good as you go wasn't easy.'

'Because I heard a rumour recently. That someone here had been feeding information to a reporter.'

'I thought you'd moved on.' Commander Abner smiled.

'So did I. But when you suddenly realize that maybe your career didn't end the way you thought it did . . . '

'It's possible, I suppose. Leave it with me, Reuben, I'll keep my ears open. I owe you that much.' Commander Abner flicked at some small specks of white on the shoulder of his black uniform. 'So, what are you up to at the moment?' he asked.

'The only things I can do.'

'Which are?'

Reuben sighed. The questions had barely let up since Sarah had arrived at the lab. They would have made a good double act, if they had got on, and if Sarah had been capable of taking orders from anyone, including her boss. 'Identity. Paternity. Fidelity. Whatever comes along. Private cases, commercial cases, you name it.'

Commander Abner stood up and walked over

to the partially blinded internal window that faced into Reuben's old laboratory. Through it, scientists were pipetting, chatting, assessing and comparing. He beckoned Reuben to join him. Reuben watched them; some he recognized, some he didn't. He was suddenly struck by the thought that they looked like lab rats, sniffing their way round as if searching for an exit. Among them Reuben saw Judith, who was flushed after her moped journey, her cheeks reddened by the biting wind.

'You know, Reuben, before I came over to Forensics, I never realized what a dirty science it was. Grubby, oily, filthy. Blood, semen, saliva . . . vaginal, anal, buccal . . . Mopping up other people's spills.' Commander Abner's tone was gentle and contemplative, an off-the-record frankness to it. 'And every day as we get smarter, the criminals get more careful. Sure, miscarriages of justice occur. Sometimes we get the wrong man. And as you know, on occasion this hasn't always been by accident. Which is why I'm here. To sort this mess of a division out. And it's also why I've asked you here.'

'Sir?'

'You know I appreciate what you did for us after you left. Helping bring a corrupt officer down . . . Believe me, Reuben, if it was within my power, I'd reinstate you today. But rules, as we're fond of reminding the public, are rules.' Commander Abner looked absently through the glass. 'Still, there are other ways.'

'What are you getting at?'

'That sometimes as a police force, we can't go where we want to go. Sometimes we can't do what we want to do. We're the good guys, Reuben. We have strict procedures and protocols to keep us on the straight and narrow. Outside GeneCrime as well as inside it.'

'So?'

'So maybe sometimes they're too strict.' He sighed, a low moan of career-long frustration. 'You take the sickos out there raping and murdering seemingly at will. And all the time we're being held back, slowed down. Forms to fill in, boxes to check, health and safety, ethics committees, civil liberties . . . I'd like to just get out there, do some covert testing, rattle a few cages.' Robert Abner rubbed his face wearily. 'Sarah Hirst is smart though. She keeps tabs on you. And not just for your advice. She can see what I can see. That one day we might need you, Reuben. Because you're the only person in the world with a predictive phenotyping system that actually works.'

'Which is why I don't come cheap.'

'I'm serious. One day, I'm going to come knocking. Everything will be *sotto voce*, and there will never be any traceable lines of communication. But the way events are unfolding . . . Well. I'm just saying.' Commander Abner smiled, almost apologetically. 'You know how things are.'

Reuben nodded. He'd felt exactly the same when he was running the forensics section of GeneCrime.

Lost in overlapping thoughts, they continued

to watch the scientists ensconced in their antiseptic cage below. Reuben stared at Judith, who glanced up momentarily. But the window was a two-way mirror, and her eyes failed to track him down.

5

A tracksuited, athletic and well-presented man steps off a quiet tube train many metres beneath the crowded streets of West London. His hair is curly, dark, and shines as if wet. Just behind him, Reuben Maitland and Moray Carnock exit from a different door moments before it closes. The train slides out of the station, a piston within a cylinder, dragging warm, thin air behind it, which ruffles their clothes.

The man turns into a corridor, heading for another platform. The corridor is divided, those coming on the right, those going on the left. Reuben and Moray hug the wall and keep left. The glistening mosaic tiles on the wall catch Reuben's shirt and Moray's jacket. The man peers quickly back, as if aware that he is being followed, but the curve of the corridor protects Reuben and Moray from his straight line of vision. Reuben checks Moray's face. It is etched with concentration and intent.

The passageway continues to bend and twist deep beneath the city. Moray glances behind, making sure the coast is clear. He nods to his partner. Reuben takes a small gun-like object from his pocket. It is warm in his palm. Still walking, he aims it at the neck of the tracksuited man. Ahead is an opening, the junction of several passageways and escalators. Moray has a final look around. There are no direct witnesses.

He taps Reuben on the shoulder. Reuben hesitates a second, sighting down the barrel. There will be one shot, a single opportunity. He knows he must not miss. And if he hits, it has got to be silent and undetectable. Small round CCTV cameras are everywhere, bolted to the walls, taking everything in.

Moray steps in front, shielding Reuben from direct view. Reuben directs the implement over Moray's shoulder. Then, just as the man begins to exit right, Reuben pulls the trigger. The man turns into the corridor and disappears. Moray stops and bends down, examining the floor carefully, picking up a small plastic object the size and shape of a match head. Reuben keeps walking, tracking the target, making sure.

Around the corner, the tracksuited man steps on to an escalator. As he does so, he scratches his neck irritably, a delayed reaction, as if bitten by a mosquito. Reuben knows it doesn't hurt. The man looks around, but sees nothing untoward and continues on, Reuben edging along further behind and allowing Moray to gradually catch up.

★　★　★

Judith Meadows gripped the small plastic probe with a pair of disposable forceps. Her hands, usually steady, trembled slightly, and she struggled to hold the object. She was well aware that working for Reuben was the wrong thing to do. Judith knew she was a trusted and respected technician within GeneCrime, a safe job in a dangerous world, watching murderers and rapists appear as bands on gels and sequences on screens. Remote from the carnage, but watching it all the same. She dropped the probe into a bullet-shaped Eppendorf tube, and bathed it with several drops of a red liquid which smelled vaguely of antiseptic. Judith glanced over at Moray Carnock, who was lounging on a sofa in a grubby overcoat, examining the intricacies of the SkinPunch gun, which was capable of firing a tiny probe and snatching a microscopic sample of skin. But the real action, she thought with a frown as she slotted the tube into a hot-block, lay outside the FSS. It lay in the passions and obsessions of her former boss.

Judith looked at Reuben, who was pushing his arms into a lab coat. He was putting on a little weight, she noted, and she saw this as a good sign. Maybe he was taking things easier, lightening up. But even as she thought the words, she dismissed them. Reuben was always one step ahead, caught up in the next case, the next problem to be solved, just as he always had been when he ran the forensics section of GeneCrime.

'So, remind me again,' she said, to no one in particular.

'This is Mr Anthony McDower,' Moray replied without looking up.

'And his crime?'

'Possibly having an affair with the wife of a Mr Jeremy Accoutey.'

On the far side of the room, Reuben extracted a slide from an elongated cardboard box. He walked over and picked up Judith's tube, peering deep into it. As he did so, Reuben pictured the sinister beauty of the microscopic world of forensics. He saw the human skin cells rushing out of the probe and dispersing, bursting open like grenades, spraying their contents like organic shrapnel, double helices of DNA dancing in the solution, thrashing around one another like aquatic snakes, slowly and inexorably falling to the bottom of the tube.

'As in Jeremy Accoutey the Arsenal defender?' Judith asked.

'None other.'

'Jeremy Accoutey the ex-jailbird?'

Reuben slotted the warm tube into a small blue centrifuge on the lab bench. 'Reformed character, apparently,' he said.

'I don't know,' Judith smiled. 'If you'd seen the game the other night . . . '

Moray treated himself to an extravagant yawn. When he had finished, he said, 'Yeah. The ref blew so much he looked like Louis fucking Armstrong.'

'Well, saint or sinner on the pitch, it's his wife's behaviour that concerns us now.'

'Aye, true enough,' Moray muttered, rummaging in the folds of his substantial coat. 'Here,' he said, passing Reuben a muddy brown envelope, 'this came for you.'

Reuben guided his gloved thumb under the flap and opened the envelope. Inside was a note, thin white paper, Times New Roman font. He read it silently and passed it to Judith.

'What is it?' she asked.

'Read it.'

'"Michael Jeremy Brawn, Prisoner #362847, Pentonville; False genetic identity; More deaths will follow; Find the truth."' Judith raised her full dark eyebrows. 'What's all that about?'

'Beats me. Moray?'

Moray sat partially up on the sofa, battling the considerable gravity of his abdomen. 'Just came via the PO box. Your guess is as good as mine.'

Reuben retrieved the note from Judith and pocketed it. 'Name rings one. Judith?'

Judith shrugged, adjusting the hot-block temperature. 'Maybe.' She took the tube from the centrifuge and placed it into the small metal heater. 'Maybe not. You got the suspension buffer sorted?'

'Must be out of practice. Give me a minute.'

Reuben weighed out a gram of white powder with a spatula. The electronic scales took a moment to settle, digital numbers flickering as the balance fought for calm. Reuben stared down at the powder and licked his dry lips. He then glanced up at the shelf in front of him. On it, among bottles and beakers and jars, was a small white vial marked 'Oblivion'. Reuben dragged his eyes away, forcing them instead to scan the labels of the cold, colourless solutions there, which read NaOH, EtOH, HCl, Tris, NaAcetate, EDTA and TBE. On the shelf above, a large dewar flask bore a peeling sticker which announced 'Liquid Nitrogen'. Reuben ground his teeth as his eyes once again hunted down the vial called Oblivion.

'That's the minute,' Judith said, bringing him round.

Reuben half smiled, tapping the fine white powder into a tube of water, and shaking it vigorously. He appealed for inner calm.

'Well, for now,' he muttered almost to himself, 'let's find out what stories Mr Anthony McDower's DNA can tell us.'

6

The streets close to GeneCrime were a tangle of human movement, people walking, riding, running, driving and fighting their way to their next destination. Roads battled to funnel the movement into ordered directions, white lines keeping the masses apart, yellow lines preventing them stopping, hatched boxes barring their entry. Overall, Sarah Hirst thought with a shrug as she left the war zone of the pavement and entered a glass-fronted café, this was life. Most people on the straight and narrow, some crossing the line, a minority doing just what the hell they wanted.

Inside, Reuben was sitting at a table so square it almost looked sharpened. He was reading a newspaper, its upside-down headline LEADING CID OFFICER RAPED AND MURDERED. Silently, she took in his fair hair, his green eyes, his lean frame with its wide shoulders, the cleft of his chin, the almost perpetual frown of concentration. A sharp mind, a genuine radical, an obsessive visionary with police hang-ups. Be careful, she told herself.

Sarah stepped forward and drummed her chewed fingertips on the cold surface of the table.

'Dr Maitland.'

Reuben took a second to look up, deep absorption clawing at him. 'Detective Chief

Inspector Hirst,' he said, shaking himself round.

'May I?'

'What?'

Sarah nodded at a chair.

'You're late.'

'Things are crazy at GeneCrime.'

'More crazy than normal?'

Sarah sat down heavily. 'Multiple crime scenes, huge sets of forensic samples, the usual backlog grinding through the system.'

'Hell, it's a big unit, I'm sure you'll cope.'

Sarah reached forward and grabbed a couple of chips from Reuben's bowl. 'You mind? I'm starving.'

'Go ahead. Enjoy yourself.'

'Barely enough time to eat at the moment.' Sarah swallowed the deliciously greasy fries. 'So, what did the big man want?'

'Commander Abner? Something and nothing.'

'What was the something?'

'Said he might need my services one day.'

'And the nothing?'

'The usual. How he wished I hadn't taken matters into my own hands and got myself sacked.'

'Any idea what he might need you for?'

'Who knows.'

'But something unauthorized?'

'Guess so. Can't imagine it appearing on any official audits anywhere.' Reuben slid the remnants of his lunch towards Sarah. 'Especially since I'm persona non grata with all of GeneCrime's senior staff.'

Sarah plucked another chip from the bowl.

'Not *all* of them,' she said.

Reuben folded his newspaper and leaned forward. 'Listen, Sarah, what do you know about someone called Michael Jeremy Brawn? Currently serving time in Pentonville.'

'Dunno. The name sounds familiar. You got any more info?'

Reuben hesitated a second. Then he pulled a piece of paper out of his jeans pocket and passed it across to her. 'This came through the post.'

Sarah scanned its contents. ' 'Find the truth.' ' She broke into a smile which made her eyes glisten.

'What?'

'Someone knows how to press your buttons.'

'So?'

'So ignore it. It's a note. Plain and simple.'

'But don't you think — '

'Look, Reuben, not everything has to be some sort of conspiracy. Chill out for once.'

Reuben slid his bowl back and out of Sarah's reach. 'If you're going to be like that.'

'So I'm working on a no-win-no-chip basis now?'

'You scratch my back . . . '

'I'm a trained firearms officer, Dr Maitland. It might pay you to be nice to me.'

'That's more like it. The old Sarah Hirst. Cold, calculating and heartless.'

There was a snap to Reuben's words, making them sound as if they'd been spat directly from his thoughts. He was regretting the outburst almost before it reached Sarah's ears. She stopped, the playfulness disappearing from her face.

'Bit low.'

'I just meant . . . '

'Things change, move on.'

She fell silent. One of her earrings caught the light, winking in the sun, flashing as she moved her head. Reuben marvelled at the vivid reds and deep blues hidden in the pale rays of spring, split and refracted, rescued by the diamond. It was an expensive item, the sort of thing someone else buys you. He wondered for a second who had given the earrings to Sarah, and when.

'Sorry. Crossed that line again,' he said with a sigh.

'I hope I don't need to spell it out.'

'I know. What happened before — '

'I take a calculated risk with you, Reuben, every time I see you. As you say, persona non grata. Disgraced police civilian whose activities I shouldn't turn a blind eye to.'

'Oh come on, Sarah. You get as good as you give.'

'How so?'

'The advice, the technical input. How many times have I helped you?'

'And how many times have I ignored the fact that you have GeneCrime samples in your freezers, a member of GeneCrime doing your dirty work; that you're associating with gangsters like Kieran Hobbs . . . ' Sarah made a show of checking her watch. 'Look, I'm late. I'd better run.'

Reuben unfolded his newspaper. 'Sure.'

'OK, take care of yourself, Reuben, because you're in a very precarious position.' Sarah stood up to leave. 'Seems to me that if you work for gangsters and investigate the police, you've got things all wrong.'

As she strode out, Reuben muttered to himself. Sarah Hirst, as hot and cold as ever, a fragile relationship built on mistrust. Each needing the other, each uneasy with their role. But Reuben was smart enough to know why he unnerved coppers, and what he had that they needed so much.

7

Reuben loitered on the doorstep of a smart suburban semi, dodging a freezing spring shower. He examined his watch, and ran a hand through his damp hair. He glanced around at the tended garden, the immaculate German car, the recently swept pathway. It irked him momentarily that his wife had swapped her quest for domestic perfection so easily from his house to someone else's. Orderliness almost seemed to emanate from her, symmetrizing everything in its wake. He took another deep breath, scanned his watch again, noticed that the hands had barely moved, and finally pushed the doorbell. There was a pause, then the sound of movement, the rumble of carpeted stairs taken in stockinged feet. Reuben stepped back a pace. Keys rattled, the lock fumbled, and then the door was pulled open by a smart-looking woman with a dark bob and piercing green eyes.

'You're early,' she said.

'Good to see you too.'

'Look, there's a problem.'

'What?'

'Josh isn't well.'

'Again?'

Lucy Maitland sighed, sweeping at her disciplined fringe. 'It's nursery. Breeding ground for germs. Anyway, I'm not sure I want him going out, especially in this weather.'

'But we agreed.'

'Before there were germs.'

Behind Lucy, Reuben noticed for the first time the shape of a man lurking deep in the hallway. He approached, the light gradually revealing his brown hair and tanned skin. Reuben raised his eyebrows briefly at him. 'Hello, Shaun,' he said flatly.

'Reuben,' Shaun replied.

'Look, Reuben, I'm sorry your journey has been wasted,' Lucy continued, 'but that's the way it is. Surely you don't want him getting worse?'

'Can't I even see him?'

Shaun paced forward so that he was standing shoulder to shoulder with Lucy. Together, they filled the doorway, a human barrier.

'You know, legally,' Lucy answered, 'you shouldn't even be within four hundred metres of him.'

'But I thought we'd agreed — '

'Or this house.'

'You said you would be flexible.'

Shaun took a step towards Reuben. 'The answer is no. Not when he's sick.'

Reuben held the stare, his eyes wide, his muscles tight, his jaw clamped. Large, fat drops of rain soaked the denim of his jacket. Then Shaun stepped back and slammed the door.

Reuben stood still for a few seconds, facing the door. In its shiny black paint he saw his helplessness staring back, distorted and rejected. Then he turned to walk down the drive and towards the street. But as he passed the front of the house, he glimpsed his eighteen-month-old son through the streaming bay window. Reuben stopped. He tapped his fingernails against the thick double-glazed glass. Joshua looked up from the plastic car he was crashing into the skirting board, and started to totter rapidly and eagerly towards him. 'That's my boy,' Reuben whispered to himself, his breath on the window. 'You still recognize your old dad.'

Then Joshua came to an unsteady halt, caught up in a coughing fit. Reuben watched as his son screwed up his eyes, his mouth wide, his chest silently spasming. He fought the impulse to kick open the front door and hold him. Instead, Lucy entered the room and picked Joshua up, turning him away from Reuben, shielding him with her arm, kissing the back of his neck. She stared coldly at Reuben. He touched the glass with his fingers. Between the double-glazed panes was a fine film of moisture. He saw layers of glass and air, distorting his vision, deadening noises, separating the warm from the cold.

Reuben turned and paced disconsolately back down the short spotless drive, through the lacquered gate and on to the smart South Kensington street that Lucy now called home. He swore under his breath, moist air defeated by the rain. She had only moved a mile and a half since they had separated, but this part of the city was as alien to him as Novosibirsk.

As he crossed the road and headed towards the shelter of an Underground station, Reuben's mobile rang, disrupting his gloominess.

'Dr Maitland?'

Reuben paused. 'Hello, Sarah,' he said.

'About that note.'

'Which note?'

'The one you showed me earlier.'

Reuben turned down a side street. 'The one I should ignore on account of being perpetually suspicious?'

'Right.'

'Well?'

'According to Metropolitan records, Michael Jeremy Brawn got four years for sexual misdemeanour. Pleaded guilty to assaulting a woman on a train. Must be ten or eleven months ago.'

'I'm touched. But why are you ringing me?'

Over the line came the sound of keyboard tapping and coffee being slurped. 'Perpetual suspicion. What else do *you* know about Michael Brawn?'

'Nothing, except his name rings a bell, and the note alleged he has a false genetic identity. Why?'

'Because he's an interesting one. I've had an ask around. Touched a few nerves, especially with senior uniform.'

'Really?'

'Really.'

'Look, about earlier — '

'Forget it.'

'I just . . . considering what we've been through, sometimes I forget the rules.'

'Well, there's a simple way of remembering them. *Professional* and *personal*. Two different things.'

'I know.'

'I don't have a lot of time right now, bigger fish to fry. But I'll try and pull Brawn's record.'

'Very good of you.'

'You're going to be paying me back for this.'

'I was worried about that.'

Sarah took another swig of coffee. 'Be afraid, Dr Maitland,' she said, 'be very afraid.'

Reuben closed his phone and frowned. Mostly, he understood people. How they worked, what they wanted, what they needed. But not Sarah. A Ph.D. in biology and years of detective intuition and still Sarah remained a mystery to him. Unreadable, inconsistent, contrary. And very beautiful. Almost gratefully, Reuben allowed Gloucester Road tube station to beckon him into its dry subterranean world and swallow him up.

8

The Underground lifted Reuben up and nudged him out on to a slowly drying street. Tyres were cutting into the remaining moisture and spraying it into the air. On the pavement, the tread of shoes picked up droplets of water from saturated paving slabs and moved them to new locations. Reuben's jacket tried to rid itself of its invading wetness, an almost invisible steam coaxed out of it by the emerging sun. He shrugged his shoulders, shifting the clammy denim momentarily away from his skin.

He crossed the road, and tracked left and right through a succession of junctions, echoing through an underpass and emerging on to a wide straight road which contained a row of uninspiring shops. After a furniture store, Reuben paused in front of a tall, fortified metal gate. He heard the buzzing click of acceptance and pushed through. A long narrow alleyway took a kink to the right and ended in front of a steel door. Reuben pressed the buzzer twice, waited a second, and then walked through.

Inside, the factory floor was concrete and empty. Strip lights hung down at regular intervals from the low ceiling. There were no windows. At the far end, a lorry-wide shutter was bolted shut. Several industrial tables occupied one corner. They were stainless steel and countersunk, with gleaming taps at each end.

Kieran once told him the area had originally been used for gutting fish, and the rest of the factory for packaging, before the business went bust. Reuben scanned the room for the ruined corpse, beaten and pulped, bleeding into the porous ground, almost expecting it still to be there. He sighed to himself, repeating his mantra under his breath. The ends and the means. The ends and the means.

He spotted Valdek towards the rear of the building, leaning against the same table that had held a bloody iron bar a couple of days earlier. Reuben walked towards a dark green door halfway along the opposite wall. As he did so, Valdek straightened and began lumbering towards him, aiming to cut him off. Reuben slowed his pace, allowing him to catch up. He glanced around. There was no sign of blood on the ground now, the floor scrubbed meticulously clean. An area of darkness was the only sign, still wet where it had been scoured. Reuben wondered whether Valdek had disposed of the dead man himself, dumping him in a river or feeding him to pigs, or some other such underworld treat. What Reuben had found out about the deceased man had lessened his sympathy. Still, nobody deserved to be slowly battered to death in a dingy warehouse by a psycho like Valdek Kosonovski. Reuben tried not to let his disgust show as Valdek reached him.

'What do you want?' Valdek asked.

Reuben said, 'Is your boss in?'

Valdek frowned, his jaw locking. 'He's busy.'

Reuben had met Valdek a handful of times and

had failed to warm to him. He had an Eastern European look which verged on the Slavic, his nose blunt, his face square, his hair receding and lank, longer on the sides and back than was truly fashionable, as if compensating for its retreat. His neck was thick and firmly set, his ears, under his hair, big and bold. Reuben saw the iron bar, clenched fists and leather boots. He pictured muscles swelling and contracting. He imagined flesh bruising, blood leaking, bones cracking.

'How long for?'

'You got an appointment?'

Valdek's English was perfect, despite his roots. He spoke in a low rumbling monotone, verging on the hoarse at times, a canine growl you instinctively didn't want to get on the wrong side of. Reuben wondered whether the steroids he undoubtedly took were fucking with his voice box.

'Yeah,' Reuben answered, stepping over to lean against the bare brick wall.

Valdek followed him. 'Well, while you're not doing anything . . . '

'What?'

'I want to know about it. Forensics.'

'In what way?'

'How long do DNA samples last?'

Reuben squinted at him. 'Depends. Minutes, hours, days, years.'

'Where are people's DNA samples kept?'

'What do you want to know for?'

'And what information do the police keep?'

'Anything else?'

'How do you know if you've been DNA

45

tested? I want to hear all of it.' He glanced around the empty warehouse. 'Here. Now. You and me. Man to man.'

'Why?'

'Because I'm asking you and you're standing here.'

Reuben shrugged. 'Not a good enough answer,' he said.

Valdek appeared to swell. Maybe he just changed his posture, pushed his chest out or lifted his shoulders. But beneath his World Gym sweatshirt there was a standing to attention of muscles, an urgent readiness for action that Reuben knew he was supposed to notice. The guy was on a very short fuse.

'What kind of fucking answer do you want?' Valdek asked, stepping closer.

The air had changed. Menace. Straining at the leash. A finger trembling on a hair trigger. Valdek glared down at him. Reuben met his eyes head on. Blazing, full beam, wide pupils.

'Something better than that,' he answered.

Valdek stood toe to toe with Reuben. 'You arrogant cunt,' he spat, drops of moisture spattering Reuben's face. 'What's your problem?'

Reuben refused to be intimidated. 'My problem is that I don't want to talk to you about forensics.'

'You got an issue with me?'

'I've got an issue with your attitude.'

A door opened ten metres away. Out of the corner of his eye, Reuben recognized Kieran's other minder Nathan strolling over.

'What's going on?' Nathan asked.

46

'We'll come back to this,' Valdek whispered, scowling, his teeth bared.

Nathan approached and Reuben knew that Valdek had had his moment. Valdek stepped away, keeping his distance, brooding, the low ceiling holding the intensity tight.

'Hey, doc,' Nathan said, 'how're you doing?'

Reuben glanced back at Valdek, who avoided his eye. He made a mental note not to antagonize him again. Witnessing the aftermath of a Kosonovski beating had been shocking, but seeing Valdek up close and on edge had surprised him. How quickly things could escalate from nothing, how little provocation was needed. Reuben suspected that Valdek wouldn't have hurt him. Kieran had him on a tight leash. And it had been too tempting not to push him, to see what it took to get him angry. Reuben sensed that one day in the near future, when Kieran had no use for him any more, Sarah Hirst might be getting an anonymous tip-off about Valdek Kosonovski.

'Fine, thanks,' Reuben said.

Nathan was mid-thirties, a serious weight-lifter like Valdek, just as wide but slightly taller. He was the friendly face of Kieran's ever-present minders. Nathan seemed to grin almost permanently, as if he was practising the look for a bodybuilder competition.

'What were you talking about?' Nathan asked. 'I bet it was what you do, wasn't it? Forensics and all that?'

Reuben nodded.

'My missus loves all those shows. With those

shiny labs and the way they outsmart the bad guys. Can't get enough of it.' Nathan had the kind of chirpy cockney accent that almost seemed to have died out in the capital. 'That how it is in real life?'

Reuben glanced around himself, at the factory interior, the two minders, the scrubbed floor, the grubby stench of crime. 'Just like it,' he answered.

'Great. Well, he should be ready for you now,' Nathan said. 'Go on up.'

Reuben pushed through the green door. He thumped up the stairs and paced along a plushly carpeted corridor. At the end, Kieran's office door was open. Reuben found Kieran sitting upright in his leather chair, leaning slightly forward, his blond eyelashes flickering in the bright sunlight like butterfly wings.

Reuben sat down opposite him and said, 'You should keep your boys under control.'

Kieran grinned, a flash of teeth to go with the glint of Rolex and the bling of jewellery. 'They're OK, aren't they? So one of them's a bit, what? *Excitable*. Nothing wrong with that in my business. Sends out the right message to the right people.'

'And everyone else?'

'You get a bit of rough treatment?'

'Something like that.'

Kieran leaned forward and opened a drawer. 'I'm sorry, Reuben. I'll have words. Here, maybe this will help.' He pulled out a thick wad of pristine twenty-pound notes, and slid them across the empty desk.

Reuben hesitated, rubbing his face and sighing.

'What's up?' Kieran asked.

'I'm not proud of what I do for you.'

Kieran puffed his cheeks. 'I'm hurt.'

'Let me tell you a story, Kieran.' Reuben frowned at the bundle of notes, as if they were in some way repellent. 'When I started out in forensics, you were exactly the kind of villain I was after. In fact, I actually spent time on a case involving one of your many syndicates.'

'And then?'

'And then I came to see that what's good and what's bad isn't necessarily so clear cut. I saw coppers beating people up, innocent people. I saw criminals helping others in times of need. And then I started to see something worse.'

'What?'

Reuben moved his eyes away from the money and stared out of the window, looking at the flat, soiled roofs of two-storey shops. 'Around the time I left GeneCrime, a copper began using forensics to put people away. He reasoned that forensics is the one thing juries don't question, the one infallible truth among the chaos of evidence. And it was easy. As long as you had access to the databases and the specimens, you could do what you wanted. Identities could be traded, samples could be inserted or deleted, matches could be found. Science is just people. And people are a mixed lot.'

'There's always been bent coppers,' Kieran shrugged. 'Here, I'll write you a fucking list.'

'But now they're smarter. A new breed using

new tools to get what they want.'

'Forensics, you mean?'

'Sometimes. And as a result, innocent punters languish in jail to further careers, or to substantiate hunches, or to punish suspects in unsolvable crimes.'

'Can't be *that* widespread though.'

'Not necessarily. But it's out there. And I'm worried it might be happening again. Single coppers rarely act alone.'

Kieran Hobbs caressed the smooth skin of his cheeks, feeling for the meaning of Reuben's words. 'So, basically, if I've got this right — and tell me if I haven't — you waste your time running round trying to solve crimes that have already been solved?'

Reuben made a sound halfway between a grunt and a laugh. 'Something like that. Because no one else does. No one else seems to care about the fact that science can be used and abused. No one else seems to care about the truth any more. Just arresting punters and putting them away.'

'So things change, move on. It's life. This place for example.' Kieran waved his arm around the office. 'Nowadays, most of the capital's fish comes already gutted and prepared, a lot of it even flown in from all over the world. Friend of mine runs an import business. It's how I found this place. Nice and quiet and out of the way. And it don't even smell too bad!' Kieran chortled to himself, his smile fading over three or four seconds. 'So new circumstances get exploited by new men. Why you though? What do you care?'

Reuben sighed, blinking away the sunlight. 'Because occasionally things happen that change the way you think. You either ignore it, or you do something about it.'

'Oh fuck. An ex-copper with principles.'

'The rest is only a sideline to finance the big stuff. Paternity suits, industrial espionage' — Reuben took a piece of paper out of his jacket — 'tracking the identities of assassins . . . I mean, no offence, Kieran, but it's small potatoes.'

'It ain't small potatoes when someone comes to kill you.'

'Thought that was just an occupational hazard.'

'So who was he then?'

Reuben squinted, recalling the warehouse below and rubbing his cottonwool bud slowly over the open eyes of the pulped man lying on the floor. 'Ethan de Groot. Dutch in origin, but lived here for some time. There's his last known address and phone number. Thirty-two, single, one previous conviction for possession of cocaine, two for ABH and another for intent. Nice guy.'

'I've seen worse.' Kieran casually scanned the piece of paper, before slotting it into his shirt pocket. 'What I don't get is who sent this Dutch cunt after me. Who is it wants me finished that badly?'

Reuben stared balefully out of the window. 'I'll write you a fucking list,' he whispered to himself.

51

9

Sarah Hirst loitered in the doorway of the flat, a metal cylinder marked 'Cryo-Store' in her hands. From it, a heavy white vapour leaked slowly down towards her stockinged legs and over her leather shoes. Reuben watched her for a second as she walked past him and into the room, vaporized nitrogen swirling behind her like a cloak. There was a fluid loveliness in the way she moved, as if she'd been poured out of a bottle, viscous and honeyed, which the gas exaggerated, like the vapour trails of a banking aircraft. 'Professional and personal,' he whispered to himself. 'Professional and personal.' He locked the metal door and turned to face her.

'What you got?' he asked, pointing with his eyes at the cylinder she was holding.

'I thought you might be asleep.'

'So why did you come?'

Her eyes widened. 'Because what I've got here is good enough to wake you up.'

Sarah paced over to the lab bench. She placed the Cryo-Store carefully down and opened it. Reuben took a pair of elongated forceps from a shelf and retrieved a frozen and preserved Eppendorf tube from the volatile liquid.

'And this is?'

'A DNA sample from none other than Mr Michael Brawn, Pentonville's finest felon.'

'How the hell did you sanction that?'

'Sanction? You don't sanction the removal of a classified forensic sample into the wider community.' Sarah propped herself against a stool, half leaning, half sitting. 'Thought you might have a dabble with your wonder technique of predictive phenotyping. You never know what it might find.'

Reuben ran his eyes quickly around the lab, over its busy shelves, its blank surfaces, its humming freezers, its anonymous equipment. 'Sure. It's that or get a good night's sleep.'

'Anyway, I've got to shoot. We've just had reports of a potential victim, dredged fresh out of the Thames.'

'Like Tamasine Ashcroft?'

'Got to go and oversee the prelims.' Sarah glanced directly at Reuben. 'But, yes, could be another.'

'What have you got so far?'

'Not a fat lot. Except there may be more than one man involved.'

'How so?'

Sarah straightened, the stool complaining as it scuffed the vinyl floor. 'Sorry, Dr M. Need to know basis.' She tugged at the sleeves of her black jacket and smoothed her dark skirt. 'Gotta dash, otherwise the FSS will have already started bitching about GeneCrime taking over. Good luck with the predictive phenotyping.'

'If I decide to do it.'

'Oh, you will.'

Sarah unlocked the door and left the lab with a sad smile which seemed to linger in the room after her. Reuben paused a few seconds, thinking, wondering, trying to decide what made Sarah tick, and what she truly wanted from him. As he slowly inserted himself into the stiff restraint of his lab coat, he whispered, 'I know I should trust her, but . . . ' And then he grunted, taking in the empty space around himself. Whispering to yourself. That was one step closer to lunacy than talking to yourself.

★ ★ ★

The idea behind predictive phenotyping was a simple and brilliant one which had done much to ruin Reuben's career and personal life. The science was good, unexpectedly robust and unerringly accurate. What hurt with predictive phenotyping was the potential for misuse. The ability to determine what a stranger looked like from a microscopic sample of their blood, or hair, or saliva even, brought with it a number of temptations Reuben had been unable to resist. For when your wife is having an affair with an unknown person who leaves hairs behind in your bed . . . Reuben shuddered for a second, revisiting the events of the previous year which had precipitated his sacking from GeneCrime. Sarah's words tracked him down a final time. When the personal and professional get mixed up in a sticky tangle, that's when you know you're in trouble.

As Reuben popped open the tube and extracted a small sample of its contents with a pipette, he felt the spark of the technique's possibility ignite once more. He knew he wouldn't sleep, and that he would work through the night. It wasn't that Michael Brawn interested him per se — a single piece of paper with a few words on it was only a minor red rag — but that the excuse to delve, to probe, to use the technology that only he had access to, bit into him like a snare. Besides, the purity of doing something for the sake of its methodology appealed to him after the grubby, filthy commercial cases he was pursuing. As he flicked a sequencer on, he once again recalled Commander Abner's words, his assertion that predictive phenotyping could be the answer to his problems.

The hours began to get soaked up in an enveloping series of activities and actions: tapping information into a laptop; lying horizontal on a sofa reading a book; taking down the vial marked 'Oblivion' from a shelf; flicking tubes with his index finger; using the same finger to rub amphetamine into his gums; slotting the tubes into a machine; chewing his teeth; reading data off a screen; pipetting coloured fluid on to a DNA chip; staring into screens of numbers; mapping facial coordinates . . .

Reuben pulled his head back from the glow of his laptop. A clock in the corner of the screen read 13:27. He'd worked solidly into the next day. He hesitated, savouring the pause, and then pressed the return key. Slowly, on the screen, a 3D face began to come to life.

Reuben watched, fascinated. Textures and colours, contours and coordinates, depth and tone, pushing and receding, narrowing and widening, lightening and darkening, shaping and defining. He stretched, amphetamine muscles relishing the chance to extend and unfurl. The computer stood still, its result illuminated on the screen. The face was that of an Afro-Caribbean male, mid-forties, mildly obese. In a text box in the corner was printed 'Psycho-Fit of Michael Jeremy Brawn: moderate intellect; schizophrenia negative; likely benign'. Reuben squinted at the 3D image, rotating it with his mouse so that it seemed to be shaking its head.

'So, Mr Brawn,' he frowned, 'nice to meet you at last.'

10

Twelve faces glanced up at Prison Guard Tony Paulers with a dozen expressions ranging from expectation to hatred. Among the negligible middle ground were irritation, apathy, disdain and guilt. Tony Paulers had become adept in his twenty-one years of prison service at simultaneously noting and ignoring what he saw staring back at him from the inmates of Pentonville. Those who beamed were generally up to something, those who growled and snarled either weren't or didn't care who knew it. Either way, he had been spat at and sworn at and kicked so many times in the last two decades that it had become a matter of survival simply to avoid confronting what he saw in the eyes of his inmates.

The TV room was half full, prisoners slumped on plastic chairs, absorbing the daytime trivialities of a world they were locked away from. Tony would be happy if they watched television all day. The lulling, soporific immersion in home improvement and cookery programmes seemed to dampen their spirits. Tony had never been assaulted in the TV room.

He allowed himself a moment to examine the assembled ranks in front of him, naming them in his head, being quietly vigilant, seeing who was where. Hardened cons, care-in-the-community cases, lads who were only months too old for borstal. Tony appreciated that status in here was not a winning smile, or a professional job, or a beautiful wife, or a platinum credit card, or anything else you might strive for on the outside. No, status here was simple and brutal. It was in the twinkling of a bicep, the girth of a chest, the length of a charge sheet. And as he focused on the prisoner he had come to fetch, he realized that this one was different. This one was outside the normal rules of categorization. This one was the exception that proved the rule.

Tony cleared his throat, most prisoners having already switched their attention back to the screen. 'Michael Brawn,' he announced, 'you've got a phone call.'

Tony watched Michael Brawn stand up. He was slow in his movements, almost compellingly so. He recalled the first time he had seen him, nearly a year ago. Tony had been mesmerized from the start, unable to keep his eyes off him. They were drawn to Michael Brawn, fascinated, incapable of moving away. Moths to flames, rabbits to headlights. Tall, lean and intense. A bony hardness about his face. Calm, ordered, in control, and extremely psychopathic. The kind of man who unnerved prison warders, whom they tried to stay on the right side of.

Michael Brawn looked Tony in the eye, standing still in front of him. Tony nodded at the waxen face, pale and gaunt, almost stripped of expression, something unbreakable in the boniness of the cheeks and forehead. He saw the impression of power, almost inviting Tony to try him, and that was what unsettled him. His silent confidence. Tony knew that Brawn rarely spoke, seldom even acknowledged those who talked to him. He just watched them with fixed eyes, and a slight twitch of the eyebrows. As Brawn stepped forward, Tony appreciated that there was intellect there as well. You knew that this man saw into people, understood their motives, read their body language, sized them up before they were even aware of the scrutiny. And that this man had been in situations. He had been beaten, kicked and threatened. He knew what pain and suffering were, and what effect they had on other people.

Michael Brawn passed close, the air from his tall, lean body breezing across Tony's face. Tony turned and followed him, a couple of yards back. Brawn walked briskly along light green corridors and through sets of prison doors. Tony watched from behind, taking in the expressions of prisoners as Brawn passed them. He was no body language expert but had spent enough of his career observing the interactions of criminals to know that Michael Brawn didn't just worry the guards.

They entered a wider corridor housing a series of wall-mounted phones, each with its own graffitied metal hood. Tony watched Brawn snatch the receiver, glance up and down the walkway, and listen intently. He sauntered past, stopping to pass the time of day with a fellow officer. Swivelling slightly, he continued to monitor Brawn. He was hunched over, his head pressed hard into the metal hood, extracting all the privacy he could from it. And then he began to speak, slowly and deliberately, his accent dry and Mancunian. Tony strained to hear over the bland nothingness his colleague was spouting.

'Yeah?' Michael Brawn whispered. 'December. The seventh. Third Sunday. Second Monday. The fourth. Tuesday. August seventeenth. May twelfth . . . '

The other guard continued his spiel, and Tony turned back to him momentarily. 'But the governor wants an anti-smoking initiative, apparently. Some national scheme. And him on, what, sixty a day? Easy. Like to see him come down on to the shop floor reeking of fags and booze and try and implement that one.'

But Tony wasn't really listening. Once again, Michael Brawn was dragging him away, his very presence captivating. This time, it wasn't simply his indefinable difference from the other prisoners. Tony had just learned something new: Brawn was passing code out of the prison.

He watched him hang up and walk nonchalantly back the way he had come. Tony Paulers ended his half conversation with a noncommittal smile, and headed off to his office. He had a phone call of his own to make.

11

He was breathing quickly, but this was good. He liked to feel his lungs expand in his chest, cold with the ache of stretching slightly too hard. The second one had been easy. She had made it possible, had put herself in the right position, given him her vulnerability on a plate. The only problem had been the mugger, the scumbag who had wanted her purse, or whatever he was after. He spat out a wet, sour-tasting ball of phlegm. Wankers like that made him mad. And when he was mad, there was no one who could harm him. When he was angry, truly angry, he was on fire. Untouchable.

The mugger had seen it, and had turned and fled. Half of him had wanted to chase him, hunt him down, punish him for scaring the woman half to death. But then again, the mugger had presented him with an opportunity he couldn't overlook. He had almost made the decision for him. Sometimes all it took was a small nudge, and suddenly you were standing on the other side of the line that most people won't cross. And with the first and second decisions, a series of events was now inevitable.

He watched and waited. The thing was timing, not availability. Lots of women were available. It was not being seen. In a city of eight million pairs of eyes, there were eight million chances to get caught. You had to be selective. Many nights he would go home having accomplished nothing. Having taught no one any lessons at all. But remaining at liberty, free to try again another night.

He knew things would change. At the moment, it was straightforward. No one was hysterical yet. But give it two or three more, the police would finally link them, they would begin to understand what they were up against. Then different rules would have to apply.

Lights bounced off the Thames, dulled by their association with the browny grey mass of water. He watched it silently flowing by, cold and uncaring, keeping a chill wind tightly wrapped around it like a scarf. On the opposite side were new blocks of flats, supposedly interesting in shape — wedged or curved — designed to seduce the eye rather than assault it. Not like the blocks where he had grown up. Big, straight, towering monstrosities, most of which had now folded in on themselves, dynamited to make way for the smoother shapes of designer living. But at least the old blocks had character. You knew who you lived next to. No need for video phones or remote entry. Just flats full of people getting on with their lives while the Thames quietly went about its business.

He heard a horn . . . then he shook himself round, glancing at his watch in the gloom. Not quite a black-out. Just a few seconds of tuning out, being elsewhere. Small wedges of time which seemed to go missing occasionally. Where they went he didn't know. He didn't physically move anywhere or do anything, his mind just wandered. A side-effect, the doctor had called it. She had said a lot of things about side-effects. But he had kept his cool. The medical profession didn't understand much about living, about being truly and utterly alive. They were more concerned with lessening symptoms, patching you up, making you feel that you were better. Not with actually making you better. There was a difference, a large difference, which seemed to be lost on the GP. Being good and feeling good, being healthy and feeling healthy, being alive and feeling alive.

And she had spoken names. Big, ugly, strung-together medical names. Words like car crashes, smashed into long pile-ups. Hypothalamo-gonadal-pituitary axis. Follicle-stimulating hormone. Hypogonadotrophic-hypogonadism. A leaflet spelling it all out. He had looked the terms up, Googled them on his computer, learned how to say them, and what they meant. He repeated them rapidly under his breath, waiting and watching. Follicle-stimulating hormone . . . '

He shook his head, his hair damp, cold against his face as it moved. Back again. More lost seconds somewhere. The burning itch that needed to be scratched brought him round. He checked his watch. One thirty-four. Very few people around now. Just the odd one or two shuffling home, or looking for cabs, or drawn to the Thames. He stamped his feet. Keep moving, stay ready, be alert. His breathing was still quick. He was excited and on edge.

63

He closed his eyes and listened. Noises across the water, drifting, swirling in the air, being blown from who knew where. He blinked. Among them the hypnotic tick-tock of high heels. He clenched his teeth, rolled his neck, opened his eyes wide and stepped back into the shadows, ready.

12

'Mock fucking Tudor,' Moray groused, his voice as rough as the gravel drive which stretched before them.

'Who'd have guessed?' said Reuben, his footsteps crunching in unity with Moray's, echoing their arrival.

'You coming in?'

'I'll lie low. Let you earn your money.'

'Great,' Moray replied. He examined the house in more detail. 'Footballers. Was there ever a group of people less deserving of over-payment?'

'Lawyers?'

'Ach,' Moray said with a grin, 'the familiar sound of Dr Maitland's axe being ground.'

Reuben smiled back. 'I'll wait here.'

'Cheers.'

Moray pulled an envelope out of his coat and tramped towards the front of the house. As he did so, he swore under his breath. An eight-bedroom mock-Tudor Barratt home. No class, no character, no soul. He stopped by the door, which had a dark glass panel at head height. Moray quickly glanced away from the reflection of his untidy form. Below was a spotless doormat, inviting him to clean his shoes before he entered. Moray inspected his tatty foot-wear for a second, sighed, and rang the over-sized doorbell. After a couple of moments it was pulled open by a man in smart jeans, a tight jumper and pristine shoes. Moray took in the square jaw and the highlighted hair, the post-ironic mullet and the previously broken nose.

'And?' the man asked, holding a large black remote control in his hand like a weapon.

'I've got your results.' Moray nodded towards the envelope, which he was swinging between his forefinger and thumb. 'Can I come in, Mr Accoutey?'

Inside the lounge, an enormous flatscreen TV was illuminated green. Figures in red and yellow tussled across its shallow glassy surface. Jeremy Accoutey pointed his remote at the screen, freezing the image. Moray glanced from the TV to Jeremy and back. On the screen, Jeremy Accoutey was in the process of taking a penalty kick in front of a packed crowd. The ball remained frozen, stopped midway on its trajectory towards the goalmouth, oval and distorted in its movement.

'You like to watch yourself play?' he asked.

Jeremy grunted. 'Depends on the result. Do you want a drink?'

Moray shook his head.

'You sure? I've just opened a bottle.'

'No thank you, Mr Accoutey.'

Jeremy hesitated, then picked a bottle of Courvoisier off a coffee table and poured some into his glass.

'So,' he said, swirling his drink, 'you've got my answer.'

'Yeah.'

'And?'

Moray pushed the envelope towards him. 'Inside you'll find screen-shots of all our analyses. Everything should be self-explanatory.'

'So what does it say?'

'It's best you read the full report. But any questions, contact us via the usual PO box.' Moray let go of the envelope, allowing Jeremy to take it. 'And we'll need the remaining three and a half thousand.'

Jeremy Accoutey snatched the envelope, his fingers immediately moving to tear it open. Then he stopped, his jaw twitching, appearing to change his mind. He walked over to a dark office desk which sat brooding in the corner, surrounded by lighter Scandinavian furniture. Moray pictured the desk lurking in an antiques shop somewhere, solid and defiant, happily gathering dust. Jeremy unlocked a drawer and pulled out a bundle of notes.

'Should be all there,' he said, passing it to Moray. 'Three and a half.' Jeremy then reached into his jeans, and with a practised movement pulled out a couple of additional twenties. 'And here, this is for you and your partner. Get yourselves a drink or something.'

Moray didn't look up from leafing through the wad of notes and silently counting them. 'We don't do this for the tips,' he said.

'So what do you do it for?'

'It's a long story, Mr Accoutey. And just as we respect your privacy, we expect the same in return.' Moray finished counting, and glanced at Jeremy, who was still holding the purple and blue notes, unsure what to do with them, unused to having his money refused. 'A two-way street,' Moray added with a smile.

'Right.'

'And remember, if you have any questions, you know how to get hold of us.'

Moray made his way to the door, past the screen image of Jeremy Accoutey — his penalty kick in mid-flight, an instant of expectation pixilated and frozen — and walked out, crunching back up the sandstone drive.

Behind him, and with the door still open, Jeremy stared hard at the envelope. He closed his eyes for a second and crossed himself. He took a heavy swig of his drink, baring his teeth as it burned its way down. He took a deep breath which stretched the ribbing of his jumper. And then he tore at the envelope with trembling fingers.

13

DCI Sarah Hirst hesitated for a second, her arm stopping mid-motion. Rules and regulations, a voice whispered.

'I shouldn't really,' she said.

Reuben stared through the windscreen. A thin rain was falling, mist-like, layering the glass with a film of almost imperceptible droplets. He counted four seconds between sweeps of the intermittent wipers.

'Do you want my help or not?'

Sarah allowed her arm to complete its journey, handing the photograph over to Reuben. 'OK, but prepare yourself. Some of these aren't nice.'

'Compared with what I've seen recently . . . ' Reuben began, but then he stopped. The colour photo showed a naked female corpse with strangulation bruising and a sick pallor which spoke of a breathless death.

'We've tried extracting from all six of the blue regions here.' Sarah pointed with slender unpainted fingers. 'But no joy. We're absolutely stumped.'

Reuben focused into the picture, examining the blue spots of negative DNA testing. She was lying on her back on a cold white table, lifeless and inert. Sometimes all it took was a photograph, and he was there. In it, seeing it, feeling it. The arteries gorging, the muscles clenching, the airways fighting, the heart spasming. Alive and thrashing, the single most animated instant of life always in the seconds before death.

'The body was discovered in water?'

'The Thames, no less.'

'And for how long?'

'We think she's been dead for three or four weeks. This is just a hunch, but she could be linked to the DI a few days back.'

'Tamasine Ashcroft?'

'That's the second time you've mentioned her by name. Did you know her?'

'Not really. Think I might have met her once or twice on an investigation a few years back.' Reuben cleared his throat. 'Up-and-coming DI taken out in her prime. Any connection between her profession and her death?'

'How do you mean?'

'Could she have been working on something . . . '

'Nothing that checks out. Some paedophile stuff, but it doesn't look to be linked. Even coppers end up in the wrong place at the wrong time.'

'Yeah, well.'

Sarah reached for the picture, holding her hand out, palm up-turned. 'Could I?'

Reuben passed it back, frowning. 'You're saying it might have been the first?'

'I'm not saying anything. But you're aware what happens with first-time murders.'

'Like first-time lovers. Don't really know what

70

they're doing till they've done it and it's over.'

'So this could be important.'

'If it's linked.' Reuben rewound to the case that still haunted him. No mistakes then with the first one. Just slow, methodical torture and death as Reuben's career fell apart and his marriage disintegrated. 'But it doesn't always work like that. You remember?'

Sarah half turned in her seat. The bad memory was still raw. 'Sorry . . . '

The wipers dragged again across the windscreen, shuddering and screeching in protest. It had stopped raining. Reuben blinked a couple of slow blinks. It was amazing. You could stare through a windscreen for long sluggish minutes and not notice that the wipers were still flicking back and forth, the wetness having dispersed, the glass no longer needing clearing. The brain and its ability to miss the obvious and lose itself in memories you hoped you'd buried.

'Sometimes,' Reuben said after only a brief pause, 'if they've been in the water a while, particularly where there are boats, you get this weirdly impenetrable mix of oil and algae.'

'Oil?'

'From outboard motors. This is good because it preserves the DNA, but bad because it makes it almost impossible to get at.'

'So what do we do?'

'Ask the lab to try again using a dilute ethanol solution. Then precipitate with sodium acetate and re-sequence. Might need five per cent glycerol in the PCR mix as well.'

71

'You think it will work?'

'It's the only thing that stands a chance.'

Sarah frowned. 'We'll give it a shot. Thanks. Now, I've got something for you.' She pulled another colour photo out of the pocket of her charcoal jacket. 'Have a look at this one. Recognize him?'

Reuben squinted at the mugshot of a dark-haired Caucasian prisoner taken at the time of arrest. 'Possibly . . . '

'You *did* carry out your predictive phenotyping on those samples last night?'

'You're joking. This is Michael Brawn?'

'None other.'

Reuben patted the pockets of his denim jacket, then slid out his pheno-fit of Michael Brawn. He searched the digitized features: the shallow nose, the rounded pudgy cheeks, the distended earlobes, the anterior curve of the chin, the slight overbite. But mostly Reuben stared into the blackness of the face, with its dark pigmentation, pure-line Afro-Caribbean, unmistakable in its ethnicity. He placed the picture next to Sarah's mugshot, shoulder to shoulder, head to head.

'White Michael Brawn, meet black Michael Brawn.'

The wiper juddered across the dry screen again, and Sarah finally turned it off.

'There's something else, something more important than this,' she said.

'What?'

She bit into her lower lip. 'He's one of ours.'

'Shit. I thought the name — '

'This changes things, Dr Maitland.'

'Fuck, yeah.'

'I used Charlie Baker's access to check back through GeneCrime records.'

'Charlie Baker?' Reuben sucked in a breath that held a faint tinge of Sarah's perfume. 'Are you sure that's wise?'

'As I say, I am trying to catch what looks like a serial rapist at the moment. You'll forgive me if I take short-cuts.'

Reuben surveyed DCI Hirst's flushed cheeks and flared nostrils. 'Sorry,' he said.

'GeneCrime performed the forensics on him, the forensics which sent him down.'

'And if they're bent . . . '

Sarah whistled, a low note somewhere between a sigh and a hum. 'I need to have another ask around, see what people know. Pull his file and have a proper look.'

'It doesn't make sense,' Reuben said, partly to himself. 'We profiled him, and his phenotype and genotype are entirely opposite.'

'Just as the note suggested.'

She flicked at her hair in the mirror. Reuben continued to focus on his pheno-fit, a million unsettling notions blurring his vision. Michael Brawn. A false genetic identity. DNA used and abused. It was still going on. Sarah's mobile rang, and she answered with a quick series of yeses and nos. Reuben scratched his forehead hard, trying to dismiss the notion. Sarah ended her call.

'No rest for those who hunt the wicked,' she said. 'Drop you somewhere?'

Reuben shook his head slowly. 'Here's fine.'

He climbed out of the car, slotted the pheno-fit away, and allowed himself to be swallowed by the sea of bodies flooding the pavement, immersing himself in other people's rights and wrongs, in their truths and inconsistencies.

14

Reuben lined up four colour photographs on the white lab bench. The first was a picture of Lucy, of her shoulders and her head. He recalled taking the photo, Lucy reluctant, self-conscious from the attention. They were on holiday somewhere, Portugal he guessed, and she had a reddening tan from too many hours in the sun. Her sunglasses were in her hair, which was slightly lighter than normal. Reuben estimated that it was near the end of the holiday, and they had been about to return to England, to their pre-Joshua lives, which seemed to revolve almost entirely around work. Lucy's eyes were smiling, despite the reluctance. The light which bounced off them projected carefree happiness, a future together, marriage and children, endless possibilities. Reuben scrutinized her face, absorbing every detail of the moment, a shutter's blink of everything that used to matter.

Joshua's photo, in comparison to his mother's, was slightly blurred. There was almost a halo around him, the haze of movement of his pale body lending an ethereal aura to his skin. Reuben estimated he was around fifteen months. When he saw photographs of his son, he half wished he could fast-forward them to an age when his features would start to really crystallize — five or six maybe. Even now, when he looked at him, he couldn't be sure. The darkness could just as well be from Shaun Graves as from Lucy. The nose was still a snubbed mound of tissue waiting to bud. The mouth and ears, the chin, the line of the eyebrows, the cheeks . . . all were beginning to talk to him, but would always remain supporting evidence. The eyes held the real clue. They were a light blue, with, from some angles, a hint of grey-green, and Reuben never tired of staring into them. But eye colour, he was well aware, could change up to the age of two. After that he would have a good idea. Reuben's irises were green, as were Lucy's, and Shaun's were hazel. He had done the maths, performed the permutations for the two locus trait with its three alleles. A complex inheritance with some guesswork involved. But a lot hinged on whether Joshua's eyes remained blue or began to turn more green.

He put Joshua down and picked Shaun Graves up. He was in a dark suit and light shirt, caught unawares, frowning slightly, his face almost square on to the camera. A Moray special, snapped covertly from some distance, one of a series of shots he had taken for Reuben in the days when the exclusion order had been rigidly enforced, and his only contact with Joshua was holding illicit photographs of him. Shaun had, Reuben was forced to concede, charismatically good looks. His chin was long, with the hint of a dimple in it. His ears were relatively small and symmetrical, and his cheekbones high and prominent for a male. Shaun's light eyes offset his golden skin. His hair was dark brown, but not quite as dark as Lucy's. Reuben focused on the face which had taken everything away from him, forcing himself to be cold and scientific, to map the details of his features rather than glare at them with lasting bitterness.

Closing his eyes and imprinting Shaun's characteristics, Reuben dropped his photo and picked up the final one. It was a perfunctory picture of his own face, expressionless and deadpan, taken from his old GeneCrime ID card. A terrible photograph, but ideal for the purpose at hand. There was no dishonesty of a forced smile or any other expression developed for the camera, just his nose, mouth, eyes, chin, ears, hair and cheeks. It was almost like an autopsy picture, so lifeless and drained of colour by a bright camera flash.

As he examined it, he recalled the period when it was taken. GeneCrime had just updated its already heavy security and had required new photo-ID cards for all personnel. It was three months before his dismissal. Reuben sensed the wildness in his own eyes, tried to immerse himself for a second in the suspicions, the pressures, the abrasive atmosphere of the division, at a time when everything was starting to go wrong. The root cause of where he was today. The seeds of protracted suspicion, the need for results starting to push one or two of his colleagues over the line that should never be crossed by CID.

And then Reuben paying the ultimate price. He saw Commander Robert Abner, red in the face, shaking his head sadly at Reuben, while DCIs Phil Kemp and Sarah Hirst stared at him in quiet silence. Sarah Hirst, cold and elegant, undisguised resentment on her face. Phil Kemp, dark-haired and squat, an unhealthy pallor to his skin. Clearing his throat, raising his eyebrows at Reuben and reading the charges against him. Then, minutes later, when all the talking was done, leaving the room, barrelling down corridors, DI Charlie Baker standing in his way, making him scrape past, giving Reuben a slow handclap out of the building.

Reuben blinked rapidly, returning to the now. He arranged and rearranged the four photographs on the bench, constructing family trees. Reuben and Lucy, with Joshua beneath; then Shaun and Lucy, with Joshua beneath. He superimposed features, measured distances with a pair of callipers, squinted and scribbled notes into a lab book. And then he turned Lucy's photo over and moved Joshua's picture next to his own face, and then next to Shaun's, running his eyes rapidly back and forth between the images.

Reuben stood up. He slid a clear bottle labelled '100% Ethanol' from a lab shelf and poured a slosh into a Pyrex beaker, measuring out roughly a hundred millilitres. A quick calculation told him that this approximated to half a bottle of 40 per cent spirits. He pulled down the small glass vial marked 'Oblivion' from a rack of chemicals, and shook its powder back and forth. Its fine off-white grains arranged themselves into hills and valleys, ups and downs. Reuben flicked the tube with his middle finger, deciding.

He knew he could never bring himself to perform a paternity test. To sully Joshua, to drag his DNA into his lab, through his equipment, into his tubes . . . It was the purest form of hypocrisy, but Reuben had fought the impulse a thousand times. And at least this way there was still hope. To test his son and come up with a cold statistical number, the answer 'no' spelled out in a long stream of digits, truly that would finish him. He uncapped the vial, wet a fingertip and dabbed it inside. Then he rubbed the bitter powder into his gums, a small quantity which would keep him alert and awake.

Swigging from the beaker, he slotted the photos of Joshua, Lucy, Shaun and himself away, and sighed. He sat upright in the chair and pulled out two other pictures. And as he sipped the drink and felt the first tingles of the slow onset of amphetamine, he began to inspect and re-inspect Michael Brawn's contrasting photos in minute and utter detail.

15

Sarah Hirst supported the weight of her head with the fingers of both hands. A cold, gnawing headache was burrowing deep into her sinuses. On the desk in front of her lay a multitude of papers and photographs, covering almost the entire surface. The photos showed crime scenes, bodies and fragments of bodies. She felt a sense of overwhelming atrocity in the redness of the colour close-ups and the coldness of the black and white mortuary shots. Sarah pushed her fingertips into the thin skin of her forehead, lowered her chin and shifted the pressure from the top of her nasal passages. Like a ball of pain which moved position as she altered the angle of her brain, the headache seemed to relocate to her frontal lobes.

Three unsolved murders in little over a month, and now this. A body dredged from the Thames. Maybe linked to one or more of them, maybe not. There was no Missing Persons report, no search. Just a bloated corpse spotted by a woman walking her dog. Pathology had refused to commit themselves to a time of death. Three to four weeks was the best they had come up with. Sarah sighed. To disappear and to die, to have no one miss you, and to wash up naked on the brown cloying banks of the Thames . . . She rubbed her aching head, and again felt the pain move as she did so. This was loneliness on a scale even London found shocking.

Sarah had run Reuben's suggestions past Dr Mina Ali, the senior forensic technician of GeneCrime. Since Reuben's departure, the unit had promoted from within. The publicity and the sudden openness of the division had had that effect. CID, Forensics, Pathology — everyone looked inwards, as if trying to rediscover the privacy they had lost when everything spiralled out of control.

The press had swarmed all over the covert unit. In the subsequent nine months, wounds had closed and scars had formed, but actual healing was still a way off. GeneCrime's greatest strength was also its greatest weakness. A unit of élite CID and brilliant scientists, supported by gifted programmers, pathologists and criminologists, had pushed crime detection to world-leading levels. Cases previously beyond the scope of straightforward resolution had been brought to fruition through new methodologies and cross-discipline cooperation. But it had come at a price. The disparity in personality, outlook and approach between GeneCrime's police and scientist factions had sometimes threatened to overwhelm the unit. Mistakes had been made, lines had been crossed, egos had taken hold. And then DCI Phil Kemp, Sarah's opposite number, and the man who initially took over from Reuben, had begun to change the rules.

Sarah reached for her coffee, which was cold. The thought of Phil Kemp distracted her from her grinding headache. It was possible that caffeine was to blame for it, but she drank the bitter liquid anyway. Sarah knew she had to keep going; had to run through the evidence, get Forensics to cross-match samples found around each body; had to chase Mina to see if she was willing to use Reuben's method of extraction. The unit had fucked up once before, and Sarah was damned if it was going to happen again.

A knock at the door made her look up from the slim comfort of her cold coffee. Detective Inspector Charlie Baker was standing in the doorway, dark-haired, swarthy, a model IC2 if ever there was one. Sarah wondered just how hairy he was beneath his white shirt and black trousers. The short beard that covered much of his face and neck seemed almost ready to overwhelm him.

Charlie passed Sarah a heavy brown CID file, holding on to it a moment longer than was necessary. 'Here,' he said. 'This was in your pigeon hole.'

'Thanks.'

Charlie paused for a second, and Sarah knew that something was up.

'This the file Reuben Maitland's interested in?'

'What makes you think that?'

'See this here?' Charlie pointed to the title on his security badge. '*Detective Inspector* Charlie Baker.'

'So?'

'So, I *detect* and I *inspect*.'

'Well, do you think you could detect the door and inspect your way back out again?'

Charlie scratched his beard and grinned.

Sarah noted the way his teeth fitted tightly together, worn upper incisors meeting equally worn lower ones.

'Touché,' he said, before spinning round on his black heels and leaving the office.

Sarah returned her attention to the carnage in front of her, seemingly a hundred corpses lying at subtly different angles with multiple patterns of wounding. But all sharing the same horrible truth. Lives ended in unimaginable pain and violence.

She picked up a picture of the bruised corpse of DI Tamasine Ashcroft. Married with one child. Her eyes fixed open, horror in her expression. Knowing about men who did this, and finally meeting one face to face. And then the most recent discovery. Slightly bloated, pulled out of the river after a few weeks. And, as she looked more closely at the Pathology report, similar patterns of injury to DI Ashcroft. 'Killing them first and then raping them. Asphyxiation, death, and then, and only then, penetration.'

Sarah picked up her drink and forced another sour mouthful down.

'So what are you so scared of?' she asked.

16

Lesley Accoutey poured another drink, her hand shaking, the bottle clinking against the rim of the glass. Her slender fingers gripped the gin and tonic and carried it across the room, ice cubes rattling and slices of lemon slowly sinking. She sat down on the cold laminate flooring. They had chosen it together. Natural oak. And it looked good, virtually indistinguishable from the real thing. As she ran her eyes over the surface, Lesley noted the simulated imperfections which had been imprinted into its pattern, meticulously designed, a sad parody of the random beauty of real wood. She pressed her palm hard into the façade. It felt cold to the touch and didn't seem to give anything back. Not like real wood.

She glanced up at her husband Jeremy, perched silently on a large cream sofa, staring intently at her. Anthony's name came to her, and his face. She blinked him away. This was more important than anything, even Anthony. This was her marriage. And yet . . . Lesley began to cry again.

'No more lies, Lesley,' Jeremy said, after a few moments.

Lesley continued to sob, unable to look her husband in the eye.

Jeremy took a heavy slug from his glass. 'His DNA matched samples found in your underwear.' He picked an A4 manila envelope off the sofa and held it up for emphasis. 'They said the odds were ten million to one. You know me. I like a flutter now and then. And I know those odds are pretty tight. So no more lies.'

Lesley raised her tear-stained face, blonde hair tumbling into her eyes. Again, an image of Anthony hunted her down, tracksuited and smiling, stroking his trained hands over her slender body, making her laugh and exciting her all at the same time. She glanced around the room. Could she give all of this up? she silently asked herself. A footballer's salary for a physio's? She ran her fingers over the unyielding laminate flooring.

'We keep this quiet, and no more lies,' Jeremy repeated.

Lesley looked up at him and whispered the word 'sorry'. She tried to picture Jeremy taking her used panties from the laundry box. Choosing a likely pair, one of her favourites, expensive and sheer. Or maybe he had given them several sets to choose from. She was filled with a sudden disgust. Having her dirty knickers opened, revealed, examined by people she didn't know. Violated. All looking for stains, for Anthony's essence which had leaked out of her and into her underwear. Lesley felt a sudden flare of anger.

'You had no right going through my things,' she said. 'Giving them to sordid men who delve about in other people's private — ' She stopped herself, trying to choose a different word, on the verge of saying 'affairs'. 'Business.'

'Yeah, well, sometimes you've got to do these things.'

'Do you?' she asked angrily.

'When you get whispers, sniggers. When suspicions won't go away, month after month. And when you hear there's a way of telling you one hundred per cent yes or no.'

'Oh God.' Lesley swallowed her gin, the ice cubes clattering against her teeth. Such a mess. Such an ugly fucking mess.

'They got DNA from him, and DNA from inside you . . . ' Jeremy battled the anger and the humiliation. 'Look, if we're going to survive, we have to face this thing together. Openly and honestly. OK?'

Lesley stared at him, and shook her head slightly. She mouthed the word 'sorry' again and pushed her long manicured nails hard into the imitation wooden floor.

17

The secret, Reuben conceded, was always to stay one step ahead. And as he was driven east along concrete carriageways and brightly lit thorough-fares, he appreciated that sometimes this meant isolating yourself from cold, hard logic and following the random vagaries of your heart. But ahead of what? His old division was stitching itself back together. It was only with the benefit of time and distance that he was finally understanding all that had happened, and all that was still happening.

No one was sure how many miscarriages of justice there had been. Or, more worryingly, whether new ones were being perpetrated. Reuben knew it, Sarah knew it, Abner had even alluded to it. Phil Kemp couldn't have been acting alone. He simply didn't have the insight or the ability to trade genetic identities without being detected for so long. That required access to samples, to databases and to methodologies that a CID officer would struggle with. Reuben could see now that in neutralizing Phil Kemp, he had created a more subtle problem. You feel the bulging tumour under the skin, you cut it out, and you assume you've solved everything that's bad. But what about the ones you can't see? The small, thriving metastases hiding in the bones? Sometimes, Reuben frowned, the obvious symptom blinds you to the more serious diagnosis.

As the taxi turned off the dual carriageway, Commander Robert Abner's words hunted him down and found him. *Sarah Hirst is smart. She keeps tabs on you.* Reuben had never been sure about Sarah. Not in the way that you're sure that you are single, and happy half the time, and miss your son like crazy. Not in the way that in knowing your own strengths and weaknesses you also know those of others. Sarah had always been closed. Cold, distant, almost deliberately unknowable. With certain exceptions. There had been a time, several months ago, when Sarah had lowered her defences briefly, when Reuben had witnessed emotion and feeling and empathy. When they had nearly crossed the line. Nearly. But now the circumstances were different, and Reuben appreciated that he was, as Commander Abner had pointed out, being kept close. Not that close to Sarah Hirst was a bad place to be.

Reuben patted his jacket pocket for the envelope Moray had given him earlier. He examined it closely for a couple of seconds, turning it over and inspecting both sides. The PO box address was typed and printed, screaming anonymity a little too loudly. He ripped it open and retrieved a note from within. It was a slim strip of good-quality paper which may at one point have been part of a larger sheet. He read the printed words out loud to himself.

'The truth to your sacking from GeneCrime lies in Michael Brawn's identity.'

Reuben glanced again at the nondescript envelope, re-read the words of the note and put both in his pocket. When you mess with forensic scientists, he thought, it's best to do it cleanly and unidentifiably.

The taxi slowed and stopped, and Reuben looked up. They had arrived. The Lamb and Flag was buried deep in East Ham, the kind of establishment that had proudly watched the changing faces of a million men and women walking through its doors over hundreds of years. Reuben pushed through the front door as his taxi pulled away to find another occupant to transport around the capital. The bar was rough, vainly aspiring towards spit and sawdust, its drinkers raw and edgy, and overwhelmingly male. The air was sour with drink. Almost immediately, a figure who had been leaning against the wall interrupted Reuben's path. He was late twenties, medium height and very tattooed.

'You Stevo?' Reuben asked.

'Only if you're Reuben,' the man replied.

Reuben stepped further into the pub and offered his hand. It was taken by Stevo's, which was so tattooed that it shone blue in contrast with Reuben's white offering.

'Thanks for meeting me.'

'Any friend of Kieran Hobbs is a friend of mine.'

Reuben grimaced, and hoped it didn't show too badly. 'Not a friend, exactly. I sometimes do some work for him.'

'Either way. He told me to look after you.'

'How do you know Kieran?' Reuben asked.

'Done some stuff for him. Mainly through Nathan, who's an old mate.'

'What kind of stuff?'

Stevo smiled. 'Friends of Kieran shouldn't ask that sort of question.'

'So where's it happening?'

'Follow me.'

Reuben followed Stevo through the pub and out into the rear yard. It was concreted, and two powerful floodlights hung in opposing corners. Thirty or forty people were milling around, a jittery excitement in the air, their voices clipped, their movements quick and twitchy. Reuben and Stevo pushed their way through until they could see what was going on. At the centre was a crude square marked out on the floor.

'You watch. The old pros, the ones who usually win, will be sober as judges. It's the young lads, they've had a few — call it a bit of Dutch or whatever — and they're vulnerable. Bravado higher, reflexes slower — walking targets to a geezer who knows what he's up to.'

Two men appeared from opposite sides of the crowd. Both were dressed in jeans and T-shirts. They walked over and shook hands, eyes not meeting, scanning the people surrounding them, sensing the intensity. The crowd fell silent.

'What are the rules?'

'No rules,' Stevo answered, 'except when one of you's had enough the other has to stop.'

Each man took three paces back, facing the other. A whistle blew. They rushed forward, and within seconds were kicking, tearing and punching each other with a ferocity that took Reuben aback.

'Smaller guy will win,' Stevo said.

'How do you know?'

'Wants it more. Plus, you've got to have balls to be a small guy and get into this ring.'

Both men were soon bleeding, the fluid black under the artificial lighting. Sickening blows continued to be traded. The crowd shouted and cheered. The larger man suddenly doubled up, bent over, spitting blood and teeth.

'Jesus,' Reuben whispered.

'You never see the punch coming. Even with practice. Believe me.'

'No?'

'No. What you do see is the body shape. You see the cunt shaping up to put one on you. You get to know when he's about to swing. And that's when you have an instant to make that decision.'

'Which decision?'

'Do I get out of the way, or do I get to him first? And this geezer just made the wrong call.'

The smaller man paced around his fallen opponent and kicked him smartly in the head, snapping his neck up. The larger man keeled over on to his side, and the smaller man walked up and kicked him in the head again. The man on the floor raised a bloody hand before he lost any more teeth. A whistle blew from deep within the crowd. The smaller man stopped, then turned round and bowed to the crowd. A low cheer went up, echoing around the enclosed yard.

'You seen enough?' Stevo asked. 'Plenty more

where that came from.'

'I think I get the idea.'

'Right then. Maybe you're ready.'

Reuben managed a half smile. He had the sudden need for a drink.

Staying one step ahead. That had been his rationale for this. Sensing that things could turn nasty at any moment, and suspecting that learning how to fight might be a useful skill. He was increasingly putting himself on the line, and no longer able to call for automatic police back-up. A sixth sense had recently started gnawing away at him, telling him to be prepared for anything. And that was exactly what he now planned to do.

18

'Ah, DI Baker, I've been meaning to speak with you.'

'Sir?'

Commander Robert Abner closed the door to the Gents behind him and paced over to the urinal. Charlie Baker half turned, unsure how to react.

'I guess this place is as good as any,' Commander Abner commented as he unzipped his flies, noisy and exaggerated in his movements.

As he did so, he turned his avian eyes on the man standing next to him, appraising him one final time. DI Charlie Baker was bearded and sharp, with small dark eyes and a paleness which spoke of too many hours under the strip lights of GeneCrime. Commander Abner knew he worked hard, and was reasonably unpopular, with no obvious allegiances in GeneCrime. People didn't trust him, or want to share their space with him. The closest thing to a loner that the inter-reliant police unit held. But Commander Abner considered this to be a good thing. A man with ostensibly few friends was unlikely to have fostered strong alliances. For this reason, Robert Abner considered him low risk. Not that that was any guarantee, but what could you do? he asked himself. You had to start somewhere. He had pulled his file, cross-checked with a couple of old colleagues, watched him closely. There was no substitute for the copper's instinct. Especially when you were policing the police.

'What I'm about to say is in confidence, and I expect it to stay that way. You understand?'

Charlie Baker nodded, acutely uncomfortable. He had barely needed the toilet, but had decided to stretch his legs nonetheless. Now here he was, standing shoulder to shoulder with six foot four of area commander, his bladder suddenly closed off, and not knowing where to look or what to say for the best. 'I understand,' he answered quietly, looking down at the dry porcelain, empty except for a couple of blue toilet cubes.

'Good.' Robert Abner began to piss, a powerful hissing jet which filled the silences. 'Look, Baker, we need to sort this division out. We're doing OK, the situation is better than it was, but still I hear things.'

Charlie stared mournfully into his section of the elongated urinal as Abner's yellow stream flowed past him on its way to the drain. 'What kind of things?'

'Rumours, inside and out. Impropriety. Surely I don't need to say it, man?'

Charlie grunted noncommittally.

'I want you to keep an ear to the ground. No one must know. Someone in this unit isn't playing fair. Trouble is, I can't have an open audit. It's all too vague, too easy to walk away from. Unless, that is, we catch them at it.'

'And, specifically, what is 'it', sir?'

'That's my business. But I recently had an

94

idea, a way to sort things out. Someone who could help us.'

Charlie remained distinctly unnerved, barely listening to the unit commander. He had spoken to him maybe two or three times since he had taken over the jurisdiction of GeneCrime. He wasn't a boss who interacted with his staff unless he really had to. Charlie had always imagined his inaccessibility was a strategy for maintaining discipline, the unapproachable head who unsettled his staff and kept them firmly on their toes. And now this. Standing next to him, scared to death, unable to piss. The warning hanging in the sharp damp air of the toilets. Someone not playing fair. Catch them at it.

'Who have you asked to help?' he asked.

'Maybe I'm not making myself clear.' Commander Abner glared down at him. 'Your job is not to question what I'm doing. Your job is merely to report anything out of the ordinary, anything new that happens which doesn't sound right. I don't want you ploughing through past cases. We're too busy, and that's something that, as I say, I'm trying to take care of.'

'Right.'

The flow from Charlie's left was easing, trickling down to virtually nothing. And still Charlie couldn't go. He heard the commander shaking out the last drops. Amid his misery, Charlie felt a shot of apprehension. Abner poking about in the division could only be bad news. He wondered what he was really after, what had brought him to this course of action.

95

This was a long way from standard operating procedures.

'So I expect you to keep me up to speed. Anything unusual, or unorthodox, or doing the rounds — scandals, hints and insinuations — I want to hear about it. From now on, you are my ears on the inside of GeneCrime.'

With that, Commander Robert Abner hoisted his zip up as energetically as it had come down, turned and walked out of the toilets.

As Charlie stood at the urinal, partially humiliated, embarrassed and impotent, he pondered Abner's words, and worked through the implications. Why was Abner sharing this with him? Was he being set up? What was the commander trying to achieve? And what had got him so spooked? But as he thought, he quickly saw that this could become a position of trust, reporting directly to the big man, a situation of safety, of protection, of immunity. As he relaxed, he began to piss. He whistled, steam rising from the porcelain. From now on, he would be burrowing his way into the centre of GeneCrime, listening, watching, and biding his time, his every move sanctioned by Abner.

19

The footwell of Moray's ageing Saab was littered with piles of fingernails, which looked to Reuben like the bones of a tiny mammal. Some were long and femur-thick, others shorter and curved like ribs. It was clear that Moray chewed his nails as he drove, then flicked them towards the generally empty passenger side. As Reuben peered closer, he saw that the fibres of carpeting were entwined with the fragments, as if subsuming the bones into the nylon earth.

'You don't have many passengers, then?' Reuben asked.

Moray continued to chew into the tip of his middle finger for a few seconds. 'Not so many.'

'Or manicurists?'

'Mani-what-now?'

As they crossed Southwark Bridge, the Thames appeared choppy, and military grey in colour. Reuben shivered for a second, imagining being dredged from its muddy depths, the clay sediments in his hair, a mix of oil and algae coating his skin. And he wondered whether GeneCrime had successfully isolated DNA from what might be the first victim linked to DI Tamasine Ashcroft.

'Did you explain the possible outcomes to him?' he asked.

'I did.' Moray finally detached the remaining piece of nail. He plucked it from his mouth,

97

glanced at Reuben, and flicked it out the window. 'There,' he groused. 'Happy?'

'Ecstatic.'

'But you know at this rate we're going to have to set up a fucking counselling service.'

'Fancy it?'

'Yeah, right. 'Mr Accoutey, I'm afraid your wife is fucking the Arsenal team physio behind your back. Now, can I have the cash please?' Or, 'Mr Bloggs, your actual father is the man you've been calling Uncle Pete all your life. Twenties will do, or fifties if you're pushed.' Reckon you could do better?'

Reuben bit into his own nail, feeling the slight flexing, the reluctance of the hard, translucent substance to yield. 'Paternity suits aren't exactly my thing.'

Moray took a quick look sideways. 'Could save you a lot of grief in the long run.'

'I can't do it. You know that, Moray. I just can't. Call me a hypocrite. It's just when it's your own flesh and blood . . . '

'Aye. Sorry.'

'And this way, at least there's still hope.'

'It's not the despair that kills you . . . '

'I know. It's the hope.'

Reuben rubbed his face, a slow, heavy movement of his hand dragging his features down. The other side of the Thames was equally as frantic as the one they had just left. For a second, Reuben saw the myriad of bridges which criss-crossed the river as slender and elongated escapes from the mayhem, calming moments over water, before it all began again. They stuttered and barged their way through the streets of cars, buses, taxis and cyclists. Reuben made a silent promise to himself that he would retire to the countryside. Somewhere static and silent where clocks seemed to run slow, the only sound the sighing of cows and the music of birds.

He held on to this image for several quiet minutes, until they pulled up outside a café bar. It was metallic, Italian, and looked expensive, its designer modernity clashing with Reuben's daydreamed fields. Moray eyed the entrance intently.

'You sure about this?' he asked.

'How do you mean?'

'That you trust her one hundred per cent?'

'One hundred's a big number,' Reuben said, loosening his seatbelt. 'But I don't see what she would have to gain from stringing me along.'

'Yeah, well. Just be on your guard.'

Inside, DCI Sarah Hirst was sitting bolt upright at a polished aluminium table, in a polished aluminium chair, both of which struck Reuben as being wildly uncomfortable. As he walked up and pulled out a chair, he wondered if the furniture was simply too painful for slouching.

'Hello,' he said.

'Thanks for meeting on my territory.'

Sarah looked tired, but her eyes were wide and busy, taking in everything around her. Reuben glanced at her large black coffee, a legal amphetamine, with little of the pleasure but all of the heart thumping.

'So . . . ' he began.

'So indeed.'

'How's things?'

'Absolutely snowed under.'

'You said on the phone you were trying to tie it to the latest killing.'

'Ninety-five per cent. Sex post-death. It has to be.'

'Any joy with the DNA?'

'Mina Ali's on it. But no luck as yet.'

'There was one other thing. Tell her to try a pre-amplification step with random primers and low magnesium. That's about all I can think of. And if that fails — '

'I'll pass it on. If we can get it sorted, you never know.'

'What is it that you couldn't say over the phone?'

Sarah drank deeply from her coffee. Reuben sensed that she was making him wait, preparing him for bad news. She used both her hands to replace the mug, which rattled against its saucer.

'Well?' he asked.

'You might want to look closely at this.'

Sarah pulled a thick brown file out of her slim leather case and slid it across the table. Reuben picked up Sarah's coffee, took a swig and grimaced. The front of the file read 'Michael Jeremy Brawn; GeneCrime CID'. Reuben opened it and began to leaf through its thin white and yellow pages. There were more photos of Brawn, distinguishing marks, witness statements and dates of arrest.

'Who else knows about this?'

'No one.'

'You sure?'

Sarah sighed. She turned her coffee round to drink from a different side to Reuben. 'As you're aware, you can't be sure of anything in GeneCrime. You put that much ego under that much pressure and grant that many exceptional powers, you don't expect things to be straightforward.'

Reuben paused, suddenly lost in something. He stared at the Final Evidence form, scanning left and right, up and down. An inventory of samples collected from Michael Brawn and results obtained. The last piece of paper before a laboratory investigation officially became a CID one. Figures and statistics and outcomes. And there, at the bottom, his own signature. Fuck. He looked again, blinking rapidly. His brow furrowed.

'Is that what you mean?' he asked, holding the document up.

'Why don't you show me?'

Reuben pulled out a pen and scrawled two words on another piece of paper from the file. Then he turned them both round and pushed them across the table towards Sarah.

'You really do sign a shit autograph,' she said, frowning and leaning her head forward, her light hair cascading towards the papers. 'But my point was, either one of them was signed through a major hangover . . . '

'Or?'

'Or by someone else. It just struck me when I flicked through the file. That signature is

101

different from others of yours.'

'But who the fuck could have done that?'

Reuben stared at the two signatures. The more he thought about it the surer he was becoming. Dots were joining, actions linking themselves together. His sacking. The shift from the private to the public. A commander with deep-rooted suspicions about the very officers supposed to be solving crimes. A metastasis inside GeneCrime. Michael Brawn sitting in Pentonville with a false genetic identity. Someone faking Reuben's signature on an evidence document to get Brawn put there.

He looked up and frowned at Sarah. 'You want to know something?'

Sarah drained what remained of her drink. 'Why don't you spell it out, Dr Maitland?'

'Michael Brawn has just become personal,' he said.

Other decisions now needed to be made, other courses of action followed. Something deep in his coffee-sour gut told Reuben that things were going to get nasty. He took out his mobile and dialled Stevo.

20

Immediately, there was something in his nose which spoke of school PE lessons. A rough comp in West London, which had nevertheless splashed out on a state-of-the-art gymnasium, almost as if it had decided to swap physical education for mental. Although it had been built several years before Reuben began attending the school, the pinch of sweat, the sweetness of leather and the freshness of wood had hung permanently in its air. Now, as with all nasal matters, the smell seemed to travel up through his sinuses, diffusing through the sphenoid bone directly into his brain. Dusty memories were slowly coming alive, as if they had been lying there for twenty-five years waiting only for that one unique odour to wake them from their coma. Reuben saw sadistic PE teachers, shivering boys running the full gamut of pubertal development, games treated more like punishments than pastimes.

He scanned the gymnasium. All around, wooden bars lined the walls. Several well-pounded punch bags were supported from the ceiling, and battered medicine balls loitered in heavy static lines. Reuben looked back at Stevo, who was standing in front of him wearing a head-guard, his tattooed hands out front.

'We ain't talking about boxing here,' Stevo continued. 'This is different. This is *fighting*. You saw what went on the other night.'

'Unfortunately,' Reuben answered, adjusting his tracksuit top. He had wanted to witness the way men fight, knuckle to knuckle. Sooner or later, Reuben suspected, the knowledge would come in useful. Now he had decided to take the next step.

'You get punched in the ring, fine, it hurts, but you're OK.'

Stevo reached forward and jabbed Reuben in the shoulder. Reuben peered through Stevo's padded head-guard and into his eyes, trying to gauge what to expect.

'You know what I mean? You take one from a fist — no gloves now — or an elbow, or a knee . . . '

Stevo jabbed him again, harder this time.

'Right,' Reuben grunted, his shoulder complaining. Stevo was enjoying this, his eyes ablaze, and for a second the apparition of a PE teacher returned to Reuben.

'One of those and you're going down.'

Stevo stood still, in control, his hands by his side. Reuben felt his shoulder, which jarred slightly as he moved it. Then Stevo punched him sharply and suddenly in the guts.

'Doesn't matter who you are.'

Reuben bent over, caught out, winded, unable to breathe. He had barely had time to react. He fought for air, angry, his brain struggling to keep up. The rules were changing by the second. Stevo was going to hurt him.

'And forget the films. No one's coming back at you after two or three good punches.'

Reuben straightened, hands on hips, finally inflating his diaphragm. He monitored Stevo intently. He was examining his knuckles, rubbing his thumb over the point which had connected with Reuben's chest bone. Stevo looked up. There was meanness in his face. He smiled, blue eyes and yellow teeth. This was for real. Reuben lifted his hands, ready to protect himself. Stevo continued to wait, revelling in the moment, and Reuben wondered what he had actually let himself in for. People like Kieran had very nasty contacts. Men who did what you asked them to do, with no question or hesitation. Men like Valdek Kosonovski, iron bar at the ready. If these were the sorts of friends Stevo had, then Reuben should be on his guard. This wasn't a game. This was fighting. But Reuben had made the rash decision when he saw his counterfeit signature staring back at him the previous day. It was time to toughen himself up. He had a bad feeling about what lay ahead.

Stevo lowered his hands. He was grinning under his head-guard. And then he launched a punch. Reuben tried to duck, but it struck him on the side of the head. His ear rang; it was on fire. Then something changed. PE teachers, playground fights, Phil Kemp . . . Stevo aimed a kick at Reuben's gut, but Reuben reacted and grabbed Stevo's leg. He jerked it round and pushed it hard, sending Stevo reeling back, slamming on to the mat.

Stevo picked himself up, taking his time, slow and deliberate, breathing hard. 'Not bad,' he remarked with a laugh. 'Not bad.' He took off his mask and wiped his forehead with the back of a hand. 'Nathan told me you were a bit of a pussy. In fact, Kieran said so as well. But maybe not.'

'Thanks.' Reuben grimaced, dismissing the notion that he had been about to launch himself into Stevo, fists blazing, kicking and punching, on the verge of losing control.

'I guess we just have to get you angry.'

21

Kimberly Horwitz pushes through the last physical barrier clawing at her to remain at work. The revolving doors hesitate, resisting her efforts for a second, before gaining a reluctant momentum and then propelling her forcefully on to the street. Increasingly of late, Kimberly feels as if the seventeen-storey building is swallowing her in the morning and spitting her out at night.

As she walks, she swings a slim case, trying not to count the days. Three months in London had sounded ideal. A chance to get away and start again. But that was the very problem. She was alone in a foreign city, perpetually out of time-zone synch with family and friends back home in Boston. If she was entirely honest, the reason she accepted the bank's invitation to aid its acquisitions team had been more about not saying no than actually wanting to say yes.

Corporate banks seem to sway over her. Only a few persistent lights are on in the buildings which stare blackly down at her. When she looks up, she feels dwarfed by the towering office blocks which back on to the Thames. Kimberly checks her watch. Nearly two a.m. Sixteen-hour days, just like at home.

She walks around a corner, and heads towards the main road. She pictures her bed in the apartment the bank has rented for her. Her stomach growls loudly, and she is glad for the moment that she is on her own. The result of a client's attempt at an ice-breaker, a buffet of Traditional London Fare. Or Fayre. Some bizarre Limey post-war food known as tripe, a selection of severed eels in a ridiculous type of gelatin, a paper cup full of gritty shells called cockles. She smiles to herself, her digestive system complaining again. What were they trying to do, poison them, for Christ's sake?

Kimberly cocks her ear to one side. Amid the clacking of her high heels, a softer noise. She spins round but sees nothing. An echo, maybe, sharp spikes from her footwear bouncing back from the office blocks, muffled and restrained. She listens acutely. The rhythm stays fixed, the hard and the soft answering each other. But then they start to lose synch. The duller noise becomes quicker than her own pace.

Understanding is soon upon her. Kimberly glances left and right. A parallel street to the right, an intersection straight ahead. Someone who had been matching her pace for pace is speeding up. There is no one around. She suddenly feels a long way from Boston, homesickness mingling with fear, making it feel colder and more desperate.

The taxi rank is just one block away. Kimberly tells herself not to panic. She has come to London to do a job, then get the hell back again. Besides, the streets of England are safe. Downtown Boston, no way she's going to be walking the streets at this hour. Central London, however, is fine. She hurries towards the intersection, scanning the cold commercial frontages of office blocks and the dull black windows of insurance agencies.

And then, from nowhere, with no sound, a figure. Coming towards her, fast and intent. She starts to scream, but doesn't get the chance. The air is out of her before she hits the pavement.

22

The tube train surfaced in a hurry, as if it were coming up for air. Reuben blinked in the light, staring through the opposite window. The platform was bathed in a pale spring yellowness, one of the stations where the Underground poked its head out to see what was going on. He stretched, aware that he was stiffening up, leaking blood vessels forming deep bruises where Stevo's fists had rammed home. He again pictured the ruined body of Ethan de Groot, destroyed by an iron bar, a mess of internal haemorrhaging, ruptured organs and broken bones. Being beaten to death was truly horrific, and Reuben shuddered for a second with the memory of having to take DNA swabs from the corpse. But this, he acknowledged sadly, was what his life was becoming.

He scratched his chin. It hadn't always been like this. From being a junior CID officer, the return to education, a Ph.D. in molecular biology, the switch to forensics. Academic publications, pioneering research, high-profile breakthroughs. Head-hunted for GeneCrime, an élite national forensic detection unit being assembled in Euston. Rising to the position of lead forensics officer. Becoming a media spokesperson on crime. Building a loyal team who looked up to him and helped him push the science of what was possible. And then everything going wrong, with Lucy, with Shaun Graves, with GeneCrime. The very newspapers Reuben had written for demanding his dismissal for abuse of position.

The train began to move, accelerating in small electric jolts, disappearing down into the ground once again. Reuben's options had narrowed. He had lost his wife, child, job and home, in a matter of weeks. But he knew that GeneCrime needed monitoring. Rumours from his old team abounded. And so he had set up a covert lab, had begun testing GeneCrime evidence smuggled out by Judith, while pursuing private cases to finance the investigations. Holding hands with the devil in order to do what was right.

Reuben shook his head. Ten months, and he was starting to sleep properly again. But things were still messy. A new lab, new private clients, helping the gangster Kieran Hobbs figure out who was trying to kill him. The police taking a sporadic interest in the form of Sarah Hirst, keeping him under observation, tolerating his activities in exchange for his insight. None of it sat well. He was caught between just about everything: between the police and the under-world, between his wife and his son, between what was right and what was wrong. But all the time knowing that if he didn't police the activities of GeneCrime, no one else was going to, and wondering how many other Michael Brawns were out there, the scent of false genetic evidence leaking from their skin.

At the next station Reuben stood up and left

111

the train, climbing two sets of escalators to emerge into the tainted air of the city. No house, no car, no bank accounts, no nothing. That had been the idea. Invisible and untouchable, free to go where he wanted, beneath the radar of the people he investigated and the clients he served. As a disgraced police civilian, Reuben was well aware that his only protection was anonymity. That and fight training. He made his way to a bus stop and stood in line. Once famous, respected and feared, now just a scientist in a bus queue.

★ ★ ★

Moray had beaten him to the laboratory. He was sitting on the sofa fingering a padded envelope, looking apprehensive.

'Post,' he said quietly.

Reuben inspected the package. 'Funny, the print . . . '

'It's the same as the other ones.'

Reuben pulled on a pair of gloves and ripped it open, pouring its contents on to the bench. Several very tightly wrapped wads of used fifty-pound notes dropped out, along with a piece of paper. Reuben scanned the note and slid it along to Moray.

'The truth to GeneCrime lies in the genes of Michael Jeremy Brawn,' he muttered. 'Find out who he is. PO box 36745.' Moray whistled a long, low note and picked up two bundles, weighing them in his palms as if he could guess their value.

112

'What do you reckon?' Reuben asked.

'Twenty to twenty-five.'

'I mean, about the note.'

'Someone has an axe to grind about GeneCrime and is prepared to pay.'

'But who? And what are they really after?'

'They need you to get involved in whatever's going on.'

'But what *is* going on? All we know is that GeneCrime seem to have put someone away based on false DNA. And someone else wants to know the truth.'

'Who do you figure?'

Reuben picked the note up again. The same font as before, used by just about every computer in the world, probably cut from the same sheet of paper as the others. The envelope was self-sealing. He examined the adhesive flap up close, knowing that it could have trapped enough skin cells for forensic analysis. But Reuben's instinct told him that whoever sent the notes was being more careful than that.

'If I was a gambling man, I'd put my money on Abner.'

'Why?'

'Just a few things he said last week. Dropping hints like they were going out of fashion.'

'About what?'

'GeneCrime is a mess that Abner's trying to mop up. One bent officer doesn't spoil a division, but things take time to settle down. And while they do, everything has to be right. Abner needs to have independent knowledge of any potential impropriety.'

'But why not come to you directly?'

'He couldn't risk it. Anyone got wind of the fact that I was digging about in GeneCrime and he'd have all sorts of nightmares on his hands. Think about it. The press, his fellow officers, GeneCrime CID and Forensics . . . there'd be mutiny. And all this in the middle of a major investigation.'

'So what about Michael Brawn?'

'What's really weird is he pleaded guilty at his trial.'

'So?'

'A fake DNA sample should have got him off the charge. There would have been no forensic way of linking him to the crime. It's the wrong way round.'

'Maybe that's why Abner wants you to pursue it.'

'If it's him.'

'But what can you do anyway? The guy's in prison.'

Reuben shrugged. 'At least he isn't going anywhere for a while.'

'And where's a copper going to get twenty-five grand?'

'I hope you don't need me to answer that. Believe me, for paying off informants and oiling the wheels, there's always money available. Just look at the sums seized on drug raids. Twenty-five grand is child's play.'

Moray smiled. 'I always did wonder what happened to all the seizures of cash, and the sale of assets.'

'Another grey area in the universally grey area

of crime detection. Whatever you've got to do to catch the bad guys.'

Moray stood up and made a show of checking his watch. 'Should be our motto. Listen, I've got to run. What do you think, though? Twenty-five grand could buy a lot of equipment, keep us going for a few months.'

Reuben was still holding the note, gazing at it, almost focusing through its neatly typed letters. 'How could I not be intrigued?' he asked.

'Right enough,' Moray answered, heading for the door. 'But a word of caution. When someone wants you to do a thing so bad, you've got to wonder why.'

'So you're saying I should do what exactly?'

Moray shrugged. 'Fucked if I know,' he said.

Reuben pulled his gloves off. 'Thanks a lot.'

Moray grinned, opened the heavy door and slammed it as he left. Reuben glanced up at a vial labelled 'Oblivion', and licked his dry lips. There had been no point asking Moray. He knew exactly what he was going to do.

23

DCI Sarah Hirst was beginning to regret the large Danish pastry she had just eaten. It wasn't that being around the dead made her nauseous any more, or that the smells and sights of the GeneCrime morgue still unsettled her constitution. It was simply that as she watched the pathologist's retractor open the deep scalpel wound just below the sternum of Kimberly Horwitz, she knew what was coming next. There was something about viewing the contents of a dead person's stomach that resonated deep in her guts, almost as if intestines could see and had empathy.

Sarah enjoyed watching the scientists the most. They were awkward, disjointed and withdrawn during the pathological investigation, impatiently waiting to take samples — a skin punch here, a swab there, a scrape wherever possible. By contrast, CID were stolid and unmoved, cracking gags to while away the time and camouflage their discomfort. Even after so many investigations, the professions kept themselves isolated. Sarah wondered whether the gulf in personality would ever be bridged. Reuben Maitland had come close — a scientist with the loyalty of CID and Forensics alike — but then his work and home lives had collided like light bulbs smashing, imploding and showering shards of debris far and wide.

The thought of Reuben ate away at Sarah like the sharpness of the formalin invading her sinuses. She took a lot of risks on his behalf, turned a blind eye to his investigations, maintained communication with him when most of her colleagues still bore grudges. But much as she kept him where she wanted, Sarah was aware that using someone whom you only partially trusted was a dangerous way to proceed.

Sarah focused on the examination in small bursts. The Path technician held open a clear plastic bag. Symbiosis wasn't quite the right word with Reuben. He was more like a commensal parasite. Digging his way into the soft underbelly of GeneCrime. The chief pathologist slit the bluey green stomach, which was distended and bloated. And while Sarah didn't doubt that GeneCrime investigations had gone awry, Reuben's motives almost seemed too self-absorbed. There was a thin leaking of gas, putrid and sick, which nearly made Sarah retch. She glanced away, hand over her nose. That, or she had underestimated Reuben. Sarah had made that mistake once before, and it had proved costly. Still, his obsession with knowing the truth about his former unit bordered on the fanatical. The incision was widened, teased apart with two pairs of blunt forceps. A thick acrid liquid seeped out, running darkly over the surface of the gland, like a punctured animal bleeding.

Sarah watched Charlie Baker for a second. He was mesmerized by the dissection, taking it all in, eyes moist with fascination. Other members of the room were contrastingly circumspect. Working silently and efficiently, the pathologist used a sterile plastic spatula to spoon the lumpen stomach contents into the bag.

Sarah appreciated the risks Reuben was taking as well. An underground lab, associating with known criminals, the type of men he had hunted prior to his sacking — this wasn't easy. The bag slowly engorged, its corners inflating, its middle bulging. There was a slurry of orange paste, fragments of fibrous meat, a white-ish slime which Sarah took to be detached stomach lining. For a second she saw the intensity of Reuben's motivation, the willingness to sacrifice everything in order to hunt down the corrupt, the criminal and the fraudulent, those who falsified, altered and distorted, the users and abusers of forensic science, the police officers and scientists who undermined the whole of criminal detection through their deliberate actions. While Sarah knew that these people were the exception, she had seen it happen with her own eyes, but had failed to recognize it. Only Reuben had been sharp enough to spot what was going on.

The pathologist struggled for a second, digging his spatula deep into the recesses of the shrivelling organ. He gave up, instead pushing his gloved fingers inside and pulling out a series of pale stringy remnants. Sarah looked away again. And now, in a society where the underworld were wising up to the power of forensics, where police needed better and better methods of detection, where the pressure to identify and arrest those who murdered and raped had never been higher, the stakes were massive. This was what Reuben had seen from the outset. The power of forensics for good, and also for bad.

The pathologist muttered something through his mask, and Sarah's brain scrambled to process the words, trying them on for size. Then she understood. 'Tripe,' he had said. 'No idea people still ate it.' Sarah belatedly appreciated the reason for the slow progress: he hadn't been clear whether he was removing parts of a cow's stomach or the corpse's. She shook her head slightly at the thought of a stomach lying within a stomach. Sarah had seen more bizarre things come from the bellies of the dead, but still, she had yet to witness anything pleasant.

Mina Ali, senior forensic technician, stepped forward and passed the pathologist an extended cottonwool bud, which he delved deep into the open stomach before passing it back to her. She watched Mina carefully insert it into another plastic bag and seal it. Mina, petite, dark and bony, raised her eyebrows at Sarah on her way out of the morgue. For a second, Sarah longed to follow her, but she knew that she should be seen to be present.

Aside from the rare sight of partially digested tripe, nothing untoward had come out of the corpse's digestive tract yet. They had no DNA, no nothing. Just striation marks and signs of condom-protected rape. But last meals occasionally revealed things that no one alive could tell you.

24

The door crashed open, a dull thud echoing through the lab, metal plating slamming into the wall. Reuben looked up, pipette midstroke between two sets of coloured tubes. Moray was holding a bulging carrier bag in one hand, a folded newspaper in the other.

'What's up?' Reuben asked.

Moray paced quickly into the flat, locking the door behind him. 'Trouble. Big trouble.'

'Like what?'

Moray tipped the contents of the carrier bag on to the floor. A multitude of newspapers tumbled out.

'So you've got a paper-round?'

'This is serious,' Moray answered.

He stooped down and arranged the papers — the *Sun*, the *Mirror*, *The Times*, the *Mail* — so that their front pages could be seen. Reuben scanned the headlines, which screamed FOOTBALLER AND WIFE DEAD, SUICIDE RIDDLE OF ARSENAL FULLBACK, ENGLAND DEFENDER IN DEATH PACT and ACCOUTEY'S FINAL SCORE.

'Fuck.' Reuben picked up the *Mirror* and focused intently on the text sheltering under the huge headline. 'Says here the police aren't looking for anyone else in their enquiries.'

'Right, but listen to a couple of these. They don't make good reading.' Moray rummaged through several editions, licking his thick stubby fingers for grip. ''Jeremy Accoutey, who was imprisoned in 2004 for his part in a brutal fight outside a nightclub, was yesterday described by team-mates as having a long-term fascination with firearms.''

'Why didn't we know this?'

Moray continued to read from the article. ''During his Arsenal career, Accoutey was capped twelve times for his country. It appears that, after taking his wife's life, he turned the shotgun on himself.''

'Oh God.' Reuben was scanning the inside pages of the *Sun*. ''Lesley Accoutey was described by a close friend as bubbly, vivacious and beautiful, with not a care in the world,'' he quoted. There was a colour picture, an amateur modelling shot taken, he presumed from the clothes, some time ago. Reuben had never met Lesley Accoutey. She was elegant and lovely, smiling out at the camera, unknowing. A few years later, a shotgun to the head, her cranium shattering, her face collapsing, her world ending.

'There's worse. Check out *The Times*.'

Reuben picked up the paper with a look of sad premonition. He read out loud, half whispering, his voice tight with misgiving. ''Commander Robert Abner, head of GeneCrime, a pioneering Metropolitan forensics unit, commented, 'The investigation is currently centring on the circumstances which led up to and precipitated the tragic and bloody events.''

'Like an envelope full of forensics,' Moray muttered, 'explaining how his wife was banging the team physio.'

'With our prints all over them.'

'Fuck, indeed. And look, even your old mate's getting involved in the action.'

Reuben took a copy of the *Daily Mail* from Moray, folded to reveal a half-page editorial. He mouthed the words to himself. ''DI Charlie Baker, leading the inquiry, said, 'It is only a matter of time before we make an arrest.''

Reuben pulled off his latex gloves, which were grey with newsprint, and threw them in the bin. He scratched the back of his neck, angling his head to the side, biting into his top lip. This was never supposed to happen. No one was supposed to get hurt. That was the code they had adopted. Forensic detection for independent corroboration. Final proof when all other avenues pointed to the same conclusion. But nobody had mentioned firearms.

Reuben slumped down on a plastic and metal lab stool, designed more for leaning against than for comfort. As he scanned the room, he appreciated that laboratories rarely offered solace. The benches were sharp and unyielding, the machines cold and grey, the solutions stoppered and toxic.

Moray tidied the papers into a pile, equally silent and absorbed. After a few moments, he straightened and said, 'So, what now, big man?'

Reuben remained still. Two people had died as a consequence of his actions. He saw the next few weeks. CID sniffing around, finding the lab, closing him down. The balance shifting. Being compromised again. Making himself vulnerable. And all the while having to stop trawling through

GeneCrime cases, letting doctored science slip through the net, allowing it all to happen again.

He made a quick, silent decision, brutal in its simplicity, dangerous in its implication. It had been gnawing at him for days, but he had kept it at bay. Now he saw that it was the only option.

'Gotta go,' he said to Moray. 'There's someone who can help.' He smiled a sad smile at his partner, and opened the door. 'I'll catch up with you later.'

Reuben took out his mobile as he walked, and dialled a number. 'There's only one person who can make it happen,' he whispered, waiting for the call to be answered.

25

Central London at rush hour. Barging, jarring, pushing, jostling, forcing. Reuben stared through Admiralty Arch and up the long straight drag of Pall Mall. At the end, and out of sight, Buckingham Palace sat in stony defiance, gazing over the vehicles grinding their way past like a huge impatient parade. The traffic was virtually static, four lanes fighting to get home, engines running, tyres heavy, fingers drumming on steering wheels.

Reuben glanced at his watch. A light changed somewhere, or a roundabout opened up; a momentary easing, vehicles moving forward, first gear to second, then quickly back again. He watched a battered maroon Fiat Punto take advantage of a gap and pull over in front of him. A rear passenger door opened and Reuben peered inside. Kieran Hobbs was grinning at him, all white hair and white teeth. Even at dusk, he was virtually a beacon. Reuben climbed in next to him and closed the door. In the front, Kieran's minder Nathan indicated and pulled back into the traffic.

'Hey, doc,' Nathan grinned in the rear-view mirror.

'Hi, Nathan,' Reuben replied. He took a moment to survey the interior of the car, and turned to Kieran. 'Hard times?' he asked.

'Invisibility.'

'How do you mean?'

'I drive my Range Rover,' Kieran explained with a sigh, 'half the journey your boys are in my rear-view. I travel about in this, nothing.'

Reuben ran his fingers over the cracked plastic interior of the door, which had lost its fascia, its skeletal workings open to the world. He examined the window winding mechanism for a couple of seconds, with its coil of wire and corroding levers, simple and functional, never meant to be seen by the world. 'But still . . . ' he said.

'You're saying you drive something better?'

'I don't have a car, Kieran. Or a house. Or a bank account. Or anything.'

'After all the money I've put your way?'

'Invisibility.'

Kieran grinned. 'I hide from the good guys, you hide from the bad guys. Right?'

'Something like that.'

Reuben was unsettled and on edge. Images of Lesley Accoutey and her husband continued to eat into him. He knew that you couldn't legislate for the extremity of a person's actions, but still, his activities had resulted in two deaths. Even though he told himself that Jeremy Accoutey in all probability knew the identity of the man his wife was fucking, and just needed final proof, it still didn't sit comfortably. All of his career had been about taking the correct path, doing what was just and right. He looked over at Kieran. Even when that seemed to be wrong at the time. But sometimes, sometimes life isn't that simple.

'So, where are we going?' he asked.

'Thought we might eat while we talk.' Kieran leaned his chubby form forward. 'Nathan,' he instructed, 'the usual, please.'

Nathan glanced in the rear-view, his thick neck turning slightly. 'Sure, boss,' he answered. 'I'll cut down the back way.'

Reuben stared silently out of the window as they picked their way around Piccadilly Circus, exiting towards Oxford Circus, cutting down side streets. He didn't feel like talking to Kieran. Not yet, anyway. After a few stop-start minutes the ageing Fiat Punto pulled up outside a row of shops, and parked on a double yellow line. Reuben saw a traffic warden spot them and amble over, increasing his pace as he got closer, pulling out his ticket book as a visual warning.

'Don't even think about it, sonny,' the traffic warden began. 'You can't park on a double — ' He stopped. He had noticed Kieran Hobbs climbing out of the back.

'Is there a problem?' Kieran smiled.

'Oh, sorry. I never realized . . . '

Kieran waved a dismissive hand and the warden nodded obsequiously, replaced his book and sauntered away.

Reuben followed Kieran out of the car. He walked a couple of paces behind, taking a few strides to catch him up. When food was in the offing, Kieran didn't hang about. Reuben noticed with interest that during their short journey along the pavement, four people nodded, smiled or otherwise acknowledged the presence of Kieran Hobbs. This, he conceded, a genial and well-known gangster, old-fashioned, liked and respected by his community.

Kieran pushed open an unmarked door, which was sandwiched between a couple of shops. Reuben tracked him down a flight of stairs, which opened out into a dingy restaurant. Immediately, two waiters hurried over and escorted them to a table which appeared to be the best of a bad lot.

'Drinks, Mr Hobbs?' one of them asked. 'Before you order?'

'Leave us for a bit. We've got business.'

Both waiters scurried away again. This was power. Proper power. Not the sort the police wielded or governments manipulated. This, Reuben was aware, was direct and instant authority over people's actions. For a second it irked him that a man like Kieran Hobbs should have such sway over the lives of other individuals, while those seeking only to help, to enforce and to support had none. Even a copper of Commander Abner's seniority couldn't muster the influence Kieran had.

'So, this makes a change,' Kieran said, puffing his cheeks out. 'Dr Reuben Maitland, famous forensic scientist, ex of Scotland Yard, comes to me, asking a favour.'

'Believe me, I don't feel good about it either,' Reuben answered sadly. 'And I need it to be a free favour.'

'That's what I like about you, Reuben. You've got balls.'

'At the moment, anyway.'

'So, what can I do for you?'

Reuben glanced around the restaurant, making sure he couldn't be heard. This had to be done discreetly. No one must know, or else the whole thing could go dangerously wrong.

'It's really a case,' he said quietly, 'of what your friends might be able to do for me.'

26

Moray Carnock summed up the punters in the bar with the bitter word 'aspirational'. Moray hated bars. What was wrong with pubs, old-fashioned cosy retreats, warm beer, a warm fire, a place to wallow in what was good about the country? Not the country he still called home, of course, his accent refusing to lie down and surrender to pervasive English vowels and softly spoken consonants, but his naturalized home, here on the wrong side of the border. Fucking London and fucking bars, he sighed.

He picked up the drinks, trying to blend into the background, being careful not to catch the man's eye. Again, he cursed the fact that this was a bar and not a pub. Who was going to notice one more overweight slob in a public house? But in a smart Islington bar, Moray was well aware that he stuck out like a tramp at a temperance meeting. Cursing his luck, he placed the glasses down in front of Reuben.

'Fucking hate these places,' he grumbled.

'So you've said. About twenty times now.'

'I mean, why does the cunt have to choose a place like this?'

Reuben glanced around at the stylized fittings, which looked to have been ripped wholesale from a series of studio apartments. Not that he would admit it to Moray, but he did have a point.

'Could be worse. What's he done?'

Moray tapped the side of his nose. 'Need to know basis only.' He took a swig of his beer. 'But it's nasty. Could get himself in a lot of trouble from the law.' Moray glanced over in the direction of the man he was tagging. 'That's if the company decide to turn him over.'

Reuben ran his fingers across the CID file in front of him. It was slightly creased, and he felt the soft undulations in its cardboard surface. He had finally persuaded Sarah to lend it to him for a few hours.

'Let's get back to this,' he said.

'OK. But when he leaves, I'm leaving.'

Opening the file, Reuben said, 'So GeneCrime helped in the convictions of forty-two criminals that year. Now, a lot of those would be as outside help — where we took over cases the FSS was struggling with and got a result for them.'

'And the rest?'

'Would have been split fairly equally between my lab and Phil Kemp's old lab.'

'And the Michael Brawn case?'

'Not one of mine. Which is why I guess the name was only vaguely familiar to me. Just one of GeneCrime's forty-two cases in an average year.'

'So what we're saying is that Michael Brawn was convicted about the time you were genetically profiling your wife's lover and getting yourself sacked for gross misconduct.'

'Thanks for the memory. But the sacking has something to do with it all. OK, I crossed the line. And when Shaun Graves announced he was bringing a public prosecution against the Met for wrongful arrest, that's when it changed from being a reprimand to a dismissal. But Robert Abner is reasonably convinced Phil Kemp forced Graves to go public, which effectively ended my career.'

'What makes you so sure Phil leaked the details? Could have been anyone.'

'Like who?'

'Like Sarah Hirst. Or Charlie Baker. Or Mina Ali. Or anyone else in GeneCrime who had something to gain from your dismissal. Kemp's the obvious one, but he's only one of many.'

Reuben took a moment for a contemplative sweep of the bar. 'I guess so. But here's the thing, Moray. Have a look at this sheet.' He extracted a thin piece of paper from the file and handed it over to him.

'What?'

'You see the scrawl at the bottom? Supervising forensic officer on the conviction. Someone ripped off my signature. It's close to mine, but too shaky, like it was traced from something.'

Moray inspected the writing closely and frowned, a succession of deep parallel creases rippling the surface of his forehead. 'Now that changes things. Why would someone falsify your signature?'

'I had the authority to pass the evidence on to the next level.'

'But how come you didn't spot it at the time?'

'Things were messy. Must have happened right when I was getting myself sacked.' Reuben breathed in the fumes of his vodka as he

131

swallowed the liquid; it was as if he was getting two hits for the price of one. He felt the anger return, the violation of having his signature used and abused. 'But what really matters is this. My authority was misused to get Michael Brawn put away on fake evidence. Meanwhile, Brawn is languishing in Pentonville making no waves about false imprisonment.'

'And the fucker who did all this?'

'Maybe still active inside GeneCrime. Now that's a scary thought with multiple other investigations going on every day.'

'And how.'

'I mean, they could be doing anything.'

Moray was only half listening, a wary eye trained on the man in the pinstripe suit talking earnestly on his mobile. He glanced back at his empty glass.

'I don't get it though. What would they gain from all this?'

'It's not necessarily about gaining anything.'

'No?'

'I reckon this is about hiding something.'

Moray stood up. The man in the suit had ended his call and was beginning to leave, his drink still half full. 'That's one for you to ponder, my friend,' he responded.

Reuben watched Moray instantly change mode, from lugubrious Scotsman to trained security expert. Moray took out a cigarette, lit it, and made for the bar. 'OK if I take this ashtray?' he asked the barmaid, picking it up anyway. While she moved off to serve someone, he gathered the man's discarded drink and carried it back to the table. 'Here,' he said, 'quick favour. Can you profile this? I think there are some sterile plastic bags in the car. The rim should be clean.'

'What are you now, a forensics expert?'

'Fortunately, no,' Moray answered, handing over his car keys. 'Catch you later.' He left the bar as swiftly as he could, heading after the man in the suit.

Reuben examined the glass for a second, noting the profusion of fingerprints on its surface. But as Moray had suggested, the rim would be where the DNA was hiding, buccal cells from the mouth caught up on the glass. He poured its contents into Moray's empty pint, and walked out of the bar with the glass in his hand.

In Moray's car, with its skeletons of discarded fingernails, Reuben carefully inserted the glass into a clear plastic bag. He tucked it away in the glove box, then drove back towards the lab, the afternoon traffic light and well behaved, large streams of hot exhaust gases churning in the wind.

He focused through the cars, buses and taxis around him, seeing back into the past, hunting down images of his previous life. He saw the other main laboratory of GeneCrime, gleaming and empty, save for Phil Kemp, leaning against a bench, short and stocky, his shirt tucked tight into his trousers, his collar un-ironed, his pallid skin haunted by a dark stubble which lurked deep in its pores. Phil Kemp chatting and smiling at Reuben, two friends who had become distanced by their career aspirations. Reuben

133

blinked rapidly, retrieving the words that had passed between them, the deeds, the actions, moments that even now loomed large, hard-wired in, like all the millions of random events of a life, just needing a spark to light them up again.

Reuben pulled on to a long stretch of dual carriageway and accelerated hard, the big thirsty engine of Moray's Saab relishing the attention. He frowned, picking through the options. Phil Kemp could have authorized the Final Evidence document himself. There would have been no need to fake Reuben's signature, except to distance his own motives from it. The dial surged past eighty, and Reuben narrowed his eyes in concentration.

What he really needed to know now, though, was what was so fucking vital about Michael Brawn.

27

Judith Meadows pushed her head into her powder blue helmet, her matching scooter gleaming in the underground lighting of the GeneCrime car park. The helmet was tight, and as she forced it on, her ears filled with the scrape of the foam lining, and her chocolate-brown hair pulled taut against her scalp, falling over her face so that she had to stop and tuck it into place.

She was cold and tired. It had been another long shift, ten hours with only one break. Robert Abner had circulated an email asking for volunteers to work double shifts, and Judith had reluctantly offered to help the following day. The thought sapped her even further. She wanted to be home, curled up in front of the TV, avoiding the news, just relaxing like normal people did, ones who weren't caught in the aftermaths of carnage on a daily basis. And with a potential rapist at large, and the investigation gathering pace, she felt the need for escape even more acutely than ever.

Judith knew that most of the details had been kept out of the press, but it would be big news soon. Evidence was falling into place. Profiling and pattern matching were confirming what the GeneCrime scientists intuitively knew already. The word 'serial' — which needed utter proof, rather than supposition, before investigations were scaled up — had begun to infect

135

conversations in corridors, in offices and in laboratories. But still there was no DNA. Despite all the double shifts, all the technologies, all the insight and experience, the advanced methodologies were floundering. At least two, and probably three, of the cases were linked; everyone believed it. But proving it forensically was hurting.

Judith pulled her strap tight, feeling it bite into the skin beneath her jaw, sensing the heaviness as she tilted her head. A headache was beginning to gnaw its way through her cerebral cortex, and the compression of the helmet seemed to be engaging it in a battle for supremacy, pain pushing in and pushing out at the same time. The unit was under pressure, and these were the times when it showed its limitations. When a serial killer was active and successful, when bodies were coming in at the rate they were, then GeneCrime started to reveal its cracks, as it always had. Admittedly, Judith told herself, pulling on a glove, things were better than they had been. Commander Abner was instilling a sense of unity, pacifying the eager CID, mollifying the gifted but fragile scientists. Bringing GeneCrime closer to its original remit — a cutting-edge unit able consistently to push crime detection beyond what was currently believed feasible.

A door opened behind her, and Judith glanced around. DI Charlie Baker stood in the doorway, his arms folded. Judith had never been sure about Charlie. He was ambitious to the point of disruption, a copper who rattled the cages of all around him. He had a knack, doubtless

136

developed from countless interviews, of unsettling people through the mildest, barely perceptible insinuation or suggestion.

'Judith,' he said. 'Glad I caught you.'

Judith fiddled with her other glove, trying to pull it on. 'Sir?'

'You wouldn't happen to have a whereabouts for Reuben Maitland, would you?'

'No, sir.' When you lie, Judith told herself, be decisive. 'Why would I?'

'I heard a rumour that you two were friends.'

'Really?'

He watched her intently. 'That's what I heard.'

'Well that's the danger of rumours.'

DI Baker scowled, a sharp grimace partially hidden beneath his beard. 'What about a fat Scotsman by the name of Moray Carnock?'

'Like I said . . . ' Judith pushed the start button of her Italian scooter. The small engine put-putted away, fast and erratic at first, quickly settling down. She wanted to be the hell away from DI Baker and his remorseless stare as soon as she could.

'You sure?' he asked. His eyes narrowed and his mouth tightened. Something told Judith that getting on the wrong side of DI Baker was not an advisable course of action.

'Like I said,' she repeated.

DI Charlie Baker continued to monitor Judith for a couple of long seconds. 'Well, if you do, you know where to find me.' He furrowed his brow and turned round. Then, almost as if he'd practised it, he half turned back, seeming to remember something. 'Maybe the cold air will jog your memory,' he added, smiling coldly at her as the door shut on him.

Judith climbed on to her scooter, beginning to shiver slightly. She revved the machine up and squealed through the underground car park, out into the icy wind and on to the dark streets.

28

If he strained, Reuben realized he could actually see the snagged fibres from the cloth which had polished the front door since his last visit. This is what the gate to hell would look like, he thought. Black, lacquered, almost mocking. He closed his eyes and words from the three notes played across his retinas. *Michael Jeremy Brawn. False genetic identity. Your sacking from GeneCrime.*

Reuben blinked rapidly, returning to the present. He rapped the knocker hard, anticipating trouble. Moments later, the door was pulled open. His ex-wife looked flushed and pretty, in a hassled kind of way. For a second, he longed to grab her, to hold her, to pull her close to him.

'What do you want?' she demanded. 'I'm late for work already. I've got a big commercial suit pending.'

Reuben half smiled at the fact that his thoughts could be so far away from hers. This had not been an unusual occurrence, at least not towards the end of their marriage, when Lucy's were presumably preoccupied with another man.

'Let me drop him off at nursery,' Reuben said. 'I've got a couple of hours and thought — '

'You can't just turn up like this.'

'I'm offering to help, Luce. What possible harm could there be?'

'I'm serious. The answer is no. And he's coming down with something again.'

'Although he's well enough to go to nursery?'

Lucy made a show of sighing out loud. 'That's my decision. My final decision. And if you don't leave, I warn you, Reuben, I'll call the police.'

'Just this once.' Reuben tried not to plead. 'It's just that I might not be around — '

'If it was up to Shaun, we'd have called them a long time ago. I mean, what the hell do you expect? You DNA-profile him, have him arrested — '

'You're making it sound deliberate. His name just ended up on the wrong list. Things got out of hand.'

'Then you keep turning up demanding to see Joshua, violating your exclusion order. Come on. We're lawyers, for Christ's sake. And you, I'm afraid, are breaking the law.'

'Your law. Not mine.'

Lucy treated Reuben to the icy smile she reserved for the defining moments of arguments. He pictured her using it in court, and it scaring the shit out of the opposition. 'Read the statutes, Reuben,' she said. 'Disgraced coppers don't get to make the rules.' She stepped smartly back and slammed the door.

Reuben remained where he was, bitter and resentful. In the background he could hear his son, somewhere behind the foreboding surface of the door. He knew it was the product of desperation, but he couldn't suppress the notion that he had heard the word 'Daddy'.

Reuben stepped away, walking quickly and angrily up the drive. He took out his mobile phone and dialled a number.

29

Sarah Hirst examined two depressing pieces of paper, both still warm from her printer. She could have read the information direct from her screen, but even in the twenty-first century, police departments ran on print-outs rather than pixels. The sheets quickly lost their heat as she held them up and read them again, and as they did so she sensed another trail go cold.

Everything pointed to the same man being responsible for at least three deaths. DI Tamasine Ashcroft. The unidentified female found after four weeks. And now Kimberly Horwitz. Everything except what really mattered. The MOs were identical: bodies discovered in the Thames or within half a mile of it, raped post-suffocation. But no DNA. And if GeneCrime couldn't find DNA, there wasn't any to discover.

Sarah pictured this for a second. Rape with no DNA. A condom — that was the easy part. But putting surgical gloves on first, without contaminating them, and then putting the condom on, seconds after killing, the body slowly cooling, becoming aroused but still being calm and careful enough to think clearly, not leaving hairs anywhere on the victim, no pubic hairs, no head hairs . . . This wasn't just difficult. This bordered on the obsessional.

Both sheets of paper yielded negative results.

On the first, no semen sample, no DNA found at any site on Tamasine Ashcroft's body, internal or external. On the second, the stomach contents of Kimberly Horwitz had come back similarly pointless. The tripe consumed at some sort of buffet, mild alcohol residue, partially digested vegetables. No deposits or silt from the river. She had been killed somewhere close to her final resting place, and dumped in the river after death.

Sarah leaned back in her chair, its springs groaning as she pushed her feet up on to the desk. Soon they were going to have to go public with everything they had. The capital's female population would be sent into panic. They would stay away from the river, avoid taking any risks at night, get chaperoned wherever they went, and the deaths would stop for a while. Sarah cursed. And then the killer would get even more careful, and would come back for more, and would be even more difficult to detect.

She shook herself, knowing that she had to stop thinking like this. People had died, and maybe others would as well. But still the detective urge made her see everything in terms of results instead of tragedy. Sarah was honest enough with herself to appreciate that this was a perennial failing. Being too hard-nosed. Breaking friendships in order to solve cases. Using people and spitting them out to achieve her ends. She thought guiltily of Reuben, of what had happened before, of what could happen in the future. The reason he would never truly trust her. Sarah frowned. One day she would kick

142

back and relax, put friendships first, become well liked, open and honest. But until that day — when people stopped mutilating others, when women ceased being dragged out of cold rivers brutalized and battered, when police morgues were empty of the hacked and slashed — Sarah's means would continue to justify her ends.

The phone erupted into close-spaced double rings, indicating an external call. Sarah leaned slightly forward, still with her stockinged feet on the desk, and poked at the speakerphone button with the end of her pen.

'DCI Hirst,' she said.

'Sarah, it's Reuben,' came the reply.

'I was just thinking about you.'

'Should that worry me?'

'Only slightly.' Sarah squinted at the clutter in her office, telling herself again that catching bad guys was infinitely more important than treating people fairly. 'So, what's up?'

There was a crackly pause, Reuben's breathing mixing with the background noises of hurried London movement. 'Sarah, can you pull some strings for me?'

'What kind of strings?'

'Difficult ones. Illegal ones.' He paused again. 'Quiet ones.'

Sarah slid her feet off the desk and sat upright, her mouth closer to the phone. 'How quiet?'

'Silent. You, me and nobody else.'

'Why?'

'I've finally decided.'

'What?'

'There's a couple of things I need to do. And

143

then . . . ' His footsteps coming to a standstill. An audible breath. The stubble from his chin scraping against the mouthpiece.

'Reuben?'

'Pentonville.' A clearing of the throat. 'I'm going in.'

It was Sarah's turn to be quiet. She chewed the inside of her cheek. Eventually, she said, 'Why?'

'Look,' he said with a sigh, 'there's something in all this that concerns me. Something serious. Something we haven't talked about.'

'Go on.'

'Let's say you have a serial case. Let's say the murders you've told me about are linked.'

'They are. So?'

'We know something in GeneCrime isn't right. Someone, maybe working alone, or maybe with others, has already doctored official forensic evidence.'

'But that was months ago. And it might have been Phil Kemp.'

'I don't think DCI Kemp did this. Or if he did, that he acted alone. Phil had the authority to pass Michael Brawn's forensic evidence through the system, no questions asked.'

'You're saying, then, Dr Maitland, that a rogue scientist or CID officer or both got Michael Brawn sent down, and is now just sitting pretty in the middle of this advanced forensics unit?' Sarah glanced over at the door, at its observation panel, the safety glass distorting the light from the corridor. 'And none of us has noticed anything? None of the senior detectives, none of

144

the experienced scientists, none of the multitude of people who are paid solely and professionally to detect wrong-doing?'

'But not within. Not inside the division. You know how it is in the force. You're always looking *out*, at the criminals out there, the ones who are perpetrating all the evil.' He sighed down the line, in danger of losing momentum. 'I'm saying that when you're caught up in a manhunt, you don't have time to look inwardly. Think about it. A rogue element slap bang in the centre of a big investigation.'

'What could they have to gain though?'

'That's exactly the point. We don't know. Michael Brawn willingly going to jail. A psycho murdering and raping women. And then person or persons unknown in the thick of it all. The question you need to ask yourself, DCI Hirst, is do you trust the way the manhunt is progressing? Why do you have no pattern matches at all? Why aren't you picking up any DNA? How is the attacker evading the country's most advanced forensics unit?'

Sarah let the words sink in. 'You're saying they could be deliberately fouling up a big investigation?'

Reuben inhaled a deep breath and took time over his words. 'I'm saying anything's possible. And the sooner we sort out who Michael Brawn is, and who put him away, the more faith we'll have in the rape investigation. One rotten apple — '

'Can do a lot of damage,' Sarah answered, almost to herself.

'Brawn was charged on false CID evidence. Someone wanted him in prison or out of the way. Whatever it is lies at the heart of what's happening in GeneCrime. Maybe at this very minute.'

'It's a sobering thought. And the answer is?'

'The only lead we have is Brawn. And that's where I'm going to start. I need you to make the call straight away.' Reuben's footsteps started up again, movement and determination coming through the line. 'I'll take to you later,' he said. And before she could react, the connection was cut.

Sarah stared at the phone, which was making the sound TVs used to at the end of the evening, in the days when schedules actually stopped for the night. She let it continue, thinking hard, wondering about Reuben's motives, deciding whether to help him, working through worst-case scenarios, reasoning whether she should inform anyone else, calculating what she would need to do to keep everything quiet, and all the time focusing on the negative pieces of evidence scattered across her desk.

After a full five minutes, during which the complaint of the phone grew inaudible to her, Sarah picked up the receiver and dropped it again, and the noise stopped. She hunted in a packed drawer for a directory of Metropolitan CID numbers, and began cross-referencing names against on-line lists of information. Soon, she was running her little finger across the screen, hostile static following its progress.

Then she used her other hand to dial a number. And as she waited for her call to be answered, she convinced herself again that friendships were expendable in the midst of a murder investigation.

30

Reuben marvelled at how quickly city streets could turn from the exclusive to the downright execrable. Even in the most desirable areas of London, you were only ever three or four wrong turns from the types of people and housing that money helped keep out of sight. Reuben didn't know the address of the shop he was seeking, but he knew the kind of road which would take him there. Within minutes, the number of shoppers had eased, the proportion of boarded or shuttered properties had rioted, and the number of youths hanging around on corners had reached epidemic proportions. He knew he was heading in the right direction.

The shop, when he found it, was more welcoming than he had imagined, but he still felt nervous. Not because he was afraid, but because this was a moment of commitment, of not turning back, of utter permanency. His hand gripped the wooden handle of the door, which was flaky and dry. He examined the pictures in the window for the one that he wanted, but couldn't see it. Reuben loitered another second, before pushing the door open and stepping inside. A facially tattooed man looked up at him from his magazine and raised his pierced eyebrows.

Sitting in the padded chair, Reuben recalled the words of his father, who had always told him that no matter what anyone else said, it hurt like hell. Even after a few drinks, and a lot of bravado, the pain was still acute. And he had been right. Reuben focused on the buzzing source of discomfort, the minute needle shooting in and out, carrying with it a dark blueness, depositing it firmly under the epidermis and out of harm's way, and in his soreness he felt a rare and sudden empathy with his father. They were finally bonding, long after his death. He closed his eyes, the hum of the instrument loud in his right ear, encouraging his mind elsewhere. They both had sons, and they had both made a clear mess of parenting. They both had weaknesses — spirits for his father, stimulants for Reuben. And they had both sat in a chair like this, feeling this pain.

Reuben shook his head. That was about it. But then a memory of his childhood tracked him down, one he had long since forgotten, pricked by the tattooing. With Aaron in the front room of their fourth-floor flat. Eleven-year-old twins in the same dark blue Adidas shorts and shirts, white stripes on the sleeves. Looking at Aaron, fair and freckled, with long blond hair, unkempt and shoulder-length. Watching him run his fingers over his father's forearm. His father, tall and fair, with rougher and more blunted features than his sons'. On his arm a fresh tattoo of a dagger, firmly in the process of scabbing over, the pattern only just discernible. Aaron asking how much it hurt, and his dad smiling and saying even more when he had to pay for it. Reuben desperately waiting his turn, wanting to

149

touch it and not wanting to, drawn and repulsed at the same time.

And then pushing his hand forward and Aaron withdrawing his. Reuben's fingertips brushing the raised surface of the tattoo, red and blue ridges budding through the damaged skin, a stubble of fine blond hairs mapping out the area, a large, angry scab forming and brooding. Almost seeing it forensically, the damage to the layers of skin, the irritated response from the body. The warmth of his father's arm beneath his fingers. Silently wondering why his father had had this done, what it meant outside the living room, outside the flat, on the streets and in the pubs he frequented. Seeing Aaron eyeing it almost enviously. His brother already knowing what it implied, and to whom, and wanting one himself. Reuben asking what would happen when the scab fell off, whether it would take the ink with it, and George Maitland laughing that fluid cackle of his, saying no, what will be left behind will be the real deal.

Reuben looked down at the needle. The real deal indeed. But this was going to be his calling card, his way in. The change in his identity that would get him what he wanted in Pentonville. The tattooist had changed needles, red shading with a finer point now filling in the gaps. Every line, every dot, every nuance would be there for life. Layers of skin would be shed, cells dying and falling away, scattering like dust. And always there, deep in the epidermis, the red and blue and black ink would shine through, getting duller and weaker with each tier of skin, but still lurking entrenched in the flesh like a memory that can't be shaken.

The tattoo artist was silent, concentrating hard, flicking his eyes back and forth between Reuben's arm and a picture in a book. Reuben was happy not to distract him. He looked away, the discomfort gnawing but not unbearable. He had experienced worse. A broken ankle, a dislocated shoulder, a spill of phenol on his hand. Physical and chemical damage. And that was neglecting the mental torture of watching a stranger play daddy with your son.

Reuben closed his eyes, wondering if Sarah was making the critical phone call on his behalf, and whether she had the authority to pull it off without alerting her superiors. Things were getting messy. When having a tattoo done seems like a step in the right direction, Reuben conceded, things were undoubtedly untidy.

31

Detective Inspector Charlie Baker brooded in the corner of the large open-plan living room. For his taste, the ceiling was on the low side, symptomatic of a new house masquerading as an old one. The furnishings were light and breezy, neutral to the point of banality, the walls cream, the flooring a patterned wood effect. It was, Charlie thought, chewing his teeth, a fucking vacuum.

He surveyed the forensics team in front of him bitterly. Above almost everything, Charlie resented forensics. It was middle-class detection, crime-solving for academics, criminality for people who didn't want to get their hands dirty. The fuckers even wore gloves all day, wrinkled white fingers inside, isolated from the truths they delved into, and the human mess they poked about in. And not just any gloves. Surgical gloves, like they were carrying out life-saving operations, with divine power over the outcome of an investigation. Charlie had never been afraid to get involved, to bang heads together, to do house to house, to work all day and all night questioning some shifty fuck who was holding out on him.

Of course, he could see that there was a place for forensics, that you needed two types of policing these days: those who got out there and rattled cages and chased bad guys, and those who skulked in laboratories looking down microscopes. The one helped the other, and this is where GeneCrime had derived a lot of its success. There was an important distinction between the different elements, however. A case could be solved without forensics, but it could never be sorted without standard, no-frills police work. Both disciplines needed each other, but it wasn't always a two-way street. He smiled thinly to himself. Let some of these overqualified nerds get out of their gloves and lab coats and chase a villain. Lock them in a cell with a wife-beating psycho. Get them to question a gang of paedos. Ask them to infiltrate a crack ring. Let's see them take an armed robber down.

Charlie snatched a wad of forms from Dr Mina Ali, senior forensic technician. She was thin and angular, dark and lopsided, and he imagined snapping her like a twig. He signed all the yellow copies and returned them silently, seeing it in her eyes, as it was in most of their eyes. The animosity, the lack of trust. Charlie thrived on it. He wanted them to dislike him, to not be sure of him.

'A couple more sample requisitions and an evidence exclusion,' Mina said, producing a thin stack of blue forms.

'And I thought CID had all the fun,' Charlie answered curtly.

Mina stared at him a second longer than was absolutely necessary. She was sharp and outspoken, a force to be reckoned with, despite her diminutive height. Charlie stared back, deadpan. Now Commander Abner had put his trust in him, he was a man with power. No one knew that yet, but they soon would. And Dr Mina Ali had better watch her forensically protected step. He scrawled his biro over the pages and shunted them back, watching Mina shuffle away, nonchalant and unconcerned but, his copper's eye informed him, ever so slightly flushed and trying to hide it.

All around the elongated living room, technicians inched along on their hands and knees, teasing out samples with plastic forceps, opening drawers, filling tubes with minute volumes of liquid and cataloguing specimens with practised patience. Charlie's gut rumbled somewhere deep inside him, an uncomfortable readjustment of his bowels. He wondered whether the forensic technicians could somehow detect his contamination of the scene if he broke wind. Charlie had sat through enough meetings on the promise of new technology, on their incredible levels of detection, on their sublime specificity of action. And yet no one ever spoke any more about the instinct of a copper, of his ability to pick one miscreant out of a crowd, or to recognize the one key fact in a whole dossier of information; of the diligence which identified the single strand of evidence among the tangle of crossed wires. The sensitivity and specificity of a chemical reaction was, he believed, nothing compared with the precision of the detective mind.

Charlie watched a junior CID officer carry something towards Mina, his movement rapid against the measured progress of the rest of the

154

team. He was instantly alert, pacing over to the far side of the room, arriving within a few seconds. Charlie saw that it was a fragment of paper, thicker than normal, photographic perhaps, and decorated with a series of slender, closely packed coloured lines. It looked like a bar code drawn with randomly assorted pens. Mina held it in her upturned palms, frowning. Charlie reached forward and snatched it from her.

'What is it?' he asked.

Three or four technicians who had shuffled over stood uncomfortably, not meeting his eye.

'What?' he barked.

'If you'd give it back,' Mina said.

Charlie ground his teeth, then pushed it towards her. Fucking forensics, a voice inside him screamed.

Mina ran her dark eyes over the piece of paper. 'An ABI 377 screen-shot,' she answered.

'In English?'

'Before you get the actual bases out of an ABI sequencer, it produces an image file. And this looks like one of those.'

'So this is sequence data?'

'Kind of,' Mina said quietly. 'Though not the sort you see every day.'

'And what the fuck would a footballer be doing with DNA sequence data?' Charlie asked.

Mina turned to him, black irises huge through her glasses. 'That, DI Baker,' she responded with a smile, handing the scrap back, 'would appear to be your problem now.'

Mina encouraged the team to return to work, and Charlie remained in the centre of the room, a name coming to him, a link where previously there had been just a dead footballer and his wife, an idea that grew and grew, a connection that made him happier the more he pulled it apart in his mind.

32

Reuben ran his hand through his short-cropped hair, getting used to the feeling. Grade 2 all over, a classic eighties crew-cut. It felt like the fur of a short-haired dog, or like stroking suede the wrong way. There was something good about the honesty of a skinhead, he felt. It wasn't styled or coloured or otherwise tainted. It was the truth, before it twisted and turned and became distorted. This was, he thought, what he should have done years ago. But until now there had been no need.

In front of him, Stevo glared back. Reuben still wasn't sure about him. He suspected that under different circumstances Stevo would have liked to hurt him for real. Stevo was helping him, but there was an undercurrent of malice in every practice punch that landed, and every kick that put Reuben on his back. Ex-coppers were rarely popular at the best of times, especially with borderline hoodlums like Stevo. The thought made Reuben shiver involuntarily. Things were going to get a lot worse where he was heading than Stevo's muzzled hostility.

Reuben glanced up as the door to the gym opened and closed. Kieran Hobbs paced towards him, flanked by his ever-present security. Nathan sauntered over to Stevo and exchanged a high-five and a hug, his large frame almost swallowing his friend between distended muscle groups. Valdek remained where he was, arms folded and eyes glaring.

'Thought we'd come and watch,' Kieran announced with a grin. 'Stevo tells me you're getting better.'

'Better than what?' Reuben asked. He was on edge, not wanting to fight in front of Kieran and his minders.

'Better than a lab monkey should be.'

Reuben once again felt the familiar unease of being around gangsters. Even Kieran, genial and good-natured, worried him. Not because of who he was, or what he did, but because every time he saw him Reuben pictured his own fall from grace. At GeneCrime, Reuben had spent a short period of time on a case involving one of Kieran's many syndicates. And now, immersed in the duality of his existence, Kieran, underworld enforcer, the type of man who had would-be assassins like Ethan de Groot tortured and pulped, was closer to being a friend than an adversary.

'Let's raise the stakes a bit,' Kieran said. 'Fifty quid on Reuben. Nathan? Valdek? You want a piece on Stevo?'

Valdek slid a note out of his pocket and silently handed it over. Nathan left Stevo and similarly gave his boss a fifty. Reuben saw that the experienced cash of hardened enforcers, of virtual street fighters, had little confidence in his abilities.

Kieran clapped his hands, firing a sharp echo through the high-ceilinged room. 'Now we're talking,' he roared. 'Come on, Reuben, let's see what all this training has done for you.'

Reuben examined his hands. This time there were no pads or gloves. Bare feet, jeans, T-shirts. They were fighting for real.

Stevo said 'Ready?' and Reuben nodded. He breathed deeply, watching Stevo, letting him attack first, as he'd been taught. Subtleties of body shape, of posture, of readiness all taken in and assimilated. Stevo switched his weight from foot to foot, his torso shifting and adjusting. He held his arms out, bent at the elbows, fists yet to form. And then he launched forward, three quick punches, right, left right. The first catching Reuben around the ear. Stepping back from the second two. His ear ringing hot. He shook his head. Stevo kicked at Reuben's midriff. He parried it and pushed him to the side. Stevo brought his right fist abruptly round. Teeth jarring together, his lip splitting, the taste of iron.

'Come on, Reuben,' Kieran shouted, 'sort the wiry fuck out!'

Reuben ignored the buzzing numbness in his mouth. Stevo came at him again, fists first. He ducked smartly and drove his knuckles up into Stevo's guts. Winded, Stevo grabbed Reuben round the neck, pulling him to the floor. Reuben's face was forced into the mat, bleeding into its shiny rubber surface. Reuben kicked and thrashed. Frantic. He broke free and spun Stevo on to his back. Reuben forced his weight down on him, straddling his chest, knees pinning Stevo's tattooed arms. Stevo was breathing hard, his ribcage heaving beneath Reuben. He looked up, eye to eye, and grinned. Bad teeth with ominous gaps stared back at Reuben.

'That's my boy,' Kieran said, walking closer. 'Now finish him.'

Reuben felt Stevo squirm. He was light and wiry, smaller than Reuben, but strong and quick. Reuben formed a fist and held it above Stevo's face. 'You want to quit?'

Stevo smiled again. 'Hell no. I'm just catching my breath.'

And then Reuben's head pitched forward, pain arriving in the back of his head in two almost simultaneous blasts. Off balance, he tumbled away. Stevo was instantly behind him. He pushed Reuben's arm straight into its socket. A paralysing agony tore through his once-dislocated shoulder. Reuben fought to spin round, clawing at Stevo. He was mute with pain, helpless and desperate. He felt the bandage on his arm rip, and then the pressure ease. There was a moment of nothingness and silence. Then Stevo let go of him and stood up.

'Jesus,' he moaned.

Reuben pulled himself to his feet, his heart racing, the fire in his shoulder subsiding, the back of his head still smarting, his ear ringing. 'What?' he gasped. He looked down at his arm, the bandage hanging off, the tattoo exposed. The scab was partially detached, revealing pristine new skin below. He noted that Kieran and his minders were examining him closely. 'What?' he gasped again, but this time with less conviction.

'I dunno.' Kieran shook his head, half serious, half mocking. 'First you lose me a hundred quid, and then that.' He pointed with his eyes at the

160

tattoo. 'I thought you had more taste.'

Reuben pulled the bandage back up, feeling naked for a second. And this coming from a borderline albino with a penchant for gold jewellery. He snorted to himself, in discomfort, feeling future bruises, wiping the redness from the corner of his mouth.

Stevo came over and wrapped an arm around his shoulder. Reuben took comfort from the fact that he was breathing hard. It hadn't been easy for him.

'Nice one,' he muttered.

'Thanks.'

'I think you might be ready.'

'I don't think I'll ever be ready. But at least I'll be prepared.'

33

Through the third-floor window Reuben spotted Sarah Hirst's barely camouflaged police Volvo pick its way across the rubbled car park. He watched her talking on her mobile, a short, terse call which made her frown. Even from this distance he could see the lines on her forehead and the irritated pinch of her brow. He wondered who she was talking to, and whether it was work or private. As far as he knew, she was still single. But there were a lot of things Sarah didn't talk about, a lot of territories their conversations were firmly steered away from. Reuben often asked himself what Sarah was protecting, why she felt the need to draw lines between people, who really mattered to her outside the job. Once he thought he had broken through, was close to seeing through the façade, but the shutters had come down again and he had been left with her three-word mantra of conduct — personal and professional.

As he waited for her to end the call and come up to the lab, he rocked the small toy in the palm of his hands. It was a Kinder egg, oval and slightly elongated, the sort which pulled apart at its equator to reveal a few small fragments of plastic which inevitably required assembling into something or other of little interest to a child once it had been constructed. He spotted an envelope on the lab bench and wondered momentarily whether he should send the egg's contents to Joshua. The words 'choking hazard' were printed on the scrap of paper which had fallen out of the egg along with its plastic innards. He frowned briefly to himself.

Laid out on a clear perspex tray beneath his hands was an Eppendorf tube, half full of a pink liquid, a minute pair of disposable tweezers, several dabs of double-sided tape, a scalpel blade, a cottonwool bud and a nylon glove. Through the rear window he saw Sarah climbing out of her squad car. Reuben worked quickly, packing the items into the Kinder egg and forcing it closed again. It was a tight squeeze, but they just about fitted. He spent a few long seconds staring at the object and slowly shaking his head. Then he slid it into his pocket as a knock sounded at the door.

Sarah appeared hassled, in a pretty sort of way, almost as if vexation suited her features. Her light straight hair, not pinned back under its usual discipline, worried her eyes. She wore very little make-up, and her clothes hadn't seen an iron recently.

'Jesus, look at the state of you,' she said.

Reuben neglected to comment on her appearance. 'Thanks.'

'What happened?'

'Training and preparation,' he answered, running his tongue over his swollen lower lip.

'I won't ask. Probably a good thing to look like that where you're heading. You ready?'

Reuben had a last scan of the lab, its fridges and freezers, its anonymous machines, its

163

industrial light fittings, its spotless benches. Containers housing solvents, buffers, powders and liquid nitrogen crowded its shelves. In the freezers he pictured thousands of small opaque tubes, each with a unique sample of DNA. He flicked off his computer and shut down the lights. 'Yes,' he answered, 'I'm ready.' Under the bandage, his right arm itched like crazy. A small pool of blood had leaked through, scabbing brown at the surface of the cotton. He checked his pockets, certain that he had everything he needed. And then, Sarah waiting impatiently by the open door, he locked up and left.

Reuben remained quiet as Sarah drove out of the ruined housing estate, with its skeletons of vehicles and carcasses of buildings. Inflated carrier bags were tangled in the branches of skinny trees. A cold easterly wind blew through the broken windows of empty tower blocks, a lifeless howl tearing at the thick glass of the Volvo. Sarah's police radio burst into life and died again, inaudible words crackling and fading.

'So this is it then,' Sarah muttered. 'Any last words?'

'It's only going to be a few days.'

'A long few days, though.'

'Maybe. But it will be worth it.'

'I guess so.'

Reuben surveyed the dismal concrete atrocity which surrounded them. He fell silent, listening to the engine as Sarah turned on to a main road and worked her way quickly through the gears.

'If there was a way of doing this through official channels . . . ' he said after a while.

'There isn't. Not without him finding out.' She drove quickly, relying on motorists to spot the understated police markings. 'In which case you'll never find out who he is and get to the truth.'

'Yeah.'

Sarah turned to him as they waited at a traffic light. 'Well it won't be your worst assignment ever. Remember what happened last year?'

Reuben fingered the Kinder egg in his jacket pocket. It was warm, unyielding, and critical to the next few days. He recognized where they were, knew they were getting close.

'Jesus, yes.'

'Just don't compromise yourself in there.'

'Compromising, as you know, is not something I do well.'

The rest of the journey passed in silence, Reuben watching the outside blur by, thinking things through, knowing it was the right course of action but wishing there was another way.

'OK, we're here,' Sarah said eventually as she pulled the squad car into an underground car park, blinking in the momentary darkness, her tired eyes struggling to adjust. She parked rapidly and brusquely, and Reuben couldn't help but be impressed.

'I'm going to have to go on one of those driving courses one day,' he said, climbing out.

'Sorry, Dr M,' Sarah countered with a smile, 'for proper CID only.' She walked around the car and stopped in front of him. 'I think you're forgetting something.'

Reuben looked into her eyes, brilliant and

clear despite the fatigue. 'What?' he asked, caught for a second in her beauty.

'Give me your hands,' she answered.

He paused, unsure. And then, almost disappointed, he understood. Reuben pushed his arms towards her. Sarah took them in her own, keeping eye contact, something playful in her face. Then she handcuffed his wrists.

'Come with me, Remand Boy,' she said, leading him towards a door and up a flight of concrete steps.

They walked along an off-white corridor which opened out into a larger hallway. At the end, they entered an office. It was small and modern, designed to be functional rather than comfortable. A duty sergeant was seated at a cramped desk. He was late twenties, thick-set and surly, clearly resenting being bound to his desk. He looked up at them with little enthusiasm.

'DCI Sarah Hirst, GeneCrime Forensics, Metropolitan CID,' Sarah announced, an abrupt and official intent to her voice. 'This is Reuben Maitland, on remand for attempted spousal murder. Hearing's been postponed for a week, and bail denied, while we repeat a series of DNA tests. He's now due to be transferred in the interim. Can I leave him with you?'

The duty sergeant sighed audibly. 'You got his forms?' Reuben noted that he had an untidy mouth, lower lip too big, teeth elongated and badly aligned.

Sarah passed him a sparse bundle of paperwork from her case. 'I'm afraid we're still

166

waiting for his I-26 and his 2052 Self Harm.'

A practised look of doubt shaded the man's features. 'Without the 2052 there's no — '

'Look, sergeant,' Sarah interrupted, 'I've got another case due upstairs. Court three. I'll have one of my team fax the Self Harm through as soon as it comes.' Her tone hardened. 'Now, let me ask you again: can I leave this prisoner with you?'

'Fine, ma'am,' he replied, straightening in his seat but avoiding eye contact. 'You uncuff him, I'll take him through.'

Reuben marvelled at the power Sarah could generate just by raising her voice a notch. Sarah turned and unlocked his cuffs. She stared into his eyes again, a long second which excited and unnerved him. There was something there, but he struggled to decide what. Sarah then moved out of the way, pausing in the doorway as the broad and looming duty sergeant stood up and gripped his upper arm.

'From now on, he's all yours, sergeant,' she intoned.

Reuben felt the tightening grip and knew that this was a taste of what he was about to face. Constraint. Restrictions. Limitations. He was suddenly nervous.

*   *   *

An hour later, in a prison van with blacked-out windows, Reuben swayed on his feet as the vehicle emerged through the double security gates of the courthouse and swerved around the

167

corner. Surrounding him, prisoners were standing, trying to peer through the obscured windows, banging on the walls with their fists, shouting and hollering. The van shifted direction again and the prisoners swayed, bouncing off one another. Reuben punched the metal lining of the van hard, his knuckles jarring, his teeth clenched hard.

He was about to take his own personal trip to hell.

TWO

1

Reuben paced the cell, restless, curious and on edge. He examined it from every conceivable angle, a habit he had developed in the many hotel rooms he had called home over the last year. There were two slender single beds, a metre and a half apart, tubular metal frames, dark green blankets and light green sheets. A partition just over a metre high abutted the pillow of Reuben's bed. Behind it sat a toilet, its plumbing open and exposed, and next to it a brown plastic bucket. There was a pair of boxed fluorescent lights, one on each wall, and the floor was sealed with a tightly glued vinyl. A white painted board attached to the wall ran the length of the bed, just above it, blank except for an infestation of drawing-pin holes. At the end of the room, a window, a metre wide, with integral white-painted bars. In between the bars resided a thick layer of perspex which felt warm to the touch.

Reuben stopped in front of a chest of drawers with inset blue handles. He examined a small sink in the corner which was full of socks soaking in the murky water. Two hot-water pipes ran through the cell, one of them feeding the sink. A few pairs of dark blue boxer shorts adorned both pipes, and were slowly drying. Over the other bed was a collage of posters: a wolf, close up and hungry; Homer Simpson, drunk and watching TV; an England flag, hand-drawn; a Liverpool

FC banner; two composite pictures of lingerie-clad women in a variety of poses; a calendar with a picture of a castle; a BMW Auto Sport sticker; a grisly bear with an arching salmon in its mouth. Reuben tried and failed to picture the man who would be his cellmate from the images he chose to surround himself with.

Since arriving he had been interviewed twice, searched naked, then asked about his health but not examined. He had filled out questionnaires, had helped complete a Shared Cell Risk Assessment form, and had barely uttered a word of truth. The induction process, which had been rumoured to last two days, had been rushed through in hours. It had been brisk but friendly, prison personnel happy to push him through the procedural stages, into the next waiting room, and into the next, until they were satisfied he wasn't going to kill himself or anybody else. Reuben had often read reports on Pentonville when he worked at GeneCrime and consigned killers there. Prisoners in bleak, often dirty cells; inadequate first-night procedures despite occasional self-inflicted deaths; night staff unaware of the location of new prisoners; lack of training in basic emergency procedures; prisoners locked up for twenty-two hours on some wings; vulnerable prisoners routinely moved into stained cells alive with cockroaches. He had known what to expect. And not just from what he had read.

Reuben recalled that feeling, alone, cut off, scared, incarcerated for the first time, surrounded by men you would pay to avoid on the outside. The intense concentration of murderers,

172

rapists and the mentally unstable. Not knowing who was who, the people to stay clear of, the inmates to not even look at. Appreciating the cold statistics of bullying, self-harm, sexual assault. Hearing the stories about men cutting themselves just to spend a night in the safety of the hospital wing, of punishment beatings, of sugarings, of buggerings. Seeing prisoners sitting in their cells smoking crack all day, indifferent warders ignoring everything except what they wanted to see. The insomnia, the helplessness, the hidden hierarchies, the all-pervasive fear.

Reuben knew, because he had been there before. A different institution, a long time ago, almost in a previous life. Three months for possession of Class A narcotics with intent to supply. Aaron's narcotics. Protecting his brother from breaching his parole and going down for five years. Identities traded, Aaron promising to stay clean and make it up to him. It had been a poor decision, one that still rankled with Reuben. But the knowledge of prison life, which he repressed and had always been ashamed of, now gave him strength. He knew what to expect, and how he would react. Reuben was no virgin. He was an ex-con.

He walked over to the metal door, which again was painted white, with an enlarged letter-box aperture, a metal flap which folded out into the corridor and couldn't be opened from the inside. There was no door handle. He ran his fingers over its cold surface wondering who was going to walk through.

Reuben turned and examined himself in the

wall mirror, which was metal, not glass. The barely reflective surface showed a man with a crew-cut, narrowed eyes and gritted teeth. A week could sometimes be a long time. Still, he would do what he had come to do, then get the hell out. Undetected and unnoticed. A viral particle that floated in on the wind and floated out again.

He glanced towards the door as its lock turned. The man who walked in was mid-thirties, scruffy and slightly shorter than Reuben. He tossed his folded newspaper down on the bed, the whole time maintaining eye contact, spending a few critical seconds weighing Reuben up. Reuben looked back at him. He wore loose tracksuit bottoms and a red hooded sweatshirt. Dense cropped hair, dark eyebrows, stocky through his clothes. He said the words, I'm Narc, and Reuben replied, I'm Reuben. The voice was north-western, Merseyside probably, but could have stretched into Cheshire.

'So, what're you in for, like?' Narc asked.

'On remand. Tried to kill my wife.'

Narc sat down heavily on his bed. 'Why?'

'She'd been cheating on me.'

'How did you know?'

Reuben had had time to invent his story, and knew it inside out. But verbalizing it suddenly felt empty and unconvincing.

'I caught her out,' he answered.

'How, like?'

'What are you in for?'

'How did you catch her?' Narc repeated.

'I don't want to talk about it.'

174

Every time he had rehearsed the words in his mind they had sounded plausible. On remand, awaiting trial on the grounds of attempted spousal murder. He had even smiled when Sarah had suggested it. Trying and failing to kill his unfaithful wife seemed to ring true, as if this was something he had thought about doing, Lucy in the arms of Shaun Graves finally pushing him to violence. But there was just something about saying it out loud which didn't sit right with him, confessing to a crime that hadn't happened.

Below dark, thick eyebrows, Narc screwed his eyes up and squinted at Reuben. He leaned forward on his bed, hands on his legs. 'You want to be nice to me,' he said curtly. 'I could save someone like you a lot of bother in the long run.'

'What do you mean, someone like me?'

'Someone who hasn't done time.'

Reuben sighed, unsure for a second what to say. It had been fifteen years ago, before the force, a short sentence. The image of his brother came to him again. But time moved on, and to someone like Narc, Reuben clearly didn't look the type any more. He wondered whether that was a good thing or a bad thing.

'That obvious, huh?' he said eventually.

'Only to the whole prison. And this ain't a nice prison. I've done Winson Green, Scrubs and Dartmoor, and this little shithole is the worst of them all.' Narc stood up and took a pace towards Reuben. 'And as for this wing, it's the shittest wing of the shittest prison. Suicide hot-spot of the whole penal system. Two people a week die in UK prisons. You know that? And some weeks

175

both of them seem to come from this cesspit. You get me?'

Reuben nodded.

'You don't fuck about in here. When someone asks you a question, you fucking well answer it.'

Reuben avoided his eye, sensing a quick temper and a refusal to give ground. There was no point in facing his cellmate down. He had to get in and out with the minimum fuss, ruffling as few feathers as possible.

'I came home early from work and found him in my house,' he began quietly. 'When he'd got the hell out I calmed down. And then I started hitting my wife and couldn't stop.'

Narc relaxed his chest and shoulders, which had been on alert beneath his hooded top, prepared for trouble. 'You see?' He grinned. 'You stick with me, you'll go a long way.'

Reuben turned and sat on his bed, staring at the blank ceiling above him. His cellmate wasn't ideal, but shouldn't present a problem. Seven days and seven nights, by his best estimate. Lying low and doing what needed to be done. Redressing the balance, searching out what Michael Brawn had to hide, snooping into the affairs of GeneCrime. And all the time closing in on the truth about his sacking from the country's leading forensics centre, burrowing into the heart of one institution to find his way into another.

2

Reuben felt acutely observed. He was in the lions' den, and knew it. Without doubt he would have put away some of the prisoners he was walking past. It was an unnerving thought. As he negotiated his way down steel stairways and along catwalks, he tried to blend in, dressed in grey tracksuit bottoms and a baggy T-shirt, his tattoo obvious, his crew-cut unremarkable.

From the inside, Pentonville was a Matrioshka doll of metal cages within metal cages, a web of suicide netting connecting everything. In between, corridors were freshly painted in pastel colours. Several of the passageways had suspended ceilings with neon strip lighting. Reuben could see where towering Victorian corridors had had their wings clipped, the arches above doors squared off. The largest prison in the country, captive in the twenty-first century, being bent and twisted into shape as it served its time.

The dining room had retained its high ceiling. Reuben received his evening meal — a cube of lasagne, a portion of carrots and a scoop of chips — and looked round for somewhere to sit. Inside, an almost insistent voice repeated the words *blend in, blend in*. Most of the plastic seats were taken. He headed towards a virtually empty table in the corner, and lowered his tray. A large, tattooed prisoner glanced up, his forehead wrinkling into a bulldog frown.

'Fuck off,' he said.

Reuben lifted his tray and changed direction, spying another empty space on a different table, this time opposite a shaven-headed inmate.

'Not there, darlin',' the man growled without looking up.

Reuben paused, about to sit down regardless. *Blend in*, the inner voice urged. He took his tray and walked away, glancing around, aware of the scrutiny. The dining room was packed, the conversation loud, inmates seated in what looked like established groups. Reuben tried for a third time, a free chair at the end of a long table. He dropped his tray down gradually, making eye contact, attempting to appear firm but not too firm. The answer came back instantly.

'No one sits there, fuck-face.'

Reuben hesitated, weighing the prisoner up. He was bearded and intense, but not too large. Reuben pulled the chair out and sat down, staring at the man, refusing to be messed about again.

'Did you fucking hear me?' the prisoner asked, his voice rising, his eyes wild.

'Yes,' Reuben replied, 'I heard you.'

He picked up his fork and stabbed it into the lasagne, slicing down and dissecting it. The man slowly rose to his feet.

'You are a dead man,' he said.

Two other inmates at the table stood up. Reuben squinted at them. They were larger than their companion. Reuben watched them check for guards before walking round the table to him. The first, a snub-nosed man with thick black stubble, reached down and yanked the fork out of Reuben's hand. The second, balding and sturdy, with a thin mouth and piercing blue eyes, lifted Reuben's tray off the table.

'You don't sit there, new boy.'

'No one fucking sits there.'

The two men walked over to the table Reuben was first turned away from, and dropped his fork and tray in an empty place. The tattooed prisoner moved to say something, but was dissuaded by the stares of the two men. Behind them, Reuben reluctantly stood up and headed over to his tray.

'You sit there and eat your dinner,' the prisoner with the black stubble instructed.

'Then we'll come and find you, explain a few things to you,' his partner added, cuffing Reuben's cheek with the palm of his hand, a mock slap used to emphasize the point.

They sauntered back the way they had come, their eyes fixed on Reuben, not letting up until they reached their food. Even then, for a few long seconds, they monitored him between mouthfuls, muttering to each other. Please, Reuben said to himself, don't let them have recognized me. The newspaper interviews, the late-night current affairs programmes, the odd appearance in court. It was more than possible. The mission would be finished before it started.

Reuben slouched over his tray, opposite the tattooed prisoner, who stared at him with open contempt. So much for blending in. He had been in Pentonville just seven hours. It would only take one attentive soul, one bright spark, one prisoner he had come across before, and he would have to get the fuck out and quick. Forget Michael Brawn, it would become a matter of survival. He had heard the stories — everybody had. Ex-coppers in prison brought the psychos out of the woodwork. He made a stab at eating his food, which was suddenly cold and unappetizing.

3

Reuben entered the toilet block, his head down, the need acute. There was a urinal which ran along the length of the far wall. At right angles to that stood four sinks, small metal mirrors above each, and opposite the sinks was a row of flimsy formica cubicles, with walls and doors which stopped half a metre above the redtiled floor. Reuben appreciated that privacy was not encouraged in the toilets of Pentonville.

He pushed his way into an empty cubicle and sat down, his stomach suddenly fluid, his colon spasming. Reuben had pictured this moment numerous times since leaving his laboratory in the morning, and none of them had cheered him. There was no other way to do what he needed to other than accept that it was going to be unpleasant and messy. He closed his eyes and pushed, hovering slightly off the seat, his hand in position. It hurt like hell, hard and unyielding, a sensation he wasn't eager to prolong. He gritted his teeth and made it happen, his eyes watering, blood on the toilet paper, an acute stinging pain making him smart.

When he had finished, Reuben flushed and left the toilet. He checked that he was alone before running the hot tap and squirting some soap into the water. Then he dropped the Kinder egg in, wedging it so that it blocked the plug hole. He squirted out more soap, washed the egg and scrubbed his hands. The door opened and an Asian inmate with two pierced earlobes wandered in. Reuben picked the egg out, sure that it was clean, and took it to the towel. The prisoner watched him. Reuben kept his back to him, dried the Kinder egg and towelled his hands. He left the toilets, the egg in his pocket, one vital part of his mission accomplished.

Reuben headed for the TV lounge. Finding the prisoner he needed to track down was going to take time. It was a big place. One needle inmate in a haystack of twelve hundred miscreants. Reuben knew what he looked like, and the wing he had been assigned, but that was it. He hadn't been in the dining room, or in any of the other areas Reuben had been able to gain access to. Now, after dinner, he was free to roam until nine p.m. That gave him almost three hours. And if there was one thing prisoners liked to do after their evening meal, he knew from experience, it was watch TV.

It was difficult to define the space as a room. Without walls, it felt more like a cage than a lounge, a metal enclosure with a concrete floor, and barred walls and ceiling. Twenty inmates were slouched on chairs, watching a TV which was mounted high in the corner. Around it, nothing but space, extending high into the atrium, suicide netting and steel walkways the only things visible for fifteen vertical metres.

Reuben skirted around the outside, careful this time to choose a seat that wouldn't raise anyone's interest. He was about to sit down on an orange plastic chair when the two men from the dining room entered and walked straight over to him.

'Oh no you don't,' the taller man said. 'You get to come with us.'

They steered Reuben out and down a long corridor to a room with brick walls and a rough plastered ceiling, part of the old communal area. Two inmates were in the middle of a game of table tennis. The hypnotic ricochet of the ball, from bat to table to bat and back again, was as rhythmic as a clock, the noise echoing in Reuben's ears, his eyes darting to follow the motion. And then, in a feat of surprising speed and agility, the shorter man with the thick stubble sprang forward and caught the ball in mid-flight. The noise stopped and Reuben's eyes came to a standstill on him.

'Match fucking point,' he said, stamping on the ball.

The two players glanced at each other. Then they dropped their bats and walked out. On his way to the door, the one closer to Reuben met his eye. Reuben recognized what his face was betraying. His expression said, I wouldn't swap places with you for the world.

Reuben clenched his fists behind his back. He watched the man who had caught the ball pick up the table tennis bat and turn it over in his hands, aware that his reactions were quick and his coordination extraordinary. His colleague closed the door, and said quietly, 'We know who you are.'

'Got word from the outside.'

183

Reuben tensed himself. He had been recognized already. The men paced closer to him.

'From now on, you do what we say.'

'And you stay the fuck where we can see you.'

'If you want to stay alive.'

They talked almost in unison, as if they had already rehearsed what they were going to say to him. He thought momentarily of the interview rooms at GeneCrime, where he had witnessed the same approach to countless cases, CID officers working as a team, insinuating and intimidating, a double act of interrogation.

'You play by our rules.'

'Or you don't play at all.'

A cold, leaking nervousness tightened Reuben's stomach. Fingernails dug deep into the palms of his hands, curled fists ready.

'But, see, Mr Hobbs wasn't very forthcoming.'

'So you tell us why you're here.'

Understanding finally came to Reuben. He let out a long breath and slowly moved his hands to his back pockets. 'I tried to kill my wife,' he muttered through a disguised breath of relief, the words again feeling false and lacking substance.

'And why should that interest Kieran Hobbs?'

'We're friends.'

'You don't look like one of his friends.'

'I've been helping him with a few things.'

'Like what?'

'Can't say.'

The two men, Kieran Hobbs' associates, glanced at each other, unsure.

'See, if we're going to look after you — '

'Someone tried to kill Kieran. I was able to

find out who it was.'

The shorter of the two scratched his dark stubble, his eyes wide. 'So you're a snitch?'

'No,' Reuben answered. 'I just know people. Kieran paid me to find out who sent the assassin, a man called Ethan de Groot, and I did. And he owes me the odd favour. So when I knew I might be going down — '

'He agreed to have you minded.' The taller prisoner softened. 'Look, I'm Cormack. Cormack O'Connor. And that there's Damian Nightley.'

Damian managed a brief half smile before saying, 'But look, see, if we're going to mind you, you're going to have to do a fuck of a lot better than you did at dinner. The last guy you sat down opposite, you want to stay well away from. If Boucher comes looking for you, we ain't going to be able to help.'

'Aiden Boucher?' Reuben asked.

'You know him?'

'I've heard of him.'

Reuben cut to a large wooden lecture theatre a few years earlier, packed with an attentive audience of police and CID. Slides flicked on to the screen, showing the face of Aiden Boucher from different angles, clean shaven and looking younger than he had in the dining room. DI Charlie Baker had been standing at the lectern, briefing CID on Boucher's possible involvement in the murders of four homeless men. What had stuck with Reuben about the talk was the way Charlie had directed his laser pointer, hovering on the pupils of the projected face, which made

185

it look like there was a demonic fire in Aiden Boucher's eyes.

Cormack cleared his throat. 'So you keep yourself to yourself, and don't step on anybody's toes.'

'Especially not psychos like Boucher,' Damian added.

'And we'll look out for you.' Cormack stepped away from the table-tennis table and opened the door. 'We can't protect you from everyone, but you'll be OK if you stick close to us.'

Reuben walked out, following Damian and Cormack, suddenly feeling immune and protected among twelve hundred restless criminals, most of whom would see an ex-copper as fair game.

4

The green phone card had the letters HMP stamped deep in black across its middle, indented, almost branded. Reuben pushed it into the slot, a process that the mobile phone had made almost obsolete, outside prison at least. He dialled from memory, slouched over so that his head was almost covered by the scratched metal hood which guarded each of the telephones in the row. The hood reminded Reuben of the imitation of privacy which Pentonville sought to encourage. Like the flimsy cubicles in the Gents, the barely partitioned toilet in the cell and the walls made of bars rather than brick. Designed to make you feel there was seclusion when really that was the last thing the prison wanted.

The call was answered swiftly with the words, 'DCI Sarah Hirst, Metropolitan CID.'

'You OK to talk?' Reuben asked.

'Sure.' The sound of a door being slammed. 'Any signs of Michael Brawn yet?'

' 'Fraid not.'

'Has anyone twigged?'

'I thought they had, that I'd been recognized. But no, so far so quiet.'

Sarah was silent for a second. 'Good,' she said eventually. 'So, what's it like?'

Reuben glanced out of his hood. A short queue of tracksuited prisoners were chatting and fidgeting, waiting their turn. The other three phones were occupied by inmates, similarly slouched over, all trying to muster some privacy for their words to loved ones, or lawyers, or associates. 'Not great,' he said quietly, acutely aware of the need not to be overheard. 'Fair share of psychos here, one or two of whom we've put away. Aiden Boucher, for example. Almost ended up being his fifth victim.'

'Jeez. Nasty piece of work.'

Reuben cupped the end of the receiver with his palm and continued to talk as quietly as he could. 'It's going to be a long week, but I'll survive. Just got to find a way of taking a DNA sample from Brawn that is one hundred per cent dependable.'

'Any ideas how?'

'I'll have to wait and see. Not sure how close I can get to him yet.'

'Don't get how you're going to do it without him noticing.'

'Nor me. But the good news is Kieran Hobbs has two of his men keeping an eye on me. Cormack O'Connar and Damian Nightley.'

'I'll look them up,' Sarah answered, 'see what they're in for and whether you can trust them.'

Reuben heard the scratch of pen on paper, and heard Sarah whispering their names under her breath while she jotted them down.

'Thanks,' he said. 'I'll call you back later.'

'When you've nailed Brawn, go see the governor. I've spoken to him and he knows the score.'

'Who else is in on this?'

'That's about it. You, me and the governor makes three. And Moray and Judith of course.

188

That quiet enough for you?'

'Any quieter and they'd need radar to detect us. Thanks.'

'Then the governor will get you transferred back to the same courthouse, and I'll pick you up from there. And, Reuben?'

'Yes?'

'Don't take any unnecessary risks.'

Reuben smiled. 'Don't worry, I won't.'

He scanned the corridor again quickly. And then he saw him. Coming his way. 'Shit,' he said.

'What?'

'Got to go.'

A tall, lean man was picking up the next phone along as the previous caller headed off. Reuben replaced his receiver. The man had his back to him. He was slightly taller than Reuben, his hair jet black and neat, his wide shoulders hunched, his sweatshirt pulled up to reveal his forearms. His face in a dozen different arrest photos. Obvious and unmistakable.

Michael Brawn, in the flesh.

Reuben picked the receiver back up and pretended to dial another number, frantically wondering what to do, all the time straining to hear what Brawn was saying. He faced him slightly, watching his jaw move, unable to see his features but catching fragments of his conversation: 'The last Friday. October. The third of the fourth. May.' Reuben pulled out a small address book and quickly started to scribble down the words. Brawn's accent was Mancunian with hard vowels and, almost hidden among them, rounded London consonants.

189

'Saturday the eighth,' he continued, 'the first of the first — '

'Oi! Virgin! One fucking call, man.'

Reuben half turned, continuing to record Michael Brawn's words while pretending to talk. A couple of prisoners were glaring at him.

'Hang the fuck up, or I'll do it for you,' the closest to him said.

'The penultimate Monday. Ash Wednesday . . . '

Reuben inscribed the last few words.

'Cunt-face! Put the fucking phone down now!'

Reuben paused, weighing up his options. The second prisoner was twitching, his teeth bared. He flashed back to Stevo's training, seeing the punches, the kicks, the actions of defence and attack. And then the mantra returned: *blend in*. Reuben replaced the phone.

Without looking back, he walked away, past Michael Brawn and past the scratched metal hoods of the phones, and loitered at the end of the corridor, where it gave way to a communal space dominated by a pool table. Two immates were playing, lost in the shot one of them was taking. Reuben watched for a second, sensing the seriousness of the game, excited that he had encountered Michael Brawn on only his second day, wondering how the hell he was going to DNA-test him.

Moments later, Brawn strode past him, turned right down an adjacent hallway and disappeared. Reuben waited a second, fingering the address book in his pocket, full of days and months from Michael Brawn's mouth.

Then he turned the corner and followed him.

5

The TV room was packed with eager prisoners, forty or fifty of them, standing and sitting. On the screen, twenty-two football players were arranged around the circumference of the centre circle, their heads bowed, wearing black armbands, observing two long minutes of silence. The TV room was hushed as well — a rare moment of reverence. Reuben had now learned which block Michael Brawn was housed in, which floor and which corridor. The exact cell, though, had been difficult to narrow down. Reuben had lost him behind a closed set of doors, but he knew he was confined to one of twelve potentials. Although Reuben had loitered in the vicinity on three separate occasions during the day, Brawn had remained firmly ensconced in his room, blank metal doors hiding him from view.

Until now. At the very front, and towards the right, Michael Brawn was sitting bolt upright on a blue plastic chair. As the two minutes' silence ground on undisturbed, Reuben, standing to the side and slightly behind Michael Brawn, observed him for a few seconds. He was inanimate, statue-like, straight and erect. His skin shone white, blue veins bulging below the surface. He pulled deeply on a skinny roll-up every few seconds. And then, with no warning at all, he jumped to his feet and screamed 'Cockney

191

wankers!' at the television. In Reuben's peripheral vision, he saw hardened lags glance at one
another. Others stared at Brawn with obvious
hatred. The organized silence continued to hang
in the heavy smoke-laden air.

Then, near the back, another shout erupted
from a thick-necked prisoner with a shaven head.
'Shut it, Brawn,' he said.

Michael Brawn swivelled to face him. 'John
fucking Ruddock,' he said with a smirk. 'Why
don't you come here and make me?'

John Ruddock stared. The smoky silence
seemed to deepen. All attention had now
switched from the screen, prisoners mesmerized
by the two inmates. Brawn was taller than
Ruddock, but less bulky. His was a lean
frame, all bone and sinew. In contrast, Ruddock
was thick-set, a weights-room physique,
someone who had turned civilian flesh into
prison muscle.

From the TV, a loud whistle cut into the room.
An ironic cheer went up. Michael Brawn
returned his gaze to the game and the
commentator continued his interrupted football
commentary: 'And it will be interesting to see
how Jeremy Accoutey's unfortunate death last
week affects Arsenal's performance tonight.
Certainly Manchester United will be looking at
that area of central defence and wondering — '

The TV voice was drowned out by a shout
from Ruddock. 'Come on Arsenal!' Several other
prisoners repeated the refrain. It was clear to
Reuben that Pentonville was a prison which
would favour anybody over Manchester United.

192

And in North London, Arsenal was virtually the home team.

Reuben rolled up his right sleeve, slowly and deliberately. He took a packet of cigarettes that he had traded with Narc from his front pocket. With an almost practised casualness, he passed a cigarette forward to Damian. Damian glanced at Reuben's tattoo and shook his head. And then Michael Brawn noticed it, out of the corner of his eye. He turned and looked slowly up at Reuben. The look was cold and appraising, an expressionless reading of Reuben's face. Reuben was suddenly on edge. This was the man he had come for, the prisoner whose DNA evidence had been falsified, the inmate someone wanted investigated, the criminal who might hold the key to Reuben's sacking and GeneCrime impropriety. Brawn's wide-spaced eyes revelled for a second in Reuben's discomfort, and then returned to the game.

*　*　*

Reuben squinted at the digital counter in the corner of the elevated screen. The game was fast approaching half-time. All around him, prisoners continued to be nervy and excited. He guessed they didn't see many live games, especially not clashes between footballing enemies, the big grudge matches of the season. He continued to focus most of his attention on Michael Brawn. A short-haired prisoner was leaning over and speaking to Brawn, who was taking very little notice, absorbed in the game. Occasionally he blinked, but other than that, he was inanimate. On the screen, a Manchester United player surged into Arsenal's eighteen-yard box, and a mis-hit shot deflected into the net. Suddenly, Brawn was on his feet, arms in the air, shouting.

'Fucking get in there!'

No one else moved. Brawn turned around, arms still aloft, teeth clenched, eyes ablaze. Mostly, prisoners avoided his gaze. Reuben stared at him, taking everything in. For the first time, he appreciated that there was something unhinged about Brawn, something outside the normal rules, something that was best left alone. Reuben also sensed that the other inmates knew this already. While he tried to sum up what exactly it was that was different about the man, Brawn shifted his head slightly to look hard at him, and Reuben found himself caught in the headlights of his eyes.

In the background, the commentator was beside himself with excitement. Reuben grinned slowly at Brawn, an expression designed to say, our team has scored. Brawn stared back, waxen and cold. Reuben scratched his tattoo, almost involuntarily. The other prisoners fidgeted quietly in their seats. Then Brawn left Reuben's face and ran his eyes around the room. The commentator was saying, 'And the unfortunate lad at the back, Jeremy Accoutey's replacement, seems to have deflected that past his keeper and into his own net.'

The peep of the referee's whistle sounded. Michael Brawn swivelled round and sat down again. Reuben waited a couple of moments before leaving, shouts once again erupting in the room, inmates screaming at the TV; twenty-two players running to the baying of the crowd, one of their number lying dead inside a morgue, gunshot wounds to his head, samples of his wife's DNA sitting in Reuben's freezer, a large sum of his money in the glove box of Moray Carnock's car.

6

Judith Meadows rotated the slim platinum band of her wedding ring with her thumb and index finger. It was a nervous habit, something she often caught herself doing when her mind was busy, or she was unsure, or she was impatient between long stages of laboratory protocols. She pictured her husband for a second, sitting at work, chair tightly pushed under his desk, maybe twirling his own wedding ring absently, wondering whether it was really working out or not. A fresh start, they had both agreed. A time to reappraise their relationship. What Judith needed, he had suggested, was a baby. And whereas Judith would have happily slapped him for such a brazen lack of insight into her desires and needs, the words had instead hit her a smarting blow, which still stung three months later. The insensitive bastard was right.

Judith followed one step behind Moray Carnock as they exited the lift and made their way down the long, plush corridor of the hotel. She let go of her wedding ring and continued to think. It was as if her finger had finally slipped off the mute button of her alarm clock. The suppressed buzzer had begun to sound and there was little she could do to stop it again. She was in her mid-thirties, soon it would be too late. And now, slightly nauseous and feeling tired, Judith realized that things might be about to

196

change. The sick feeling in her stomach was compounded by guilt, and by the knowledge that her work would inevitably suffer. Days spent pulling double shifts in the hunt for a serial murderer would be numbered. And there would be other issues.

She knew she would give her heart and soul to Reuben's cause as long as she could. She believed in her former boss and what he did, knew that it excited her and kept her alive, understood that scientific impropriety within GeneCrime could blow holes in UK forensics which might never be repaired. Judith just hoped that if her tiredness and queasiness were anything more than fatigue and a rushed lunch, she still had enough time to make a difference.

Moray stopped outside a blank door and inserted a card in its slot. They pushed through and into the room, which housed several heavy pieces of gym equipment. A floor-to-ceiling window revealed a couple of miles of London rooftop. The carpet was thin and hard-working, and contrasted with the rest of the hotel's deep luxury. Judith reached for her wedding ring, and cursed, stopping herself just in time. Moray walked forward and extended his hand in Kieran Hobbs' direction.

'Mr Hobbs,' he said.

Kieran took his hand and shook it. Judith deliberately held her arms by her sides. It was not good practice for forensic technicians to shake hands with known criminals.

'Hey, Judith,' Kieran said with a wink. 'How're you doing?'

Judith smiled back, a cement mixer of emotions churning her stomach. Her husband wanting a baby, fighting to disagree and not really winning, beginning to feel strange, long shifts hunting killers spacing her out, meeting real-life gangsters in the flesh, her former boss undercover and in prison. None of it sat right when she put it all together, but individually, things seemed to make sense.

'Fine,' she said.

Kieran extended his pink fleshy hand, a twinkle of gold catching the light. Judith shook her head, quickly and demurely, her hair amplifying the refusal.

'From such a beautiful woman, that hurts,' Kieran grinned. 'But fair play. Still, you can't be telling me CID are interested in semi-legitimate businessmen like me.'

'Semi? That's pushing it,' Judith answered. 'But no, not so much. Bigger fish at the moment, I'm afraid.'

She turned her attention to Nathan and Valdek, who were pushing free-weights. Nathan was lying down on a bench, forcing a monumentally stacked bar upwards, with Valdek standing at the side, his arms hovering close, ready to help if necessary. All that muscle, Judith thought, and so few neurons. For a second, she allowed her eyes to enjoy the spectacle. The rippling, engorging flesh, sinews straining, veins enlarging, teeth clenching, eyes bulging . . . she took in Nathan's face, his locked jaw, his grimacing smile, his creased forehead. Nathan caught her eye momentarily, and seemed to flinch, almost embarrassed by his exertions. Judith glanced quickly at Valdek. He winked at her and flicked his tongue around his lips. Judith returned her attention to Kieran, suddenly feeling uncomfortable. He was taking a tightly wrapped bundle of notes out of an inside pocket and handing it to Moray.

'That's what I owe Reuben up to date.'

As Moray struggled with the cellophane binding, intent on counting the money, he asked, 'You found out who sent the Dutch guy to kill you?'

'Working on it.'

'And?'

'Slowly slowly catchy monkey. But I've got something here that might just help.'

Kieran pulled a small plastic bag out of his inside pocket and passed it to Moray, who examined it briefly and gave it to Judith.

'What is this?' she asked.

'A mugshot of yours truly. God knows where it came from. But we found it in the lining of the Dutchman's jacket just before we burned his clothes the other day.'

Judith peered through the plastic. A thin red residue coated its inner surface, the black and white image of Kieran's face tinted pink by the blood.

'So?' she asked.

'Someone must have given it him, right? And that someone might be who wants me gone.'

'Who's touched it?'

'Just me,' Kieran answered. 'And those two.' He nodded in the direction of his minders.

Judith frowned, thinking, wondering what Reuben would do. 'I might have to get DNA swabs from all of you for elimination,' she said. 'Then we'll test it, see if there's anything worth looking at. Might need a few days though.'

'Fine, darling,' Kieran answered. 'You're the boss. Whatever it takes to wrap this thing up.'

Moray peered uneasily in the direction of Valdek. Reuben had almost been shocked by what was left of Ethan de Groot.

'Nasty business,' he said.

'Yeah, well,' Kieran responded. 'The man tried to kill me. Purely self-defence. You think your lot would take a harsh view of someone defending themselves from a hitman?' he asked, turning to Judith.

'You leave me out of this,' Judith replied quietly. 'I'm hardly a spokesman for the police.'

Kieran scrutinized Judith for a second, running his pale blue eyes over her. 'No problem,' he said. 'No problem at all.'

* * *

In the lift back down to the lobby, Moray said, 'That's Hobbs' private gym. Not that he uses it too much himself, by the looks. Just a perk for his boys.'

'Why in the hotel though?' Judith asked.

'He's got financial stakes in a lot of property round here. The ultimate aim of the money launderer — to convert it into bricks and mortar, in legitimate businesses.'

'I don't like working for him.'

'You don't say. But it's fine for me and Reuben. Hobbs is one of a dying breed, an old-school gangster. You know where you are with him. He's big enough not to have to go looking for it, if you know what I mean. Stable and sorted, with no axe to grind.'

'Until someone comes along who wants to kill him.'

'Which is where we come in. And without his money, we wouldn't be able to do the important things.'

Judith was silent. She knew the arguments, had heard them over and over, and appreciated their stark truths. But they never reassured her. If she was photographed shaking hands with a man like Kieran Hobbs, or even within his vicinity, her career would be over. Covert surveillance was a matter of fact. It happened, on both sides of the law. Just like the picture of Kieran she had in her pocket.

'I know,' she muttered. 'We've just got to be careful not to get mixed up in the things he's mixed up in.'

'That,' Moray shrugged, 'is the tight-rope we walk.'

The lift pinged, its door slid open, and Moray and Judith walked out through the lobby, surrounded by tourists, staff and businessmen, multiple worlds converging in the bright foyer of a London hotel.

7

As he walked, a fine mist permeated the air and slickened Reuben's face. It was the kind of borderline rain which closes in, turning everything grey, making you squint. He wiped his eyes, still staring down at his trainers. The tarmac, usually lifeless, was glistening. Cormack O'Connor, pacing shoulder to shoulder with him, his head similarly bowed, continued where he left off.

'Officially, money laundering. Five years. But let's say there might have been a bit more to it.'

'How do you mean?'

Cormack smiled at his feet. 'You'll learn not to ask those sorts of questions.'

'So, what about you?' Reuben said, turning to his left.

Damian Nightley cleared his throat, a low rumble through his voice box. 'Gun smuggling, you know, firearms offences. We had half of London sewn up. You name it, we could get hold of it.'

There was nothing boastful in Damian's tone of voice, just a matter-of-fact statement of the truth. And Reuben knew it was the truth. He already understood exactly what Damian and Cormack were in for, and what they had done in the past. Sarah had recited their litany of criminal activity down the phone to him, and it had taken several minutes.

'Pretty straightforward,' she had said. 'Nothing unsolved or untoward. Just bad boys who got caught out and are doing their time, until they're released back into society and we lock them up again.'

'What makes you sure they'll re-offend?' Reuben had asked.

'Call it a DCI's intuition. Career criminals from Kieran Hobbs' organization. Take away the criminal part and they've got no careers.'

Reuben stole a surreptitious glance at the prisoners on each side of him. Human beings, people who had drifted into illegal actions, men who risked their liberty and lost. Until ten months ago, Reuben's contact with criminals had mainly involved the microscopic parts of themselves that they left behind at crime scenes. More recently, he had been dealing with them in the flesh, and what had shattered his preconceptions was their ordinariness. Criminals were normal people who had different moral outlooks. Forensics, as well as police detection in general, demonized men like Damian and Cormack. Reuben had often stared at DNA sequences or profiles and seen not the human but the satanic, a molecular reductionism which shrank a criminal down to the one act they had perpetrated, the one evil they had given in to. But Reuben was increasingly coming to see that it wasn't quite like that. And while he would happily have hunted both men who were protecting him, and would have been eager to avoid their company outside Pentonville's walls, he couldn't escape the conclusion that Damian,

Cormack and their ilk were not evil so much as misguided and morally askew. Just like his father.

Cormack lifted his damp face towards Reuben, then thumbed in the direction of Damian. 'Ask him how long he's got left of his ten-year stretch,' he said.

Reuben glanced at Damian. 'How long have — '

'No fucking remission,' Damian spat, his tone suddenly harder. 'I got two months left.'

'He's almost a free man. And do you think he's happy about it?' Cormack turned his face to Reuben again. 'Ask him if he's happy about it.'

Reuben did as he was told, wondering why Cormack felt the need for an interpreter. 'Are you — '

'Drop it, the both of yous.' Damian's cheeks flushed with anger, his eyes narrowing. An undeniable darkness surfaced on his brow. He bent his head down and kept walking, veering off the exercise path towards a door marked 'Block B'. Reuben watched him go, puzzled at how quickly he had changed.

'Miserable sod,' Cormack muttered. 'If it was me, I'd be counting the days.'

Seconds later, a whistle was blown some-where, and the forty minutes of exercise came to a halt. Cormack told Reuben he'd meet him after lunch, once he'd made a couple of calls, and they agreed to track Damian down. Reuben headed straight for the canteen, his stomach rumbling.

Already, after only three days, he felt firmly on the road to being institutionalized, food the trigger that kept him regimented, synchronized and under control. It was like hospitals, or old people's homes. Ridiculously early lunches and dinners, which always left you on the verge of hunger, perpetually waiting for the next meal, in line and orderly, obedient and submissive. Reuben shrugged as he walked, an involuntary twitch, feelings rising to the surface. Sometimes, on important cases, he had worked for sixteen hours straight and had barely eaten a morsel. But that was the all-consuming nature of forensic detection — the cooling body, the scattered skin cells, the drying blood. And the amphetamine had helped, from time to time. Now, however, locked up with nowhere to go and little to occupy him, he was ravenous, as if eating were a substitute for living.

Reuben entered the high-ceilinged dining room, with its flaky paint and warming odours. He stood at the back of the queue, waiting his turn to receive several ruined lumps of food on a plastic tray. Someone joined the queue behind him and Reuben turned slightly, monitoring him in his peripheral vision. He was well aware that this was a safer option than staring directly. The grainy, blurred edge of his sight sensed something important. He turned a little more, the man coming increasingly into focus. Reuben's heart began to pound, his stomach forgetting about lunch. Michael Brawn was standing next to him.

Reuben shuffled forward in silence, closer to the food. He weighed his options. An unambiguous sample of DNA wasn't something you could easily take at the best of times. And without someone knowing, it was virtually impossible. Michael Brawn was two or three inches taller than Reuben, expressionless, his wide eyes sucking everything in. Reuben's tattoo — the crest of Manchester United Football Club — was facing him, clearly visible on the forearm sliding an aluminium tray along the steel rails of the serving counter. From Reuben's angled view, he could see Brawn's similar but lower-quality depiction on his right arm. He silently thanked Sarah for providing his CID file, which detailed the distinguishing mark.

Reuben knew he had to get close to Brawn, to find out where he went and when, and which of the small cluster of cells was his. Only then could he plan how to snatch a pure sample of him without his knowledge.

'Good result last night,' he muttered.

Michael Brawn remained quiet, just staring. It was clear to Reuben, as it had been in the TV room, that Brawn was a man who controlled every situation he was in. His silence undermined, hanging in the air, making men talk when otherwise they would be mute. But Reuben needed a result.

'Now it's just Chelsea to try and catch,' he said.

Again, Brawn glared at him. Reuben remained half turned, trying not to look directly at him, feeling the discomfort of the scrutiny. They shuffled a couple of paces closer to lunch.

'But with our away form this season, who knows?'

Brawn cut into him with his eyes. Reuben held his tray firmly as a dollop of vegetable landed on it, a similar portion left clinging to the ladle. The clank of metal on metal. A background hum of chatter. A soft whoosh of steam from a water heater. Utter silence from Michael Brawn. Reuben's trainers squeaking as he stepped up to the next server.

'I heard we might get bought out again, though. Did you hear anything?'

Michael Brawn dropped his tray beside Reuben's. A similar dollop of greenness landed on it, the server avoiding his eye. And then the sound of a snort, barely audible, but unmissable to Reuben's ears. Michael Brawn blowing air through his nostrils. The suggestion of don't-make-me-laugh.

Reuben turned away, focusing on the next server in line. Hidden from Michael Brawn, he allowed himself the briefest flicker of a smile.

8

The low-ceilinged room thundered and cracked, gunfire ricocheting off its surfaces, funnelling the fury so that it pounded DI Charlie Baker's ears until they felt as if they should be bleeding. He ripped a pair of ear defenders off a rack and paced quickly along the row of shooters. As he fitted them over his ears, the noises dulled, their edges rounded off, though still forceful enough to rattle his skull.

There was room for six officers at a time, the stalls divided with rough planks of plywood, looking to Charlie as if they had been knocked up in someone's spare time. He walked along the dark green carpet. Above, the ceiling was strip-lit and suspended, like in a cheap shop. Even by Metropolitan standards, this was an untidy gun range. He peered at the damage as he passed each stall in turn, two female officers and four male. The targets were black bowling-pin shapes on a fawn background, successful hits appearing as specks of white where light poked through from behind. He reached the final marksman in line and waited, allowing him to discharge a volley of shots in quick succession. Then Charlie reached forward, his arm angling up to tap Commander Robert Abner on the back.

Commander Abner turned his head, then swivelled his upper torso round, a two-stage process which seemed to Charlie slightly robotic, as if one cog controlled another. He pulled his own ear protectors away. 'What is it?' he asked.

'Sorry to interrupt you, sir. Just thought you should see this ASAP.'

Charlie held up a clear plastic bag, which contained two fragments of a sheet of paper. He glanced past his superior officer at the target near the end of the room. Robert's shots were clustered in two regions, one in the rounded head area and the other in the approximate torso. Charlie noted with satisfaction that the torso holes were in a tight cardiac formation. He also observed with interest that the skull shots were in no way random, and appeared to concentrate around the area where the right eye would lie. The commander hadn't lost his touch. And while Charlie considered himself a good shot, and had been trained to roughly the same standard, he knew that he wouldn't fancy his chances against him in a twenty-five yard competition. The old man was still a star.

'What is it?' Commander Abner asked again.

'I retrieved them from the house of Jeremy Accoutey.'

Robert Abner laid his pistol flat on the deep wooden shelf in front of him, making sure its short, chopped nose was pointing away from Charlie. He took the evidence bag in both hands, savouring its silky plastic feel, layers rubbing and sliding over each other. The paper inside was thick and vaguely familiar to him.

'So . . . ' he said.

'It's output data from a sequencer. The screen-shot patterns you get for quality control

209

prior to sequence analysis.'

'I'm more than familiar with what gel files are, detective inspector.'

'Sorry, sir.'

Commander Abner shouted to be heard over another barrage of shots. 'But I don't recognize the format.'

'That's because it's probably from an ABI 377. Still in operation, but less fashionable these days. The dog's knackers a few years back, and not the sort of equipment generally used by amateurs.'

'Do we use them currently?'

'Decommissioned our last one about ten months ago, sir.'

'Ten?'

He peered down at Charlie, a stern uncle with a glint in his eye. Charlie did his best not to be unnerved by Commander Abner's reputation for detail, or his status as one of the country's leading detectives, or his decorations for smashing gun rackets and drug gangs, or his no-nonsense progress in the world of forensics. It was, Charlie was forced to concede, a lot to try not to be daunted by, and it left him with the worrying fear that Abner saw right through him and into his motives and actions. It was bad enough a criminal getting on the wrong side of Commander Robert Abner. But a policeman . . . Charlie moved his thoughts to safer ground.

'Give or take a couple of weeks, sir.'

'So, let me get this clear,' Robert Abner growled. 'A footballer kills his wife, then turns the gun on himself. Some time prior to this

210

event, he has been given sophisticated forensic information which hasn't come from ourselves.'

'Exactly, sir.'

'Charlie?'

'Sir?'

'Drop the sirs. We're both on the same side here.' Commander Abner raised his eyebrows, a brief smile twitching on his lips. 'Besides, it unnerves me. Now, what kind of information do you think Mr Accoutey received?'

'Impossible to tell.'

'But if you had to guess?'

'The obvious, given the death of his wife, would be some sort of infidelity test.'

'And who do we know who is currently offering such a facility?'

Charlie felt as if he was being tested, a senior officer asking what he already knew. 'Well, commercial outfits — you know, private labs that advertise in the back of magazines and just cover paternity tests, that sort of thing. If it was something to do directly with Lesley Accoutey, and that's simply a guess, there's only a couple of names that spring to mind.'

'Which are?'

'There was a private lab out near Heathrow, set up by some ex-human genome staff from the Sanger Institute — ' Another volley of rapid gunfire burst through Charlie's words and he waited for a period of quiet. 'You know, when the human genome was essentially mapped, a few punters branched off into more exotic stuff. Screening for inherited syndromes in potential partners, picking up viral infections at an early

211

stage, HIV testing, deciding which partner had got the virus first, a few borderline activities for employers and insurance companies . . . '

'And they're still active?'

'Very much so. We've been keeping a quiet eye on them.'

'Good. Maybe it shouldn't be so quiet from now on. Go over and see them, have a nose into their business.'

'I will. Only . . . '

'What?'

'There is the other possibility.' From the outset, a name had come to him thick and fast. A bell ringing, a nerve firing. 'There are whispers about Reuben Maitland,' he said. 'That he's still sniffing around, and offering forensic services.'

Robert Abner's face hardened. 'I want you to leave Reuben Maitland out of this.'

'But, sir. Surely he's a potential suspect.'

'I have my reasons,' he said, picking up his gun again. 'And that's all you need to know for now.'

He emptied the chambers, and Charlie watched him slot six new rounds in their place. Commander Abner replaced his ear protection and turned back to the target, and Charlie appreciated that his audience with the big man was over.

He walked back the way he had come, once again running the gauntlet of multiple weapons being discharged, and seeing tiny bright holes appear in distant targets, almost as if light itself was forcing its way through the cardboard in spontaneous bursts. He wondered why Robert Abner was protecting Reuben Maitland, and whether there was a bond between the two he didn't know about. It was not a thought that cheered him. The chance to squeeze Maitland was one he would have relished. And if it was true that he was still poking his nose into prior GeneCrime business, then having him put out of harm's way would have been a massive bonus for Charlie. As it was, he decided to convince Abner that he wasn't interested in Reuben Maitland, while all the time getting closer to him.

I know this smacks of you, Charlie thought, examining the evidence bag one more time as he left the range, and now, Dr Maitland, I'm coming to get you.

9

Joshua Maitland lay serenely asleep on his back, a blanket half on and half off him, a stuffed dog which had seen better days just out of reach. As his right arm stretched, it pulled a thin clear tube with it, which entered a vein on his wrist. The cannula was disproportionately large, and held in place with a plaster decorated with cartoon robots. A small amount of dried blood surrounded one edge of the plaster, wrinkling its surface.

While Joshua slept, a nurse approached his bed and adjusted the flow-rate of a bag of saline hanging from a small metal frame. 'Just keeping an eye on his fluids,' she said with a smile. Lucy Maitland attempted to smile back, a terse flick of her lips revealing a glimmer of teeth. When the nurse had left, Lucy glanced anxiously at her watch, and then at the clock on her mobile phone. She sighed, and looked back at Joshua, peaceful and still, with all the untouched beauty a sleeping child possesses. She stared in wonder for a second, the way she always did when Joshua was asleep, his noisy exuberance gone, leaving behind only a delicate loveliness in its place.

Sometimes, from a certain angle, he reminded her of Reuben. She saw it more when he was still. But when Joshua was charging around the place, boisterous and rowdy, Lucy thought he looked more like Shaun. But still, at eighteen months of age, she was unable to tell definitively. And the more quiet he had been recently, the more withdrawn and the less likely to run about screaming Shaun's house down, the more he had seemed to resemble her estranged husband. Lucy smiled briefly to herself, that illness could change the way her son looked to her. In rude health he was Shaun's son; in ill health he was Reuben's.

Lucy stroked the warm softness of his skin. She desperately hoped that Joshua wasn't Reuben's son. It was impossible to be certain either way without a DNA test. But Reuben didn't seem keen on the idea, and, though she battled to suppress it, neither was she. At the moment they had a status quo, which, given the last ten months, was a hell of a lot more acceptable than further turmoil. What she did hope, however, was that the hospital tests on Joshua would be rapid, and as decisively negative as she knew they would be. These days, doctors seemed to test for anything they possibly could, desperate to avoid the career-threatening instance when they missed something big. As a practitioner of law, Lucy knew that medics were petrified of meeting her ilk in any context other than the doctor-patient relationship. She secretly believed that this was why Joshua was being singled out for such invasive testing, given two or three months of just being mildly under the weather.

Lucy checked her watch again. Where are all the bloody staff? she asked herself. Her mobile rang. Work would be hunting her down, wondering why she wasn't keeping any of her morning appointments.

'Hello, Lucy Maitland,' she answered, trying to sound upbeat.

On the other end, from a corridor in Pentonville, Reuben said, 'It's your ex-husband.'

Lucy gave a half laugh. 'Not till the paperwork comes through, sonny. Until then, estranged would be more accurate.'

'Anyway . . . ' Reuben paused, his breathing scratching through the receiver. 'Look, I just wanted to know how Josh is. Last time I saw him he had a bad cough.'

'He's fine,' Lucy replied flatly. And then, 'Actually, he's not fine.'

'What do you mean?'

'He's in hospital having blood tests.'

'Hospital?'

'Don't panic. Just as an out-patient, referred by the GP. Useless bugger that he is.'

'But what are they testing for?'

'Christ knows. But I wish they'd get on with it. We've been here so long Joshua has fallen back to sleep. Tell the truth, I wouldn't mind joining him.'

'If you had to take a wild guess though?'

Lucy noted that Reuben sounded edgy. 'Like I said, probably nothing, simply a precaution. Bloody inconvenient — I've got an eleven o'clock. Actually, I don't suppose you could . . . '

In Pentonville, with his head pressed close to the metal hood, the phone jammed in the crook of his neck, and a phone card pushed in the slot,

216

Reuben watched a succession of prisoners pass him by. 'I'd love to,' he said with genuine regret, 'but I can't. I'm a bit . . . ' Aiden Boucher walked past. He glared intently at Reuben and gave him the universal throat-cut sign. 'A bit busy at the moment. For a few days at least.'

'Fine,' Lucy muttered.

'Look, when will you know?'

'When I've managed to see a bloody doctor, which in this place might not be any time soon.'

'I'll ring you,' Reuben said. Aiden Boucher was disappearing into the distance, swallowed up by other inmates. Reuben pictured his son in the hands of medics, wanting only to hold him himself. 'Good luck, Lucy. And will you give him a kiss for me?'

In the brightly lit hospital room, Lucy ended the call with a curt yes. She bent down to Joshua's face and gave him a very brief peck on the cheek. 'That's from Dr Maitland,' she whispered, not wanting to wake him. 'Which is about all he's ever given you.'

A medic entered the ward and she straightened again. She knew she could be fearsome if she put her mind to it. Colleagues at her law firm often joked about it. 'Being Lucied' was the phrase they had invented — on the wrong end of one of her tongue lashings. She stood up and straightened her skirt. Woe betide the doctor who came between Lucy Maitland and getting her son tested and out with a clean bill of health as fast as possible. In fact, woe betide anyone who came between Lucy and anything she wanted.

10

Moray Carnock ambled his considerable bulk along the pavement. A light rain that didn't seem to carry wetness with it, just freshness, was beginning to come down. His clothes stayed dry, barely touched. Yet the droplets continued to fall, whipped up by the wind. Fifty metres in front of him his quarry was making similarly unhurried progress, untouched by the moisture, talking on a mobile, stopping occasionally in front of shop windows, gesticulating with his free hand. Moray noticed that a good deal of his attention was focused on checking his own reflection. He seemed to focus particularly on his hair, with its permanent wet-look and irritatingly rakish sweep. Moray ignored what he saw in the windows he passed. It was, he told himself, what lay on the inside that mattered. His stomach began to rumble. Moray allowed himself a brief smile. A pasty and two sausage rolls were what lay on his insides, and they rarely helped matters at all.

Anthony McDower started walking again, and Moray continued his progress. From what he could gather through Judith, the police conclusion had been murder followed by suicide. Jeremy Accoutey possessed an illegal firearm, had been in trouble with the law before, and knew with one hundred per cent certainty, thanks to Reuben, who his wife was fucking.

Stranger things had happened, however. And Mr Anthony McDower, the team physio, examining his profile in a series of high-street shop windows, certainly didn't look overly distraught. He had been questioned and released by the police. But at the very least, Moray and Reuben had concluded, he was worth keeping an eye on. So Moray had decided to devote his afternoon to seeing exactly what Mr McDower did during his time off.

Moray watched Anthony enter a sunglasses and watches shop, the kind of place you go when you want to buy something but can't really figure out what. He checked his own watch. Three thirty-six. That awkward period between lunch and tea. He rummaged in the folds of his coat, but his fingers discovered only empty wrappers, the plastic remains of saturated foodstuffs. McDower was taking his time. Moray imagined him trying on a series of similar sunglasses, relishing the chance for more self-examination, paying more attention to his face than to the potential purchases. Although Moray was 95 per cent sure he was innocent, obvious vanity only days after the death of his lover seemed inappropriate at best. He tried to imagine how he would have felt if his ex-wife had died when they were still together, and reasoned that he probably wouldn't have been able to drag himself out of bed for a week. McDower's behaviour was different, however.

The howling of sirens pierced the air. Moray appreciated that this always meant bad news for someone somewhere. That omni-present

219

London noise had become exactly what pain, misery and tragedy sounded like to Moray, an anthem of distress, an electronic wailing of misfortune. Ambulances, fire-engines and police cars rushing to the scene of somebody's bad luck.

A dark blue Ford Mondeo pulled up sharply next to the kerb, and Moray cursed under his breath. 'Here we fucking go,' he muttered with a sigh, pretending not to have seen it. He began walking, but only managed a few strides before a CID officer he didn't recognize began to match him pace for pace. He was in plainclothes, and seemed to have taken the description almost too literally. The logo-less jeans and ironed shirt screamed copper louder than any uniform would have.

'Care to come for a ride?' he asked.

Moray scanned the window of the car behind the officer. There was a figure he recognized in the back, and he knew the game was up.

'Aye,' he said, 'why not? My feet are killing me.'

Moray sauntered over and climbed in through the rear door. The plainclothes CID officer sat in the front, and the car pulled off. Moray looked over at DI Charlie Baker and smiled. DI Baker was in full uniform, the severity of his black jacket combining with the sharpness of his beard to formidable effect. He didn't smile back.

'You a football fan, Mr Carnock?' Charlie asked.

'Only the proper stuff.'

'The proper stuff?'

'Kilmarnock, you know . . . '

'And do many Kilmarnock players shoot them-selves?'

Moray raised his eyebrows, thick folds of skin rippling his forehead. 'It would be no bad thing if they did.'

DI Baker stared back, impassive and deadpan. 'We found some very interesting documents at Mr Accoutey's place, documents that reek of you and Reuben Maitland.'

'Really?'

The car cut through the traffic and took a roundabout at speed. Moray realized that they had failed to spot Anthony McDower. For a second he felt put out that he had been followed while he was following someone else. He heard a clichéd Hollywood voice-over in his head: *And then the hunter became the hunted*. It was an amateurish mistake that might have proved costly under different circumstances.

'And how do you figure that out?'

'I think you'll find, Mr Carnock, that we're able to figure a lot of things out.'

'Now this is interesting,' Moray muttered. 'And is that all you have?'

DI Baker appeared to redden under his beard, an angry scarlet topsoil just about visible through the undergrowth. 'We are talking here about the violent deaths of two people. Have you seen what a twelve-bore does to a human face?'

Moray shook his head. He had seen a lot of unpleasant sights, but had been spared that particular one.

'It's not fucking pretty. This is serious and high-profile. A shock to the public. One of the tabloids is apparently about to print some very disturbing pictures. Don't know how the fuck they got them. But this ain't fun and games, Carnock.'

'I still don't see — '

'Now you tell Reuben that he'd better watch his back. Old loyalties are one thing, but the press are scratching this like the pox. And sooner or later they're going to want to see some blood. As you well know, taking DNA from people without their knowledge is an illegal activity.'

Moray turned away, scanning the streets. CID were on to them, and it had happened quicker than he had guessed. True, they didn't have enough evidence yet, but they were obviously close. He wondered for a second why DI Baker was warning them, and concluded that he wanted to watch them squirm, needed to see what they would do now, had been eager to witness their reaction. He also realized that they didn't know Reuben's current whereabouts.

'I wish I could help you,' he said, turning back to face him, 'but I haven't the faintest idea what you're talking about.'

DI Charlie Baker held his gaze for several long moments, the look cold and appraising, an intensity gained from years of cross-examining liars and deceivers. Moray tried not to flinch. The bastard knew something else. It was there in the thin smile lurking in his beard. Something that could conceivably sink them.

Moray turned away and chewed his lip. He needed to contact Reuben and let him know that his old unit was coming for him.

11

Sarah Hirst closed the door of the records room behind her. Had there been a lock, she would have gladly used it. The windowless subterranean room was one of only a handful which escaped the all-pervasive air conditioning of GeneCrime. The building, only three years old, had been constructed with security and biological safety in mind. This meant that none of its small number of windows opened, and the laboratories were kept at a slightly higher air pressure than everywhere else, to prevent the ingress of airborne contaminants every time someone entered through a door. However, the fine balancing act that the four-storey, hermetically sealed building had to maintain resulted in air-conditioned rooms which were perpetually too hot or too cold. Nowhere seemed to be just right. Her own office was ridiculously cold, no matter the time of day or year. Even in summer Sarah had to wear a jacket or a coat as she sat in front of her computer.

Walking through the floor-to-ceiling stacks of records, Sarah ran her index finger over the paper and cardboard files almost absently, enjoying the still, natural air. She had requested Michael Brawn's record the previous week, but hadn't pulled it herself. From now on, she decided that if the opportunity arose she would hunt out what she needed without requesting support staff help. Just getting out of her office for half an hour felt like a major escape act.

The records room housed all the case notes, files, general information and forensic evidence available, around a third of which wasn't housed on the GeneCrime server. Even in the hunt for a modern serial killer, Sarah was well aware that there was no substitute for the depth and sheer volume of knowledge that old-fashioned paper filing systems housed. Currently, she was cross-referencing witness statements from the three murders, and examining the last-known routes of each victim. Sarah pulled the files she needed and lugged them over to a small area which housed a number of chairs and a couple of desks. Again, she could have carried them back to her office, but the thought of staring into her computer screen and shivering herself towards another biting migraine filled her with dread.

Sarah was deep into the testimony of the man who had discovered the body of the second victim, DI Tamasine Ashcroft, when the door opened. She looked up and saw the neat, crisp form of Commander Robert Abner. Sarah had vowed from day one not to be intimidated by him, and so far had been reasonably successful. There was something strong and paternal about him which she found somewhat difficult to deal with. Her own father had, even through the eyes of a devoted daughter, been weak and inconsistent.

He approached her desk, almost hesitantly.

'DCI Hirst,' he muttered, 'do you have a moment?'

'Of course, sir.' Sarah glanced down at the files strewn everywhere, the photos of the victims, the typewritten statements and the photocopies of evidence. 'Excuse the mess.'

'Sorry to disturb your work.' Robert Abner indicated a chair. 'OK if I park myself?'

'Sorry. Of course.'

Sarah detected the slight awkwardness in her boss's approach, and the automatic diffidence in her own behaviour. Since he had arrived to oversee the division and put it back on track, she had never spent more than a few minutes alone in his company. He was a remote boss whom she respected, and who in turn allowed Sarah to get on with her work. From this, she surmised that the commander trusted her, largely because he wasn't interested in her daily activities. And she was more than happy with the arrangement.

'I'll come straight to the point,' Commander Abner said. 'When was the last time you saw Reuben Maitland?'

'Two or three days ago, sir.'

'Do you have a current whereabouts for him?'

''Fraid not.' A small voice inside told Sarah not to say anything daft. She had barely breathed since the first question. 'All I know is that he's away on a job.'

Commander Abner frowned, and Sarah noticed that the crease of his forehead and the wrinkling of his eyes made him almost handsome.

'What kind of a job?'

Sarah exhaled, hoping to God that she wasn't blushing. She had arranged Reuben's entry into Pentonville without her boss's knowledge. Maybe the commander knew more than he was letting on. But it was too late to tell him now. She decided to feed him a vague and unincriminating version of the truth.

'I'm not sure,' she answered. 'Just heard along the lines that it was something underground, you know, out of the way.'

'Out of the way,' Commander Abner repeated, partly to himself. 'Anything else?'

'Not that I know.'

'But you're in touch with him?'

'Sometimes, yes. I know he's not necessarily welcome around here, but his depth of forensic knowledge is legendary. And, of course, he still has access to predictive phenotyping. Plus he's given us some potential avenues in the hunt for DNA from what we think might be the first victim.'

Robert Abner tipped his head back and regarded Sarah for a moment, his eyebrows pulled so tight together that they almost met. 'Don't worry,' he said. 'It's no bad thing to have Reuben on our side. I dealt with him myself recently.'

Reuben had told her all about the meeting, and about Abner's assertion that he might soon be requiring his services.

'Just wanted to know where he was at the moment, and what he was up to. That's all.'

Sarah folded her arms in her lap, forcing them still so they couldn't betray her with a sudden twitch or scratch of the face, or any other of the subconscious tics of the liars she questioned on an almost daily basis. 'Like I say, some sort of job, I think, sir.'

Commander Abner stood up again and straightened himself, smoothing the creases of his uniform. 'Right.' He aimed a smile at her and turned for the door. 'I won't disturb you any more.'

When he had left, Sarah rubbed her head and stared down into the folds of her skirt. Lying to an area commander was not good. She rewound through the conversation, trying to gauge whether she'd left enough grey areas, and whether she'd been vague and noncommittal where it counted. Then she wondered whether she should just have come clean. After all, if Reuben was right, Abner was actually behind the internal investigation into Michael Brawn. Although this made a lot of sense, she had no direct evidence of it. But this was her case, and the fewer people she told the better. And when Reuben completed his mission in a couple of days' time, and they had the result she needed, she would take all the glory, and no one would ever care that she had gone behind Abner's back.

12

Reuben realized it was getting close. The time to take a sample from Michael Brawn was fast approaching. Every extra day he spent in Pentonville increased the chances of disaster. Twelve hundred inmates; surely someone would recognize him soon. He had to take an unambiguous DNA sample from Michael Brawn, and then get straight to the governor. But as he sat on the toilet seat of a flimsy cubicle, examining his Kinder egg and picking out its forensic contents, he knew he was going to have to be an opportunist. When the moment arrived, any moment, he would have to seize it quickly and without hesitation. And also without Michael Brawn or anyone else knowing.

In many ways, the SkinPunch weapon would have been ideal. Reuben had designed and built it for just such an eventuality. The anonymous and certain removal of a skin specimen, a few thousand fibroblast cells, pure and untainted DNA. But Reuben knew he could never have smuggled the gun through the searches. And if he had, it would have been substantially less fun to remove than the Kinder egg. He continued to play with a small pair of tweezers and a short cottonwool bud, lost in thoughts of how and when. While he pondered, Joshua's face drifted in and out, lying in a hospital bed somewhere, the terrible word 'tests' hanging over him.

Reuben was about to pack his kit away when the door to the toilets opened and closed, and he heard a voice he half recognized, echoed and distorted by the high ceiling. He peered through one of the many deliberate gaps in the cubicle's structure. Standing in front of a long row of porcelain sinks, Damian Nightley was washing his hands quickly and hurriedly. Reuben sensed someone else in the toilets too. Damian turned his head towards the urinals, which were hidden from Reuben's view.

'Just leave me the fuck alone,' he said.

Reuben strained to see who he was talking to. Running water obliterated the reply, which was short and sharp.

'I'm connected,' Damian replied. 'You should think carefully about that.'

He turned the tap off and walked over to the hand-towel. From his movements, Reuben sensed he was acutely uncomfortable, but unwilling to back down and leave the toilets in a hurry.

And then the voice came again. This time Reuben heard it clearly. 'I've got my eye on you,' it said. It was a hard, dry Mancunian accent. It was Michael Brawn.

'And what's that supposed to mean?' Damian asked.

Reuben focused intently through the space between the door and its formica wall. The sound of footsteps. Not trainers, like most of the rest of the prison, but leather shoes, slapping the tiled floor, ricocheting around the hard surfaces. Then he saw him. Michael Brawn walking over to Damian, face to face. Peering slightly down, sneering and pale. 'If you don't know by now, son, you haven't been paying attention.'

A toilet flushed close to Reuben's, and its door banged open. A man Reuben didn't recognize walked over to the sink and began washing his hands. Reuben returned his attention to Damian, who remained motionless, staring long and hard at Brawn, before eventually walking out. Brawn lingered a moment, looking blankly in the mirror. He didn't smile or alter his expression. He just took it all in, his own mouth and hair and eyes, a statue facing a statue. Reuben wondered what the hell he was thinking. What would be on my mind if I was Michael Brawn? Reuben asked himself. And then Brawn spoke into the mirror. Three short words which Reuben strained to hear. But they were unmistakable.

'Not long now,' he hissed.

He turned and disappeared from view.

Reuben packed the forensic contents of his egg away. This could be it. The moment. He waited a beat, then flushed the toilet. If he could follow Michael Brawn to his cell, he would stand a chance. He slid the bolt back and pocketed the Kinder egg. All he would need were a few hairs or access to his toothbrush.

And then the door flew open and Michael Brawn stood in the door-frame, wide-eyed and bristling with violence. He shoved Reuben back, stepped inside the cubicle and locked the door.

'Let's have a look,' he said.

Reuben had no time to react. Brawn's long

straight arm pinned him to the wall, his open hand pressing into Reuben's sternum. With his free hand he reached forward, still holding eye contact, and forced Reuben's right sleeve up. Then he licked his index finger slowly. A thousand fears flashed through Reuben's mind. Alone in a cubicle with a psychopath. Off balance and trapped. The porcelain of the toilet cold against his leg. Brawn ran his wet finger across the surface of Reuben's tattoo. A light seemed to go on in his eyes, sparkling in the gloom, never moving away from Reuben's.

He pulled a small penknife from his trouser pocket. Reuben tried to edge back, but there was nowhere to go. Brawn's strength defied the relative leanness of his torso. He lowered the blade until it touched Reuben's tattoo. He pushed it down, and Reuben felt the sharp nip of the cutting edge. Then, slowly and deliberately, Brawn sliced the blade across the tattoo. A cold sting, a tingle somewhere in his groin, a biting pain opening up along the line marking the knife's progress. The burning tear of skin, the spasm of slit muscle, the deafening scream of bisected nerves. Droplets of red pushing their way through the dark inky-blue epidermis, lining themselves up into an angry stripe, merging into larger drops, oozing over hairs, funnelling along the pattern of the tattoo, dropping on to the floor. Michael Brawn, his eyes enjoying the sight of blood.

'I don't know what you want,' he whispered, folding his knife in a quick, seamless movement.

231

He slapped Reuben half seriously, half mockingly around the face. 'But you keep the fuck away from me.'

Michael Brawn unlocked the door, stepped out and walked smartly away, his footsteps echoing behind him.

Reuben clenched and unclenched his right hand, feeling for damage. His grip was fine, as were his movements. He looked down at the cut, straight and sharp, through the heart of his tattoo. Superficial damage only. Blood continued to fall on the tiles, and Reuben stooped to clear it up with some toilet paper. He wrapped another wad around his arm, pulled his sleeve over it and left, gritting his teeth, blocking the pain.

The mission had just become a lot more complicated.

13

Damian's cell, like most of the others in the block, was defined almost exclusively by the pictures stuck to its walls. The images reminded Reuben of tattoos. They were the visual story you wanted to tell, the parts of your life projected for public consumption. And whereas Narc's pictures were eclectic and virtually unreadable, Damian's were obvious and straight to the point. Reuben felt that he knew Damian's entire life story from one glance at his wall, and that Damian wanted it that way. Three children, two boys and a girl, at various stages of development; school mugshots in front of identically blurred backdrops; holidays on beaches and at campsites; a smattering of weddings, parties and family occasions. In some shots a squat, dark-haired woman stared bleakly into the camera, never quite smiling. Reuben wondered who had taken most of the photos. Damian had spent long years under detention, so it certainly hadn't been him. But the message was there all the same: this is my family, and this is what really matters to me.

Reuben couldn't help but wonder why, if that was the case, Damian had risked everything by being so deeply involved in the supply of firearms. He hoped Sarah was wrong, and that former associates of Kieran Hobbs wouldn't go straight back to their criminal ways. With a bit of luck, Damian would change careers when he was released in a few weeks. Certainly, Reuben wouldn't want to see him arrested by any of his ex-colleagues at GeneCrime.

Reuben decided to ask the question that had been refusing to abate for the last two hours, while the cut on his arm throbbed acutely and refused to stop bleeding.

'What do you two know about Michael Brawn?' he asked.

Damian caught his eye, a flash of hostility. 'What's it to you?'

'Just curious.'

'Best kept clear of,' Cormack answered, turning the page of his newspaper. 'He's got form and a half. Involved in a lot of not-nice things.'

'Like what?'

'Who knows? You just hear rumours. That's all you do hear in this place. Rumours. How someone bumped someone else, or is connected to the guts, or takes it in the greenhouse . . . ' Cormack glanced up from his paper. 'Trouble is, you never get to know what's right and what isn't.' He smiled, a boyish, cheeky grin that Reuben imagined had saved him from the odd bollocking at school. 'Take Laughing Boy, for example.' Cormack jerked his thumb in the direction of Damian.

'What?'

'I heard the other day he accidentally smiled.'

Damian scowled at him. 'Cocksucker.'

'And that as well.'

Despite himself, Damian broke into a brief

234

grin, which quickly faded. His characteristic apprehension returned with a vengeance. He stood up, smoothing the crease on the bed where he had just been sitting.

'Anyway,' he said quietly, pacing to the door.

'What?'

'Don't wreck my cell. Leave it tidy.'

'Where you going?' Cormack asked.

'Visiting time.'

'Who's coming?'

Damian's sigh was more visible than audible. His whole chest heaved up and fell back again. 'My old lady.'

He left the room, and Cormack raised his eyebrows at Reuben.

'What's the story?' Reuben said.

Cormack returned his attention to the paper. 'Some things are best left unasked,' he muttered.

Reuben lifted his sleeve a couple of inches, keeping it out of Cormack's view. The toilet paper was dark red, the blood dry and brittle. Between bouts of pulsing and throbbing, the wound had begun to itch. Reuben lowered his sleeve, ignoring the temptation to scratch it. As he did, an image hunted him down, sparked by two words Damian had said.

Visiting time.

Seated next to his brother Aaron, fidgeting, thirteen-year-old boys unable to sit still. A sparse room with empty tables and chairs. His mother Ina opposite, sharing her scolding looks between the two of them. Appreciating that his mother looked drawn, her fine features burdened by bags and wrinkles. Looking uncomfortable and out of place. Waiting and waiting, the room gradually filling up. The noise level rising, whispers turning to murmurs becoming chatter rising to shouts. And then Dad approaching, shuffling, his head down. Dressed in drab blue clothes, picking his way between tables towards them, gruff and awkward. Wanting to hug him, to hold him, anything. But something in his eyes holding Reuben back. His mother asking, so how are they treating you? His father replying, fine.

Oh, George . . .

I said, fine.

Aaron asking, when are they going to let you go?

And Reuben chipping in, soon, Dad?

His mum and dad exchanging quick glances.

Ina Maitland saying, we'll talk about this later, boys. But for now, give your dad a hug.

Reuben rubbed his face slowly, his eyes screwed tight with the memory. The place was starting to fuck with his head. This was the problem, he understood, the very thing that happens in prison. You fester. All the time in the world to sit and think does you no good at all.

Reuben stood up. 'I've got to get out of this place,' he muttered.

'Haven't we all,' Cormack replied laconically. After a couple of seconds he asked, 'What were you asking about Brawn for?'

Reuben rolled up his right sleeve and pulled the wad of tissue away. It clung to the wound, and congealed blood came away with it.

'He ran a knife through this.'

Cormack sat up on the bed and leaned

236

forward for a closer look. He whistled through his teeth. 'You're kidding.'

Reuben shook his head, defiant and angry, something he didn't like the feeling of welling up inside him.

'And I'm going to make the fucker pay for it.'

He walked out of Damian's cell and back towards his own, where his small scalpel blade lay, ready to be used for something a good deal nastier than he had originally intended.

14

Laura Beckman, a petite female in a tight red cardigan and dark blue jeans, stands up and waits by the doors for the night bus to stop. The brakes grind and squeal and the vehicle shudders to a halt. There is the sharp hiss of pneumatics and the doors fold open. He stands up and follows her off.

She leaves the vehicle and turns down an empty street. On the other side to her lies a school. There are zigzag lines in the road, multiple signs and speed bumps. A white painted railing on a small wall runs almost the length of the two-storey building. He remains twenty paces back, blotting out memories of his own schooling, suppressing his own pathetic and ineffectual efforts inside the classroom and out of it, still seeing the playground fights, the crush of eager pupils chanting 'Scrap, scrap, scrap!' while on the inside he or someone else was pulverized by boys who knew they wouldn't lose.

He doesn't know what time it is, except that the pubs kicked out seemingly an age ago. They are on the other side of the Thames and moving away from it. It is warmer tonight than it has been, but is still by no means pleasant. He wonders momentarily whether the woman is cold, and why she isn't wearing a coat. He knows that if he had dressed more . . . nothingness. And back again. A short blankness. He shakes his

238

head. He is still walking, on automatic pilot, the woman just about in sight. He quickens his pace. The black-outs are becoming more frequent and less predictable. He has no idea what happens or where he goes, but he knows they can't last more than a few seconds at a time.

The rules should have changed by now, but they haven't. He takes some reassurance from this, gradually closing in on the red cardigan ahead. There have been theories in the papers, but nothing more, no details. Besides, they have been consumed with the death of a footballer and his bimbo wife. But no official statement. No warning to stay off the streets. Just vague articles saying the police are still trying to link the death of this one with that one. And so the women of London continue to roam the streets, all dolled up, looking their best and remaining available.

He squeezes his fists tight, muscles hardening. She is ten paces ahead now, turning past a row of terraced houses. He glances around. The street is empty. There are no CCTV cameras and no cars. Most of the houses are unlit. The moment is coming. The surge, somewhere deep in his stomach. A tightness in his groin. Chewing his teeth hard. The show is about to begin. Time to make one more of them understand the truth about power.

The tablets from earlier are fully in his system now. He senses the energy they bring, expanding his chest, breathing deeply and quickly. The doctor talked again about side-effects, but that's all they are. It is the main effect that really matters, not the small and unimportant changes they smuggle along with them for the ride. And what a ride. He is, he firmly believes, unstoppable. What would it take to bring him down when he is in full flow? A van-load of coppers might be in with a chance. But a large proportion of them would end up with broken skulls and smashed-open noses.

The slag in front takes a left turn up a side street. The lighting is worse, the houses sparser and separated by commercial buildings and lock-ups. As she walks, she spins her head sharply round. Through the dark, he sees her face for the first time. It is pale, pretty and etched with concern. She is on to him. It is time to do it. Her pace increases, the heels of her shoes stabbing hard into the pavement. No black-outs, he says to himself. No black-outs.

He concentrates, the anger rising, the sick dread, the nervous anticipation. He starts to run, full tilt, leaning forward, his arms thumping through the air. She looks back again. He sees the fear, and it turns him on. He sprints faster, a lion in the chase, utterly focused on the kill. He feels light and strong, pounding towards her. Seven or eight paces back. Gaining with every stride. He can see she doesn't know what to do, other than run for her life. Again, this spurs him on, sends his excitement up a notch.

And then she stops. Turns round and faces him. She is breathing hard, mustering some defiance. He doesn't hesitate. She raises her hands, palms up. He leaps forward, lunging through the air. Flattens her, like at rugby. Her skull thuds into the pavement, a hollow sound, a coconut dropped on to concrete. He is on top of her, tearing at her clothes. She is dazed, maybe even concussed. He leaves her jeans and slaps her round the face. Come on, bitch, come on, he says to himself. Wake the fuck up.

There is blood in the back of her hair. He looks at the surgical glove on his right hand, which is smeared in red. He slaps her again in the face, shaking her body. Nothing. She is out cold. He glances around. The street is quiet. 'You have to wake up,' he growls. Her breathing is shallow, despite the chase. He feels the side of her neck for a pulse. It is difficult to detect through the gloves. This is no good. He screws his eyes up. It cannot be accidental. You have to know what I'm doing to you.

Suddenly he wonders, what if she doesn't come round? What then? She dies outright from a head injury. He knows the excitement is ebbing. He has lost control of the situation. And with no control, there is no point to be made. He wipes the bloody glove across her breasts, still tightly wrapped in the cardigan. Slowly, he stands up. If he blacks out again now . . . He turns and walks away, angry, frustrated, upset. Not looking back and staying in the shadows now. A lesson learned. Sometimes showing a woman too much power can be a bad thing.

15

Reuben strode into the pool room, an unhealthy anger raging. It had refused to abate, just as his wound was refusing to scab over. Inside, fifteen prisoners were standing or leaning, quietly smoking, intent on the game in progress. Michael Brawn languished in the corner, holding a pool cue, his hands in front of his chest. By the look of him, Reuben guessed that he had just played his shot and missed. A well-built inmate with dreadlocks was leaning over the table, taking his time. The atmosphere was tense with the suggestion that this was more than merely a game of pool. Something was riding on this. Maybe money, maybe cigarettes, maybe favours, Reuben didn't know. But a couple of paces to the right of Brawn, Reuben noticed Aiden Boucher among the spectators, intense and wide-eyed, his beard sharp with hostility.

Reuben walked round the table and stood in front of Michael Brawn.

'I want a fucking word with you,' he said.

Michael Brawn surveyed Reuben. The room fell silent, Brawn's opponent slowly straightening from his shot. All attention transferred from the game and on to Reuben. Brawn passed his cue to the inmate closest to him and stepped closer to Reuben.

'I'm all ears.'

'You put a knife through my tattoo.'

Reuben pushed his arm towards him, the evidence in red, an angry slit five inches long, bleeding thin, watery fluid.

'You're lucky it wasn't your heart,' Brawn said.

A couple of the spectators wolf-whistled, and Reuben sensed that this was going to get nasty.

'Now I'm going to fuck *your* tattoo up,' Reuben continued.

Michael Brawn laughed, his face never changing expression, his mouth barely open.

Reuben darted his left hand forward and grabbed Brawn's forearm. He pulled the scalpel blade from his back pocket with his right.

'Still think it's funny?' he asked, burning into his eyes.

'Hilarious.'

'You're not so tough.'

Brawn snorted. 'Tougher than you.'

'You think so?'

'Come on, streak of piss. Do it.'

Reuben moved the blade closer to Michael Brawn's arm, holding it above one of his tattoos. It was a crude skull, the standard bluey green of prison tattoos. The orbits of the eyes were red and the lower jaw bone missing. The thickness of its lines spoke of a blunt needle and repeated puncturing of the skin.

Brawn fixed his stare. The spectators stood in rapt attention. Reuben was aware that this was a hell of a lot more important than the game they had been watching. He gripped the scalpel blade perfectly still, the fingers of his other hand digging into Brawn's wrist.

'Because, deep down,' Brawn taunted him,

'you ain't got the balls.'

Reuben held his nerve. 'Only one way to find out.' He lowered the blade until it was touching the fine dark hairs of Brawn's arm.

'That's it, new boy. Nearly there.'

Reuben scanned the room with his peripheral vision. In the prisoners' expressions he detected a hunger for blood. Aiden Boucher monitored him intently, almost quivering with expectation. Reuben glanced back at the blade. His fingers had started to tremble slightly. As he watched them, fighting it, they shook more obviously, almost as if someone else was controlling their movements.

Don't panic, he told himself. You can do this.

'I mean, fair's fair,' Michael Brawn sneered. 'I cut you, and now it's your turn.'

Reuben pinched the small blade hard. All around, prisoners craned their necks for a direct line of sight. Michael Brawn's eyes continued to bore into Reuben, willing him to dare. Despite gripping harder, Reuben failed to stop the shakes. The anger was still there, but it was becoming muddied by events and feelings beyond his control.

'Shut the fuck up!' he shouted.

Brawn raised his arm slightly. 'I'll make it easy for you, yellow boy.'

The blade touched skin, juddering on the flesh, making a shallow depression in the inky tattoo. Reuben was sweating, telling himself he was waiting for the right moment. He needed to do this.

There was suddenly something ablaze in

244

Brawn's face. 'Come on, you motherfucker! Cut me! Cut me!' he screamed.

Behind him, Boucher shouted, 'Slice him, for fuck's sake!'

A few more spectators joined in the chorus. The words 'Slice him!' echoed around the walls of the room.

Reuben looked up from the blade and into Michael Brawn's psychopathic face. The pupils were huge, the pale cheeks filling with red, the stained and worn teeth clamped together. He sensed the sweat from his fingertips wetting the blade, loosening his grip. He held it tighter and ground his teeth. He closed his eyes and pushed deeper. Into Michael Brawn's tattoo, into Michael Brawn's skin.

And then he stopped. Something somewhere said, 'Enough!' There was nothing more to gain. He lifted the blade, pocketed it and glanced around the room, sensing the reaction. There was an instant outpouring of derision, inmates booing, laughing or making the universal 'chicken' noise. Reuben turned from Brawn's pitying grin and walked away. His chin dug into his breastbone, his head held low, his walk slow and dejected.

But as he turned the corner, Reuben smiled, his lips pulled back, his teeth bared. He punched the air with his fist. He brought the fingers of his left hand up to his face and examined them intently. A small dab of double-sided sticky tape was still in place on each fingertip, and each held a hair or skin fragment or some other microscopic part of Michael Brawn tightly to its

245

surface. Reuben punched the air again. He had DNA-sampled Brawn in front of a room full of witnesses without anyone knowing. Including Michael Brawn.

Reuben made his way to his cell. Thankfully, Narc was elsewhere. He sat down on his bed, the door swinging shut behind him. Leaning forward, he took the Kinder egg out of a pair of socks under his pillow and placed it on top of the chest of drawers. He used the small pair of tweezers to remove the strips of tape from his fingers, manoeuvring them into the Eppendorf tube with the pink fluid. Then he carefully removed the scalpel blade from his pocket and rubbed a cottonwool bud along its surface, before snipping the bud into the Eppendorf tube.

Monitoring the door, Reuben unfolded a letter he had written the previous night. He carefully poured a few drops from the tube on to each corner of the page, wafting it for a couple of minutes to allow it to dry. Then he folded it back up and slotted it into an envelope.

He glanced up as the door opened, quickly hiding the contents of his forensic kit in a drawer. Narc entered, a rolled-up magazine under his arm, whistling contentedly.

'What time's the post?' Reuben asked him.

'Six,' Narc replied, between tuneless bars of a song Reuben didn't recognize.

Reuben licked the envelope and sealed it, leaving the cell at a brisk walk. The postbox, a hangover from the jail's Victorian days, was ornate and bore the embossed words 'Her

246

Majesty's Prison Service'. Reuben hesitated a second, savouring the victory. Then he slid the letter into the sealed metal box. Job done. He sauntered down to the dining room where dinner was about to be served.

16

In the morning, Reuben ate breakfast then made his way to the governor's office, as agreed with Sarah. A weight had been lifted from somewhere and he walked with the easy nonchalance of someone about to be released. The only problem that remained was his son, who had been lying in a children's hospital the previous day having a series of tests. Lucy had been vague, but from what Reuben could tell, the GP was playing it safe. Lucy had that effect on men. But not, it turned out, on Reuben. Perhaps if she had, he conceded while queuing for a phone, he might still be a dutiful husband in a respected job.

As far as he knew from his restricted contact, Joshua had been unwell for around three months. Nothing more than a series of colds and other nursery-borne ailments, all of which had sapped his strength and slowed him down. But he was secretly pleased that Joshua was having the tests anyway. When he had the allclear, there would be no more excuses for blocking access, no more being turned away from Shaun Graves' immaculate house to trudge back down that immaculate drive, Joshua supposedly too unwell to stand a day out with his father.

A phone became available, and Reuben went through the rigmarole of phone cards, of dialling through the prison operator, of waiting to be connected. When the call was answered, it was clear that Lucy was fighting her way through the early-morning traffic.

'I'll get straight to the point,' she said.

Her voice sounded deeply sincere. It was unlike Lucy to be anything else. In fact, this had been one of Reuben's favourite things about his wife when they were together. Just coming out and saying what was on her mind, with no agenda or prevarication. Although she had, of course, failed to mention the small matter of the affair she was having.

'What?' he asked.

'Joshua. The tests. Where are you, by the way? Maybe we should meet up.'

Reuben knew at that instant the news wasn't going to be good. Lucy suggesting that they get together hadn't happened since the day Reuben had moved out.

'I can't,' he said. 'What is it?'

'Look, the consultant implied that things have been going on a long time without us realizing.'

'What sort of things?'

There was a pause, an intake of breath. 'Reuben, they think it's leukaemia.'

Reuben stood motionless, the word freezing him to the spot. He appreciated what the disease was and what the implications were.

'Which type?' he asked.

'They're not sure. I've got to take him back tomorrow. He's booked in for more tests.'

'Fuck.'

'But things aren't great.'

249

'How do you mean?'

'Some of the things they said . . . '

'Like what?'

'He's failing fast, Reuben. He needs help. They said something about his white blood cells reaching the point of being overwhelmed.'

Reuben pressed the receiver into his face, as if this could bring him closer to Lucy. The background noises grew louder. But also, somewhere deep among the cacophonous sounds of London, he detected a change in Lucy's breathing. Long, broken inhalations, and sharp, sighed exhalations. She was crying.

'Look,' he said, 'it will be fine. We'll cope. We'll manage.'

'We?' Lucy asked quietly.

'You, me and Shaun.'

'Quite a trio.'

'You know what I mean.'

Lucy sniffled, the noise exaggerated by the speaker. 'I guess so. I mean, until the next set of tests . . . But now I think of it, he hasn't been himself for so long now. I just hope it's not as bad as they made out yesterday.'

Amen to that, Reuben thought.

'Look, I've got to sort something, then I'll come and see you tomorrow. Which hospital is it?'

Lucy told him the details of the ward and Reuben wrote them down. He hung up, distracted and on edge, a heavy grey sadness tightening his brain. He walked slowly, thinking through the implications, wondering whether it would be acute myeloid leukaemia or some other

250

variant, desperately flicking back through university lectures on medical biology and the immune system. Reuben realized his knowledge was patchy at best.

He turned out of the old high-ceilinged corridor of the telephone area and into a newer-looking block, with pastel walls and strip lighting. The governor's office was at the end of the hallway. Reuben knocked on his door and waited, shaking his head, trying to rouse it from its melancholy.

Inside was a small waiting area, with three seats and a couple of potted plants. A guard sat at a modern pine-effect desk in a blue swivel chair. His name-plate read Prison Officer Simms. He was thin and weaselly, and Reuben guessed that his moustache was an attempt to compensate for the fact. Officer Simms wore black trousers, a white shirt with black numbered epaulettes and a black tie with the HMP insignia. He was by far the smartest guard Reuben had encountered so far.

'And you are?' Simms asked.

'Reuben Maitland, prisoner 4412598.'

Prison Officer Simms regarded him keenly. 'And what do you want to see the governor about?'

'A private matter,' Reuben answered.

Simms wrote Reuben's details down, slowly and carefully, taking his time.

'A private matter?' he repeated.

'Something important.'

Simms sighed, then nodded sharply in the direction of a chair. Reuben walked over and sat down. He glanced at the door marked 'Governor', which lay to the right of Simms' desk, then scanned the clock impatiently.

'You're next,' Simms added a few seconds later. 'But he hasn't got much time.'

'I know how he feels,' Reuben whispered to himself.

★   ★   ★

Ten minutes later, Reuben entered through the door and sat down opposite the governor, who was studying a piece of paper. The governor was relatively young — early forties, maybe — and almost entirely bald. In fact, Reuben noted as he watched him, his scalp was so shiny it looked wet.

When he had finished reading Reuben's details, he looked up. There was, Reuben noted, an almost nervous air about him, which clashed with every mental image he had ever stored about prison governors.

'So, Mr Maitland,' he began. 'Remand, awaiting trial dates. What can I do for you?'

'My colleague Sarah Hirst has been in touch?' Reuben said.

'I'm sorry?'

'DCI Sarah Hirst, Euston CID.'

'Remind me again,' the governor said with a smile. 'It's a big prison.'

'I'm finished here. I need to be shipped back out to the courthouse. As arranged.'

'OK. I see the problem.' The governor raised his eyebrows sympathetically and offered

Reuben a cigarette, which he refused. He took a long drag on his Marlboro Light, his words exhaled through a stream of smoke. 'Mr Harrison was taken ill at the weekend, suspected stroke.'

'Mr Harrison?'

'I'm the acting governor in his absence.' He flicked some ash into a small plastic ashtray. 'So there's been some contact with — '

'You mean you don't know who I am?'

'Not apart from what it says here on your charge sheet.'

Belatedly, the implications of the governor's words hit home. Reuben appealed for inner calm, the news of his son clouding his thoughts.

'Let me explain things to you,' he said quietly. 'I came in here to perform a job with the cooperation of the Met. I've now finished, and I need to be transferred back out.'

The governor's expression changed to one of suspicion, his eyes narrowing through the smoke. 'What sort of job?'

'I'd rather not say.'

'And now you'd like to be released?'

'Not released, exactly . . . '

'Well, form a queue, Mr Maitland.'

'But — '

'You may have noticed that most of the men in here are rather keen on being let out.'

'But DCI Hirst — '

The governor cut him short again. He appeared to be relishing his authority. 'Is there anything else I can help you with?'

'For fuck's sake!' Reuben stood up and banged the desk. 'This is a joke!'

'Sit down, please.'

'Look, ring the DCI, see what she says.'

'Calm it, Mr Maitland. And, for the second time, sit down.'

'My son is ill. I need to get the hell out.'

Behind Reuben, the door started to open. Reuben had to convince the governor, had to make him understand, had to get the fuck out of Pentonville.

'Sit down, Mr Maitland,' the governor repeated, his cheeks reddening.

Reuben spoke slowly and clearly, desperate to get his point across. 'I'm an ex-police officer, for fuck's sake. Forensics section. All you have to do is make some calls.'

'Sir?' Prison Officer Simms asked from the doorway.

'Escort Mr Maitland back to his cell, please.'

Reuben banged the desk hard. 'Come on. For fuck's sake. My son — '

'Mr Maitland! In here you play by my rules. You don't come into my office and raise your voice. And until you understand that, I have nothing more to say to you.'

The governor stubbed out his cigarette and closed Reuben's file, swivelling to return it to a filing cabinet. Officer Simms stepped towards Reuben, one hand on the truncheon lurking in his belt.

'Don't make me use this,' he said.

Too many fucking films, Reuben thought, a large part of him wanting to see Simms try and

254

swing at him before Reuben floored him. Instead, he walked out of the office and, slowly and dejectedly, back towards his cell, his shoulder scraping the wall, his anger subsiding, a sick feeling of defeat settling in his stomach.

17

'You should have cut me when you had the chance.'

Michael Brawn was standing in the doorway, tall, looming, intense. He pulled the door to behind him.

Reuben sat up on his bed, knowing the answer but asking anyway, 'What do you want?'

'To see a copper die.'

'I'm an ex-copper,' Reuben answered.

There was a glint in Brawn's eye. 'That's the general idea.'

Reuben stood up slowly, a couple of paces back from Brawn. He saw quick flashes of his final training session with Stevo. The wooden-lined gym, Kieran and his minders watching, things played out for real. Stevo saying, 'Let him come at you. Use his momentum against him.' Stevo swinging a punch, Reuben sidestepping it and grabbing his arm. Tugging smartly, pulling Stevo forward and on to a low body blow. Winded, Stevo trying to catch his breath.

'Word travels fast,' Reuben said to Brawn.

'The speed of sound, when it's important.'

'And why is it so important?'

'I think I remember telling you to leave me the fuck alone.'

'Fine. I'll leave you alone.'

'Oh, you'll do that all right.' Brawn took a step forward. 'Only people you're going to be bothering for a while work in the hospital wing.'

'Officer Simms,' Reuben said, partly to himself.

'See, information goes both ways when it needs to.'

Reuben tensed his body, subtly shifting position, readying himself. Brawn took another pace forward. His arms were by his sides. He was in utter control and knew it. His features were on fire, his eyes wide, his nostrils flaring, his teeth bared. Reuben didn't like what he saw in the face standing just a single step away from his.

'Had you figured from the outset,' Brawn sneered. 'Tattoo too new, hair too short, words too long.'

'Is that right?'

'Said to myself, this one doesn't belong.'

Brawn stared past Reuben, at the scratched metal mirror on the wall. Reuben sensed for a second that he was almost talking to himself.

'So what's your point?'

'Shall I tell you what every educated man's worst nightmare is?'

Reuben shrugged, his mind racing, knowing he was trapped in his cell, Narc probably in the weights room, lunch not for a couple of hours, no likelihood of anyone entering for a long time, the chances of being heard slim at best.

'Pentonville,' Brawn continued. 'And every forensic scientist's worst nightmare? Shall I tell you, Maitland?'

Reuben nodded almost imperceptibly, barely listening.

'Alone in a cell with a man like me. And *your*

worst nightmare? Here. Now. With the door closed.'

Reuben's eyes darted quickly around his surroundings, confirming the extent to which he was trapped.

'But this is worse than that. Much worse than that.'

Without warning, and in one fluid movement, Michael Brawn grabbed Reuben's shirt and yanked him forward. His knuckles exploded into Reuben's nose. Reuben collapsed to the floor, blood streaming from his face. His nose was buzzing and on fire, an urgent stabbing pushing up through his sinuses. Brawn stood over him, mesmerized by the blood.

'Because this one needs to be shown.'

Reuben tried to stand, desperate to fight. Brawn kicked him in the face, an upward trajectory, snapping Reuben's neck back. Reuben knew he had to react now or he would be in serious trouble.

'This one needs to be told.'

Reuben lunged for Brawn's leg, but he jumped up, bringing his full weight down on Reuben's outstretched arm. Reuben cried out, his ulna and radius squeezing together, a marrow-deep ache burrowing into the bones.

'This one needs to be damaged.'

Brawn stepped back and kicked Reuben's prone form in the guts, causing Reuben to curl up like a fetus. He rasped for air, his diaphragm flattened, his lungs useless. His chest heaved quickly back into life, coughing up blood. Reuben rolled on to his front and tried to stand

258

up and defend himself. Through the quick succession of blows, he realized that Michael Brawn was toying with him. He used the white formica chest of drawers to pull himself to his feet. He was breathing hard, bleeding through his nose, and his left arm was throbbing and numb. Brawn grinned at him, then headbutted him clean on the chin.

'How was that for you?' Brawn asked, upright, fists clenched, beginning to enjoy himself. 'OK?'

Bent double, blood gushing from his nose and mouth, Reuben steadied himself. There was no point in defending himself. Suddenly, he straightened and ran at Brawn, who sidestepped him and pulled him on to a torso punch. The name Stevo lit up in Reuben's screaming mind.

Brawn walked round to stand in front of Reuben, pulling his head up by the hair. Reuben sensed that Brawn needed him to understand the full horror of what was about to happen.

'What say we step things up a bit?' Brawn said with a grin. 'Get this party started?'

He pulled out his small, sharp knife. Reuben pictured fragments of his skin still clinging to the blade, some dyed red, others blue. Brawn waited until Reuben was paying attention, angling the blade so that it glinted in the light.

'You ever had a tattoo removed?' he asked.

Reuben didn't answer, heavy rasping breaths all the noise he could muster.

'I don't suppose you have. But I warn you, it might sting a bit.'

Brawn pushed Reuben back into the corner of the cell. He thrust the knife forward and Reuben parried the blow. Brawn brought his other fist round and socked Reuben hard in the solar plexus. As Reuben gasped for air, Brawn used his strength to pin Reuben to the bed, right forearm exposed, the tattoo facing up.

'Let's see what it takes to remove one of these completely.'

Reuben tried to thrash, but Brawn was strong and was pinning him down. Reuben scanned the cell wildly for a weapon. On the drawers was his mini-forensics kit, hidden in a pair of socks. He reached his other arm towards it, pushed it out and popped the egg open with his hand. The scalpel blade clinked on the hard surface. Reuben grabbed it between his forefinger and thumb. Brawn wasn't looking. He was staring down at the tattoo, lowering his knife slowly, mimicking Reuben's efforts the previous day. Finally, blade touched skin. Reuben felt the sharp bite of the contact, an inch to the right of the long, angry cut Brawn had already given him. He saw the pulsing on Brawn's twisted neck, slow and thick. The carotid artery. A quick stab and it would all be over. Reuben gripped the scalpel hard, fingers white with the effort. Brawn was still playing with the knife. He started to run it round the outside of the tattoo, a shallow cut growing deeper. Beginning to dig into the skin, excavating, levering up a deep layer of epidermis.

Reuben took aim. He pulled his arm back to lunge. There was a bang. The door flew open. Prison Guard Tony Paulers burst in, followed by

Damian and Cormack. Reuben dropped the scalpel blade into the palm of his hand. He felt the pressure ease.

'That's enough for one day, Brawn,' Guard Paulers said, one hand on his can of pepper spray.

Michael Brawn straightened and stood up. He folded his knife slowly and deliberately, before tucking it away.

'Just a bit of fun,' he said, smirking.

Guard Paulers fingered the canister in his belt. 'Out. And don't let me catch you in here again.'

Michael Brawn sauntered slowly past the guard, winking at Damian on his way out. Reuben flopped on the bed, losing blood. He heard the voice of the officer requesting medical help on his radio. Most of his torso was in agony and his face felt battered. He closed his eyes and waited for painkillers to come and find him.

18

Judith Meadows carried the post through the hall and into what remained of the kitchen. The builders were late, but this was not unusual. She sat down on one of the two remaining stools and ran her eyes around the room. It had badly needed doing, had done since the day they moved in. But two public-sector wages didn't go far in London, and after the mortgage there was rarely the money for significant improvements.

She flicked through the letters. Two for her husband, one for next door, again, one from the bank. Judith didn't need NatWest to tell her how skint they were. She aimed the white envelope unsuccessfully at the bin, watching it somersault on to the brickdusted floor. Although Reuben's money was helping, with a baby coming, financial matters were now more serious. And while the cash that Reuben gave her was an undeniable bonus, it was not the reason she helped him. She thought again about the bloodied photo of Kieran Hobbs, wondering whether Reuben would be able to make anything of it when he resurfaced.

The fifth letter made her raise her eyebrows. The envelope was stamped 'HMP Pentonville'. Quickly, Judith padded upstairs to the spare bedroom. Among several tins of paint was a box of nylon lab gloves. She had brought them home a couple of days ago to use for the

262

cheek-swabbing of Kieran and his minders; now they would come in useful for the painting and decorating. She slipped one on to each hand, padded back down the stairs and returned to the kitchen. It felt early in the day to be putting her first pair of surgical gloves on, and incongruous in her small terraced house.

She opened the letter slowly and carefully, her index finger under the flap. Inside was a letter on ruled paper, faint blue lines running across the page. Scrawled in Reuben's barely legible lettering were two short sentences. 'I am safe, if a little cold. Put me out of sight.'

Judith paused, her brow furrowed. She examined the inside of the envelope again, even opening it and tapping it on the worktop, knowing it was empty but double-checking all the same. Then she examined the front and back of the envelope at an oblique angle, and performed the same careful examination of the letter.

'I'm safe, a little cold, out of sight,' she said to herself. Judith didn't imagine for a moment that he was safe. Pentonville may well be cold, and she was willing to put him out of sight, but she quickly appreciated that he was telling her something else. She repeated the words a few times, trying them on for size, imagining what they could mean.

Her husband entered the kitchen and Judith stood up. She gave him a stiff hug, and let him pat her belly. No signs as yet, nothing to show, but minute and invisible things were happening. Two parallel lines on a plastic stick the previous day had told them that. Inside, a switch had been flicked, a timer telling Judith that things were about to change. She swallowed the sick queasiness that was climbing her throat, and flicked the kettle on.

'How's today looking?' Colm asked.

'Not good. Plus I had a text request for another double shift tomorrow.'

'Really?'

Her husband, she noted out of the corner of her eye, gave her an unpractised look of concern. Two blue lines and his behaviour was already changing. The murmur of the kettle quickly became a roar, and Judith made him a cup of tea, her gloves still on.

'The extra cash will come in handy.'

'I don't want you working yourself to death. Not any more.'

'So it was OK before?'

Colm smiled in defeat. 'You know what I mean.'

'I'm not doing overtime for the sake of it. There's a killer on the loose.'

'There's always a killer on the loose. That's London. Eight million people; some of them will be psychopaths. Pure statistics.'

'Yeah, well. The difference is I get poorly paid in order to help catch killers. And when someone's actively murdering women — '

'Something sexual?'

'Yes.'

Colm lifted the mug of tea to his lips and blew across its grey surface. 'In what way sexual?'

'He rapes them after death.'

'Is that really rape?'

'How do you mean?'

'If you're dead, you can't say no.'

Colm was never interested in her cases, and Judith seldom divulged the details. It was against the rules to talk about them anyway, even with loved ones. She found Colm's curiosity unusual.

'Why are you so concerned?'

'I'm not,' Colm answered, risking a sip of his drink. 'I just thought I should take more interest in what you do. You know, now you're . . . ' He tilted his mug in the direction of Judith's belly.

'Pregnant.'

'Yes.'

'Well, it's early days. And for the record, rape is rape, whether before death, during death or after it.'

Colm leaned against the counter, one foot on the bottom rung of a stool. He was silent except for an occasional slurp. Judith continued to watch him, wondering what the hell pregnancy did to the male mind. Those thoughts fought for space with the short sentences of Reuben's letter, which still rebounded around inside her head. If it was important enough to write down and send to her, it had to mean something.

Presently, Colm walked over to the dusty sink and placed his mug in it. 'Gotta dash,' he said. 'Good luck with the builders.' He pecked Judith briefly on the cheek, gently patted her stomach again and made for the front door.

After he'd gone, Judith opened the letter again and read it out loud. 'I am safe, if a little cold. Put me out of sight.' Safe. Cold. Out of sight. At last, she understood.

Judith folded the letter and replaced it in the envelope. She took a transparent plastic bag out of a drawer and slid the letter in. Then she opened the freezer compartment of her fridge. She widened the opening of a box of fish fingers and slotted the envelope carefully into it, closing it again and pushing it to the very back.

19

Narc's first few words of the day had been prophetic. When Reuben returned to his cell after a night in the hospital wing, Narc had announced gleefully, 'So, rumour has it you're a bizzie.'

'Ex-bizzie,' Reuben had muttered.

'Oh, you're in the wrong place,' Narc grinned. 'You are so in the wrong place.'

Reuben had shrugged, not wanting to give his cellmate the satisfaction.

'They're going to fucking eat you alive.'

Reuben had then examined himself in the steel mirror. His face was battered, his left eye half closed, the bridge of his nose swollen. Five uneven dark red stitches zipped two lips of cheek-flesh together. He touched the straight nylon thread poking out of the end of the wound. It was sharp and unbending, at odds with the soft numbness of the tissue it held together. The sutures had been administered by an unsympathetic male nurse without anaesthetic. Reuben grimaced. The whole hospital wing had reeked of desperation. Three prisoners who had hurt themselves just to be locked away where other inmates couldn't get to them. A failed suicide case having his wrists sewn back up. Two men who didn't speak English, weak with something viral. A butch female nurse ignoring a request for pain relief until she had finished her tea break. Reuben had almost been glad to be back in his cell. That is until he encountered Narc.

The rest of the day had been just as difficult. He had hobbled in to join the breakfast queue, and watched prisoners move away from him. The food server had dolloped a large spoonful of scrambled egg on his tray, half of which ended up on Reuben's shirt. When he tried to find somewhere to sit, it had been as difficult as it was on his first day. And when he did eventually pull out a chair to sit down, the two prisoners there had stood up and walked to a different table.

The TV lounge hadn't proved any better. Reuben had been spat at from behind, an obvious, hawked-up ball of phlegm landing on his shoulder. When he turned round, a trio of prisoners were sneering at him. And when he swivelled back, more spit began to fly in his direction. Reuben had stayed as long as he could bear. Don't let them see that any of this matters, he told himself. But still, with his shirt festooned with phlegm, he had been forced to leave eventually.

Reuben appreciated that most of the prison would very quickly know who he was. Word had spread almost instantaneously from Officer Simms to Michael Brawn, whether directly or indirectly, and wouldn't stop there. The presence of ex-CID among the ranks, especially a forensics officer, was bound to cause a stir. Reuben realized that he had obviously been pointed out; relatively few people had known his name or what he looked like yesterday. Today, however, that had changed. It was there in the eyes of men he passed in the corridor, inmates he had no recollection of seeing before. Even the guards seemed to view him with a mix of pity and amusement.

What Reuben needed quickly were friends and information. He had to find Damian and Cormack, and had to talk to Sarah, to find out what the hell was going on. Every extra day was going to feel like a lifetime.

As Reuben turned into the telephone corridor and passed through a barred gate, he finally spotted Kieran Hobbs' men. He approached them, feeling the bruises beginning to freeze up, his walk almost mechanical, but optimism nonetheless in his stride.

'Look, about yesterday,' he said when he reached them, attempting to smile. 'Thanks for bringing the cavalry.'

'Forget it,' Cormack answered.

'I mean, if you hadn't — '

'I said, forget it.'

'Kieran said you'd help me, and he wasn't wrong.'

'Yeah, well.'

'I thought Brawn was going to kill me in there.'

Cormack's tone was harder than before. 'That's what you get when you overstep the line.'

'There wasn't a lot I could do.'

Damian turned directly to Reuben. 'From now on,' he said, 'you stay the fuck away from us.'

Cormack angled his head back. 'Kieran never

269

told us you were an ex-copper. There's no fucking way we'd have agreed to baby-sit you.'

Reuben examined the graze on one of his knuckles, smelled the sour male odours of tobacco and sweat that pervaded the prison.

'Look, I used to be a copper, then I moved over to forensics.'

'Same fucking thing,' Damian answered.

'See, we keep hanging round with you, what's everyone gonna think?' Cormack's eyes were wide and angry. 'That we're giving you info, grassing them up. You think we're going to risk our lives for you?'

'Not a fucking hope. I got eight weeks left in this shit-hole. And I'll tell you this, Damian Nightley ain't going out in a fucking box.'

'So from now on, stay the fuck away. Whoever you are.'

Damian and Cormack pushed past Reuben, one on either side, their shoulders barging into him, re-igniting the pain of his bruises. Reuben watched them go, sensing the anger in the stiffness of their walks, the betrayal in their refusal to look back. He ran his fingers over the angry wound on his cheek. Now he was truly alone. And there were other issues to take care of.

He limped on to the huddle of corridor phones, and waited his turn. An image returned to him, awoken by the blankness of the walls. Eighteen years old, sitting on the cold leather seat of an ageing Renault 12, the car parked outside huge blank gates of steel. Rain cascading down the windows, distorting the view of the prison. The passenger-side door swinging open, his father climbing in. Surveying his dad, who was resting his face against the steamed-up side window, silent and distant, water dripping from his short hair and sliding down his face, another in a long line of custodial sentences coming to an anti-climactic end.

Reuben saying, freedom. So how does it feel?

His father replying, it doesn't feel anything.

Jesus, what did they do to you in there?

George Maitland continuing to stare out of the windscreen, his head leaning against the glass of the side window.

Reuben finding a gear in the notchy gearbox and pulling off in silence.

The queue shuffled forward. After a couple more minutes it was Reuben's turn. He dialled a number from memory, and drummed his fingers on the metal hood. When it was answered, he asked, 'How much longer?'

Rapid keyboard taps punctured the short silence, then Sarah said, 'There's been a hitch.'

'What do you mean, a hitch?'

'We kept this quiet.'

'So?'

'Maybe too quiet.'

'What are you saying?'

'Look, sit tight. I'll sort it, but it's going to take a few days to get official clearance.'

'You don't understand. I have to get out now.'

'It's not that easy. We've put someone in jail who shouldn't be there. The Prison Service will go ballistic if we don't handle this carefully.'

'I'm not particularly worried about upsetting

the Prison Service. Sarah, my son is ill and I need to see him.'

'I'm sorry to hear that, Reuben, and I understand. But see it from my side.'

'Your side? There is no your side. Sarah, they know I'm an ex-copper. Twelve hundred fucking inmates know that one of their number is ex-force. Maybe even helped put some of them away. Michael Brawn almost killed me, and he's still roaming around free. So the only sides I'm interested in are me against the whole of Pentonville. You've got to sort this, and do it now.'

'OK.' Sarah breathed heavily down the line. 'I'm doing what I can. But I have to warn you again, it's not going to happen quick. Abner doesn't know you're there. In fact, I told him I had no idea where you were. If I go to him now and request special assistance — '

'I'm not bothered about whether you've compromised yourself. I'm worried about getting out of here alive and seeing my son. Do something. *Now*.'

'Like I said — '

Reuben slammed the receiver down. He knew what she was going to say. Covert operations couldn't just be undone. There were toes that shouldn't be stamped on, torn-up protocols that had to be stitched back together. He wondered momentarily whether Sarah was dragging her stiletto-ed feet deliberately. Whether she was happy Reuben was isolated and cut off. She had done worse things before to win cases and further her causes. He dismissed the notion,

272

knowing he was angry, sensing a burrowing desperation deep in his stomach. A few days might be too long.

He headed back to his cell, to the steel door and the thick walls, a prison within a prison.

20

Moray Carnock ran his foot through the sea of white Eppendorf tubes washed up on the floor. They made the sound of a brittle plastic shale. As he peered closer, he saw that each one was labelled with a letter or a number in fine black marker pen. Some were bar-coded, a short, thin strip of adhesive paper running down one side. Moray was no scientist, but he could tell that the tubes had been there for at least a few hours. Small, receding pools of water were dotted about, the Eppendorfs mainly dry to the touch. He turned to Judith.

'How long have you been here?' he asked.

'Half an hour,' she answered. 'I called you straight away.'

'Bit of a mess.'

Judith was perched half on and half off a lab stool. Behind her, three freezer doors gaped open, their drawers pulled out, their compressors desperately buzzing, trying to cool the yawning air. Thousands of tubes were scattered across the floor. Solutions had been poured over benches, leaving them dripping and hazardous. Bottles lay empty on their sides, on shelves or on the work surfaces. The place stank of antiseptics, solvents and alcohols, as if a succession of pub optics had been poured into a bucket with a litre of toilet cleaner. It was, Moray determined, a scene of methodical carnage. He closed the front door carefully, and slumped down on the sofa.

'How are we going to tell Reuben?' Judith asked.

'Guess we'll have to wait for him to ring.'

'He's going to be distraught.'

'Aye,' Moray agreed sadly. 'He is that.'

'And there's another thing. The photo that Kieran Hobbs gave us, and the exclusion samples.'

'Thawed as well? Are they going to be any use?'

'Almost certainly no.'

'You going to tell Kieran?'

'No point till Reuben's had a chance to take a proper look. And even then it might take a bit of time. I guess we keep this quiet for now.' Judith glanced at the door, which had been open when she'd arrived. 'We've got more important issues. Who do you think got in here?'

'Fuck knows. But they came equipped.' On his way in, Moray had admired the use of subtle force which had breached the entrance. There were scratches around the hinges and a dent where a crowbar had been used. Other than that, there was remarkably little to see, and not enough damage to prevent it closing again. 'You don't get through anti-squatter doors with a screwdriver and a penknife.'

'So it's not kids roaming the estate?'

'Wouldn't have thought so. Besides, this place seems virtually deserted. How many other people have you ever seen on your way here?'

'A few. I think there's a couple of families on the second floor. But they seem to want to keep

275

themselves to themselves, like they know they shouldn't be here.'

'Squatters. Just like our good selves. So where does that leave us in terms of suspects?'

Judith shrugged, a brief movement of her shoulders through her thin and stylish leather jacket. Moray suspected that when she had decided a scooter required protective leathers, she had interpreted the idea fairly broadly.

'Look, one thing's for sure. Whoever got in is used to breaking and entering. This wasn't the work of opportunist amateurs or bored youths.' Moray stood up, scratching his chin. 'But there is a more important question.'

'What?'

'Why did they break in? It wasn't to steal anything. The PCs are still here. So it's clearly about the lab, and its samples.' Moray paced around the floor, displacing ripple after ripple of white tubes. The soles of his shoes squeaked in the wetness. 'So they were looking for something. Now, the point is this. Did they find it and take it?'

'We should be able to work that out.'

'How?'

'All the samples are inventoried. Some of them are bar-coded. If you're feeling energetic . . . '

'Unusually, no.'

'We could pick all the tubes up and tick them off. See what's gone.'

'Or, option B, and the point I'm getting to, was simply destroying what they were looking for enough for them?'

Judith gently poked a low-heeled shoe into the

carnage. 'Well, all the samples *are* ruined.'

'Is it definitely a quick process?' Moray asked.

'If you thaw them out, they die reasonably soon, yes.'

'How soon?'

'Depends what they are. But a standard DNA in water, a few hours at most.'

'So what I'm saying is that even if we catalogue all the specimens, we may well be wasting our time. Somewhere in all this might be the samples they were after. And if they were smart, they'd just have left them, among thousands of others, to quietly rot and become unusable.' Moray snorted, his bushy eyebrows flicking upwards. 'Perfect and undetectable.'

'Maybe you should inhale more solvents, Mr Carnock. It obviously suits your brain.'

'I'll bear it in what's left of my mind.'

Moray continued to pace around. Now that Judith had mentioned it, he did feel light-headed and a little dizzy. Maybe he would give the pub a miss on his way home.

'Just about the only thing they left,' he said, inspecting one of the shelves, 'was this cylinder.'

Moray reached forward to open a large metal container sitting imperiously on a widened shelf.

'Don't touch it,' Judith shouted.

Moray froze. 'What?' he asked, arm still outstretched.

'Liquid nitrogen. Minus one hundred and eighty degrees. Best not opened if you value your fingers.'

Moray withdrew his hand. 'Thanks. Now, remind me again what we've actually lost?'

'Most of the archived cases Reuben was pursuing. A lot of GeneCrime samples, things he shouldn't have had anyway. FSS specimens from eleven or twelve full investigations. All of them irreplaceable.'

'Surely they're just small portions of larger banked samples?'

Judith sighed. This really wasn't good, whichever way she looked at it. 'For some of the investigations, yes. I took a few microlitres of all the DNAs, labelled an identical batch of tubes, and passed them on to Reuben. No harm done. But for a proportion of the others, what you see dead on the floor is all that remains.'

'Fuck.'

'Exactly.'

'So it's safe to assume that whoever broke in wanted rid of DNA samples that were unique and irreplaceable.'

Judith was quiet for a second, her dark eyebrows knotted. Sometimes Moray still found it hard to believe that she was actually a scientist. She was light and easy-going, a pleasure to be with. But he saw it now. Her concentration, when circumstances demanded it, was absolute, her working through of a problem logical, careful and methodical.

'Nope,' she answered, 'we can't conclude that. Why tip all the solutions out? Why not trash the computers? Why not wipe the records off the equipment? And who really knows exactly what Reuben should and shouldn't have? I can barely remember at times. If you really wanted to erase the past, you'd have burned the lab down.'

'OK, Madame Curie, what's your theory?'
'That they were after something specific.'
'Which was?'
Judith pictured the box of fishfingers lying in her freezer at home.
'I've got a fair idea,' she answered.

21

From his vantage point, a shallow kink in the corridor, Prison Guard Tony Paulers was able to monitor most of the telephones. As luck would have it, the phones were unusually empty, and he had an unobstructed line of sight to his target.

This time he wasn't talking in code. Tony couldn't make out the exact words, but there was a distinct lack of repetition about his few short utterances. The last occasion, a few days ago, Tony had called a friend in the Met, someone he could trust, someone he had been on a training course with over a decade back. Tony had told him all he knew: that a prisoner in Pentonville called Michael Brawn, a tall, sinewy psychopath with a propensity for sadistic cruelty, was passing coded messages out of the prison. His friend had been sympathetic and understanding, but said he needed more. Tangible evidence, specific information. He'd also asked why Tony hadn't informed the governor, and Tony had hesitated, and finally answered, because I want to do this my way.

Things had changed since then, however. The governor was recuperating at home, a heavy stroke having strangled his words and staggered his gait, and a new man, Robert Arnott, had been assigned to take his place. Tony had met Arnott twice, and was not impressed with what he had seen. Too young, too inexperienced, too eager. But with the sole advantage that, compared with the former governor, he was less likely to collapse into early infirmity. So, for now, Tony had resolved to keep an eye on Michael Brawn, and see what he was up to. And here, in the telephone corridor, Brawn was talking quietly, considering his words, and almost certainly doing something he shouldn't.

Tony strained his ears, flattening himself back out of view. He turned his head and monitored the corridor, eager not to be witnessed eavesdropping. It was lunchtime, and the vast majority of inmates were either eating or waiting to eat. Then a figure approached from the far end, taking his time through the gated double doors. Tony held his radio to his ear, pretending to be in conversation. The man came closer, and Tony recognized him. This is going to be interesting, he thought to himself.

The prisoner was a shade under six feet tall, relatively slender but with wide shoulders which were slightly hunched forward as he walked. Features that otherwise might have been considered fine were blunted by the swell of early bruising. The nose and chin, in particular, had taken a pounding. Despite his injuries, there was something undefeated about him. He had heard from guards and prisoners alike that Reuben Maitland was a former copper who had worked in forensics. Tony wondered how he had come to fall so low, on remand in Pentonville, accused of attempting to kill his wife. He tried and failed to picture the man in front of him in police uniform or in a laboratory coat. That was the problem with prison, Tony believed. Dress all the men in the same casual baggy clothes and you erased the subtle signs that existed on the outside which told you about a man's likely character and background. It was like a deliberate wiping of the slate to enable a whole new set of rules to be established from scratch.

As Tony watched Reuben Maitland walk past, Michael Brawn stood upright, the phone's metal lead dangling at his side, his head rotating almost robotically to follow his progress. Something in his demeanour spoke of unfinished business. Maitland glanced across at Brawn a couple of times, emotionless and unperturbed. Tony was prepared to bet that his heart was beating fast though. What he must have seen in Brawn's eyes wouldn't be difficult to interpret.

Tony knew he should have confiscated the weapon the previous day. But without back-up, there was no way he was going to risk it. Brawn had been on fire with a psychopathic zeal, and Tony, if he was entirely honest with himself, had felt a crippling tremble of fear. It had been as much as he could do to order him out of the cell. Besides, Tony suspected that a small penknife was neither here nor there. If Michael Brawn really wanted to hurt someone, the lack of a blade would be only a minor inconvenience.

Tony watched Brawn return to his call, his eyes still burning into Maitland's back as he turned at the end of the corridor. Tony pressed himself back in the alcove, listening hard. Brawn still hadn't spotted him. He was drumming his fingers on the rounded metal hood and had resumed his conversation. After a few seconds, Tony heard the sound of the receiver being replaced. Still holding his radio, he waited, praying that Brawn wouldn't walk past him. When he knew he was safe, Tony stepped out. Brawn was near the far end of the passageway, heading in the same direction as Maitland. He wondered for a moment whether he should follow him, but decided against it. He had saved Maitland once already. He would have to fight his own battles from now on.

Tony counted the telephones until he arrived at the one Brawn had been using. The receiver was still warm, and it smelled of aftershave and coffee, a sweet and sour combination that Tony found unsettling. He dialled 0 for an operator, and waited impatiently until it was answered.

'This is Prison Guard Tony Paulers,' he began. 'Who's that?' The operator gave her name, and Tony said, 'Hey, Sandra, how's things? Look, can you do me a small favour? Could you get me the last number dialled on this phone?' Tony took out his small prison notebook, with its matching pencil. 'No, it's nothing official. Just double-checking something.' After a slight delay, the operator gave him the information, and he scribbled it down. 'Got it. And, the last thing, Sandra, remind me what number the prison uses for dialling out?' Tony entered a second number below the first. He thanked her and hung up.

When Tony dialled the first number, it was answered almost immediately.

'*Bargain Pages.*'

This wasn't what Tony had been expecting.

'Oh, hello,' he said. 'I wonder if you could help me?'

'What section are you after?' The voice was on the hard side of female. Tony pictured a middle-aged smoker.

'I'm not sure,' he answered honestly.

'Well, are you buying, selling or meeting people?'

'None. Look, my name is Tony Paulers, and I'm a police officer,' he lied. 'I'm chasing up a call that was made from this phone just a few minutes ago.'

'Oh yeah?'

'I could give you the number.'

There was a barely detectable sigh, a slight hesitation, and Tony knew his luck was in. 'What's the number?' she asked flatly. Tony read the second set of digits to her, a Pentonville line reserved for external prisoner calls, a number he knew to be occasionally and sporadically tapped. He heard the sounds of keyboard activity, and a couple of barely suppressed expletives. 'Just checking the calls-received folder. Yeah, hang on. That's the one. Eleven fifty-eight. Does that sound about right?'

Tony checked his watch. 'Bang on,' he said.

'So, what do you want to know?'

Good question. All he knew was that Brawn had made a call to *Bargain Pages* at a time when the phones were empty.

'What section did the call get put through to?'

'Looks like it went through to Personals.'

'Was an advert placed?'

'And you're from the police, right?'

'Oh yes. Yes I am.'

Another pause, another sigh. 'Well, makes no odds to me. Advert in the Men Seeking Women section. Let's see.' A smoker's cough, a smoker's laugh. '*'The time is ripe. Must act now. Share your feelings with me.'* Can't see him getting a lot of replies out of that one, can you?'

Tony wrote down the words quickly, before he forgot them.

'And that was all?'

'You want more?'

'It's just . . . When does the advert go out?'

'First thing tomorrow. He made the noon deadline by a couple of minutes. So, what station are you from, so I can log this?'

Tony hung up, his mind racing. A distinctly impersonal message in the Personals. Michael Brawn was putting a communication out there for someone. He read the words again. *Must act now. Share your feelings.* What the hell was he up to? he wondered. And what did the message really mean? He tried to figure out how the response would come, whether or not *Bargain Pages* had a phone line to pick up replies. He vowed to call back later and find out.

In the meantime, he picked up the receiver again, once more catching the lingering coffee and aftershave scent of Michael Brawn, almost as though he was still standing there. He checked the corridor was empty, and then he dialled his contact in the Met.

This time, he had something substantial to impart.

22

Reuben stuck to the edge of the corridor. It was safer that way. At least one side of him was protected. Things were going downhill fast, and he needed to be out of prison. Narc's verdict had stayed with him, his jarring Scouse accent lending menace to the prophecy. *You are so in the wrong place. They're going to fucking eat you alive.*

So far, he had been attacked only once by Michael Brawn, but more bloodshed was likely. Other inmates, ones he didn't even recognize, had whistled and jeered at him, or offered specific and gratuitous threats. The prisoner serving his breakfast had made a show of hawking and spitting into his scrambled egg. Reuben had walked over to an empty table and sat alone, and a plastic mug had been thrown across the room at him. Except for exercise periods, Reuben had stayed in his cell, lying on his bed and staring at the wall, wondering and waiting.

But nearly two days had now passed, and it had got too much. He had to have answers from Sarah before Brawn came after him a second time, or some other psycho caught him in the semen-stinking showers, or his food was contaminated with something more dangerous than phlegm. And the question came to him again: what was Brawn waiting for? The right opportunity? A suitable weapon? The help of another prisoner? The way he had looked at him earlier in the telephone corridor told Reuben that something was imminent. Brawn would not be delaying for long.

As he scraped along the wide hallway, Reuben appreciated that the first three days of his incarceration had been fine. With a mission, and the support of Damian and Cormack, time had passed reasonably quickly. He had rediscovered the routines of his first sentence fifteen years ago, and had eaten, slept and watched TV in synch with the other twelve hundred inmates. Now, however, he was out of step, keeping himself hidden away, the minutes dragging by, cuts and bruises healing with slow reluctance, on guard and unprotected. He could see that his fight training with Stevo had been woefully inadequate. When a lunatic really wanted to hurt you, there wasn't that much you could actually do.

And thoughts of Joshua, pale and in hospital, cannulas in his veins, his blood being scrutinized, white cells being counted, diagnoses being discussed, treatments being debated . . . all of this attacked him with more ferocity than even Michael Brawn had mustered. He was alone and isolated, his son with suspected leukaemia, growing weak as his bodily defences were dismantled from within. Reuben shook his head as he walked. He needed to shout at Sarah down the phone. Hopefully this time Brawn would be nowhere in sight. He had to get Sarah to forget about protocol and procedure and going through the correct channels and just drag him the fuck out of Pentonville. There was no other option. The place was secure as hell. The bars to his window, the lock on his door, the height of the walls, the gates within gates, the cages within cages. Escape was a fantasy perpetuated by films. There was only one way out, and that was through high-level CID intervention.

The corridor widened and Reuben stayed to the right. Ahead and in the middle lay two pool tables, end to end. Reuben passed a guard and nodded. The guard was, he thought, called Tony, the man Cormack and Damian had alerted when they observed Michael Brawn entering his cell. He was early to mid-fifties, Reuben guessed, and looked to have spent most of his life incarcerated. He wondered whether Tony was as institutionalized as the lifers who surrounded him. Tony nodded back, a barely perceptible dip of the head which managed to be polite but not friendly. Reuben thought he detected a small hint of disappointment in Tony's face, but couldn't be sure.

He approached the first table, which was not being used. Seven or eight men were milling about. Reuben sensed that Tony might have been keeping a casual eye on them. He glanced over at the second table. John Ruddock, thick-necked and shaven-headed, was hunched down, ready to play his shot. Damian had told him that Ruddock, the only inmate to shout abuse at Michael Brawn during the Arsenal-United match, was serving time for the murder of two nightclub doormen, and ran a ruthless extortion

288

ring in D Wing. His sidekick and opponent, he had also learned, was Clem Davies, similarly best avoided. Reuben looked away, eager not to catch their eye.

The phone corridor ran through two gated intersections, and into the newer section of the wing. Reuben fingered the phone card in the pocket of his jeans, composing his words to Sarah. As he drew close to the table, Davies, who was standing upright and staring past Reuben, said the barely audible word 'clear'. Reuben tensed. Out of the corner of his eye, he saw John Ruddock straighten, a pool ball in his hand. A dark, fast-moving object whizzed past his face, cracking into the wall and ricocheting off it at speed. Reuben kept walking. Ignore it, he urged himself. A flash of Ruddock's arm and a second ball hurtled at him. Reuben flinched, dropping his left shoulder. The pool ball grazed the surface of his shirt. There was a thump and a cry behind. Collateral damage.

Reuben turned and marched over to Ruddock. Without breaking stride, he picked up a pool cue and swung it, catching him across the head with its thick end. Davies rushed at Reuben and Reuben pulled him on to a punch. A quick-moving form darted round the back. A turbaned prisoner holding a pool ball. Throw this would you, you cunt? He stamped on the prone form of John Ruddock. Two other inmates rushed over to help him, kicking Ruddock in the head. Davies straightened and aimed another blow. The body shape. Watch the body shape. Stevo's words belatedly tracked him down.

Reuben stepped into the punch, stifling it, and delivered a sharp uppercut.

Around him, the entire area sparked into uproar. Reuben punched Davies again, the last two days boiling over. The humiliation, the threats, the taunts. He saw the prison guard approach, then back away. Two or three more inmates rushed into the mêlée. Clem Davies caught him on the side of the head. Reuben's ear rang. He shook himself and reached again for the pool cue. Ruddock was struggling to his feet, aiming wild punches at whoever was closest.

The guard blew his whistle repeatedly and urgently as chairs and tables began to fly through the air. An inmate stepped up and punched the guard in the face, knocking his whistle out. Reuben knew things were getting very close to a full-scale riot as he swung at Davies with the cue. Scores being settled in the heat of the battle. Long-held tensions bursting out into the open. Blood pouring from Ruddock's shaven head. Inmates grappling and kicking, using whatever came to hand. Somewhere a bell ringing. Prison guards doubtless struggling into riot gear, their features hidden behind masks, revelling in the heavy poise of metal truncheons, holding them in both hands like baseball bats, ready to swing as they swarmed into the corridor. Reuben caught up in the fight, unable and unwilling to leave, a point needing to be proved to the scumbags who'd tried to damage him. Being punched in the back. Turning round and swiping at a prisoner he didn't recognize. Another plastic chair hurtling through the air, catching someone full-on. Wanting to walk away, but knowing that wasn't possible. That things had gone too far. That any second the hoses would come out and anonymous guards would burst through the corridor swinging their batons at whoever came to hand.

23

Seated opposite the governor, Reuben ran his tongue around the inside of his lip, which was bleeding again. The day's activities had burst the scab, the sweet metallic taste reminding him of Brawn's initial attack. The governor was taking his time, scanning a sheet of paper, letting the silence build. Classic intimidation tactic. Control the quiet and you own the conversation. Reuben let him play at junior psychology. He had been in enough police interviews to know the deal.

The governor opened his packet of cigarettes, and slid one out. He slowly put it to his lips and lit it, blowing smoke through his fingers. Reuben had a sudden urge to snatch the cigarette and stamp on it. But sudden urges, like swinging pool cues, was what had brought him to the governor's office in the first place.

Finally, the governor laid the piece of paper flat and looked up at Reuben. 'When you came to see me, you claimed to be, what was it, an ex-police officer on a covert mission.' His voice was high and pinched, a Home Counties accent.

'Yeah,' Reuben answered.

'Interesting. Because what I've seen of you so far hardly smacks of discipline.' He slanted the piece of paper up again and scanned it. 'A knife confrontation with a fellow prisoner. And then another incident with the same prisoner, in your cell — '

'When he attacked me.'

'Trouble in the dining room. A search which revealed that you'd smuggled certain contraband into the prison. Including, it says here, the scalpel blade used in the initial confrontation.' Another drag, a smoky pause before the punchline. 'You think we *approve* of prisoners smuggling weapons into Pentonville?'

'I guess not,' Reuben muttered.

'And now this. A riot. A long-serving warder in casualty, four inmates in the hospital wing.'

'It was hardly my fault.'

'You deny that you were wielding a pool cue?'

'No.'

'And that you assaulted a number of inmates, including' — he squinted at the names in front of him — 'prisoners Davies, Hussein and Ruddock?'

Reuben remained silent, pleading for calm. All of this was irrelevant. He had to get the hell out. His son needed him.

The governor took a deep, measured drag on his Marlboro Light and blew the smoke out of the side of his mouth. 'No, I'm sorry, it's time to take action.'

'What are you going to do?'

'Only thing I can. Ship you off to the next rung on the ladder. I don't have the resources to monitor you twenty-four seven.'

'Where?'

'Scrubs.'

'Wormwood Scrubs?'

'They have a room in their Secure Unit.'

'Look, I appreciate that I've forced you into

293

this. But it just isn't like that.' Reuben was desperate. Another prison would raise a whole new series of problems. 'Like I said, I was a CID officer before I transferred to the Forensic Science Service. I ran GeneCrime — you've heard of the unit?'

The governor stared back and shrugged. 'So?'

'I'm here to track a prisoner, to take forensic evidence from him. Now I've done it, and I need to be released. I'm not a criminal.'

'Like you said before. Although there is this, Mr Maitland.'

The governor opened a shallow drawer in his desk and pulled out a slim file. There was a sense of check-mate about his movements which Reuben tried to overlook.

'What is it?'

'Previous arrest record.' He leafed through a few of the fragile pages within. 'Let's have a look. Possession of cocaine with intent to supply. Three months in Belmarsh.'

Reuben slumped in his seat. The bastard had been digging. 'How did you get that?'

'Wasn't easy, but I have some useful contacts. So you *are* a criminal, in fact, Mr Maitland. And also one who has covered up his identity at some point in the past, in order to work in the force.'

'So at least you know I was in the force.'

'Oh, you were. But now you're not. A covert mission? Don't make me laugh. Where's your evidence? Where's the paperwork? Why have no CID officers come knocking on my door and begged for your release? Shall I tell you?'

'Go on,' Reuben answered flatly.

'Because you're a fantasist, Mr Maitland. Nothing more, nothing less. After our last little chat, I cross-checked. You were sacked by the FSS for gross misconduct. No one I talked to knew where you were any more or what you were up to. None of my contacts in the Met are even aware of a policy for forensics officers entering prisons. Face facts, Mr Maitland. I know what you are and you know what you are.' He made a show of signing the piece of paper in front of him, briskly and irritably, and motioned Reuben to the door. 'Go and pack your stuff. I've booked a van. You're leaving tonight at eight p.m.'

'You're wrong,' Reuben muttered, defeated and powerless in the governor's office.

'And, for the record, don't mess the governor of Scrubs around. He really is the meanest governor in the whole prison system.' He allowed himself a sly smile as he finished his Marlboro Light. 'I look forward to hearing how you two get along.'

24

Reuben checked his watch. He didn't have much time. Things had moved so quickly, from seeing Michael Brawn at the phones, to the fight in the hallway, to being summonsed to the governor. He had just under two hours before they transferred him. Reuben had tried and failed to get through to Sarah. Her mobile was off. Her answerphone told him that she was attending a crime scene. She would be unaware of his movement to Scrubs until he could contact her. And that might take days. Secure Unit prisoners, he was well aware, had to earn luxuries like phone cards.

His second choice, however, was more helpful.

'They've fucked your lab,' Moray said, matter-of-factly.

'Who?' Reuben asked.

'Interesting question,' his partner answered. 'But they were good at it. We thought you might have some suggestions.'

Reuben closed his eyes. He was going to a different prison, his son was sick and his lab had been done over. This wasn't a great day.

'Look,' he said, 'forget that for now. I need you to do something for me.'

'Name it,' Moray said.

'This is a big one.'

'Go on.'

'In fact, my fat friend, this is *the* big one.'

Moray didn't bother disguising his sigh. 'As I said, big man, name it.'

'And you don't have much time.'

'As in weeks, days or hours?'

'As in minutes.'

'I'm on it. When and where?'

Reuben told him what he knew and hung up. He glanced at his watch again. An hour and fifty-five minutes to pack his meagre possessions and say his goodbyes. An hour and fifty-five minutes to avoid a last-minute beating by Michael Brawn. If there was an up-side to his current situation, at least he would be leaving Brawn behind.

Reuben made his way back to his cell and slumped on the bed. He dozed for a while, then spent a long while staring at the eclectic series of images Narc had chosen to decorate his wall with. There he saw illustrated the conflicted state of mind brought about by incarceration. The pictures of freedom, of nature, of sexual possibility. A mental slide-show of denied opportunity, of self-imposed captivity.

The door opened and Reuben sat up. Narc eyed him almost triumphantly. Reuben realized that he had given Narc a new lease of life over the past week. He had become the copper's cellmate, his notoriety rocketing within the prison, a nobody who had suddenly become a somebody, with information and observations and stories to tell.

'So it's true?' Narc asked, looking down at him. 'You're off?'

' 'Fraid so.'

297

'Of course, they're gonna fucking *love* a bizzie in Scrubs.'

'That so?'

'You think this place is bad? I've heard stories about the secure wing would make you want to fucking die than go there. And that's normal prisoners. Not fuck-ups like you.'

Reuben stared up into his beaming face, his almost cheeky expression of joy. 'Narc, shut it.'

Narc changed instantly. 'You threatening me, copper?'

Reuben stood up. He opened his drawer and the clear plastic HMP bag he had been given and started to stuff his clothes into it.

'You threatening me?' Narc sneered again. 'Cos there's about a hundred cons in this wing would like to say goodbye to you properly. All I do is open this door and shout. You want that?'

'Like I said. Just shut your mouth.'

'The trouble with you, you don't know when you're fucked. I mean, really fucked.'

Reuben grunted. Prison was starting to mess with his mind. He gripped the handle of his bag.

'Right now, people in this wing will be ringing their mates in the Scrubs, telling them there's a smart-arsed copper on the way over tonight, telling 'em what you look like, who you are, what you've done. And you know who's at the head of the fucking queue?'

Reuben tried not to meet his eye. 'Surprise me.'

'Your mate. Michael fucking Brawn.'

Reuben continued to round up his possessions, knowing that he had to stay calm. Out of the corner of his eye, he noted that Narc was visibly gaining in confidence.

'And an educated boy like you, delicate hands, pale eyes, could be very popular over there. Make someone a very nice wife.'

Reuben suddenly snapped. A lifetime of being in control had disappeared in just under a week. He wheeled around and grabbed Narc by the throat, pushing him hard against the wall.

'I've got you a leaving present,' he spat, pulling his fist back.

Narc's triumphalism only seemed to grow. 'At last! The educated man becomes an animal!'

'I'm warning you . . . '

'This is the system you send people into.' Narc was undeterred, despite the imminence of violence. 'And what does prison do?'

'Tell me.'

'It brutalizes you.'

And Reuben saw it. He knew he was right. His father, the rain pouring down, head bowed in the passenger seat, examining his knuckles, raw and wounded. Realizing that a barrier had been put up between them, a gruffness, a sadness, which had never been there before. His father increasingly withdrawn, given to depressions and fits of temper. A different man from the one who had gone in.

'Doesn't matter who you are. If you weren't brutalized before, you fucking are by the time you leave.'

Reuben slackened his grip and turned away. Narc was smiling slyly at him, his point made.

There was a rattle at the door, and then it

swung open. Two guards stepped in, ones Reuben had seen in riot gear earlier, removing their helmets after the fun was over, wiping the blood off their metal truncheons with paper towels. One of them brandished a pair of handcuffs and sauntered over to stand uncomfortably close to Reuben.

'Who's been a naughty boy then?' he asked. His breath reeked, sour tobacco on top of wet halitosis.

'And naughty boys have to be punished,' his partner added.

The first guard grabbed Reuben's wrists and fastened the handcuffs tight.

'Time for a trip to hell,' he grinned.

25

The modified Ford Transit was a snug fit, designed to transport a maximum of two or three prisoners at a time. Its blackened windows were barred on the inside, invisible from the street. The driver sat in an enclosed compartment, sealed off in wood and metal, with a drilled plastic hatch at head-height to the side. Reuben sat between the two guards, his manacled hands in his lap, wrists already swelling and sore.

They were, Reuben appreciated, picking their way through quiet North London back-streets. He monitored their progress for a second through the tinted window. Some of the roads were familiar, well-worn routes across an area of the capital he and Moray had come to know well over the last few months. They were only a couple of miles from GeneCrime, not far from Kieran Hobb's patch, and Judith's house was a handful of junctions away. The pavements were almost empty, the darkness unappealing, the cold keeping people inside. The van passed the Italian café where Moray had dropped him just over a week ago, Sarah Hirst sitting inside, drinking coffee, Michael Brawn's file resting on the table, a faked signature inside. Reuben pulled in a deep breath and held it. The guards fidgeted in their seats, bored and listless. Reuben sighed the air out again and slumped forward, holding his head in his hands.

'That's it,' the first guard said.

'Kiss your arse goodbye,' his partner added.

'Cos from now on, it's gonna belong to someone else.'

Reuben stayed where he was, long second after long second. The guards lost interest in him. The van slowed, the driver working through the gears, the brakes complaining as they reached a junction.

And then there was an almighty thump. A screeching, grinding aftershock of metal contact. A strangled shout from somewhere, maybe the driver. Out of the corner of his eye, Reuben saw events in slow motion. The two guards careering forward like crash test dummies, in flight, ramming into the seats in front. Papers and belongings hanging in the air. Reuben, in the brace position, staying still, his movement subdued by the rear of the next seat. Shaking his head. Standing up and turning to the rear of the van. Walking unsteadily back. The guards slumped in their seats, blood beginning to pour from their faces. Reuben kicking the buckled rear doors. Glass crunching under his feet. A smell of petrol in the air. The doors yielding on the third blow. Outside, Moray jumping down from the cab of a four-tonner which was leaking fluids from the impact. Moray grabbing Reuben's arm and leading him across the empty road to a parked car. Vision still blurred, senses running slow. Buzzing in his ears. Climbing into the car and driving off at speed. Looking back through the side mirror, pale and aching, sight and sound starting to cooperate. Watching the damaged prison van slowly recede into the distance. A guard emerging, bent double and coughing.

Out of prison.

A free man.

THREE

1

. . . and back again. He takes a couple of seconds, shakes his head. Gaps, holes, rips in the present tense. No way of knowing whether they're getting more frequent or whether it has been like this for months. Very difficult to tell. But they seem to happen under certain conditions. Excitement and anticipation, at night, when alone. Then during the day, hardly at all.

He glances quickly around, checking nothing has changed. The car park still has just three vehicles in it, the lights of the surgery burning bright behind vertical blinds. He clenches his fists and releases, repeating the move several times.

The noise of a car. He looks over at the entrance, a battered maroon Polo pulling in, spluttering past and parking. A young woman, nineteen or twenty maybe, climbing out. Just yards away. On another occasion, he tells himself. Not tonight. He watches her from behind the thick laurel hedge, her body slender through her coat. Dressed tight, exhibiting what she can despite the temperature. Wanting to be looked at, inviting his stare. But another night, another occasion.

He drags his eyes away, checking his watch. Almost seven p.m. Those general practitioners are putting in the hours. Late surgeries twice a

307

week for office jockeys tied to their desks. He hunches his shoulders and pushes them back, laughing to himself. The police putting in the hours as well. Looking for him. Feeding wildly inaccurate descriptions to the newspapers. Coming up with half-baked theories and notions. And he is right under their noses, has been, all along. No one has twigged anything. It gives you faith. All that staring at computer screens and DNA sequences when a quick look around, a few questions here and there, could do the trick straight away.

There was nothing in the papers about the last one. He checked them all, reading and scanning, page after page, fingers grubby with ink. They obviously hadn't linked it. True, it was different. Could almost have looked accidental. A young woman in a red top lying on the pavement, having fallen and hit her head after a night out. But it had left him hungry. Being denied something has that effect. A missed opportunity. A reckless attack that didn't go as planned. The one that got away. He wonders whether she survived the cold, lying on the empty street, bleeding from her head, and suspects she didn't. He smiles to himself, the answer coming to him. If she had, the police would have tried to link it.

Somewhere a car alarm screams for a few seconds, before being terminated. It is cold, but not as bad as it has been recently. He guesses it is three or four degrees, about the temperature of a drink in the fridge. For a second, he wonders whether a chilled can of Coke would just feel normal if he drank it now. It's all relative, after all. How things relate to each other. How events are linked. How compounds interact. How you deal with those interactions.

Negative feedback, that was the problem. The doctor told him that. Although she'd said a lot of things. More long names and clinical conditions. What were her exact words? It increases the desire but inhibits the performance. Like alcohol or something. But what did alcohol ever do for you, apart from make you thirsty and sluggish? For a doctor, her knowledge was laughable. Two-dimensional textbook stuff. This alleviates this, but may cause this. This is associated with this, but rarely this. This interferes with this, and shouldn't be used with this.

But this, this is the stuff, this is life, proper life, as it is designed to be lived. Not scraping by, office hours, tired and bruised, weak and enfeebled, never quite catching up, never really being who you wanted to be, repressed and suppressed, unable to fight, just taking it from your corporation, your boss, your partner and your kids, a bloated punchbag, there for the kicking, waiting in the warm air of a doctor's surgery at seven p.m., praying to fuck that they'll put you on antidepressants.

But it is not enough simply to survive. You must exist. And you must demonstrate your power of existence. And if one part of your power is denied you, is lost as a by-product of who you are and what you do, you must find another way. A more gratifying way. A more permanent way. A way that shows the low-lifes and reprobates surrounding you that you are

309

more alive than the rest of them put together.

An old man hobbles across the car park to his car, and makes a meal of pulling out and driving away. His exhaust gases stay in the air after he has gone, wafting through the cold, still car park. Seconds after he disappears, the young female returns to the safety of her Polo, a prescription in her hand. She leaves briskly, no seatbelt, tyres squealing slightly. He glances around. Just two vehicles left now. Nice ones, noticeably smarter than the patients'. One with four-wheel drive, the other Scandinavian and sleek.

A light in the top left of the three-storey building goes out. He reaches into his pocket and takes out a small plastic bag. Inside are two vinyl gloves, transparently thin and lightly powdered. He pictures her taking hers off as he puts his on. He is careful, not touching the outside of the gloves, wriggling into them as he has observed and practised again and again. The plastic bag is folded up and zipped into the inside pocket of his jacket. He pulls out a woollen balaclava and rolls it down over his face.

High heels, echoing along the alleyway. He is breathing hard through the coarse material, wet, excited breaths. And then he sees her.

He knows this one will be different. Away from the usual area. No point in dumping her in the Thames. Besides, it will keep those CID boys and girls busy. This is far too early in the evening to be driving around. And the plush upholstery could do without the blood. Just do it here. She will understand.

She approaches. Tired and relieved. A heavy

black case with her. Fishing in her coat pocket for her car keys. Pushing the button, a flash of indicators on the four by four. Smaller than the one he drives, he notes, stepping out, staying in the shadows, skirting round. She pulls open the rear passenger door and slides her case across the seat. And he is there. Behind her. Gloved hands around her neck. Doesn't even have time to cry out. Babbling incoherent words through her crushed windpipe. He allows her to rotate a little, to see him. The shock in her eyes. But she is a doctor. Surely she knows about these things, and what to expect? With one hand pulverizing her trachea, he uses the other to lift his balaclava. Face to face. Red cheeks, eyes frozen wide, mouth in a silent scream. Still alive. Just. He knows she will be thinking three minutes. Two words burned into her suspended consciousness. Three minutes of oxygen starvation before permanent brain damage.

He has a quick glance around. No one. He senses the rising panic in her movements. The tensing, then the thrashing, stiff and flailing, unnatural jolting of the limbs, jerky actions through suddenly engorged muscles. He rips her coat off her. 'Look at me now and tell me I'm impotent,' he grunts. Her terror is turning him on. She knows that three minutes is not a long period of time. He pulls the balaclava back down, and unzips his trousers. 'Call this erectile dysfunction?' The condom is already on. He lets her see it, allows her to make the leap, to understand what is going to happen to her. He thinks he detects it in her face. Revulsion amid

311

the shock and the horror.

He squeezes harder, the soft cartilage of her neck yielding, windpipe and blood vessels closing. She is showing the first signs. Her three minutes are almost up. He pushes her into the back seat, so she is lying partially down. As he waits for it to end, patiently watching the colour ebb, the life slip away, he realizes that although it started out random, now there almost feels to be a pattern. He wonders whether it is always like that. Just like life. You drift into things, follow them where they take you, end up going in directions you had never thought about.

He releases his grip. The doctor, with her mocking manner and unsympathetic words, doesn't move. He opens her legs, knowing that after this one, the next is already sorted.

A female from GeneCrime, the forensics unit in Euston.

And not just any female.

2

Moray eased the car to a halt in the parking bay of the Children's Hospital. A large sign read 'No Waiting'. Reuben, stiffening up after the prison van impact, rubbed his neck and glanced up at the building. It was modern and new, all glass and steel, guaranteed to look awful in fifteen years' time. Moray killed the engine and swivelled in his seat to face him.

'You sure?' he asked. 'You've only just broken out.'

'And now I'm breaking in.'

Moray pulled a pair of bolt cutters from the side compartment of his door. 'Here, let me see those things.'

Reuben placed his hands on the steering wheel, which was still damp from Moray's grip. He knew the risk his partner had just taken on his behalf.

'Thanks,' he said.

'I haven't got them off yet.'

'I mean for the rescue.'

'Ach, it was wild. Wouldn't have missed it.'

Moray continued to work on Reuben's handcuffs, testing successive regions of the metal for hardness and ease of access, squeezing the handles of the bolt cutters together and then relaxing them again. Reuben watched him as he battled. He seemed to be getting fatter, if anything, and if Reuben didn't know better, he would have mistaken him for a lazy slob. But lazy slobs didn't rush out and hire commercial vehicles at short notice and slam them into prison vans, let alone steal cars and secrete them at pre-determined points. He had asked a lot of Moray — too much, in fact, for most — but he had planned it all and carried it off in less than two hours. Truly, despite his size, there was even more to Moray than met the eye.

Between grunts of effort, Moray said, 'As tactics go, this isn't the best.'

'It'll be fine. They won't think of looking here yet.'

Moray released the left-hand manacle, and using the same technique on the other, quickly broke through. 'There you go.' He took the various pieces of metal and glanced up at the front of the building. 'I managed to get hold of her, finally. She should be inside main reception, waiting for you.'

'Thanks,' Reuben said again, rubbing his wrists. 'What are you going to do?'

'I'll wipe the car clean and ditch it. Meet you by the entrance.'

Reuben smiled gratefully at Moray and climbed quickly out of the car. This was no time to be congratulating each other. He walked briskly to the rotating doors, a bitter wind rushing straight through his jumper. Hot air churned out to meet him as he entered. He was wary, glancing about, taking in the two security guards behind the front desk, the profusion of fake plants and vending machines, the concerned

314

parents pacing about, the general air of sad and efficient ill health.

DCI Sarah Hirst was sitting on a plastic chair reading a magazine. She stood up as she spotted Reuben and walked straight over. Against the paleness of her blouse, Reuben sensed a flush of anger in her face.

'This isn't good,' she said, up close. 'On so many levels, this isn't good.'

'It's a fuck of a lot better than where I was before.'

'I mean, what the hell were you thinking?'

'That I was going to spend the rest of my days being buggered in Wormwood Scrubs.'

'But I could have got you out.'

'It was taking too long.'

'I thought I explained. I was making progress. Gently pulling strings. It would have happened in a couple of days, max.'

There was something in Sarah's eyes that suggested she didn't wholeheartedly believe what she was saying.

'By which time I would have been in a different prison.'

'But still — '

'Look, Sarah, my son is ill and getting iller. Plus, someone's smashed up my lab, and I need to know who. I'm not blaming you for the difficulties involved in getting a disgraced ex-copper out of a prison he wasn't officially in, it's just that time is of the essence.'

'This isn't good,' Sarah repeated, almost to herself. 'Come on, let's walk and talk.'

She guided Reuben through a set of double

doors and up two flights of stairs. The corridors, like Pentonville's, like GeneCrime's, were low-ceilinged and strip-lit, with neutral colours and little warmth. Sarah turned to Reuben as she walked, her shoulders relaxing a touch, her face gaining a small degree of compassion.

'So, how was it?' she asked.

'Every bit as good as you might imagine.'

'And Michael Brawn?'

'Nailed. I guess this is where things start making sense.'

'Yeah.' Sarah gave him a once-over with her pale blue eyes and long dark lashes. 'Jeez, you look rough. And you could have smartened yourself up a bit.'

'I'll be fine. The plainclothes look.' Reuben glanced doubtfully down at his trousers and trainers. 'Besides, you think you can spot the difference between a con and a cop just by their clothes?'

'Generally, yes,' Sarah answered with a smile. 'Here we are.'

They came to a halt outside a door marked 'Acute Ward 4'. Sarah reached forward and pressed the intercom button. Reuben suddenly felt nervous. Until this moment, he had barely stopped. From his cell, into the van, into Moray's car and through the hospital. Now, standing still and picturing what he was about to see, Reuben inhaled a cold, deep breath, which seemed to drop like liquid nitrogen into the pit of his stomach.

Sarah pushed her mouth up to the speaker of the intercom and pressed the button again.

'Hello? This is Detective Chief Inspector Sarah Hirst. I called earlier.'

The door clicked, electromagnetic contacts moving apart. Sarah and Reuben pushed through. Inside, the ward was decked out in luminous colours. It had been Disneyfied, with approximately drawn cartoon characters having fun across the walls. Within a few paces, they were met by a nurse. Filipino, Reuben guessed, or possibly Malaysian.

'Can I help you?' she asked.

Sarah swiftly pulled her warrant card out of the front pocket of her trousers, as if she was about to start shooting. 'DCI Sarah Hirst,' she said. 'And this is DI' — Sarah glanced unsurely at Reuben, and then at the wall they were facing — 'Michael Mouse.'

Reuben nodded, his eyes wide at the name.

'The father of your patient Joshua Maitland has recently escaped from prison,' Sarah continued. 'We're concerned he might try to get access to his son. Myself and DI Mouse would like to have a look around, if that's OK. Maybe talk to one or two staff?'

The nurse remained impassive. 'He's over there — bed six.'

She turned and pointed towards a curtained-off section where the ward opened out, a new profusion of cartoon characters desperately trying to bring a sense of fun to acute childhood illness. Reuben walked slowly towards the veiled area of beds, excitement and nervousness fighting in his stomach.

'*Mouse?*' he whispered tersely to Sarah.

'It's all I could think of at short notice. And you're lucky it wasn't Donald fucking Duck.' She stopped, keeping her distance. 'You go in, I'll chat to the staff. But you've only got a few moments.'

Reuben steadied himself, swaying slightly on his feet, his eyes closed. Helplessness, fear, worry, love and sadness surged through him in consecutive waves. He listened for a moment to see if Lucy was there, then pulled back the curtain and stepped inside.

Joshua was sleeping on his front, his light brown hair ruffled, a tube intruding into his nose. Eighteen months old and beginning to lengthen, his arms and legs seemingly longer already than the last time. Reuben realized with shock that he was losing weight. Toddlers should be chubby and rounded, all puppy fat and soft, bowed limbs. Joshua, however, was getting thin. He must never have noticed it before, but here, naked except for a nappy, his sheets wriggled out of, there were sharp angles and prominent ribs. He bent down and kissed his hair, running his fingers over Joshua's skin, fighting his emotions, trying not to cry.

'You hang on in there, little fella,' he whispered, pulling the yellow sheets over Joshua and composing himself. 'Your daddy's going to do everything he can.'

Reuben reached over to the far side of the bed and grabbed the metal clipboard hanging there. He scanned Joshua's medical notes, flicking through the four pages of blood results, sodium levels, fluid pHs, white cell counts, temperatures

318

and case notes. Seven words in large black capitals dominated the final page: 'Acute Lymphocytic Leukaemia. Scheduled chemo. Donor negative'.

Reuben screwed his eyes up. 'Just give me another day and a half,' he muttered, stroking Joshua's hair. 'Daddy's got to sort some nasty people out. And then I'll be back, and no one will be able to touch us.'

Joshua remained still, his breathing slow and regular, immersed in the dead sleep of children. Reuben replaced the notes and kissed his son again, this time on the shoulder. His skin was hot and smelled of the pure, innocent, undiluted love that cuts right through you and stops you breathing for a second. Truly, he thought, his face bent over Joshua's skin, the scent of a woman was a weak sensation in comparison. He stood up slowly, lingering in the close presence of his son.

'And then we'll be together,' he whispered. 'You and me. Fit and well. Happy ever after.'

The curtain was pulled back and Sarah poked her head through.

'Sorry,' she said, 'but it's time to go. I'll get my car, see you at the front.'

Reuben hesitated a long couple of minutes, burning the image of Joshua into his retinas, before reluctantly walking out. He returned the curtain to its position of privacy and headed sadly away, through the ward, along the hospital corridors and into the biting cold, silence hanging over him like a premonition.

3

The traffic was sparse, and Sarah carved through what little there was with her customary confidence. Reuben remained quiet, thinking things through, trying to catch up with the events of the last eight hours. The implications of his actions were starting to make themselves clear to him, and when Sarah began to talk, she merely voiced his misgivings.

'You're going to be high priority,' she said, taking a roundabout at speed.

'I can see that,' he responded, sliding around the back seat, Moray blocking most of his view through the windscreen.

'For all the force knows, you're a dangerous criminal who has murdered his wife, escaped prison, and is now on the run.'

'But you can sort it?'

'Wrong. I can influence specific officers here and there, but I can't protect you from a manhunt.'

'You can put the word out, though?'

'Look, even if I do break cover and tell my commanding officers what has happened, they're still going to want to see you brought to account. Since you and Brains here' — she jerked her thumb dismissively in Moray's direction — 'decided to smash up a prison van and injure its guards.'

Moray shrugged, unconcerned. 'Omelettes

and eggs, Sarah. Omelettes and eggs.'

'No, your best bet is to lie very low. Let me do what I can do.'

'Where have I heard that before?'

Sarah's features hardened, her concentration fixed on the road. 'Fuck off, Reuben. You think it's easy, in the middle of a serial killer investigation, to be running round helping you out?'

Reuben stared forlornly through the rear passenger window, thoughts of Joshua darting in and out of his head. The words acute lymphocytic leukaemia played themselves over and over, bringing images of irregular white blood cells slowly dying in veins, arteries and capillaries and not being replaced.

'I guess not,' he said.

'The papers will be swarming all over you by now.'

'Yeah, I guess they will. Look, we're here. Take the next left and pull over.'

Sarah glanced in the rear-view, maybe to check on traffic, maybe to check on her passenger. She screeched across a junction and pulled smartly up. With the engine idling, she swivelled in her seat to look at Reuben.

'You sure about this?'

'You can't lie much lower than here.'

'How long's it been since you saw him?'

'Year or so.'

Reuben pulled out his mobile phone and dialled a number. After a few seconds, he said, 'Aaron? It's me. I'm here. Right.' He flipped the phone shut, sad and slow in his movements, a resignation weighing him down. 'Said he'll be straight out,' he muttered.

Reuben monitored the street. Victorian terraces with white frontages. Cars parked nose to tail on both sides. The occasional tree, leafless and shivering in the cold. Streetlamps with their heads bowed in defeat. An OK place to live if you couldn't afford anything better.

Out of an alleyway between two blocks of houses a man dressed in baggy clothes appeared.

'We're on,' Reuben said.

Moray pointed at the man. 'That him? Jeez, he's the spitting image.'

'You know many twins who aren't?' Reuben asked.

'It's still uncanny,' Sarah said. 'Apart from the long blond ponytail, of course. What's he up to these days?'

'I dread to think,' Reuben answered, climbing out of the back seat. 'And I probably shouldn't say in front of a serving officer. I'll see you both later. And, Sarah?'

'What?'

'You know.'

Sarah raised her eyebrows at him. 'I know.'

Reuben shut the car door, then Sarah revved the engine and pulled away at speed.

★　★　★

Reuben ran his eyes around his brother's front room. He had often pictured what Aaron's squat would be like, and he could see now that he had

322

been wildly inaccurate. Apart from the scruffiness of the furniture, and the slowly dying carpet, the room was like most of the country's living rooms: more cluttered than it might be, less clean than it should be, and with almost everything pointing in the direction of the television. A wooden table in the knocked-through dining room supported a mass of books and CDs, and looked never to have been used for its intended purpose. A couple of plants were forlornly wilting in the dry central heating. Full ashtrays and empty cans colonized any remaining surfaces. As squats went, though, this was fairly comfortable.

Aaron was silent, sitting on the sofa, rolling a joint. Reuben knew that too many things had happened for them to be entirely comfortable in each other's company. He saw his arrest file in the governor of Pentonville's office; he'd been stopped with over fifty grams of cocaine in Aaron's car, and taken the blame for his brother to save him breaking his parole. Reuben realized he still hadn't truly forgiven Aaron. And there were other factors. The way they had ruthlessly explored opposing sides of the law; Aaron's decision to stay at home while Reuben went to university; the death of their father, a habitual and petty criminal whom Reuben had begun to distance himself from during his early years in CID. All in all, the family had fallen apart, Reuben and his mother on one side, Aaron and his father on the other. Legal and illegal, law making and law breaking.

Aaron lit the joint. After several deep drags, he

offered it over. Reuben took it from him and pulled on it, stale air rushing through the papery structure, bitter smoke filling his mouth and entering his lungs. He held his breath for a couple of seconds, and as he exhaled, he said, 'You hear about Jeremy Accoutey?'

'Who didn't?'

'I kind of got involved in it, just before everything went pear-shaped.'

'In what way involved?'

'Forensic testing of his wife's lover.'

'Fuck.'

'Yeah.'

The image had stayed with him. A petite blonde with a large exit wound in her scalp.

'The tabloids had a field-day with the fact she had a boyfriend. You know, *Footballers' Wives* and all that. And you were in on it?'

Reuben took another drag and passed the joint back to his brother. A warm tiredness began to wash through him, and he sensed a sudden weight to his skull.

'It's not something I want to talk about,' he said. 'People died in nasty circumstances, indirectly related to my activities.'

'Shit. That's scary stuff.'

'That's not the half of it. I needed to get away for a bit, and someone was very interested in a prisoner in Pentonville. Twenty-five grand interested. Only things didn't go as smoothly as I'd anticipated.'

'How?'

'I got myself in a very bad situation, isolated in Pentonville, people knowing my background.'

'And now you're on the run.'

'I guess so.'

Reuben swigged from a can of beer and massaged his aching neck. Generally, he preferred stimulants. Dope slowed you down, made you sluggish and unfocused. Alcohol didn't help either. But for some reason the two depressants mixed together seemed to warm him up and melt the tension that had been squeezing his insides for several days.

'And you?' he asked, moving the conversation on.

'Same old,' Aaron answered.

'No girlfriend?'

'Women aren't exactly my strong point.'

Aaron handed the joint to Reuben again.

'But what are you up to?'

Aaron flashed his half joking, half serious expression. Reuben knew it well. He had an almost identical one. 'That depends whether you're going to arrest me.'

Reuben sighed through a long, smoky exhalation. 'As I'm growing tired of explaining lately, I'm no longer a copper. So?'

'The odd car here and there. Spot of five-fingered discount. Small-time stuff.'

Casting his eyes around the squat, Reuben was suddenly struck by the realization that Aaron was thirty-eight, and still living outside the bounds of normal society. Squatting was, he believed, something you eventually grew out of, like spinning your wheels or doing handbrake turns.

'Hell, Aaron,' he said, handing the joint back,

'what happened to you?'

'What do you mean?'

'I mean, look at this squat. Look at you. Where did everything go wrong?'

Aaron dragged deep into the joint, his brow furrowed. 'You're the geneticist. You tell me.'

'You can't blame Dad for everything.'

'OK, let's start with genes and environment.' Aaron sucked back some beer and pulled on the remnant of the joint before poking it through the hole of the can, triggering a loud and angry hiss. 'Nature and nurture. What other blame is there? Either way, Dad's fucked.'

'But you're thirty-eight — '

'Exactly the same age as you. And where's *your* cosy life, suburban house, cushy job and faithful wife?'

Reuben glanced down at the carpet, with its small army of burn holes, noting how they were clustered towards one end of the sofa. He remained silent, biting his tongue.

'I may be a loser, Reuben, but I'm one by choice.'

'What are you saying?'

'That you, on the other hand, have fucked everything up without even trying.'

Aaron let his words do their damage, monitoring his brother keenly, antagonism and resentment burning bright across his features. Reuben stared into the pale green eyes of the face on the opposite sofa. The mirror image that belied a lifetime of perplexing differences. The same, but not the same.

'And now you come to me with the fucking

police on your trail. Glass houses, brother.'

Reuben stood up, stinging and angry, the sedation evaporating. Pacing into the kitchen, fists clenched. Old scores unsettled. Rivalries resurfacing. Stitched-up wounds tearing themselves back open. Knowing that no one can cut you more precisely than your brother. Knowing that twin brothers are even more adept at it than normal siblings. And knowing that Aaron was right.

4

The usual bony hardness of Judith's hug was missing. Today, she was softer somehow, more gentle, less vigorous. Reuben wondered momentarily whether something was wrong, whether she was having second thoughts about working for him. He wouldn't blame her. A critical member of the GeneCrime forensics squad, his former loyal deputy, she was in an impossible position most of the time. But as she stepped back, he could see in her eyes that she was genuinely pleased to see him again, and this gave him some hope.

Judith walked over to sit on the sofa, and Reuben perched on a lab stool.

'So, the prisoner returns,' she said.

Reuben frowned. 'Something like that.'

When he had first entered the lab, he had been amazed at how little damage there was. The only visible signs were a front door that didn't close quite as well, and a faint smell of spilled chemicals. Judith and Moray had obviously been busy, sweeping up Eppendorfs, replacing boxes, tidying everything to its usual state of uncontaminated efficiency. If Reuben was a gambling man, he would have bet that this was more down to Judith's efforts than Moray's.

'You think the police know about this place?' Reuben asked.

'Only Sarah. And she's OK.'

'No one at GeneCrime has mentioned its whereabouts?'

Reuben watched Judith intently. Not because he didn't trust her, just for any sign of hesitation or uncertainty. He needed to know that she was one hundred per cent convinced.

'Not to me.'

'You're sure you've never been followed?'

'As sure as I can be. You ride a scooter, you keep a very close eye on the cars around you.'

'I guess so.'

'Colm reckons it's a death-trap.'

'But a very pretty one.'

'Yeah, well.' Judith treated him to one of her distant half smiles. Reuben chose to overlook the fact that the dreamy look gave her an enigmatic beauty, an unknowable and demure distance. 'I guess you shouldn't spend too much time here if you can help it,' she said.

'Just a few hours, that's all. But you're right, we'd both better only be here for the minimum time we can. Even between procedures, we should bail out. I've made myself — what did Abner say a few days back?'

'Vulnerable.'

'That's the fella. Made myself vulnerable. Half the city's police hunting me down. Violent escape from custody. They're going to be coming for me, Judith. And we can't ignore the possibility that someone in the force knows where the lab is.'

'As well as Sarah.'

'You trust her, though?'

'You know what she's like. You've observed

what she's capable of at work. It's not that she's dishonest . . . '

'What?'

'Well, to make something her own. To solve a case. To advance her career. We've both seen it. Trampling on people, messing them around, not being entirely open and honest.'

Reuben was silent. Beneath her occasional dreaminess, he knew that Judith's cogs turned with remarkable speed and accuracy. Sarah had been involved in all the events of the last week. Was it possible, Reuben wondered, that he was somehow serving Sarah's needs? Why the sudden offer to help with Michael Brawn? How did she gain such quick access to his arrest details, not to mention his DNA specimens? How had she managed to insert Reuben into Pentonville so easily, and then be so apparently powerless to pull him out again? What did Sarah have to gain, especially in the middle of a large manhunt? Reuben turned these thoughts over in his mind for a few moments. Sarah and Michael Brawn. How could she have stood to profit from Reuben's involvement? He scratched his face irritably, knowing that he was wasting time, and sensing once again that the longer he spent in the lab the more exposed he was.

Glancing around again at the tidied surfaces, he felt once more a rush of relief that Judith had understood his cryptic instructions, as she'd confirmed earlier on the phone.

'You got the sample?' he asked.

Judith patted her handbag. 'In here.'

'Smart girl. What about the rest?'

330

'Systematically ruined. Thawed and destroyed.'

Judith ran her eyes around the floor of the lab, as if pointing out to Reuben the last resting places of the thousands of DNA specimens which had died in the heat. Reuben saw the wasted hours of work, the irreplaceable samples of psychopaths and sociopaths, the meticulously labelled and inventoried investigations leaking away on a laboratory floor. Of course, some of them were just aliquots of specimens that were safely housed in the temperature-controlled store rooms of GeneCrime. But others, ones that Judith had taken in a rush, were all that remained. That was the obvious risk of taking fragile items out of their laboratories and into the wider world. And you could have all the back-ups and security doors you wanted, but if someone truly wanted to destroy something then that's what would happen. Reuben found it suddenly perverse that DNA was happy at body temperature for a whole lifetime, yet extracted and placed at room temperature it fell apart in hours.

'Fuckers,' he said, mainly to himself.

Judith pulled Reuben's letter, still bearing the Pentonville postmark, out of her bag. It was sealed in clingfilm inside a clear plastic freezer bag, surrounded by frozen peas which were showing signs of thawing.

'This wasn't a bunch of kids breaking in,' she said. 'Most of the equipment was left untouched. But the samples . . . '

'What did Moray have to say?'

'He had a theory that the intruders may have

331

left the very thing they were after. Letting it thaw out with the rest. Undetectable.'

'Well I have another theory.' Reuben took the freezer bag from Judith. 'They didn't find what they were looking for. Because this is it here, hidden among these few words.'

'Short and sweet. Who says the art of letter writing is dead?'

Reuben opened the bag, extracted the letter and held it up to the light, which was bright and blinding, the halogen bulbs of the industrial fittings almost piercing the thin prison writing paper.

'It all depends on the message you're trying to put across,' he muttered. 'And how good the recipient is at understanding.'

'I'll take that as a compliment.'

Reuben pushed his fingers into a pair of vinyl gloves and cut the corners of the letter into a tube, pipetting a series of fluids on top.

'Let's give these a while to soak,' he said, 'and then we'll begin.' He turned to Judith. 'We should get out of here. See you back here in three hours?'

Judith picked up her gloves and helmet, and Reuben followed her out, locking the damaged front door and making sure that no one was watching them.

5

'Look, just because you're on one side and I'm on the other, doesn't mean it has to be like this.'

'And what side are you on?'

Reuben shrugged, looking down at his empty hands. The conversation had been slow and awkward, with long, tense gaps. The question surprised him. Aaron saw the law as an arbitrary concept, a logical fallacy used to repress the timid and the weak. A discussion of its boundaries suggested he might finally be taking the idea seriously.

Reuben opened a fresh can of beer, pausing to think. The last week had reminded him that the law wasn't something you could just cross for fun. Every time you passed from one side to the other, you left a little piece of yourself. You ended up blurred. Bits of you abandoned on either side for ever. That's how Reuben felt, sitting in Aaron's squat — blurred, distributed, diluted, two identities, neither of which he was particularly comfortable with. And seated next to his brother, their elbows almost touching, tickly arm hairs occasionally meeting, Reuben sensed that Aaron saw it as well. But Michael Jeremy Brawn had had something that Reuben needed. His blood, his skin, his hair, anything would have done. Small fragments of a psychopath that Reuben had stolen and mailed back to his lab. Crossing from the legal to the illegal and back again.

'It's complicated,' he answered.

'Only this Jeremy Accoutey thing disturbs me.'

'Probably not as much as it does me.'

'I mean, what you did was illegal, right? Taking DNA from a woman without her knowledge, testing it, and then giving her husband the results. Not to mention stealing a sample from the team physio in a public place.'

Reuben shrugged.

'And those actions precipitate a murder. Then you enter prison under a false identity, before crashing your way out. So I ask you again, brother, what side of the law are you actually on?'

Reuben rubbed his face. He flashed through the undercover missions he had carried out during his career and after it. Pretending to be bad when he was good, lying to superior police officers to get jobs done, feeding criminals small truths to gain bigger ones. Reuben sensed his brother — sitting on the same tatty sofa, facing the same direction, avoiding direct eye contact — waiting for an answer.

'Difficult to tell these days,' he replied quietly. 'But the aim is always good.'

'Helping footballers kill their wives?'

'Channelling money into investigations that no one else carries out. Abuses of power. Misuse of technology. Tracking criminals the police can't touch. I mean, we put a CID officer away last year who had tampered with the DNA evidence of four nation-wide manhunts. Cases collapsed, the real perpetrators remained at large, the victims were denied justice. A police officer taking short-cuts to manipulate convictions. It's murky, at times, but what we're trying to do . . . '

Reuben petered out, ill at ease, appreciating that things had become complicated. The TV was off, but he found himself staring at it, as if it would spring to life at any moment and save them from each other's company.

'OK. What you do these days is up to you. It's past events that really fuck me off.'

'Like what?' Reuben asked, suddenly angry and defensive and trying to hide it.

'Dad.'

'What?'

'When he went down the final time, you virtually cut him off.'

Reuben scratched his hair, fingernails finding skin through the crew-cut. 'What could I do? I pleaded with him to clean his act up. For his sake, for Mum's sake, for everyone's sake. I was a copper, catching the bad guys. And there's my own father, a career criminal, in and out of prison.' Saying the words out loud made his actions sound harsh and predetermined. Trading his father for his career. But it hadn't been like that. 'It was beginning to undermine me. The implications, the scenarios. 'Squad, let me introduce you to Dr Reuben Maitland, lead forensics officer, section head of GeneCrime. Oh yeah, and son of a crook.''

Aaron sniffed. 'Didn't mean you had to abandon him.'

'I didn't. I just . . . stepped back a bit.'

'And let me pick up the pieces.'

335

'You make it sound like I wanted that.'

Aaron lit up, and pointedly kept the joint to himself.

'You're saying you didn't?'

'Of course not, Aaron. It just happened. Like families do. Things falling apart, people moving away, circumstances changing.' Reuben drank from his can, hoping the cold lager could extinguish the searing frustration. 'And I've more than served my debt to you, brother. You remember?'

Aaron blew a long stream of smoke into the living-room air. 'Yeah,' he answered eventually. 'Whatever.'

A fidgety silence closed in on them, oppressive and uncomfortable. Arm hairs touched again briefly, sending shivers through Reuben's body.

'Look, I've got to get back to the lab.'

'And then what?'

'It'll all die down as soon as I've run the lab test. Then I'll sort Joshua out, which is all that really matters at this moment. After that, I'll go back to my life, and you . . . well, you've got my number.'

Reuben stood up, draining his can and finding an empty surface to stack it. He double-checked his watch. Moray would be waiting, an anonymous car, a couple of streets away, the engine running.

'I guess this is it.'

Aaron got up slowly, his eyes narrow, his brow furrowed. For a second their eyes met, pale green to pale green, the same but different, staring at each other across a divide Reuben

336

knew would never be bridged. He felt like hugging his brother, grabbing his arms and wrapping them around him, the twins reunited at last after years of sporadic contact and icy bitterness. Instead he turned and walked towards the door.

Aaron's voice stopped him. 'Here,' he said, 'take this with you. See what they're saying about you out there.'

He handed his brother a copy of the London *Evening Standard*. Reuben took it, the final contact between them.

'Bye,' Reuben muttered.

'You made page three,' Aaron said.

Reuben opened and closed the front door without looking back. The documentaries, the articles, the all-pervasive notions of society assailed him as he walked. Identical twins and spooky coincidences, being separated at birth and then discovering they had identical lives with identical partners and identical children. Twins who still lived together in their mid-eighties. Mirror-image brothers and sisters who dressed alike and finished each other's sentences. Pairs even their parents couldn't tell apart. Having the same thoughts, the same tastes, the same wants and needs. Being the other half of something which looked and felt exactly the way you did. And then there was Aaron. Perplexing, diffident, too clever for his own good, itching powder on Reuben's conscience. The closest person to him genetically, but seemingly the furthest away from him.

Reuben opened the paper at page three,

annoyed and depressed in equal measure, Aaron once again having climbed under his skin, delved into the past and found conflict. Moray, a hundred metres away, flashed the lights of a car Reuben didn't recognize. But Reuben had seen something. Below the quarter-page article headlined MURDER SUSPECT FLEES SCENE OF CRASH. Underneath the byline proclaiming 'Former leading forensic scientist is hunted by police'. A smaller sister-article, bold font, just two short columns. The headline, PENTONVILLE INMATE FOUND HANGED.

'Fuck,' Reuben said to himself. 'Fuck.'

He scanned the article, double-checking the name, making sure. This changed things. An idea was beginning to form. An idea he didn't like the feeling of. He pulled out his phone and dialled a number, his thumb quick across the keys, rising excitement and fear in his chest.

6

Sarah Hirst had been sitting with her hands cradling her head for the best part of ten minutes. The skin of her cheeks was pulled tightly back, her eyes fully open, her brow creased with a series of fine parallel wrinkles. DI Charlie Baker, his arms straight, continued to lean against her desk, giving her the impression that he was looking down at her. As he talked, a myriad of scenarios jumped and danced around inside her skull. She saw names and descriptions and wounds and motives and statements and violence and desperation. But mostly she saw empty database files; sequencing traces with depressingly irregular peaks; patchy stretches of coloured bands on profile read-outs; neutral blue DNA swabs; empty agarose gels; matching patterns which failed to match.

The fucker, she had recently decided, knew about forensics. He understood how to keep out of trouble. He appreciated how to avoid contaminating a body. And then Reuben's notion came to her again as it had done almost hourly since he mentioned it a week or so ago: whoever had put Michael Brawn away was still inside GeneCrime. And if they had doctored one investigation, what was to say they wouldn't alter others? Maybe they were tampering with evidence right now, swapping samples or muddying the truth while she sat and stared into the middle distance. It was only a hunch, with no facts to support it, but it was beginning to eat away at her with unsettling regularity.

Sarah glanced up at DI Baker. He was talking rapidly, his mouth barely seeming to open behind his sharply trimmed beard, his eyes dark and distant, as if he was visualizing something as he spoke. Sarah saw him as a threat. Twice recently she had seen him coming out of the secretary's office which buffered Robert Abner from the rest of GeneCrime. Prolonged contact with the big man was generally an event reserved for bollockings, sackings or promotions. She wondered momentarily whether Charlie was after her job, but quickly dismissed the notion. Commander Abner understood policing too well to mess his staff around in the middle of what could be their largest case for years.

Charlie was now quiet, staring down at her. Sarah lifted her head from the support of her hands and mumbled, 'Sorry, Charlie, you lost me.'

Charlie narrowed his eyes. 'I was saying, Path are still a bit fifty fifty about it. The other four women are definites, including Joanne Harringdon, killed, we think, in the car park of her surgery. All held down and strangled first, raped second. But Laura Beckman doesn't fit the pattern.'

'Except that she was killed late at night, on her own, half a mile from the Thames.'

'Half of London is half a mile from the Thames. Besides, Path can't confirm it as a murder yet.'

'Smashed cranium, broken ribs?'

'She could have been knocked down. Fallen off something. Whatever. No witnesses, just a young woman bleeding from the back of the head into the pavement. There's no way we can link it.'

Sarah sighed, showing Charlie without saying it that she was prepared to back down. 'OK. But if it's not our man, and it's not an RTA, then the likelihood is that we have another killer on the loose.'

'Nah, I don't see it,' Charlie said.

'Why not?'

'I just don't. No way.'

Sarah looked up at him. He could be irritatingly dismissive at times, a slamming of the door which endeared him to few. Before DCI Phil Kemp's sacking and arrest, Charlie had been one of his closest allies. Relatively new to GeneCrime, and making very few friends, but always there when Phil needed the support of a CID stalwart. And it was now, for the first time, staring into his eyes, seeing the mix of defiance, contempt and detachment which always seemed to dwell there, that the words came to her. *You're up to something, Charlie. You're involved in something you shouldn't be.* It was intuitive, illogical and without foundation, but it struck her with all the certainty of a stone-cold fact.

Charlie turned his head, glanced around the office, bit into his top lip through his beard. 'Either way,' he continued, 'it's irrelevant. It's unlikely to be our man, there's nothing to link him, and we need to be focused on the job at hand.'

Sarah flashed him a short, insincere smile. *I've got my eye on you*, she said to herself as she asked, 'So what now?'

'Fuck knows. Four definites in the morgue. We keep looking at what we've got, hope he makes a mistake.'

'Great.'

'Maybe he'll stop. Take a break.'

Sarah grimaced. 'I don't know. Our sick friend seems to have got a taste for it.'

'Yeah, well.' Charlie straightened, stretching, pushing his shoulders back. As he did so, his jumper lifted, revealing a mat of dark hair across his belly which Sarah tried to ignore, the thick primal blackness unsettling her. 'Look, I'm going to get Mina Ali and some of the forensics section together with senior CID later this afternoon. Kick some ideas about. You OK with that?'

Sarah nodded. Technically, it was her job to coordinate the disparate factions of GeneCrime, to make sure Forensics were updating CID, that Pathology was talking to SOCOs, to help IT and Technical Support integrate all areas of evidence collection. But she let it go. There were more important issues than protocol.

The phone rang, and Sarah picked it up.

'DCI Hirst,' she said.

'Sarah, it's me.'

Sarah looked at DI Baker, cupping the mouthpiece with her hand. 'Charlie, I need some privacy.'

Charlie sucked his cheeks in, lingering, taking

his time. 'Now?' he asked.

'Now,' Sarah repeated. She watched her colleague leave the room, slowly and defiantly, and waited until the door was closed before putting her mouth to the receiver. 'What is it?'

Traffic noises and Reuben's breathing. Maybe the rustle of a newspaper held close to the phone. He sounded excitable, his words quick and direct.

'I don't know if I should tell you this, but what the hell. There's no one else.'

'What is it?'

'Damian Nightley has committed suicide, just weeks before his release date.'

'Nightley? Ten years for weapons trafficking, right?'

'Yeah. What can you find out about suicides in Pentonville?'

'In case you'd forgotten, I'm in the middle of a murder hunt here.'

Reuben sighed. 'Sorry. Any news?'

'Look, your advice on what we think was the first death — you know, the one with the oil and algae issues — helped, but not enough to say one way or another.'

'What's the problem?'

'We're getting DNA but it's more degraded than we'd hoped. And because we're still having difficulty purifying it, it's proving unreliable.'

'Is it good enough for matching?'

'We've got partial matches to four hundred profiles. But as you know, we don't deal in the currency of partial matches. So we're playing a waiting game. Testing and re-testing, and almost

343

hoping he strikes again and makes a mistake.'

'So you'll help me?'

'I didn't say that.'

There was the sound of a car door slamming, and the background noise instantly disappeared.

'Look,' Reuben said, 'I've got a fair idea Nightley's suicide may turn out to be important.'

'Well it had better be, Dr Maitland. I'll get back to you later.'

Sarah replaced the receiver. She held her head in her hands again, feeling the weight, annoyed at the distraction, but interested anyway. Nightley had flagged up a couple of interesting issues when she'd run his file for Reuben. Contacts and acquaintances across the capital. And now he was dead. An alarm bell was ringing somewhere inside her but she couldn't quite track it down. Damian Nightley. Where else had she heard that name?

Sarah turned to her computer and began pulling records and requesting files, suddenly alive and animated, a new urge surging through her.

7

Reuben tried to make his troubles disappear into the protocols of forensic detection. The fact that Joshua was ill and fading fast; that the police had launched a manhunt for him; that Damian Nightley had committed suicide; that his lab had recently been ransacked; that a footballer and his wife were dead. All of these gnawing, seeping wounds were soothed by his utter concentration on the task at hand. It had to be done quickly, and done well.

Reuben pulsed Michael Brawn's dissolved DNA specimen in the noisy bench-top centrifuge, decanted off its supernatant and suspended the remaining pellet in 70 per cent ethanol. He labelled a series of sterile tubes, flicked them open and added minute quantities of colourless fluids to each. He then vortexed the tubes and set a hot-block to fifty-five degrees. The methods and procedures were imprinted in his brain, each step coming to him as he needed it, as if he was running a mental finger down a vastly elongated recipe. Amid the volumes, temperatures, ratios and molarities, thoughts of his son remained controlled and disciplined. By imposing order on one part of his consciousness, Reuben kept the rest in check as well.

While a PCR machine hummed through a pre-amplification step, Reuben pulled his gloves off and scratched his face, before biting into a sandwich. He was acutely aware that being in the laboratory was risky. It was more than possible that its location was known to CID. But Reuben needed to grasp the answer. Who the hell was Michael Brawn? Solve this and he could go straight to Commander Abner, who would be able to use the information to validate Reuben's mission and call off the manhunt. But without Michael Brawn, Reuben would be detained, maybe shipped on to Wormwood Scrubs, locked up while his claims were investigated, testimonies taken, evidence considered. All of which would take precious days, even weeks — time that Joshua didn't have. He swallowed his sandwich and pulled on a fresh pair of gloves. Until he could take his answer to Robert Abner, everything else was just about manageable, an unavoidable limbo from which he would soon be emerging.

Three hours into the process, Judith entered. 'Got a few hours between shifts,' she said, swapping her leather jacket for a cotton lab coat and joining Reuben at the bench. Just like the old days, Reuben thought with a smile. Side by side in the GeneCrime laboratory, pipetting samples and solving cases, Reuben occasionally cracking jokes, Judith quiet between bursts of laughter. They loaded the sequencer together, Reuben injecting the sample, Judith the controls. While it ran, they tidied up, scrubbing the bench with paper towels, returning reagents to freezers and restoring solutions to shelves.

Reuben then sat at the bench and doodled on a piece of paper, his drawing skills rusty, the faces he conjured rough and uneven. Through-out his career it had been his habit to restore some dignity to the dead, people who had met obscene and violent ends, penetrated, hacked and mutilated. He would paint them late at night in his study, picturing them as they were before the atrocity that drained them away. It had been therapeutic, a way of coming down from the adrenalin rush of each crime scene. He resolved to take up painting again. His hobby had bitten the dust of late, and Reuben suspected he knew why. Every face was haunted by the fact that he was somehow caught up in the death.

'You got access to the national database?' Judith asked, bringing him round.

'Sarah's ID and password.'

'You could have used mine.'

Reuben glanced down at the sketch he had started. Lesley Accoutey, as she had appeared in the papers, blonde and effervescent, a toothy smile, a sparkle in her eye.

'Sarah reckoned it would be better this way.'

'Are we done?'

'Looks like it.' Reuben examined the sequence profile, scanning through the multicoloured lines on the screen. 'Quality fine, no bands maxing out, background low. A reasonable profile. You ready to find out who Michael Brawn really is?'

'When you are.'

Reuben copied the sequence file on to a memory stick, and inserted it into the networked PC which sat on a small wooden desk in the corner. He typed some commands, copy-pasted the information into a text-box and pressed a

347

button on the keyboard to begin the database search. The computer murmured into life, its hard drive buzzing and crackling, galloping through the database and grabbing for similarities.

'What do you reckon, Rube?' Judith asked.

'Dead cert we find something. A match to someone already on file. And then we start closing in on whoever in GeneCrime put him away.'

'Why so confident?'

'Why else use a fake profile? I think we're about to find some surprises about Michael Brawn.'

Judith made herself comfortable on the couch. 'OK. I'm going to bet we draw a blank.'

'How come?'

'Because science is like that. Ten negatives for every positive.'

'The usual stake? Loser buys the beers?'

Judith hesitated for a second, before answering, 'Deal.'

Reuben and Judith remained silent, sensing the technology of detection, the algorithms and pattern matching, the invisible binary digits, the plundering of datasets held somewhere else, on ethereal servers, insubstantial and otherworldly, intangible processes they knew were happening but which they barely understood, the only evidence of any action the noise of a computer hard drive vibrating and humming. Human time passing slowly while unimaginably vast amounts of communication raced back and forth along telephone cables.

An insistent beeping broke the silence. Reuben and Judith rushed over to the computer. On the screen was a list of numbers and names and, by one of them, a small button marked 'Update'. Reuben glanced at his watch.

'Twenty minutes,' he announced. 'The searches are getting slower.'

'The databases are getting longer,' Judith said, through an elongated yawn.

'Well, moment-of-truth time. You ready to buy the drinks?'

Judith nodded. Reuben pressed the 'Update' icon, then double-clicked on a tab marked 'Classified'. After a few seconds of rapidly scanning the information, he let out a slow, extended whistle.

'Last known address, telephone number, criminal record, the lot.'

'Is it unequivocal?'

''Fraid so. Stats of ten to the minus seven. You'd better have been paid this month.'

'Any chance of taking it out of my earnings?'

Reuben didn't answer. He was scrolling through records, arrest dates, background info, physical characteristics.

'And haven't we been a busy boy, Mr Cowley?' he said quietly.

'Who's Mr Cowley?'

'Michael Brawn. His real name. False genetic identity, false criminal identity. Michael Brawn doesn't exist.'

'No? What else does it say?'

'Here, I'll print you a copy. You pass a postbox on the way?'

349

'Several.'

Reuben pressed 'Print', and the printer hummed into life.

'If I pop this in an envelope, could you send it to the PO box number on the last note? Give the man his twenty-five grand's worth.'

'And then what?'

Reuben quickly jotted some of the details down on a yellow Post-It note and slotted it in his back pocket. As he wrote, his brow furrowed in concentration, and he said, 'The search gets called off and I can actually go and help my son.'

'How so?'

'We now have evidence that Michael Brawn has been using a false identity. Sarah will be able to use this to convince the Met that I was in Pentonville on police business, and that I don't need to be recaptured.'

Judith picked a copy off the printer and scanned it. 'Guess so. But this is interesting. A false profile gets him a false ID, which is convenient given the seriousness of his previous offences. Still doesn't add up though. Juries aren't allowed to know previous. Why go to the trouble of changing your whole identity, genetic and otherwise?'

'I guess that's the whole point.'

'Anyway, I've got to dash. Late for the next shift. It's brutal at the moment. You seen my helmet?'

'On the sofa.'

'I'd leave my head if it wasn't screwed on.'

'In which case you wouldn't need your helmet.'

Judith scanned the lab. 'I'm bound to have forgotten something.'

'As long as you post the letter.'

Judith picked up the envelope, slotted it into her upturned helmet, smiled briefly at Reuben and left the lab. Reuben barely noticed. He was absorbed, his eyes wide, sucking all the information in, the possibilities and the meanings. He stared into the screen, a summary view of Ian Cowley's previous convictions. Numbers and figures which told short, staccato truths: Agg Burglary, Conv. July 5 1988, 1yr susp 6mo. ABH/GBH, Conv. Aug 12 1989, 9mo. Manslaughter, Conv. Jan 23 1990, 6yr 6mo. ABH, Conv. March 19 1996, 2yr. Attmptd Murder, Conv. Feb 27 1999, 5yr 8mo. Reuben rubbed his face, thinking. He glanced at the newspaper that had announced his escape from the prison van. Dots were beginning to join, the truth starting to dawn.

Behind him, there were a couple of light taps on the door. He walked over, brow furrowed, swimming in ideas and notions.

'Judith,' he said, pulling the door open, 'I think I know the truth about Michael Brawn.'

He looked up. He was standing in the doorway, pushing a gun into Reuben's chest.

'Do you now?' he asked.

Reuben stared into the face, shocked, disbelieving, his brain fighting for sense. For a second he was blank. He looked into the eyes, cold and dark and wide. The name and the face suddenly merged.

Michael Brawn forced Reuben back into the

351

lab and kicked the door shut.

'Should be interesting,' he said.

'But . . . '

Brawn gestured with the pistol for Reuben to sit down.

'Right, plod,' he spat. 'Let's sort a few things out. Man to man.'

8

Lucy Maitland loitered in front of a hospital vending machine, surveying its rows of multico-loured snacks and chocolate bars, each assigned its own unique number and letter. She bent forward until her forehead pressed against the cold, isolating glass, her eyes screwed tightly shut. She needed sustenance — a cheap carbohydrate high or a greasy saturated fullness — but she had never quite trusted this type of machine. It reminded her of being six or seven, of school trips to the local swimming baths, of standing forlornly looking up, her money swallowed, the spiral not quite turning far enough, the bar of chocolate clinging sadly to its metal corkscrew, unavailable and unobtainable. Slowly, Lucy reached out and gripped the sides of the vending machine as if she wanted to shake everything loose, violently and desperately, a cascade of long-denied promises thudding into the empty catchtray. She held still for a second, swamped by recollections, her own childhood summed up for her by chocolate bars that refused to drop.

A throat cleared behind her and she straightened, swivelling her head. The house officer, three or four years out of medical school, still slightly unsure of himself. She brought her body round to face him, looked him straight in the eye, saw his barely suppressed nervousness.

'What?' she asked.

'I just wondered whether you're ready to come back in,' he said.

Lucy frowned. Of course she wasn't ready to go back in, to stand beside the bed of her only child, who was failing by the day. She had needed to escape the gaudy colours, the hospitals-can-be-fun cartoon characters on the walls, the stifling air of cheerful efficiency, and had found herself irresistibly drawn to the vending machine. But the medic had already begun to walk, less a question than a request, and Lucy reluctantly followed him.

The house officer was positioned at the end of Joshua's bed, pretending to flick through a brown file marked Joshua Fraser Maitland. Lucy took her time. When she arrived, he glanced up from the notes with what Lucy took to be practised concern. For a moment, her legs trembled beneath her suit trousers, and her stomach seemed to leap and fall in the same instant. It was bad news. More bad news. She glanced down at Joshua, serene and sedated, lying on his back, blinking slow, heavy blinks.

Lucy regained her composure and asked, 'What is it now?', crushing the tremor from her voice, the uncertainty from her manner.

'As you know, Mrs Maitland, the latest batch of tests won't be back until tomorrow.'

'And?'

'Well, whatever the results, there is something we need to do with increased urgency.'

'Which is?' Short sentences, clipped words, holding it all together.

'What we need to find now is a marrow donor.'

'As you said before.'

'Ah yes.' The house officer opened the file again, giving the impression he was simply reading out facts and figures rather than having to impart the news himself. 'The blood tests from yesterday are back. And what they show is not terribly great news. The HLA types suggest that you are not, in fact, a good donor match for your son.'

'Fuck,' Lucy whispered. 'But I'm the mother. Surely — '

'It doesn't always work like that. In the meantime, we're trawling the databases, searching for potential matches.' He lifted his head, tried to engage with her. 'There is, however, another route.'

'Go on.'

'What about the father? Could he help?'

'There are issues there. Difficult, complicated issues . . . ' Lucy Maitland stared down at Joshua, uncertainty and panic in her moist eyes, unable to fight it any longer, clumsy, sticky words getting caught in her throat. 'I told the other doctor the day before yesterday . . . ' She pulled out a tissue and blew her nose, grinding to a halt.

'Right.' The young medic returned his attention to the file. 'The consultant will see you tomorrow morning, go through all the options with you. We're expecting the final test results by then.' He snapped Joshua's notes shut. 'OK?' There was the briefest of smiles before he walked quickly away, leaning into the corner of the corridor, tilting his whole body as if it would help him go round faster, escaping the awkward scene of a mother and her dying infant.

Lucy watched him go. She blew her nose again. Her stomach rumbled and she glanced through the double doors in the direction of the vending machine. She hesitated for a second, before taking out her mobile, dialling Reuben's number and waiting impatiently for him to answer.

9

Reuben knew enough about firearms to recognize that the gun was genuine. It was a revolver popular on both sides of the law. Its snub nose stared back at him, bleak and unforgiving, absolute and inarguable. This is what death looks like, Reuben thought. The black promise of the barrel of a gun.

Michael Brawn was smarter than before. A pale shirt poked out of the top of his black leather jacket, and his charcoal jeans had been recently ironed. The straight lines and folds lent him a further severity that had been lacking in prison. He continued to stare down at Reuben, gun arm steady, face waxen and unemotional.

Reuben fidgeted on the sofa. How the fuck had this happened? Michael Brawn escaping as well. Tracking him down and entering the lab. And all because Reuben had DNA-profiled him. A multitude of notions continued to swarm around inside his head, insect ideas that buzzed and teemed and crawled and stung. A cacophony of thrumming thoughts in a still and silent lab.

Brawn took a step closer. 'It's time for you to end your life,' he said. 'Get on your feet.'

Reuben stood up, scanning the lab, desperate for anything that could help him. Brawn wasn't fucking about. He had tried to kill him once already. Reuben knew that without intervention he would have died in his cell. And now there

357

would be no help, no Damian or Cormack to alert anyone, no guard rushing in to save him. Just Reuben and a psychopath in a small series of rooms in a virtually empty building.

Brawn nudged a lab stool until it lay underneath the light fittings bolted into the ceiling. He pulled a plastic bag-tie out of his jacket pocket.

'Hands behind your back,' he instructed, 'wrists together.'

Reuben did as he was told. Brawn walked behind him, confident, in control, showing that if it came down to it, he would simply put a bullet through him. He wrapped the slim, stiff band around Reuben's wrists, slotted it through its aperture and tugged. He was obviously in no hurry. Reuben's forearms still had some movement, which he was happy about. Then Brawn grabbed the end and pulled hard, Reuben's wrists forced together, the tie burning into his skin. Brawn paced back round in front of him, reached into his other jacket pocket and pulled out a length of rope. Keeping the gun on Reuben, he climbed on to the stool and looped the rope around the brushed steel lighting attachment. He made a crude noose, yanking it to test its strength, the pistol momentarily under his arm. Then he jumped down and bared his teeth at Reuben.

'Poked your fucking nose in, didn't you?'

'How did you find me?'

'I know a lot more about you than you know about me.'

'I doubt it,' Reuben countered.

Brawn snorted, his nostrils flaring. 'I've got contacts, informants in the right places. If you know who to follow you can find a lot of people. Just like I found you.'

'So now what?'

'I finish what I started in Pentonville.' Brawn nodded his pistol at the stool. 'Now you have a go.'

Reuben stepped forward, taking his time, hoping to fuck he could think his way out of what was about to happen. For a second he longed for the police to come and find him, the manhunt actually getting the scent at last, tracking him down like it had failed to do so far. But Reuben knew he had been careful, staying in Aaron's squat, Moray driving him around in anonymous cars and staying out of sight of the police, Sarah keeping her mouth shut. As he climbed on to the stool, Reuben realized that Michael Brawn was watching him intently, his features almost gleeful. He had done this before.

Reuben's mobile vibrated silently in his pocket six or seven times. A call from who knew who that would never be answered. Brawn motioned with his pistol for Reuben to place the noose around his neck. He poked his head through it.

'You see how this thing works. Now, lean forward and tighten the fucker. That's it.'

Reuben did as he was told. Experience told him there was no benefit to antagonizing Brawn. What he had to do instead was talk his way out, sidetrack him, shift the balance. He recalled his early years in CID, learning about negotiating, looking for a route out. It was his only option.

He knew Brawn wouldn't hesitate to fill him full of bullets. Reuben had to take the longest course he could that gave him time to think.

'Come on, Ian,' he said, feeling the rope against his skin, 'we don't need to do this.'

'Oh yes we do.'

'It is Ian, isn't it?'

'We're getting to know each other now, are we?' Brawn grinned up at him. 'Coppers. All the fucking same.'

'Don't you want to know what I've discovered about you? Your real name, and what you've been up to?'

'I'll have a look at your computer. While you're swinging.'

'But you escaped from Pentonville?'

Michael Brawn gave a gruff half laugh. 'You really don't know fuck all, do you?' He stepped one pace closer. 'None of this. What's going on. You know fucking nothing.' With his right leg, he measured up for a kick of the lab stool. 'And you never will.'

Reuben stared frantically around the lab. At the shelves beside him. At the scalpel lying on the bench. At the glass bottles on the side. One jolt of the stool and it was all over. A three-foot drop. Maybe enough to snap his neck. If not, a slow few minutes of strangulation, Brawn leaning against the bench and lighting a cigarette, smoking it down as Reuben thrashed away. He glanced up at the light fittings, bolted into the joists above, knowing they would hold his weight. Reuben had salvaged them from a gutted factory to give the lab the harsh white light it thrived on. He had never pictured himself hanging from them.

Brawn was sizing the stool up again. Reuben scanned the room with growing desperation.

'OK, tell me then. What is it I don't know?'

'Goodbye, copper,' Brawn growled, stepping forward.

Reuben swung his left leg round to the nearest shelf, aiming a kick, dislodging empty bottles. Brawn lifted his right leg up, bent at the knee. Reuben lashed out again, more solutions raining down on to the floor. Brawn kicked the stool hard, jolting Reuben back. He tottered forward, rocking on the balls of his feet. Fall off and he was dead. He regained his balance, and aimed his foot a third time.

Brawn steadied himself. Knocking a stool from under a fourteen-stone man needed the right amount of force. Reuben noted the split second of hesitation. His shoe crashed into the large, heavy cylinder of liquid nitrogen on the shelf beside him. It lurched and fell, its lid coming off, fluid cascading out, litres of volatility splashing over Michael Brawn's left arm and surging on to the floor, the metal drum knocking him off balance. Brawn slipped and went down with it, into a hissing, fizzing pool of liquid nitrogen vaporizing and lifting the floor tiles.

A second of silence, of nothingness. Reuben fighting to stay upright, Brawn on his back, staring at his hand lying in the fluid. Standing up. Dropping his gun. Then screaming. Brawn holding his arm in shock. Fingers whitening and glaciating. Reuben wriggling out of the noose,

361

jumping down, picking up the scalpel and using it to cut his tie. Freeing his hands and grabbing the gun.

Still screaming, Michael Brawn lunged for him. Reuben smashed the pistol butt into his injured hand. An icy cracking, shattering sound. The tips of two frozen fingers snapping off, rolling on to the bench. No blood, just dead white flesh. Bone poking out, stripped of its tissue. Pointed, skeletal metatarsals under the harsh strip lighting. Brawn falling back to the floor clutching at his broken hand.

Reuben suspected he wouldn't be subdued for long. He picked up the lab phone and dialled the number of the one man who could help him, keeping the gun trained firmly on Michael Brawn.

10

Commander Robert Abner entered the lab warily and gestured towards the sofa. 'Do you mind?' he asked.

Reuben shrugged. 'Who's the back-up?'

Robert Abner raised his eyebrows in turn at the two men who had come in with him. 'Detective Superintendent Cumali Kyriacou, and Assistant Chief Constable James Truman.'

Both of them stepped forward and shook hands with Reuben. Senior brass. Thickset men who had seen it all before and had managed to come out the other side, as if their solid frames were resistant to the hurt and the damage.

'I know back-up is usually a little younger and fitter than this,' DS Kyriacou said with a smile, patting his plump abdomen, 'but we were with Commander Abner when you requested help.'

'And a bit of action is a rare treat these days,' Truman acknowledged, almost sadly.

Reuben glanced at Michael Brawn, who was silent and pale, shivering on the floor, hunched over, his ruined hand wrapped up in a lab coat. He held on to the gun regardless. Brawn was injured, but a wounded psychopath was an unpredictable entity.

'So this is the lab,' Commander Abner said. He cast his eyes around. 'Nice set-up.'

'Thanks.'

'And this, I guess, is the prisoner. Want to tell

me what's going on, Reuben?'

'I called you because I think you're the one person who can sort everything out.'

'Let's see what I can do.'

'OK, here we go.' Reuben closed his eyes, getting everything straight in his head. 'Using the alias Michael Brawn, Ian Cowley here was sent down ten or eleven months ago for sexual misdemeanour. Pleaded guilty, among other things, to the attempted rape of a woman on a train. GeneCrime were called in to tie some of the strands together. However, for reasons I won't go into now, his DNA evidence — our GeneCrime evidence — was faked. Michael Brawn couldn't possibly have carried out those attacks.'

'You're saying our proof was bent?'

'Looks that way.'

Abner's forehead creased, thin folds of skin darting upwards. 'Not good. What else have you found out?'

Reuben glanced over at Brawn. 'He's been passing messages out of Pentonville.'

'Pertaining to what?'

'I don't know. He used some sort of code which I couldn't crack.'

Brawn stared over at him, brooding, the colour returning to his cheeks, slowly sitting up, a Dobermann beginning to take interest in an intruder.

'That's everything you know?'

'More or less.'

'And now you've nailed him. I guess we should call off the hunt, eh?'

Commander Abner nodded at DS Kyriacou.

'I'll phone it in,' the DS answered. 'We'll still need to clear it with Scotland Yard, and we'll have to do some face-to-faces. But yes, let's get the ball rolling.'

'I've got to see my son without being arrested and taken back to Pentonville.'

'As DS Kyriacou says, a few hours and we'll have it all wrapped up.' Abner scratched the short grey hair at the base of his neck. He cleared his throat, looking down at the floor. 'I heard about your lad. Sarah told me. She's been bloody evasive recently. But it's a bad business, Reuben.'

'He's beginning to get critical. Got a message from my ex-wife twenty minutes ago. She sounded pretty . . . ' Reuben had been about to say the word 'hysterical', but let it go. 'Days and hours, that's all. I need to go and see if I'm a donor match so they can begin the chemo.'

Robert Abner glanced over at Brawn, who stared back with palpable hatred. Reuben noted that Brawn was now poised, on one knee, ready.

'As I say, we'll sort something. Maybe get you a car down to the hospital.'

'Thanks.'

Commander Abner stood up and stretched, his large shoulders rising and falling inside his uniform. 'OK. Pass me the gun. I'll bag it up and send it for ballistics. You never know what stories it might tell.'

Reuben checked Michael Brawn one final time. Surely even Brawn wasn't going to try to attack four men, one of whom was armed. But he looked like he fancied his chances. Reuben gave his former boss the pistol quickly and handle-first, so that Brawn could be instantly subdued if necessary.

Commander Abner examined the gun with deft expertise, checking the safety catch and the number of rounds in the chamber. 'Nice weapon,' he muttered, walking over to Michael Brawn. 'Well, Mr Brawn, or Mr Cowley, or whoever you are. I think we have a few issues to sort out, don't you?'

Michael Brawn stared intensely up at the commander.

Robert Abner turned to his colleagues. 'Either of you have any questions for Mr Brawn?'

Both silently shook their heads.

Commander Abner then pushed the gun into Michael Brawn's chest. 'Sweet dreams, Mr Cowley,' he whispered. And then he pulled the trigger.

A loud, dull shot, muffled by proximity, boomed through the lab. Michael Brawn's body lurched back from the impact, and fell on its side. He groaned, breathing desperately through empty lungs, dying into the floor.

Reuben stared at Commander Abner in horror. The two senior officers remained silent and still, unmoved by what they had witnessed.

Robert Abner turned to Reuben. 'Let's go for a ride,' he said, a thin wisp of smoke trailing from the barrel. 'Turn your phone off and slide it into a drawer. You're not going to be needing it where we're going.'

Reuben sat in the front seat. DS Kyriacou drove. Commander Abner was in the rear, behind the driver, and next to ACC Truman. Reuben glanced quickly back, Commander Abner in his peripheral vision. A head-fuck was in the process of happening, a reappraisal of everything he believed, a spin cycle of feelings and truths and assumptions.

The Volvo D90 sped through a junction, joined a wider carriageway, negotiated a couple of roundabouts, cruised along an overpass in a built-up area, and merged effortlessly into the fast lane of the motorway. They passed knots of traffic, coagulated around slow, sticky lorries. Inside, the car was silent. From time to time DS Kyriacou licked his lips, a quick flick of the tongue, out and in. Reuben noted its sharpness, pointed and triangular, a dry pinkness to it.

Gradually, tarmac and concrete became trees and grass. Reuben stared out of the window, his breath on the glass. Most of life, he appreciated, we don't know the truth. We think we do, but we don't. And when something startling happens, that's the reason it hits us so hard. Because it is a yes or no, a black or white, a definitive certainty. And those moments are rare. Reuben's guts rumbled like thunder. He knew that a lot of his convictions about his existence were about to be challenged.

Before long they were driving on a bumpy stone surface bordered by tall hedges, and then they emerged into a clearing. DS Kyriacou

367

skidded the car to a halt, tyres slewing across gravel. The three senior officers climbed out. Commander Abner opened Reuben's door and pointed with the gun. A few metres ahead lay a small concrete outbuilding, windowless and solid, with a rusted metal door. Reuben was escorted towards it. Robert Abner stopped just in front of the door and turned to him.

'Before you go in, I want you to think about something, Reuben. You know how leukaemia works. Your son has a cancer deep in his bones which is eating his immune system as we speak. Chomp. There goes another white blood cell. Munch. There goes another macrophage. Not that a toddler has much of an immune system to start with. You're the only person who can help your son now. And yet, and yet . . . '

Commander Abner ushered him forward with the gun.

'When he has succumbed to the cancer in his bones, we'll be back for you. You will die in the knowledge that you failed to save your only flesh and blood. We'll be monitoring Joshua's lack of progress keenly.'

'You sent me the notes, didn't you?'

'What notes?'

'About Michael Brawn. So you could get to him.'

'Way off beam.' Abner looked confused, his brow ruffled for a second. 'I'm the last person who would have sent you after Mr Brawn.'

'Then why kill him?'

'Do you think a man like Michael Brawn

368

deserves to walk the streets?'

Reuben was consumed with questions, but he knew that Abner would tolerate his curiosity only so far.

'And, shit. It was you who forced me out of GeneCrime. Not Phil Kemp, not anyone else. It was you.'

'Nudged, Reuben, not forced. You made yourself vulnerable. And when you do that, you deserve all you get.' Abner flushed, losing patience. 'Now, inside. It's time to face your own personal hell.'

Reuben turned away from Commander Abner. A kick from one of the senior officers plunged him into the darkness. Off balance, he fell to his knees. The door slammed shut and a key turned. A shaft of light poked between the roof and the top of the walls. There was a damp, human smell that Reuben didn't want to think about. Feet crunched over the gravel and car doors slammed. The large unmarked Volvo pulled away, kicking up stones.

Reuben got to his feet and rushed at the door, shoulder-first. It didn't budge. Leaning against it, he saw Joshua, pasty and listless, his eyes closed, eyelids so pale that a multitude of tiny blood vessels showed through. A rapid and insubstantial heartbeat leaving a faint green trace on a monitor. A nurse replacing the saline bag feeding his cannula. He saw days of confinement, of isolation, of helplessness and starvation. He knew that he had fucked everything up and that there was no way of fixing it.

369

Reuben pounded the door, over and over, slamming his fists into it, possessed and crazed, imprisoned again, the words of Robert Abner echoing in the din, knowing that he had it right.

This was his own personal hell.

11

The Thames Rapist. Who the hell had christened him that? Judith wondered, head squeezed tight inside her helmet. Rapist implied sex and nothing else. This was a killer, pure and simple. She zipped up her jacket and pulled on her gloves. The rape seemed to Judith almost incidental — a violent act among other more violent acts.

She pictured Commander Robert Abner writing names on a whiteboard, his crony Charlie Baker nodding his hairy face, or shaking his bearded chops. The still air, the squeak of marker pen cutting right through them. The Riverbank Murderer. The Thames Killer. The Riverbank Rapist. Give him a name, a tag for the papers. Something catchy, something that will lodge in people's minds. A moniker that tells a story all by itself. She thought of the pride involved in being the one to name the serial killer, to attach a sobriquet which would burn bright long after the details of the crimes or the victims' names had faded into obscurity. The Yorkshire Ripper. The M69 Rapist. The Boston Strangler.

Judith blew air out of the side of her mouth, feeling it warm the foam interior of her helmet. Abner had stuck to the rules. First the geographical location, then the act. The killer had been christened, and now he was more than just a man: he was a public figure, with an appended personality, a household name. Finally, he existed. But still it rankled with her that the word 'rapist' had been chosen, as if rape was somehow more serious than having your windpipe crushed or your neck broken or your ribs snapped.

Judith pressed the start button on her scooter, the small engine catching first time. She remembered how, a few days before, Charlie Baker had approached her in the car park, asking her about Reuben and Moray. Something about him that always suggested more, his words only half of the meaning. Like there were two messages, one verbal, the other secreted in his tone, or in his body language, or in the way he looked at you.

Judith climbed on, revved hard and pulled off, the scooter almost sliding from under her. She was tired, her eyes blurred, her hands aching against the vibration of the handlebars. They were closing in, that's what she heard more and more. But Judith knew the final couple of pieces of evidence were still not there. Hundreds of potential suspects, but nothing to separate them. Vague vehicle makes, conflicting witness statements, poor physical descriptions, scant forensics. Without a positive DNA they were drowning in circumstantial quicksand. And despite double shifts and extra personnel, GeneCrime, the country's leading forensics unit, was basically going nowhere.

Judith swung out of the car park and down the long straight ramp, letting the engine hold her speed back. That was the problem with forensics. You could be as advanced as you wanted but if your killer knew what he was doing, or had some basic knowledge of science or police procedure, you were in trouble. Test after test was coming back negative, or unreadable, or outside the confidence intervals. Stretching the limits of detection to the point where they became inaccurate or unrepeatable. False positives, potential breakthroughs which couldn't be corroborated. It was hell. Mina Ali barking orders, feeling the strain. Bernie Harrison, Simon Jankowski and the others coming up with ideas, new approaches and incisive strategies, but no tangible data. The first body proving difficult, DNA possibly there, but of low quality and partially degraded. Reuben's suggestions help-ing, although the raw material remaining elusive in terms of progress. A whole unit tearing its hair out as women were raped and murdered and dumped in the river. Maybe Reuben was right after all. Maybe the killer had protection from within.

The air that penetrated the gap in her visor was cool and refreshing. At least it was real air, not the filtered, sterilized and recirculated version which permeated the laboratories of GeneCrime. Judith stopped at some traffic lights and raised her visor, breathing it in. There was no other traffic, sensible people in normal jobs having long since turned out their bedroom lights and drifted off to sleep.

The image caught Judith for a second as the red light burned into her. Colm would be asleep, spread across most of the bed, maybe snoring quietly to himself. He was still acting strangely, and Judith found the thought of not having to talk to him when she got home a positive one. Surely pregnancy was something that most men dealt with better than this. She sighed. And with the thought of her husband, and the red light pointlessly barring her progress to an empty road, Judith also thought briefly of Reuben. He had failed to return her last three calls. This was unusual. He was generally the sort of person who got back to you no matter what. Even in prison.

Judith revved the engine, hoping to wake the light up. Really, she should just jump it, but she had always felt —

Blackness. A ripping, tearing feeling. Off the scooter, the bike crashing to the ground. Being dragged head first. Arms and legs failing to grip anything. Shoes and gloves bouncing along the tarmac. Muffled noises through her helmet. A defeating strength. Scuffing along and then stopping. Silence. Fear kicking in. A slow realization. This is him. The man Abner christened the Thames Rapist. Photos in operations rooms. Dark strangulation marks. Brooding organ damage. Sick stomach contents. Fractured X-rays of broken ribs. She knows she is next.

A heaviness, dragging her down. Cold concrete through her tights. Pushed into the ground. An unbelievable pressure. A hand clamping around her throat. Two deaths, she realizes. One adult, one fetal. Everything quiet and stifled, her helmet covered with something. An incredible pain in the front of her neck. Helplessly crushed. Breathing stopping. The pain intensifying, the pressure clamping harder. Going. Not gently but violently. Smothered. An insect squashed. Pressed into the ground. Life squeezed away. An unanswerable force. The end of everything. Two lives slipping away . . .

12

Two metres by three metres. Barely room to lie down. Pacing back and forth through the pitch darkness. Stopping every now and then to attack the concrete. Intense and frenzied bursts of activity. A small silver coin scratching at the wall. Short, concentrated movements, side to side. Fingers bleeding, multiple grazes and cuts from the rough, sharp surface. Knuckles and fingertips stinging with the blood and the contact. Pausing to wipe the fluid away before beginning again.

The smell intensifying. Human and sour. Evidence that someone has been here before, locked up, isolated, for long periods of time. The stench of suffering. Not death, necessarily. Not the reeking fleshy nausea of corpses or rotting body parts. More a sharp acrid scent of wasting away, of fear or of torture. Instinctive odours that track you down and tell you a story you don't want to hear. But something else in there as well. Another bitterness that lies silently in the darkness, waiting.

Feeling into the concrete, suspecting that it is hardened or reinforced. The coin making little difference, its edge flattened and becoming blunter. Continuing anyway, faster and with more force, knowing there is no other option. The floor is made from the same material, the ceiling also, the door utterly unmovable, with no handle or lock on the inside. A hollow concrete block with no obvious way out.

Slumping down on the ground, head in hands, the coin hot from the friction. Sucking at bleeding fingers, the sweet iron taste flooding in. Thinking and trying not to think. A world turned upside down. Events escalating beyond control. A son in trouble, a dead man in the lab, a senior policeman tying up all the loose ends. Breaking into prison and breaking out. And now locked up for good.

Attacking the wall again. The same place, a hand's width from the door hinge. Grunting and crying out with the effort and the pain. Skinning fingers, shredding nails. Feeling into the shallow gouge and knowing that it isn't working. But trying all the same. Refusing to quit or acknowledge the terrible possibilities. Just scratching and scraping and digging with utter desperation.

Stopping mid-stroke, breathing deep, lungs working hard. Suddenly understanding what the smell is. Not just urine or sweat or human terror, also something inorganic. A fluid from a laboratory hovering in the mix. A heavy, vaporous gas, hanging low, near the floor. Bending down and sniffing, mentally flicking through solutions and reagents. Alcohols, esters, phenols, hydrocarbons, acids, solvents, bases . . . an acid. A thick, noxious, stomach-churning acid. Getting closer to the floor, the sense of smell fatiguing, but knowing it is still there, hiding in the damp, pungent stench. The pitch blackness making the odours come alive, pure and undiluted by other sensory distractions.

Acetic, nitric, boric . . . sulphuric. A light bulb of recognition. Sulphuric acid. Concentrated sulphuric acid. Slightly yellowy, a whiff of vapour around the mouth of an open bottle, always attacking the air that dares come near it. Images of flesh and bones and clothes being sucked into the fluid and dissolved molecule by molecule, devoured and liquefied, melting into the hungry acid. And among the visions, a haze of questions. Who is next? Michael Brawn? Or simply anyone who stands in the way? What of, though? What do senior CID want? What are they after? What does Abner need? Who else has he brought here? Who has been liquefied on this very floor?

Standing up again, away from the floor, away from the horror, still gripping the coin. Feeling for the superficial hollow in the wall. Pushing the coin in and starting again, faster, more desperate, knowing that an appalling and sickening death is the only other option, darkness closing in around, the blackness stripping every fibre of hope like acid.

13

She grabs at the plastic and pulls. It stretches and tears, streetlights spilling in through the hole. As she drags it away from her helmet, she sees that it is a black bin bag. She scrambles to her feet, panting, breathing through desperate lungs. She coughs hard, a dry, uncomfortable hack which won't go away. Bent double for a second, unsteady.

He is just standing there. Looking almost confused. Vacant and staring.

Sense returns to her. A stark clarity kicks in. She turns and sprints. Out of the walled car park, into the street. Her scooter is still ticking over. On its side, the handlebars twisted. She glances around. The roads are empty. Don't panic, she says. Decide. Quick. The long ramp up into GeneCrime. A street of metal shuttered windows. Vacant pavements. He is frozen. Still in the car park. Staring into the ground. Close to the only car in there. She has time. She grabs the handlebars and pulls. The scooter lifts up and drops again. It is very heavy, unexpectedly awkward. She tries again, getting lower, her back straight. It slides a few inches across the tarmac.

She looks up. He is shaking his head, rubbing his eyes through the gap in his balaclava. It is too dark to see him well. She curses. *This is him.* A positive ID, a clear description, and they will take a massive step forward. But all she can see is

379

a shadowy form in baggy clothing with a balaclava over his head and white latex gloves. There is one detail, however. Light blue shoe covers. Used by forensic teams for contamination avoidance. The sort Judith wears half of every day.

Judith knows that her mobile is switched off, zipped into a pocket of her jacket, senses that there wouldn't be time. She crouches down, trying to push the handlebars up. She keeps her back straight and uses everything she has. The fast pulse, the rapid circulation, the glut of adrenalin sluicing through her body, all of it straining and wrenching, desperate to get the scooter up. Slowly rising, inch by inch, righting the machine in a gradual, controlled movement.

Behind the bike, she sees his body shape change. He is looking around, alert, back in the present. Judith tries to put it all together. He must have come up behind her, placed a bin bag over her head and dragged her into the car park. Then the crushing weight, the strangulation. He must have known that she was working late. He was waiting for her. Forensic scientists in murder hunts don't accidentally become victims. She coughs again, uncontrolled, her throat tight and sore, her breathing still laboured. A revelation: this is someone she has encountered before, or is even acquainted with. Accepting it is not random, it follows that he must know her. A name flashes through her mind like a neon light.

He is coming. Slowly at first, but now fifty metres away. Not running, just pacing. Leaning slightly forward, aiming directly at her. Large strides full of intent. Judith pushes with everything she has. The scooter is almost upright, but still as heavy as hell. She shifts her grip. The engine continues to tick over, oblivious. She is pulling it up now, rather than pushing. He is twenty metres away. She can see him more clearly, but doesn't recognize him.

As she puts her leg across the scooter, he starts to run. Powerful and quick. Nearly upon her. She opens the throttle. The bike lurches forward, not quite vertical. It takes off in an arc, passing close. He grabs for her but misses. Judith leans against the pull and gets it up. She ploughs through the intersection, starting to gain control. Swivelling her head, she sees he is running after her. Sprinting across the road. The scooter gathers speed and she knows she is safe. Both of her.

She twists the throttle as far as it will go, the engine whining and complaining, and looks back. He is giving up, slowing down. She unzips her mobile from her pocket as she rides. When she is far enough away, when she has stopped coughing, and when she knows she can speak, she will turn it on and dial 999.

There is still a chance that they can catch him.

14

The Operations Room clock read 9.15, slender black hands lying prone across its centre, cutting the steel face in two. Commander Robert Abner monitored it for a second in silence, waiting for the stubborn hands to move. Out of habit, he glanced at his watch, and noted that its hands were horizontal as well. He sighed and ran his eyes slowly around the Operations Room table, naming names. Sarah Hirst. Charlie Baker. Mina Ali. Bernie Harrison. Helen Alders. An assistant pathologist whose surname he didn't know. Generally, he kept the hell away from operational meetings if he could help it. From now on, though, it was in his interest to know what was going on the second it happened.

Sarah Hirst cleared her throat, the usual signal she was about to say something he didn't want to hear.

'Sir?' she said. 'Shall I continue?'

Abner frowned. DCI Hirst. Young, ambitious and dangerous. Difficult to judge, up to things she shouldn't be, exactly the kind of person Charlie Baker should be keeping an eye on.

'Go on,' he muttered.

'So, Judith is at home, shaken but OK, badly bruised neck, under twenty-four-hour guard.'

'Same kind of neck wounds as the corpses?' Abner asked.

'It appears so. Steve?'

The young pathologist with short cropped hair shuffled in his chair. Commander Abner noticed that he didn't look directly at him, which was good. Most of GeneCrime were still uncomfortable in his presence, which pleased Abner a lot. His large, imposing frame, the distance he kept, his terse pronouncements, all these had helped. And he knew that this might come in handy in the following weeks.

'I examined her a couple of hours after the attack. It's difficult to be one hundred per cent before the bruising develops more fully. But yes, I think it's probably the same shape of hand and angle of attack. From behind, finger marks along the length of the trachea.'

Sarah glanced at Commander Abner, then back at the scientists and police in front of her.

'We can't neglect the possibility that we are somehow the target now,' she continued. 'When someone working on a case is attacked . . . well, you know what I'm saying.'

'What about the other police officer?' Abner scanned his notes, double-checking the name and rank. 'Detective Inspector Tamasine Ashcroft. Did she ever have any dealings with GeneCrime?'

'We think she may have had some minor contact with the unit. Nothing unusual, and therefore hard to make a link. Plus, we haven't been able to find anything in her recent caseload that could have explained her death.'

'And the others?'

'Kimberly Horwitz, American citizen, working over here in banking. Laura Beckman, a postgraduate student — but remember, there was no sign of rape, just crush injuries to the ribs. Joanne Harringdon, a partner in a general practice. And our still as yet unidentified first one. Five women who seem almost entirely different, and in no specific way linked to Judith, who nearly became number six.'

'So these could still just be random attacks, women in the wrong place at the wrong time?' Abner bit hard into the end of his biro and grimaced at Sarah. 'I'm playing devil's advocate here.'

'I appreciate that, sir. And what you say is right, apart from Judith. I can't help but think the answer lies with her. It can't be pure coincidence.'

Commander Abner turned his attention to Mina Ali, senior forensic technician, who was sitting opposite. So far, he was pleased with Mina's appointment. She was entirely focused on one case at a time, and didn't go poking her nose where it wasn't wanted. Not like the previous incumbent. Commander Abner shut Reuben Maitland out of his thoughts and asked, 'Mina, how is the inspection of Judith's clothing panning out?'

Mina Ali beamed bright, as if she had been saving her news, letting CID waste their breath with half-baked supposition. She looked to Commander Abner like she had been up most of the night and would soon need some rest. But for now, she was obviously too excited to feel the fatigue.

'I have something,' she said.

Abner watched CID sit up, a couple of them straightening in their seats. Since Maitland had left and she had been appointed in his place, the pressure had seemed to grind into her. And with no definitive DNA from the five bodies, Mina had been tearing her long black hair out. But now he guessed she had something positive to say.

'We have DNA,' she stated. 'Two hairs caught in the zip of Judith's motorcycle jacket. We're extracting them at the moment. But we're sure they're his.'

'How?' Abner asked curtly.

'They don't match hairs from Judith, her husband Colm, anyone in the lab, or any other people Judith can recall spending time with yesterday. The hairs had to have physically got caught in the zipper; they didn't float there by accident. We're ninety per cent on this one.'

'Fine. We'll see.'

'But you know what we should do now?' Mina continued.

'What?'

'As soon as we have a profile and are throwing it through the searches, we should send a sample to Reuben Maitland.'

'Why would we want to do that?' Charlie Baker asked, suddenly attentive.

Abner peered over at him, still trying to sum the DI up, and decide whether he had made the right choice of informant within the division. Difficult to tell, but he seemed loyal enough so far.

'Get a visual, in case we don't get any matches.'

'You mean via his predictive phenotyping?' Baker said.

Mina blinked a couple of times and answered, 'Yes.'

Commander Abner bit the inside of his cheek. Here was the moment he had waited for.

'You reckon that will help, Mina?' he asked.

'It can't hurt us. Could save a few days, by which time — '

'Another strangled corpse in the morgue,' Robert Abner mumbled. He tried not to appear too keen on the idea. 'OK. Now this is tricky. Maitland is the subject of an ongoing manhunt by our colleagues in the wider Met. We know that he's clearly in hiding somewhere. But if we could get him to perform his specialist analysis for us . . . Well, you understand what I'm saying. The lesser of two evils and all that.' Abner turned his large hands over, palms upwards, as if illustrating the balancing act. 'And the Met don't need to hear that we've been in contact with someone they're actively pursuing. So, who's currently in touch with him? Anyone? Sarah?'

'Not recently,' Sarah answered.

Commander Abner's intuition told him she had replied too quickly. He stared hard at her, wondering what the story was, and knowing that Maitland was out of harm's way now.

'Well, ring him,' he said.

Sarah nodded, a stiff and rapid movement of her tightly pinned hair. 'I'll try him later.'

Robert Abner felt a surge of anger. 'Now.'

He watched Sarah take her mobile out, scroll through a long list of contacts and dial his number. He pictured Maitland's phone in a drawer in his lab, and Maitland himself in the forest lock-up. Once again, he cursed his luck that the fucking scientist had been led towards investigating Michael Brawn, digging into things he would never understand, stumbling into truths that must never surface. He remembered the feel of the Smith and Wesson, still warm from Reuben's hand, pulling the trigger, the heavy jolt, the dispatching of Michael Brawn, the solving of a problem. Nothing, Abner was well aware, solved a problem like a bullet. Small pieces of lead fracturing and ricocheting, tearing through flesh and ending disputes.

Sarah raised her eyebrows, showing that the number was at least ringing. Abner scrutinized the occupants of the room. Bright and serious coppers and forensic scientists. But none of them with the balls to truly make it. The guts to go all the way. The fight to get where he had got. He tried to hide his contempt, checking the clock again. Nine twenty. A series of meetings beckoned, press briefings, senior brass, liaising with other forces. A day of telling partial truths and careful lies.

'Answer machine, sir,' DCI Hirst announced.

'Keep trying,' Abner instructed. He visualized the inside of the concrete outbuilding, flashed through some of the previous events that had occurred there and tried to sound upbeat about Maitland, who was spending his last few days on earth in utter pain and misery. Shooting him straight away would have been too kind. Waiting until his son was dead, that was where the fun was. A nice touch which had kept him warm inside all the way back to London. 'Be good to get Reuben's input into this.' It was as much as he could do not to smile to himself.

Soon, it would be time to take DS Cumali Kyriacou and ACC James Truman back there, to sort out what needed to be done, to solve another problem, to close another door, to finish what needed to be finished.

15

At least this one probably knew what he was talking about. Lucy had witnessed enough medics, architects, accountants and other so-called professionals being cross-examined in court to know that even the most highly qualified of them was just two or three questions away from complete ignorance. Ask the right questions and you could trip anyone up. There was an art to it, a method of countering generalities with specifics, and specifics with generalities. Lucy yawned and shook her head, her dark bob swaying, a stiff movement signifying the liberal application of hairspray. Stop thinking like a fucking lawyer, she told herself. Listen to what he says, and what he can do to help you.

The consultant was standing unbearably close, a balding man, fit and clean-shaven, positively bristling with irritating good health. His name tag read Professor C. S. Berry. Lucy suspected he was on the young side to have progressed so far in paediatric medicine, and saw this as a good thing.

'So, then, Mrs Maitland,' he said, glancing up from his pager, which had just sounded, 'as my colleague intimated yesterday, this is serious. The diagnosis has come rather late in the day. You said he'd been ill for some time?'

'Just nursery stuff, you know.' Lucy stifled another yawn, her eyes watering, a restless night proving hard to shake. 'The usual random infection on top of random infection.'

'And for how long?'

'A few months. I don't know. We never thought it might be — '

'We're not here to play the blame game. But we're going to need to be aggressive. We now have all the bloods back from the lab, and are pretty sure of where we're at.'

'*Pretty* sure?'

Professor Berry smiled quickly, almost a twitch. 'OK, we're very sure. His best chance is an intensive course of chemotherapy coupled with marrow donation. Now we've been checking our database for matches and have drawn a blank. I understand the biological father is out of the picture?'

Not this again. Lucy grimaced. Did these medics not talk to one another?

'The biological father . . . it's not that simple.'

'I see.' Professor Berry's eyebrows raised, disrupting the smooth skin of his retreating hairline.

'I mean, there's a fair chance that Joshua's father . . . ' Lucy took a deep breath, telling herself to lower her defences for once. 'Look, I don't feel good about this. But when Joshua was conceived, well, there was another man on the scene.'

The consultant flicked back through his notes, the same pages that had so occupied his junior colleague the previous day. 'And this would be Shaun Graves?'

'But his tests came back negative. So he can't

be the biological father, right?'

'Just because he's not a good donor match doesn't mean he's not the father. But this other man . . . '

'Reuben Maitland, my husband. Technically at least.'

'He could be the father?'

Lucy Maitland dragged her high-heeled shoe along the shiny floor. This was verging on a cross-examination, and she was not happy to find herself on the wrong side of it. 'Yes. Yes, it's possible.'

'How possible?'

'Just possible. I don't know. I honestly don't know.'

'Look, without prying too much, you're saying that you aren't sure who the biological father of Joshua is? This could be important.'

'Do you think I don't know that?' Lucy snapped. 'Do you think I haven't obsessed about this since he was born? Do you think this doesn't matter to me?'

She peered over at Joshua. He was taking quick shallow breaths, but other than that, other than the fact that he was hooked up to several machines in a ward full of sickly kids, you wouldn't know that he was so ill. And as for the other question, how did you tell? How did you really work it out, without resorting to the kind of methods even Reuben wouldn't perform on Joshua? After all, what parents could recognize with one hundred per cent certainty visible characteristics that had emanated from them? Particularly when children changed so quickly, when hair colour was a continuum throughout life, and eye colour could alter until two, and the gaining and losing of weight could bend and stretch your features so profoundly. Shaun had thankfully assumed that Joshua was his, in his seemingly black-and-white take on the world. But Lucy knew that Reuben was still fixated and that she couldn't rule the possibility out. She looked back at the consultant, who was chewing on a pen, frowning at the notes.

'I'm sorry,' she said.

'What really matters at the moment is getting him tested.'

'OK. I understand.'

'Then, if he is a good match, the treatment options we can pursue will be much more aggressive and likely to work. The percentages will shift dramatically from where they currently are. And where they are currently is not very good.'

'I'll do everything I can.' Lucy scratched her scalp irritably, the thick stickiness of the hairspray fixing to her fingers. 'Trouble is, I haven't been able to get hold of him for a day or so.'

The consultant placed a hand on Lucy's shoulder, and she fought the urge to shrug it off. 'I'm sure you don't need me to tell you this, but time is marching on. You'd better find him. He's our best hope. Or else . . . '

'Or what?' Lucy asked, her eyes narrowing.

The consultant didn't answer. He squeezed her shoulder twice, let go and walked off, the warning in what he didn't say, the threat in the way he averted his eyes.

16

The first twenty-four hours, Reuben had attacked the walls and floor and ceiling with coins, shoes, even his watch. He was frantic and impulsive, speeding without amphetamine, snatching rest between bouts of frenzied activity, a myriad of unsettling notions driving him on. He bled and swore and screamed, furious and desperate, a caged beast. There was a way out. There had to be. There was always a way out.

By the second morning, amid the slow emergence of a new gloom, Reuben had started to work in shifts. He hadn't slept, and recognized the queasy signs of exhaustion. His mouth was dry and he was thirsty. He realized he needed a strategy. He had to think logically and focus on the task. He dozed fitfully on the damp floor for two hours, then worked for two hours. On and off, the kind of system that transatlantic rowers use, or the military in extreme conditions. A method of working all day and night in bursts. Scratching and scraping at the walls, choosing a number of sites, testing them out, pursuing the ones where even the most negligible progress seemed possible. Digging around the door hinges, sensing for loose concrete or patches of damp. Urinating in the far corner of the shed, hoping his piss might soak into the surface and make it more vulnerable. Trying not to defecate, fighting it, placating his bowels, knowing that conditions would quickly deteriorate, that flies would find their way in en masse, that the task would become harder.

The third day saw an intensifying thirst, and a hunger that came and went on waves of tiredness. By the end of it he calculated that he'd gone seventy-two hours without food or water. His palms were cracked, his fingers blistered, his knuckles skinned. A cloudburst beat down on the roof, making him shiver. He huddled against a wall, wrapping his jacket around him. When it had finished, Reuben crouched by the door. Its rust was immediately in his nose and in his mouth. He extended his tongue until it touched. A tingling metallic twinge, like licking the terminals of a nine-volt battery. But there was moisture, condensation from the rain. Reuben flicked his tongue across the surface. The dry flesh began to rehydrate, cracked furrows filling with the precious droplets. He swallowed, the taste making him gag, his throat sucking down the fluid. Not enough to keep him alive indefinitely, but water all the same.

Days were measured by thick, shadowy gloom giving way to utter darkness, a browny greyness leaking inevitably into black, and back again. In the murkiness, he saw images, snapshots of the last three weeks. In Commander Abner's GeneCrime office, Abner with his arm around Reuben's shoulder, saying, 'One day, I'm going to come knocking.' Moray Carnock holding the tight bundles of fifties from the padded envelope, saying, 'Someone wants this guy bad.' Kieran Hobbs in the dingy restaurant, saying, 'My boys will look after you on the inside.' Flashes of moments and lives. Damian Nightley, hanging from a rope in his prison cell, silent and ended. Leafing through photos of the latest Thames Rapist victims in DCI Sarah Hirst's car. GeneCrime forensics trying and failing to isolate DNA. A severely wired Michael Brawn running a blade across his tattoo in a Pentonville toilet. Joshua lying asleep in his curtained-off hospital bed. Michael Brawn lying dead on the laboratory floor, staring at Abner in horror. Abner and his colleagues silent in the car, knowing where they were heading and what would happen.

Reuben paced the building, intense and angry. He muttered to himself, almost delirious. It had to be linked. Everything. There had to be something or someone. Too many people on both sides of the law crossing back and forth again at will. And whoever it was had wanted him involved. Why? To make him vulnerable? To go where they couldn't? To distract attention from something else? So that he ended up here, in a windowless prison, waiting to die?

And who would miss him? he wondered. Who would truly grieve for him? A son he hardly knew. An estranged wife who was edging him out of her new life. A brother who blamed him for the break-up of the family. A DCI who kept her feelings bound tight under starched white blouses and angular trouser suits.

Sarah.

Controlled and ruthless, but somehow always there. Holding him close, but not too close. Striking, when she smiled. Intoxicating, when she laughed. Sarah Hirst. Something in her eyes sometimes. Lingering a fraction longer than they should, her guard dropping, her cheeks alive with the faintest of blushes. Maybe Sarah would grieve, for a missed opportunity, for a man she could have loved under different circumstances. Reuben allowed the thought to grow, picturing them together, wasting time, wrapped up in each other, her exterior melting, her features blossoming in the summer. The thought held him for several hours as he sat in the dark, the moist air surrounding him and seeming to seep into his body, kept at bay by thoughts of Sarah Hirst.

The fourth day began as the third had. An early spring chill, his body damp, his mouth parched, his teeth on edge. Reuben dragged his coin back and forth along the wall for as long as he could, sensing the futility but refusing to give up on Joshua. I have to survive, he told himself. I have to get out of here and save my son. But the concrete remained sharp and impenetrable. He was suddenly overcome by the need to defecate. Just over three full days and his body was switching modes, from passive to active, from being controlled to taking control. Survival mode. Reuben knew that fat reserves had been burned, and that protein was turning to carbohydrate, He wasn't starving yet, but after about eighty hours and extended bouts of activity his metabolism was beginning to change. Decisions were being made on his behalf. Again, Reuben wondered who had been in this windowless cell before him, and how long they had been kept, and what had become of them.

The day was interminable. Long stretches of nothingness. Haunted by Abner's words. *We'll be back for you. You will die in the knowledge that you failed to save your only flesh and blood.* Seeing Abner checking on Joshua's progress. Using his police access. Sitting in Reuben's old office and dialling the numbers, explaining that it was relevant to the case of an escaped prisoner. Joshua silently fighting, but all the time being attacked deep in his bones, his immune system being eaten away, his tiny eighteen-month life ending before it really began. Reuben wiping streams of tears from his face, angry, upset, frustrated, helpless tears, the type only a parent can cry when a child is dying. Standing up and running headlong at the door. Gratefully taking the pain, running at it repeatedly, slamming into the surface.

Reuben awoke, stiff and aching, his shoulders throbbing. He paced back and forth, muttering and whispering, shaking the dawn from his bones. He didn't believe in Satan, but he knew that this was hell. Here, now, entombed, unable to save his child, with no food or water for four days, waiting to die. This was Reuben's Hades. Forget the clichéd scenarios of flames and torture, this very moment was what hell felt like.

Reuben stopped pacing. He placed his sleeve across his nose and mouth. The stench was unbearable. The caustic nip of sulphuric acid had been replaced by something far more immediate and overwhelming. Reuben had been forced to shit in the corner of the tiny concrete building the previous day. But something

397

worried him. There were no flies. He was deep in a wooded area, and there were no flies. He listened intently. The buzz of curious insects was just audible. No rain had permeated, and now no bluebottles. If flies and water couldn't breach a building, then it was effectively sealed. The toughened concrete was standing its ground. Reuben was trapped, and he knew it. This was a fortress. No one got in, and no one got out. He realized with an even clearer certainty that he was fucked. He slumped against the wall, which scratched at his jacket as he slid down it and on to the floor.

A noise. The crunch of gravel, the rumble of an approaching engine. He screwed up his face and screamed. 'No, no, no! Joshua, no!' With his head buried deep in his hands, he whispered, 'What the hell have I done to you?' The tears came properly. Joshua was dead.

What he had to do now was make sure that the men who let this happen were punished. The rules had suddenly changed. This was no longer about survival. It was about revenge. He pulled himself together. A plan was needed. A strategy of attack.

Three car doors slammed in quick succession. Abner and his colleagues would be ready for him. But he would be more ready. Reuben stood up. He felt the coin in his hand, which he had spent half the night sharpening. It was like a razor. He paced over to the door and stood to the side. There was a series of scraping noises at the lock. Reuben summoned the energy he would need. He saw his fight classes with Stevo, recalled what he had learned from Michael Brawn.

There was a banging, echoing thud. The door flew open. A shotgun appeared through the opening. Then an arm, and then a shoulder. And Reuben leapt at it with every ounce of strength he possessed.

17

'Fuck off me! Fuck off!'

The large arm swung back and forth, the shotgun flashing through the gloom. Reuben dug the coin in, ripping flesh, blood seeping over his hand. He swung a punch with all his might, his fist connecting with jaw, the man reeling. Reuben brought his other arm round, a glancing blow which ricocheted off ribs.

'Reuben, Jesus!' A voice from outside. 'It's OK!'

Gruff and East End, something familiar in its grittiness. Reuben paused. The man with the shotgun righted himself. 'Easy, doc.' He came into full view. Nathan, Kieran Hobbs' minder. And behind, the man himself, grinning in the light.

'Shit. I thought — '

'Gotcha! My old mate Reuben. Gawd, you don't smell too good. You coming out, are you, or do you like it in there?'

Reuben stood still, blinking in the light for a second, before stumbling out. He glanced at Nathan, who was running a hand over his right cheek.

'Nathan, sorry. I didn't realize it was you.'

'Quite a punch,' Nathan said with a grimace. 'You work out?'

'Not exactly. And sorry about the cut.'

Nathan followed the direction of Reuben's

eyes, noticing the slash in his tracksuit sleeve, presumably for the first time. He dabbed at it with his fingers and said, 'No damage done.'

'All the same.'

'Just glad the boss stopped it when he did. I'll have to pass the good news on to Stevo.'

Nathan grinned, and Reuben tried to calm down, the adrenalin taking its time to subside.

'Look,' he said, turning to Kieran, 'I've got to get back to London. Now.'

Kieran turned and pointed to the silver Range Rover Valdek was leaning heavily against. 'Your carriage awaits.'

Wordlessly, Valdek climbed into the front passenger seat. Reuben followed Kieran into the back, and Nathan backed the large four by four out of the clearing.

★   ★   ★

On the motorway, Reuben turned to Kieran and said, 'So you wrote the notes to me about Brawn?'

Kieran frowned, taking a thoughtful time over his words. 'Let me explain a few things to you. Back where I grew up in the East End, a lot of people knew Ian Cowley. He's come from up north somewhere, Mossside maybe. Starts getting a bit of a reputation. Hard bastard, but not in the normal way. Not like my boys in the front there. Although after what you did to Nathan . . . Anyway, Cowley just had something about him that told you not to mess, something that said this guy

401

would fuck you over if it killed him doing it.'

'But why not just ask me to do it?'

'I'm coming to that, my friend.' Kieran span the bevelled dial on his Swiss diver's watch, each click sounding slick and oiled. 'So this cunt Cowley is in and out of prison. Serious stuff. A lot of people in the know reckon he's bumped a few geezers for cash. And not just for the cash. For the love of killing. For the thrill it gives him. He's never banged up for any of this — just ABH here, attempted murder there. But as I say, word gets round.'

'So why would Commander Abner want to kill him?'

'Here's the thing with Abner. Before he joined Forensics, he was a tough bastard. Serious Crime Squad. Had a few run-ins with him over the years. Decade ago, mid-nineties, Abner's on Firearms. Always had a fascination for weaponry.'

Reuben took another swig from the bottle of mineral water Kieran had pulled from a chilled compartment in an armrest and pictured the plaques in the commander's office, the practised way he had checked Michael Brawn's pistol over before firing it at point blank.

'His squad track gun shipments, seize them, accept their commendations. Only their actual and declared seizures are very different beasts, if you get my drift. Bit by bit they start to get a stranglehold on the UK gun market.'

'They were selling them on?'

'Not directly. They're coppers. They've got to be careful. So what do they do? They approach one of my outfits, get them to do the distribution. And it's win fucking win. Abner's cronies seize the guns and take the glory. Then they pass the rest on to my outfit, pocket a hefty slice, and come down mercilessly on any other fucker trying to sell firearms to the public at large. None of the saps they arrest complains too much, because they only get done for the weapons Abner's lot don't cream off.'

'I can't believe Abner . . . ' Reuben shook his head. 'Look, can this thing go any faster? I need to get to Joshua.'

Kieran leaned forward in his seat. 'Nathan, you heard the man.' There was no response from the front. Kieran jabbed a thick, stubby finger into Nathan's shoulder. 'Step on it,' he urged. 'Nathan!'

The bulky minder, still bleeding slightly from his right arm, sat suddenly up in his seat. 'Sorry boss, miles away.'

'You see? One bang on the jaw and you're fucking useless. I don't know what I pay you boys for. Now put your foot down.'

'I'm nudging the ton already, boss.'

Kieran flushed, his pink cheeks reddening. 'Well fucking nudge it harder.'

The Range Rover accelerated gracefully, its bonnet rising, and Reuben returned his attention to Kieran.

'So, what changed?'

'What always happens. Politics. A new Home Secretary, gun crime out of control, a severe crackdown on the cards. Abner's gang are looking exposed, and need someone to take the fall for them. So they set my outfit up as the major supplier of weapons in the capital. A lot of accusations at the trial, but Abner's been clever. Saw what was coming and began supplying my boys with marked firearms. Passed off former dealings with them as entrapment. And who's a jury gonna believe? Decorated officers or . . . well, you've seen the state of some of my punters.'

'So this all happened ten years ago. What now?'

'It's obvious. My syndicate have served their time. They're on the verge of being released back into the community. Abner and colleagues start to panic. Their reputations, careers and lives are under threat. They've done well for themselves in the intervening decade. Hence they call on the services of Ian Cowley.'

Reuben glanced out of the window, willing the vehicle to go faster but lapping up the information, and desperate to know more. 'Because he was already serving time?'

'Look, Cowley's presence in Pentonville was no accident. He was placed there to do a job.'

The penny was beginning to drop. 'The false genetic evidence . . . '

'He was given a clean identity, Michael Brawn, and set up for the sort of crime that could get him close to my boys. He was inserted there to kill them, how would you say, *in utero* — an abortion, ending them before they're spewed back into the real world.'

'Nice image.'

'You know what I'm saying. Brawn had been

put into Pentonville to get a job done, slowly and without suspicion, and now he's done it. The strings are pulled and he's magically released. And who's going to lose sleep over two or three suicides during the course of a year in a suicide hot-spot?'

'Damian knew it was going to happen,' Reuben said, almost to himself. He slugged back the rest of the water, draining the bottle, seeing again the headline PENTONVILLE INMATE FOUND HANGED.

'I'd twigged all this months ago, I just didn't have the proof. I needed to know without ruffling any feathers. Abner had to be in the dark. And with your links to the Met, and to Abner, I couldn't risk it. But now with your help, it's all stitched together.'

Reuben span round, suddenly angry, implications catching up, his brain beginning to fire again. 'And now my life is a fucking mess.'

'Which is why I bunged you twenty-five large.' Kieran smiled appeasingly. Reuben pictured this smile sorting out arguments, papering over rivalries, placating policemen. It was practised and ruthless, eyes twinkling and teeth shining, and difficult to dislike. 'Not bad for a week's work. And as for your son, we're gonna get you to him fast as we can. Don't forget who's just saved your life.'

Reuben sighed. Kidnapped by coppers and rescued by villains.

'How did you find me?'

'Heard along the line that you were missing. Your fat Jock friend put the word out. Since then

405

we've been combing known haunts and lock-ups of Abner and his colleagues.'

'You knew about that place?'

Kieran stared out of the side window. 'See, cops always think it's one-way traffic. They're monitoring us, and that's that. But they forget we spend just as much time watching them. Be professional suicide not to know what the fuzz are up to and how they do it.'

The Range Rover was now picking through the outskirts of London, houses becoming thicker, traffic heavier. Reuben felt a tight knot of apprehension in his stomach, his fists clenching and uncleching, his palms wet.

'And when I've dropped you at the hospital it's time to deal with Abner once and for all.'

'What are you going to do?' Reuben asked.

'The cunt who has faked the suicides of my friends is going to get sorted himself. No minders. Just me and him. Man to man.' Kieran fingered the shotgun lying upright between his legs. 'And that's all you should know.'

18

Reuben slammed the Range Rover door and sprinted into the hospital. The last time, Sarah had been inside. His neck had been stiff from the prison van impact, his heartbeat furious, a fugitive desperate to see his son. This time, things were different. He might be too late. As he pushed through the revolving doors, he asked himself, what if he is dead? How will I live with myself? How will I cope?

He ran to the large round reception desk. An auxiliary worker in a light blue uniform looked him up and down. Reuben ran a self-conscious hand through a week's stubble as she checked a list. Then she pointed towards the lifts. Reuben took the stairs. On the second floor he sprinted along an off-white corridor which reeked of antiseptic. A sign marked 'Acute Theatre 4'. Lungs cold and empty. A set of double doors. Heartbeat frantic. A gowned surgeon, his sleeves rolled up, his eyebrows raised. A blue door, with the words 'Hospital Personnel Only'. Throat aching in anticipation. Pushing it partially open, peering through the slit, seeing them in there, lying side by side, motionless. His eyes welling, understanding coming almost instantly, his tired, traumatized brain making the connection. Closing the entrance again, ignoring the surgeon, walking slowly away, his head and stomach and heart and emotions seemingly all connected, his skin tingling, his lungs now breathing fast. Joshua unconscious, a tiny form on a special operating table. Deathly pale, tubes seemingly sucking the life out of him. And next to him, on a full-sized bed, a man, also unconscious. Reuben rubbed his eyes.

By the time he found the canteen, which was on the lower ground floor, Reuben had calmed down slightly. He was still amazed, but it was a composed amazement, restful and still, the aftermath of dissipated panic. Reuben took a tray and picked out a range of food and drink: chocolate and fruit, a bottle of Lucozade, a portion of hospital stew and chips. He had several days' nutrition to replace. He sat at an empty table, barely noticing his surroundings, making up for lost time.

His brother and his son side by side. Aaron. He could kiss him.

Reuben took a break, knowing he shouldn't bolt his food. He scanned the canteen, with its buzzing staff and its silent parents: doctors, nurses and support workers glad of the break, mothers and fathers knowing there was no break, eating only through necessity. Children's hospitals were truly harrowing places, regardless of the bright colours and cheerful personnel.

And then Reuben spotted someone who made him stop, midchew. She was carrying a chocolate bar and a can of drink, zig-zagging between close-spaced chairs, seemingly oblivious to everything and everyone. Reuben guessed she was making for a vacant table near the corner. He stood up and waved at her. It took her a few seconds before recognition dawned. And it wasn't, Reuben noted, a happy recognition.

'Where the hell have you been?' Lucy Maitland asked, pulling out a chair opposite. 'I've been trying your phone for days.'

Reuben pictured his mobile sitting in a laboratory drawer, switched off, Abner's fingerprints all over it. 'Away,' he answered.

'For Christ's sake. Where do you go, Reuben? Where is it that you disappear to?'

'Just away.'

'Well it doesn't seem to do you much good. I mean, I know you don't exactly thrive on being smart, but God, you look like shit.'

'Thanks.'

Reuben was well aware that four and a bit days of captivity would have done little to improve his personal grooming, and he suddenly craved a shower and a change of clothes. He scrutinized his ex-wife for a moment. She looked tired and vague, like she was running on empty. Her eyes were bloodshot, her normally rouged cheeks pale and flat. Only her hair maintained any vigour. Reuben suspected this was more down to whatever product she applied to it than its inherent condition.

'Well, while you've been enjoying yourself, I've been stuck here.'

Reuben picked at a couple of soggy chips.

'So,' he said, 'I guess this changes things.'

'This changes nothing.'

'My twin brother is a donor match.'

'So?'

'You now know that Joshua is my biological son.'

Lucy nodded her head slowly, and Reuben anticipated trouble. 'And I also know that you abused your position within the Forensics Service, placed Shaun's name on a sex offenders database — '

'That wasn't directly my fault.'

'So I don't see how this changes anything.'

Reuben rubbed his face. It was impossible to win an argument with his former wife. Even when you were right.

'Look, Lucy, I want more access. That's all.'

Reuben glanced at her and she quickly looked away. He wondered whether she had been secretly disappointed at the news. Maybe she had hoped all along that Shaun was Joshua's father. Things would have been simpler that way. But he could now afford a broad smile in the knowledge that the single question that had haunted him since the birth of his son, since he had discovered that Lucy had been having a long-term affair, had been answered. It was official. He was the biological father of a beautiful young boy. It had taken severe illness and a donor match with his brother, but he knew the odds against it were phenomenal.

'So how did you track Aaron down?'

'I didn't,' Lucy answered flatly. 'Some Scotsman with a pie habit came to me and put us in touch.'

Moray Carnock. The man who could fix just about any mess you cared to get yourself into.

'How long till they come round?'

410

'The nurse said the operation will last about four hours, then they'll keep them pretty much sedated until tomorrow morning.'

'And when will we know more?'

'Not for several days. They've begun the treatment now, so things are heading in the right direction. But he's not out of the woods yet.'

'I guess not.'

Reuben finished his drink. It tasted pure and beautiful, even though it was stacked with additives. Compared to water from a rusting door, it was wonderful.

'Look,' he said, pushing back his chair and standing up, 'there's something I've got to do in a hurry.'

'What?' Lucy asked.

'Something urgent. One last thing. I'll be back before Joshua and Aaron come round tomorrow.'

And with a sense of rising apprehension, Reuben left his ex-wife, strode out of the canteen and exited the hospital.

19

Judith's hug was shaky. A little stiff, a slight tremor in her chest, her arms wrapped tight for a couple of seconds before letting go and stepping back.

Behind her, Moray said gruffly, 'I don't do hugs. And I will fight you if you try.'

Reuben grinned. 'Not a problem,' he said. 'Now, this might sound like a daft question, but what have you done with the body?'

'You're right,' Moray answered, his face serious.

'What?'

'It does sound like a daft question.'

'Really, though.'

'What body?' Judith asked.

'Michael Brawn. You're telling me there was no body here?'

'Afraid not.'

'And the lab door?'

'Unlocked.'

'So they came back and tidied up.'

'Who?'

'Robert Abner and friends. After they took me for a ride and put me away.' Reuben retrieved his mobile from the drawer and turned it on. It vibrated, indicating that he had messages to view. 'Look, this is all fucked up. Brawn was working for Abner, deliberately placed in prison, executing a gang of inmates one by one before

412

they could be released.'

'Why?'

'Abner was bent. He ran London's gun market in the nineties, made a mint out of it, and then needed some scapegoats to do his time. But he made the mistake of crossing Kieran Hobbs. Who, at this very moment, is exacting his revenge.'

'What's Hobbs going to do?' Judith asked.

'I don't know. Even Hobbs isn't big enough to take on senior Metropolitan brass. Christ knows what he's hoping to achieve.' Reuben paced over to the lab bench that Brawn had lain under, his fingertips ruined, a gun exploding in his ribs. There was no obvious sign now, the floor wiped, probably even fingerprints cleaned away. 'But I guess we'll find out soon.'

He thought of Brawn, and whether he had already been disposed of, melted down, poured away. The damp sulphuric smell of the concrete outbuilding seemed to be burned deep into Reuben's nostrils. So much life and menace seeping into the ground somewhere. But at least with no corpse in his lab, one serious problem had been averted.

'So, what else has been going on?' he asked.

There was a pause, Judith looking into the floor, Moray finding other things to occupy him.

'So?' he asked.

Judith cleared her throat. 'I . . . he attacked me. The man.'

'Who? The Thames — ' Reuben didn't say the rest of the name.

Judith nodded quickly, her eyes fixed on the

413

floor. 'After work. Late. Near GeneCrime.'

'Fuck.' Reuben walked over and put his arm round her. 'Are you OK?'

'Fine,' she said.

Reuben glanced at Moray, who shook his head.

'But what — '

'I'm fine,' Judith repeated. 'I got away. I was lucky.'

She started to cry, and Reuben held her close. Soon, her breathing became slower and less jerky, as if she was trying to control her tears, fighting to stem the outpouring.

'But there was something good.'

'What?'

'They finally got DNA. A couple of hairs caught in the zip of my jacket in the struggle.'

'Really?'

'No matches yet. But they have a sample.'

Judith said this triumphantly, as if she almost believed her ordeal would have a positive outcome. Almost. Reuben noted a pair of dark red marks on her neck, just visible above the collar of her white blouse as she moved her head.

'What are they doing?'

'Just prelims at the moment. A crude run, plug it through the database. When we found it was negative, yesterday morning, Mina decided we should do it properly, which will take another few days.'

'How are they certain they're his,' Moray asked, 'and not some random hairs you picked up along the way?'

'Fragments matched the sample from what we

think was the first victim, the one Reuben helped with. Just a couple of loci, but enough to get stats on.'

'And what do you guys do when you've confirmed that the murderer's DNA doesn't match anything in your database?'

Reuben was quiet. Excited, thinking through the possibilities.

'We start screening. You know, working our way through the hundreds of suspects we've identified from witness statements, car registrations, descriptions. The net begins slowly to tighten. But of course there is another way, now Reuben's back with us.'

'Which is?' Moray asked.

'Predictive phenotyping,' Reuben answered slowly. 'So we can see his face. But we'd need access to the DNA.'

Judith smiled. 'Catch,' she said, tossing an Eppendorf tube through the air. 'Dried down, desiccated and ready to go.'

Reuben caught it and brought the tube up in front of his eyes. The DNA of the Thames Rapist. Molecules of the man who had been terrorizing London for weeks. Fragments of the psychopath who had tried to kill Judith, microscopic pieces she had carried with her in her pocket. He flicked a hot-block on and began programming a thermal cycler. The last time, predictive phenotyping had shown him that Michael Brawn was a black man. This time, there would be no mistakes.

★ ★ ★

415

Reuben took a breather, leaning against the bench, a phospho-imager scanning two thousand spots which were crammed on to a nylon membrane the size of a postage stamp.

'Who wants a cuppa?' he asked.

Moray, who was slumped on the sofa reading the paper, answered 'Aye' without looking up.

'If you're offering,' Judith said, pulling off a pair of lab gloves.

Reuben slid a clear bottle marked 'Ethanol' from the shelf above him. He poured a slosh into three Pyrex beakers and handed one each to Judith and Moray.

Judith eyed the liquid suspiciously. 'You drink this stuff?'

'Why not?' Reuben asked, taking a swig.

'Management always told us that laboratory ethanol was spiked with meths.'

'And why would they do that?'

'To stop us drinking it.'

'Exactly.'

Moray straightened slightly and raised his beaker in front of him. 'To scientists. Who'll believe anything except the obvious.' He took a healthy gulp, then his cheeks reddened and his eyes widened. 'Fuck me,' he muttered. 'Not exactly single malt.'

'One hundred per cent pure alcohol,' Reuben answered. 'An acquired taste. Don't you think, Judith?'

Judith placed her beaker on the bench. 'I've changed my mind. Look, I'll get the wash steps ready.'

Reuben watched her pull on fresh gloves and

busy herself. She had come through a head-fuck of an ordeal. The only one to survive. The only one to get away from him alive. He knew that she would have made the same deduction he had: that the killer had already met Judith, or was familiar with GeneCrime's personnel. This was not coincidence. He marvelled that she was coping so well, but then, she had always been tough. It was one thing you never suspected of Judith. She might be petite and demure, but she was as gutsy as hell.

Reuben took another swig, savouring the warmth, wondering what the predictive pheno-typing would show him. Faces and names flashed through his mind. He glanced at his watch. In three more hours, he would know for sure.

20

There was a noise, a scratching and scraping sound, and the front door swung open. Kieran Hobbs was standing in the doorway, brash and bold, grinning from earring to earring. He walked in, nonchalant and relaxed. Reuben pressed the 'Start' icon on his laptop and turned to face him.

'Kieran,' he said, slightly taken aback.

Kieran extended a smile around the room. 'Reuben. Mr Carnock. The lovely Judith.'

Moray and Judith smiled back.

'You make any progress with that mugshot of mine?'

'We've had a few technical problems,' Judith answered.

'You win some, you lose some.'

'So you haven't found Abner?' Reuben asked.

'Oh yeah, I found him all right. Do you mind?' Kieran gestured towards the sofa, then lowered himself down.

'What happened?'

'Went straight there. Sorted a few things out. One to one. Just me and him.'

Reuben pulled his gloves off and put them in the bin. His laptop was busy, grinding through algorithms, beginning to construct the human face responsible for weeks of subhumanity.

'Such as?'

'You know how these things work. Revenge

being served cold and all that.'

'Yeah?'

'Trouble is, sometimes you don't have the stomach for cold food. Sometimes you fancy something from the dessert trolley instead. You know what I mean?'

'Can't say I do.'

'See, the thing is, no one, no matter how big, kills three senior coppers to get what they want. Am I right?'

Reuben took in the winning smile, the expression of quiet, forceful bonhomie. 'Obviously.'

'These days, you have to be smarter than them.'

'And how do you do that exactly?'

'You have to ask yourself, what's more use, owning a dead copper, or owning a live one?'

Out of the corner of his eye, Reuben noted the scaffolding, the contours, the 3D outlines. A mesh of intersections steadily gaining texture, depth and colour. A network of coordinates being mapped and re-mapped until the software was happy with itself. 'So what happened?'

'What always happens. We cut a deal. In return for silence, certain activities of mine will gain immunity from prosecution, while the Met comes down hard on my competitors.'

'But he killed your men,' Reuben said.

Kieran stood up, edgy and menacing all of a sudden, the smile gone, the mouth tight. 'A lot of people kill my men. It's dog eat dog out there.' He slid a pistol out of his jacket. 'And now there's only one problem left.'

419

'What?' Reuben asked, appreciating that the rules were about to change for good.

'I want my twenty-five grand back.'

'Why?'

'Plus all the other money I've given you recently.'

'We had a deal.'

'And now I have a different deal. I've got the boss of GeneCrime in my pocket.' Kieran waved the pistol about with practised detachment. 'I hardly need some two-bit forensic scientist to sort my problems, do I?'

Reuben straightened, ready. He eyed Moray and Judith, sensed where the door was, flicked through his options. Kieran Hobbs with a gun was not good news.

'See, by my estimates you've had the best part of twenty grand from me over the last few weeks, plus the twenty-five I sent you . . . we're looking at forty-five large. *Please.*'

Kieran pointed the gun directly at Reuben's head. Reuben paused a second, again glancing at Moray and Judith. Then he paced over to a chemical bin in the far corner.

'And don't try anything silly,' Kieran said.

Reuben opened the metal bin slowly. It held half a dozen nasties: phenol, mercaptoethanol, sodium hydroxide, glacial acetic acid, ethidium bromide. And sulphuric acid. Reuben paused, his fingers close to the brown bottle. A label marked 8N H_2SO_4. Highly concentrated. To be handled with utterly paranoid care. Brooding among liquids of lesser evil. The smell from the concrete building. A fluid that melts bones for fun.

Reuben glanced over his shoulder at Kieran. The gun was pointing at Judith. Reuben reached his hand in slowly, changing direction at the last second. He felt for a padded envelope sellotaped next to the sodium hydroxide. It came free with a small ripping sound, and Reuben stood back up. For a second, he had been tempted. Until he'd seen the weapon aimed at Judith.

'Here,' he said, holding the thick envelope out.

Kieran snatched it from him and nosed through its contents with the barrel of his pistol.

'Look, there's other money in there,' Reuben said dejectedly.

'How much more?'

'Three or four grand.'

'What a fucking bonus! Interest on my investment.'

Kieran slotted the envelope into an outside pocket and slapped Reuben around the cheek. 'You over-educated mug,' he said with a smile. Standing toe to toe with Reuben, he pulled out a fat cigar and lit it with a gold lighter. 'B.Sc.' He blew a long stream of smoke into Reuben's face. 'Ph.D.' Kieran chewed his cigar, grinning at Reuben. 'M.U.G.' He waited a second, letting the message sink in. 'You mug.'

Reuben stared back at him, his eyes narrowed, utterly powerless. Behind him, the face on his laptop was taking shape, colours and tones subtly shifting, features beginning to stick.

Keeping the pistol trained on Reuben, Kieran edged back towards the door. 'See ya,' he said, before heading out and away, his footsteps echoing along the concrete walkway, nearly fifty thousand pounds richer.

Judith and Moray slumped on to the sofa almost simultaneously. Reuben stayed where he was, his head bowed, focusing into the vinyl floor. He had been used, a scientific pawn in a game with secret rules, where the good guys and the bad guys swapped sides for fun. And what had he achieved? A senior police officer had covered his tracks, and a well-known gangster had bought immunity from prosecution.

'Fuck,' he said. 'My enemy's enemy — '

'Has a new friend,' Judith muttered.

Moray glanced up at Reuben. 'And it ain't you.'

'Ever get the feeling you've been taken for a ride?' Judith asked.

'Not until now,' he answered, dejectedly.

Reuben walked over to the computer. If he squinted, the face almost looked like a photograph. In a few more minutes it would be ready; 3D, with texture and depth, a pheno-fit face of the Thames Rapist.

Reuben knocked back the remnants of his ethanol and paced to the rear of the flat. Below, he watched Kieran Hobbs climb into the driver's seat of his silver Range Rover. Reuben looked more closely. There was someone in the passenger seat. Commander Robert Abner, in uniform, even his hat on. A folded copy of what appeared to be the *Bargain Pages*. Noticing Reuben and waving with the folded newspaper. Reuben watched the vehicle pick its way across the rubbled car park, and shook his head sadly.

'I've got to get back to the hospital,' he said.

Moray stood up, between Reuben and the door. 'I don't know, Reuben,' he said. 'You're going to have to watch yourself.'

'What are you saying?'

'Things have changed. Abner knows you've seen too much. And Hobbs, his new best buddy, isn't averse to having Nathan and Valdek beat people to a pulp. Not to put too fine a point on it, you, me, Judith, the lab . . . it's finished.'

Judith didn't look at him. 'Face it, Reuben, they're going to come for you. Maybe not today, but it won't be long.'

'And don't forget, all the archived samples have been ruined.'

'Moray's right. There's not a lot left, and now you've made yourself dangerous and vulnerable.'

'Again.'

Reuben ran his nails over an impenetrable section of lab bench. Fuck. Fuck. Fuck. He had been used up and spat out. Too quick to follow his hunches, too eager to take the bait. Sensing cover-ups and impropriety but missing the point. Entering prison on a whim and paying for it now. The detective urge strong, the obsession for the truth almost overwhelming him at times. Reuben bit deep into the inside of his cheek. Defeated, lied to, taken for a ride.

The face on the screen stared back at him, deadpan and indifferent. Reuben pressed 'Print' and waited for the photo to emerge, thinking, glancing hard at the patch of floor where Michael Brawn had been slumped in death. He frowned at Moray and Judith, took the picture, paused for a quiet moment and then made for the door.

It was a long shot, but an idea had just come to him. Maybe the laboratory was not what it seemed. Maybe he had been wrong about events. Maybe, just maybe, his eyes had deceived him. He slid a folded yellow Post-It note out of the back pocket of his jeans. As he left the lab he pulled out his mobile phone and dialled a number, praying after every ring that it would be answered.

21

Sitting between them, listening to their breathing, one long and slow, the other quicker and more shallow, both peaceful, almost serene. Reuben glanced back and forth, holding their hands, Joshua's tiny and unblemished, Aaron's larger and rougher. Watching them gradually return to him, a closed circle of father, son and brother. In the background, two sets of monitors fired green traces from left to right, digital numbers ebbing and flowing, varying around fixed constants. The blank, windowless ante room magnified the noises and images of recuperation around its walls. His two closest relations sleeping off the effects of the operation, lying on adjacent beds, their cardiac traces duetting.

Reuben wondered what his own heartbeat would look like. It seemed to have raced for days, with little let-up. Maybe it was used to it, he reasoned — the days of amphetamine, speeding through crime scenes, concentrating for sixteen-hour stretches, pupils wide, consuming each scrap of information, understanding everything, making the case stick. The last week had been different though. Breaking out of Pentonville, the Met launching a manhunt, Michael Brawn turning up, being driven to the woods by Robert Abner and locked up for four days and nights. Reuben asked his pulse for calm, begging it to slow to normal speed, trying to persuade it that all the bad stuff was over.

While his heart continued to ignore the request, he took out the pheno-fit and stared grimly at it. Who the fuck are you? he asked. The face stared back impassively. There was something in the eyes, maybe, or in the shape of the ears that spoke to him. Fragments of someone he knew or had met. But the visage as a whole drew a blank. It was not a man he recognized. Reuben pondered this for a second. It was like identifying the windows and wing-mirrors of a car, but not being able to discern the actual model. He replaced the pheno-fit, deep in thought.

And then he had a sudden urge to feel his brother's skin, to see if it was the same as his own, or smoother or hotter or somehow strange to the touch. He hesitated, and then reached forward and placed his fingers on Aaron's forehead. It was cool and sticky, verging on the wet. Aaron opened his eyes, stared at Reuben for a second, and then closed them again.

'You think I'd let you down?' he muttered.

'You want me to answer honestly?'

Aaron managed a drowsy smile. 'Probably not.'

'You OK?'

'Tell the nurse I need more drugs.'

'Nice try.'

Aaron tried to force his eyes open. 'There has to be an up-side to this.'

'There is,' Reuben said. 'You just saved your nephew's life.'

Aaron's heavy eyelids slid shut again, the

426

anaesthetic dragging him back under. Reuben closed his eyes as well, the last few days catching up. He was overtaken by an overwhelming heaviness, a desire to be where Aaron was, semi-conscious, and all the world's problems irrelevant.

★　★　★

A noise outside brought him round. He had been asleep. His neck ached, his hands still intertwined in Joshua and Aaron's. He yawned, massaging the back of his shoulders, which were tight, as if he'd just come off a long-haul flight and had stiffened up. He watched the door open, surgical staff checking up, or a nurse taking notes. Aaron stirred, mumbling something under his breath, finally starting to come round. But it wasn't a nurse or a medic. It was a senior CID officer. Behind him, lurking in the corridor, two uniformed officers standing with practised stillness.

'Hello, Reuben,' the CID officer said, walking over and standing in front of him, staring down.

'Hello, Charlie,' Reuben answered. He rubbed his neck. 'It's been a while.'

'Word is you've developed a taste for prison food.'

'Yeah?'

'And that you want some more.'

Charlie Baker pulled a pair of handcuffs out of the back pocket of his jeans. Reuben glanced down at his wrists, fingers still holding Joshua's hand. Charlie's forearms appeared contrastingly hirsute, broader than Reuben's, a dark width to them, magnified by the hair.

'I'm arresting you on suspicion of perverting the course of justice in the murder of Jeremy Accoutey's wife Lesley, and Mr Accoutey's subsequent suicide.'

'Learn that off by heart?'

'You can have the full caution, if you need it.'

Reuben grunted. 'This you, Charlie?' he asked.

DI Baker shrugged, glancing back at his supporting officers. 'Abner sanctioned it,' he said.

'Really?'

'He's got a hard-on for you all of a sudden.'

'Sounds about right.' Reuben nodded at Joshua. 'You've got family, Charlie. Just give me a few minutes here. For old times' sake.'

Charlie Baker hesitated, winding the handcuffs around his index finger, his brow creased. He scanned the room.

'Ten minutes to say your goodbyes.'

'Right.'

'Then I'm coming back in.'

'Great.'

'And these two will be outside.' He took out his mobile phone and waggled it in front of his ear to show Reuben what he would be doing. 'I've got to make some calls. Some important calls. Don't do anything daft.' DI Baker motioned his head in the direction of the static coppers, who were staring evenly at Reuben. Then he turned on his black heels and walked back out of the windowless ante room, a police

428

radio crackling away, echoing into the corridor.

Reuben saw that Aaron was awake. He checked on Joshua, who was still under, his heart-rate steady, his features beautiful and calm.

'You heard all that?' he asked.

Aaron nodded. 'Unfortunately. Looks like you're fucked.'

Reuben didn't answer. He pulled out the pheno-fit again and scrutinized it. Ten minutes and it was all over. Abner would have him questioned, charged, sent back to Pentonville, or on to Wormwood Scrubs, the place he had been heading to anyway. In prison, possibly for a few years. Perverting the course of justice. Precipitating the deaths of two public figures. Sports-mad tabloids screaming for blood.

For a second, he saw himself and Aaron as twenty-five-year-olds, dressed in identical black suits, at their father's funeral, standing in front of the freshly dug grave, an intense rain with fat, penetrating droplets cascading over the few mourners. Between them, their mother sobbing quietly. Reuben wrapping an arm around his mother, accidentally touching Aaron's hand as he did so, and recoiling. He stared at his brother now. The brother whose bone marrow was inside his son, helping him live.

Reuben checked his watch and returned to the pheno-fit, bending it back and forth. As he did so, the face became convex and concave, wide and narrow, fat and thin. Reuben stopped. He held it in the convex position and scanned its features again. An image was starting to crystallize, an idea, a series of interlinked events. Gathering speed, falling into place, times and places and actions. He stood up excitedly and paced the floor, checking it through, making sure it fitted, examining and re-examining the picture. Whispering 'Fuck' under his breath over and over. The murders, the rapes, the lack of DNA evidence until now . . . It wasn't that Abner or someone inside GeneCrime had been subverting the Thames Rapist investigation. No, the truth was much closer to home.

'What is it?' Aaron asked, propping himself up.

Reuben stopped in front of Aaron's bed.

'Brother, I need one final favour from you. And it'll be just like the old days.' He glanced over at a pair of scissors on a tray of bandages and syringes. 'But it has to be now.'

22

A silver Range Rover idles. The alleyway is narrow and blocked at one end. Ahead, a small sign reads 'Private Property of the Forensic Science Service'. Dual exhaust gases slink low to the ground, the sweet, heady pinch of petrol thick in the air. Two men in the front seats shake hands and make muffled assurances.

A figure approaches quickly and from behind, close to one wall, ducking low, under the side mirrors. He waits a couple of moments, inhaling the fumes, listening to their quiet words. The fumes make him slightly giddy, a light-headedness he doesn't like. He stands up quickly, jacket sliding against the polished metal of the over-sized vehicle. He pushes a gun through the window and smiles briefly at each man in turn. Then he fires two silenced head-shots. The noises are quick and muted, but there is still a small echo through the dead-end alley. Both bullets enter through the men's foreheads, almost dead centre. Their mouths remain open in surprise.

He grips the pistol hard in his right hand. Waiting. Ready to shoot again. He sights down the slim barrel with its wider silencer. A couple of rasping breaths, small choking noises, and then nothing. Standing and looking, he replays the last few moments. The heads turning, the eyes widening, the jaws slackening. And then afterwards, a pause of nothingness. Fine sprays of red catching the light. Small bits of blood and bone and brain appearing on the cream leather. One of the rear windows shattering. Two heads slumping, neck control gone, final gagging breaths, life over. Pitching forward towards the dash, seatbelts tensing and catching them. A slow-motion crash.

He smiles and reaches a bandaged hand into the car. He flicks open the glove box. A folded copy of the *Bargain Pages*, a pistol and a padded envelope. He leaves the weapon and takes the package. Peering inside, he smiles again. Then he glances left, up towards the road, forty metres away. A couple of cars pass, a woman hurries by with shopping. The noise of the silenced shots play themselves again in his brain. One. Two. Not like in the films. Louder and duller, less whistle. But pleasing anyway.

He looks back inside the Range Rover, double-checking. The key in the ignition, the engine purring away. Everything else is still. No twitching, no writhing, no futile, desperate spasms of life. Just nine-millimetre pieces of metal ricocheting around inside skulls, fragment-ing and tearing, setting up shockwaves, ripping through, hot and excitable. One piece of metal obviously escaping the cranium, continuing on its way to crack the back window. Thick cherry blood starting to appear, running over an earlobe, dripping on to a shoulder.

He pulls his head back out and checks the road again. He tucks the padded envelope inside his jacket. His mobile is in his trouser pocket and he thinks about making the call. The one person he had never expected to contact him. The man who gave him this job. The man who had helped him do what otherwise would have been almost impossible. He changes his mind. He will ring in a few minutes, when he is clear, out of the vicinity and away from the bodies.

He scrapes his way back along the wall, slow and unhurried, just another person in the capital going about his business. The pistol is still in his right hand. He savours the warmth of the barrel through his gloves, unscrewing the silencer slowly and carefully, wincing as he does so. He slots each piece into separate pockets of his jacket as he nears the end of the alleyway. The pavements are half full, the road a mess of bikes, cars and buses. He turns right and allows himself to be swamped by office workers and shoppers.

There are now just two more cunts to deal with. A couple of minders. Valdek and Nathan, scum who protect Kieran Hobbs. And then all ends will have been tied. No trace back to him, no vested interests to make him vulnerable. He heads for his car, ready to sort the final duo out.

In the alleyway, the five-litre petrol engine continues to idle as Commander Robert Abner and Kieran Hobbs bleed into the luxurious interior of the Range Rover.

23

The old fish-gutting factory. A dampness that
reminded him of the days he spent locked up in
the woods. The kind of building that wore its
history on its walls like tattoos. Faded patches
where signs had once hung, unfilled holes where
shelving had been attached, speckled stains
where innards had clung stubbornly to the
interior. The sluicing channels in the floor, the
drains every five paces, the large metal tables
with their gleaming plumbing and elongated taps
still intact. It was unnervingly similar to the
GeneCrime morgue, all designed to get unwanted
flesh and unneeded fluids out of sight as quickly
as possible. He wondered where the drains led.
At GeneCrime, there were strict rules on blood
and tissue disposal. But here they could go anywhere, even direct into the Thames. Reuben pictured
Ethan de Groot, leaking into gullies, flowing along
pipes, dripping into the river.

He made his way across the floor, his shoes
echoing against the concrete, wanting to
announce his arrival. Kieran might well be in the
building and Reuben had no intention of
creeping up on him. That could give out the
wrong signals entirely. But he had no way of
knowing for sure where Kieran was. Or if Kieran
was still alive. He hadn't answered his phone,
but that wasn't unusual.

Reuben recalled him leaving the lab, the smirk

of it's-only-business across his face, a thick wad of fifties in his pocket. He was nervous. This went beyond money. This was serious. He saw the recent terror in Judith's features, her pale nervousness, the hangover of being attacked and nearly killed. Across the capital, women in fear, a psycho on the loose. In his pocket, the pheno-fit, its picture suddenly crystallizing in the hospital ante room, the implications still buzzing away at him. And then, for a second he allowed a pleasant memory in, almost laughing under his breath. Swapping clothes with Aaron, trimming his brother's hair, Aaron being taken away by Charlie Baker's henchmen while Reuben lay on his hospital bed next to Joshua. Waiting and then leaving, relishing the change of identities as they had done a thousand times as adolescents.

Halfway across, and a door in the wall opened slowly. It was a room originally used, Reuben guessed, for cold storage. He stopped, surprise blowing the reminiscence away, suddenly awkward and on edge. This wasn't in the game plan. Valdek Kosonovski striding over to him, iron bar in his hand, flushed and angry.

'What the fuck do you want?' he growled.

Reuben took in the dark matted hair, the large rounded forehead, the threat of violence that emanated from his wide-shouldered bulk.

'Kieran,' he answered.

'We don't deal with you any more.'

'No?'

'So fuck off.'

435

'Where's your boss?'

'Out somewhere.' The eyes blazing, the mouth tight. 'Business.'

'Whereabouts?'

'Like I said, business.'

'Because he came to my lab and then went off with Commander Abner.'

'So?'

Reuben knew he was pushing it, but kept going regardless. 'So, did he say where he was heading?'

'He rang a while back. Said you might come sniffing around. Had a few things to take care of.'

'How long ago?'

'A piece of advice round here.' Valdek held the iron bar horizontally with his left hand, tapping it into the palm of his right, emphasizing his strength, his superiority, his command of the situation. 'Don't ask me any more questions. Turn round, forget all about it and fuck off.'

Reuben's phone rang. He ignored it.

'OK. But before I go, one final one. When did you see your boss last?'

Valdek blew air out of the corner of his mouth, just about keeping his cool. 'He dropped Nathan and me, and then went to do what he had to do.'

Reuben decided to change tack. 'Doesn't really matter. It wasn't just Kieran I came to see.'

Despite himself, Valdek said, 'No?'

The phone burst into life again, and Reuben fumbled for the 'Decline' button.

'No. After him, I wanted to talk to you.'

'What about?'

Judith's words echoed in his head. A big man. Strong enough to lift her clean off her moped. Holding her down and crushing her with his weight. And then the Path reports Sarah had shown him from Tamasine Ashcroft, from Kimberly Horwitz, from Joanne Harringdon. Broken ribs, collapsed windpipes, deep tissue bruising.

'About the rape and murder of several young women.'

'I don't know what you mean.'

Reuben frowned at the large man in front of him, realizing that if it came down to it, Valdek would tear him apart, or turn him to pulp, like Ethan de Groot. That is, if it wasn't for Reuben's hidden weapon. Ten minutes in the laboratory on his way over, and he had rounded up what he needed.

'I think you do.'

Valdek Kosonovski scanned the factory floor, checked the two entrances and flicked his eyes from the iron bar to Reuben and back again.

'Let's say I do,' he snarled. 'What are you going to do about it?'

For a third time, intrusive as hell, vibrating with urgency, Reuben's phone interrupted him. Cursing, he pulled it out and checked the incoming number. Staring evenly at Valdek, he said, 'We'll get to that. But first I've got to answer this.' Reuben pressed the button, cleared his throat and asked, 'You finally got what they owed you?'

'Some of it.'

'And Abner?'

437

'Finished.'

Reuben turned partially away from Valdek and lowered his voice. 'Hobbs?'

'Finished.'

'Finished?'

'As in brains rearranged.'

Reuben let this information sink in. It was queasy news, the stuff that made you question your motives and wonder whether there could have been another way, while at the same time exciting. His stomach surged and fell in waves.

'So what now?'

'You get your tattoo removed, copper, and I get another one done.'

Reuben nodded, despite being on the phone. He hoped to fuck that Valdek wasn't understanding this. As a confirmed weight-lifter and user of steroids, Reuben thought his chances were good. But if he twigged, picked through the implications and realized what Reuben's role had been, Reuben was fucked.

'Fine,' he muttered.

'And if I ever see you again, I'll rearrange your brains as well. From now on, stay the fuck away from me.'

'I'll see what I can do.'

There was a noise behind him. Footsteps, a double echo in his ear. Reuben span round. A man making his way in through the factory door. Tall and lean, walking quick, head bent forwards. One hand bandaged, slotting his mobile into his leather jacket, taking out a pistol.

Michael Brawn.

'You don't seem to be trying very hard,' he said to Reuben.

Valdek lowered the iron bar and took a few steps back. Brawn stopped five paces in front of him, sneering.

'Valdek Kosonovski,' he said with a smile. 'I've heard a lot about you.'

24

Reuben senses the pounding of his heart. It is so strong he can almost hear it. Two psychos, two men with a confirmed taste for killing. Both armed. In Reuben's pocket, the only thing that can help him. But against a pistol or an iron bar . . . He watches Valdek closely. No glimmer of recognition as he stares back at Brawn. Reuben surmises that Valdek doesn't know who is standing in front of him waving a gun about, or that this man has just killed his employer.

As Brawn takes a cigarette out and lights it, slowly and calmly, revelling in the moment, Reuben wonders how he has found the factory, and whether he has been here before. It is possible, but from what Kieran Hobbs said, Brawn was not someone he had associated with. And then, as Brawn blows a long stream of smoke out of the corner of his mouth, a more pressing question comes to him.

Why is he here?

'How did you know?' Brawn asks.

'What?' Reuben says.

'That I was still alive.'

'Just a hunch. No blood residue anywhere in the lab, no stains anywhere, the bulky jacket you were wearing at the time. And then, of course, the fact that you answered your mobile.'

'I was sincerely hoping never to set eyes on you again. But now we find ourselves in the same

440

place at the same time, well, that changes things.' Brawn gestures with his gun. First Reuben, then Valdek. 'Walk backwards,' he says. 'Both of you.'

Reuben glances over his shoulder, stepping back, short paces. In his jeans pocket, he still carries the folded yellow Post-It note. Brawn's address, phone number and likely haunts, copied from his arrest file. Getting hold of him had been straightforward. Guessing he was still alive and unleashing him was the easy bit. Standing in front of him again now, backing up and staring into the short, brutal nose of his gun, is another matter. Reuben rewinds to his cell in Pentonville, the merciless blows, Brawn waiting for him to get up before knocking him down again, the jarring of teeth and the tearing of skin, the knife ripping into his tattoo, the utter control, the purest sadism widening his eyes and making him grin.

Reuben sees that Brawn is backing them into an enclosed section of the factory. Two large countersunk tables section off an area the size of a small dining room. Reuben retreats as far as he can, his back touching the clammy wall. Valdek stays in front of him, standing closer to Brawn, still holding his weapon.

'Before we start,' Brawn says, 'there's something you need to know.' He turns to Valdek, the gun pointing at Reuben. 'Kieran Hobbs is dead. Killed him myself a couple of hours ago.'

Valdek stares blankly back at him.

'He had some money a copper called Abner owed me. And Abner had tried to end me with a bullet to the guts. So, like I say, Hobbs and

Abner are both finished.' Brawn takes a long, deep drag. 'Business, that's all, Valdek. Just so you don't hear it from someone else first.'

Valdek holds his gaze, unmoved by the news. And then, after a few more seconds, he says, 'Appreciate that.'

Brawn returns to Reuben. 'So, here we are.' He spits on the floor, taking a couple of paces forward. 'No guards, no rules, no nothing. Just you and me and some unfinished business.'

Reuben takes in the wide eyes, scanning around. They are cold and glassy, a distance to them. That is, until they turn on you. Then they suck at your features and rip at your composure, dazzling you till you squint, reading you as you squirm. Reuben again detects the unorthodoxy which slices clean through the normal rules of engagement. He battles flashbacks from Pentonville. Brawn is peeling back the bandage of his left hand, blood seeping into the gauze, the white bones no longer visible.

'Got a mate to round the ends off. Fingers in a vice, electric saw, clean off. Took about ten seconds per bone. Any idea how that feels?'

Reuben gives a small shrug.

'Not fucking good. Think about it. The bone sticking out, being ground through by a power saw. Whining and screaming. The smell. The burning . . . ' Reuben notices a fine perspiration on Brawn's forehead, as if reliving it hurts as much as the event. 'Then casualty. Had these nice bandages put on. Bit easier to explain than some fucking scientist took the tops of my fingers off with liquid fucking helium.'

442

'Nitrogen,' Reuben mutters.

'You see my fingers?' he screams. 'They're fucked. And now it's your turn. I don't want this to be quick. A gun's no good for what I've got in mind. Valdek, pass me the iron bar.'

Valdek stands still, his muscular frame twitching.

'It's OK,' Brawn says, 'my problem's not with you. It's with this cunt.' He waves his gun at Reuben. 'We're on the same side here. I actually came to discuss some business with you and Kieran's other minder. Ex-minder now. Is Mr Bardsmore around?'

'Nathan's got a hospital appointment,' Valdek answers.

'Home address Colmore Garden Towers. Flat 113, isn't it?' he asks. 'I'll catch up with him later. But pass me the bar and you take the pistol. It's time to start the fun.'

Valdek sums him up for several long moments. He is taller and wider than Brawn, and as mean as they come.

'Gun first,' he says.

Brawn turns the weapon round and passes it to him. Reuben again pictures Valdek beating Ethan de Groot to death, repeated body blows with the iron bar, and is almost glad when Valdek hands it over in exchange.

'Right,' Brawn instructs. 'Keep that fucker on him. If you have to shoot, make it somewhere painful.'

Reuben watches them both, edgy and alert. The low ceiling of the factory presses down. He is fucked, and he knows it. Brawn winks at him.

'You see, if you really want to damage someone, a gun is useless. Doesn't hurt enough. And if you're wearing a Kevlar vest, just feels like a bad punch in the guts. Bruises, that's all, even when Abner shot me from point blank. Couple of cracked ribs at worst. But half an hour with an iron bar, that's different. There's no vest for iron bars. You just fucking take it, and your body falls apart. Ain't that right, Mr Kosonovski?'

Valdek nods, gun hand dipping with each movement of his head. Stupid, violent and very strong. A bad combination.

Reuben has one chance, but it won't be enough. His chemical weapon will only disable one of them. The SkinPunch gun in the right-hand pocket of his jacket. The tiny probe holding a minute amount of aqueous potassium cyanide. Enough to kill a man in seconds. But he will only have a single shot. Reuben hasn't banked on facing more than one maniac.

Michael Brawn raises the iron bar, running his eyes along its surface, enraptured for a second. Seeing the damage it will do, the bones it will crack, the flesh it will mash. 'Nice weight,' he says, almost to himself. 'And the edges . . . ' He turns to Valdek. 'The edges are what makes it.'

Valdek stares back, impassive.

Reuben hopes he will pass out before his limbs are crushed. He moves his hand into position, gripping the SkinPunch weapon in his pocket. And then Brawn spins round in an instant flowing move and crashes the bar into the side of Valdek's head. Valdek drops to the floor, poleaxed, out cold. Reuben struggles to pull out the SkinPunch. It snags as he rips at it, catching on the lining of his pocket. Brawn spinning back round. Reuben levelling the gun, aiming. One shot. Sighting along its thin aluminium body, the hammer cocked, the probe and its poison ready. Brawn lifting the bar, a glint of metal. Focusing on his face, his tight, pale, psychotic face. Pulling the trigger, feeling it click, the whizz of the probe through the air. A crashing, grinding explosion in his arm, bones cracking. The SkinPunch falling. Reuben dropping to the floor, breathless with agony. Trying to focus on Brawn's face, desperate to see where the probe hit. Reuben's arm a funny shape. Bent where it shouldn't be. Through his jacket, a throbbing, swelling bump urgently pushing to the surface. His right forearm, beneath the tattoo. Grinding his teeth, shock giving way to incredible bursts of pain. Vision narrowing. Looking up. Brawn lighting a fresh cigarette, his eyes on fire, reflecting the match. Calm and measured, seeming to stand taller. If the probe hit, he would be dying now. Choking and writhing, coughing his guts up. Reuben knows it must have missed.

He watches Brawn take the gun from Valdek and slowly load it with six rounds from his pocket. The smell is ground into the floor. No matter how many times it has been mopped. Death. Gutted fish and violent death. He wonders where the hell the SkinPunch probe ended up. Reuben looks at Brawn again and knows for certain it didn't hit him.

Brawn turns around and walks away, quick and purposeful. 'Got something in my car,' he

445

calls back over his shoulder. 'Meant for Valdek and Nathan, but you can have some too.'

Reuben stares at Valdek. He is motionless. Reuben wonders whether his skull is cracked. Thick redness is starting to pool under his hair. Reuben sits up, unable to stand for the time being. He senses instinctively that bones have breached skin. He is bleeding into his jacket, ulna and radius poking out. He grits his teeth. A wave of nauseous agony burns deep in his arm. He feels cold. The fracture is disabling, making his whole body feel shivery and useless. He knows this is just one blow with the iron bar. One heavy blow. For a second time he prays he will pass out rather than be beaten to a conscious death. And he wonders what the fuck Brawn has brought for Valdek and Nathan.

Reuben cannot see Brawn or hear him. He looks through the steel legs of the nearest table. He is nowhere to be seen. 'Valdek,' Reuben gasps. 'Valdek. For fuck's sake.' There is no answer. Valdek remains motionless, his breathing hard to detect. Reuben scours the floor around him for the probe. If he can find it and reload it, he has a chance. Blood drips out of the cuff of his denim jacket. It is running inside his sleeve. Crashing waves of sick torture, making him weak. He grabs at the table with his good arm and tries to pull himself up. He has to get out. Every movement is paralysing agony. He makes it to his feet, dizzy for a second. The table is thirty centimetres deep, almost like a sink. He grabs hold of its chrome plumbing and uses it to steady himself. Then he starts to walk.

As he reaches Valdek, there is a noise, a scraping sound, punctuated by grunts. He swivels his head. Michael Brawn lets go of the large metal cylinder he is dragging and takes his gun out.

'One more fucking step and I'll fuck your other arm.'

Reuben stops, rocking on his heels. He forces himself to focus, knowing he could go into shock. A bad fracture, losing blood, locked in a factory with a killer . . . it is more than possible.

He watches Brawn struggle to lift the cylinder on to the table. Brawn is gripping it with his right arm, his left there more for balance and support, wounded fingers kept well away from the lifting, but the gun kept pressed in the palm, safe and ready. Reuben guesses the barrel is forty or fifty litres, weighing roughly the same in kilos, and again appreciates Brawn's wiry strength. Sweating and manic, he positions it on a firm base under the taps. He appears energetic, excited, up, as if he is on drugs. A dangerous high. Reuben pictures Ian Cowley's charge sheet, the multiple convictions for wounding, and remembers Kieran's prophetic words in the back of his Range Rover. *Cowley just had something about him that told you not to mess, something that said this guy would fuck you over if it killed him doing it.*

Reuben peers at the cylinder. His first instinct is liquid nitrogen. But there is no way Brawn could have got access. It is a chemical of some sort, though, its markings removed, a round, silver barrel with an aperture in the top for pouring.

447

'Come here,' Brawn instructs, breathing hard. 'I want you to watch this.'

Reuben takes an unsteady pace forward, knowing that something very bad is about to happen, something worse than being beaten to death. Brawn pushes the gun against Reuben's broken arm, feeling along its length, finding the spot. Then he slams the butt of the pistol hard into the exposed bones.

'Next to the sink, just there,' he says. 'Let's run you a little bath.'

Reuben is almost paralysed with pain, his vision blurring for a second, fighting the urge to cry out. He smells the distinctive odour as Brawn carefully unscrews the top of the metal container. He watches him slot a large plug into the gutting table. Brawn tips the metal cylinder, right arm around it as if he is propping up a drunk, his injured hand still nursing the pistol. Reuben listens to the glug as the fluid spills out, thinking, I should lunge at him, this is the moment, right now. But he is unable to move, the gun telling him not to, his arm gushing out blood, its shattered bones grating against the denim of his sleeve.

The countersunk table begins to fill, five centimetres, ten centimetres, fifteen. Deep enough. And now Reuben is certain what it is. Fizzing, burning, scorching. Attacking anything in the gutting table it can get its acid teeth into. Snarling like a dog, hungry for flesh. Brawn tips it up, shaking out the dregs of the sulphuric acid, using his left hand as well, now that the weight has gone. He has done this before, Reuben realizes. Maybe not here, but somewhere. He wonders where Brawn has been able to get hold of the stuff, and comes up with the name Abner. Laboratory grade, highly concentrated, used for making buffers and solutions. But never without very careful dilution and protective wear.

Reuben's arm is cold, and he is trying not to shake, his body wanting to go into shock, Reuben refusing to let it.

'You fucker,' Brawn snarls, nodding his head. 'Stand fucking here.'

Reuben steps slowly forward. The gun or the acid? he asks himself. The gun will be quicker, but he knows what will happen. Brawn will shoot him somewhere disabling, a knee or an elbow, then throw him in anyway. The table is low, a metre off the ground. Reuben could easily step into it.

He scans the factory desperately, thinking, clutching, knowing he is about to die. With his last broken breaths, he sees Joshua, coming round from his operation, the chemotherapy commencing, and longs to be there. He pictures Judith, deep bruises in her neck, passing the pheno-fit of her attacker to Sarah Hirst. He sees CID and Forensics running the picture through their databases and drawing a blank. He imagines Charlie Baker realizing he has been duped, and that Aaron, with his freshly cut hair, is of no use to him. He sees frantic, pointless endeavour across the capital. GeneCrime, CID, Forensics, all missing the point. He flashes through years of laboratory work, of lessons and lectures, of academic progression. Formulae

449

chalked on blackboards. Scratchy white letters copied down into his school book. Basic chemistry, the beginning of his scientific journey. He grits his teeth, ready, still dizzy and numb with pain.

'Now, I shoot you first, in the bollocks. Then I take the tips of your fingers off. And when you're paying attention, I put you in.' Brawn bares his teeth, alive, on fire, a zealous excitement igniting his face. 'Or you just get in yourself. This can be easy or difficult. Your decision. But you've only got five seconds.'

Brawn steps closer to the table, ready.

'One.'

He nudges the empty cylinder out of the way with his leg.

'Two.'

He aims the gun at Reuben's groin.

'Three.'

His finger tightens on the trigger.

'Four.'

He sights along the barrel, one eye closed.

'Five.'

He pulls the trigger.

25

Reuben hears the word 'five' and dives forward, through the air, muscles launching him, bones grinding, reaching and lunging, his fist punching the flat paddle of the tap, knocking it fully open. A shot being fired, the echo in his head, Reuben crashing down and hitting the floor hard. Above him, the one reaction that should always be avoided — pouring water into a concentrated acid. Water continuing to gush out of the taps and into the volatile liquid. A pause, the reaction spreading and intensifying, unstable molecules unleashed and on the rampage. Sudden oxidation on a massive scale. A deep whooshing noise. A volcano of boiling acid tearing through the air. A sharp, stinging burn in his nostrils. A scream from Michael Brawn.

Reuben is lying on his shattered arm. He turns on to his back, grunting with pain. Brawn is grasping his face, still shrieking. He has the gun. He turns blindly and fires at the floor. The shot misses Reuben and ricochets off the second gutting table. Brawn is clawing at his eyes with one hand, the other waving his pistol around. Reuben drags himself under the table. Another bullet randomly fired, this time closer. He glimpses Brawn's face as he spins wildly round. It is red and blistered, patches of chemical burns. Reuben glances over at Valdek. He is starting to come round.

A stinging burn in his hair. A screaming man firing shots at the floor. It takes a minute, and then Valdek remembers. Michael Brawn.

Valdek's head is ringing and buzzing and bleeding. He feels into his hair and inspects his fingers. A lot of blood. He sees the iron bar lying on the floor and shudders. A weapon for psychos. Fine as a visual warning, but actually using one . . . He thinks of Nathan, the iron bar his favourite plaything, and shakes his aching head.

Valdek pulls himself slowly up, blurry and disorientated. He spots Maitland sheltering under a table. Fucking copper. Not to be trusted. And just because he isn't in the force any more is no reason to let up. All coppers are cunts, never to be helped in any way. But compared to Brawn . . .

Valdek is on his feet. He rolls his head, his thick neck clicking as he does so. The vision in one eye is blurred and his hearing is patchy. But he is OK. Good enough to take care of business. He walks slowly towards Maitland and Brawn. Brawn spins round but doesn't see him. He is swearing and spitting and screaming, deep red craters in his face, fingers rubbing his eyes. Valdek watches Brawn shout Maitland's name and fire another shot. This one is not far away, inches at best. The copper, to give him his due, doesn't flinch.

Valdek stares at the back of Brawn's head. He flexes his biceps and his lats, and tenses his abs.

452

He reaches slowly forward, grabs the left arm that Brawn is shielding his eyes with, pulls it back hard, and instantly snaps it to the right. Brawn doesn't have a chance. The movement is too quick, the shoulder having no strength in that position. Valdek pictures his sessions in the gym with Nathan, working on the shoulder groups, smaller weights used in awkward positions to build tone rather than mass. Brawn screams, louder this time, his arm going slack, dislocated at the shoulder. He twists round with the gun but Valdek catches his other arm. Brawn is strong, but he is no match for Valdek. Day after day in the weights room, legal and illegal supplements, years of bulking up and working out. For just such a moment.

Valdek performs a similar movement on the left. It is more difficult, Brawn now aware of what he is doing, the element of surprise gone. Up, back and out, rotating at the end. Ten seconds of struggle before Brawn is off balance, hurting from the first one, with no leverage or means of protection. He feels a satisfying pop through the sleeve of Brawn's jacket, the gun falling down, his arm hanging loose at the shoulder. Brawn is unable to rub his eyes. His coat hangs long, his arms closer to his torso, his hands lower down his body than normal, his shoulders baggy at the sides. Double dislocation. A move that has proved useful to Valdek over the years. No need to tear people to pieces. With both arms out of their sockets, very few men persist in lying to you.

Valdek strides over towards Maitland. He

453

looks pretty bad, a lot of blood, an arm almost at right angles to where it should be. Maitland grimaces up at him, and Valdek fights the urge to make eye contact. Kieran is dead, and the ex-copper is involved somehow. He wonders for a second what to do to him, whether to dislocate his undamaged arm, or whether to leave him alone. Cunts like that who come round asking questions deserve everything they get. And then the words from earlier eat into him, washing around his ringing skull. The rape and murder of young women in the capital.

Valdek ponders his options. Brawn is shouting and screaming, blindly pacing around, yelling Maitland's name, still desperate to destroy the fucker. Valdek walks up to him. He glances at the gutting table. It is boiling and alive, a whitish vapour hovering over it. Valdek guesses it is acid or something similarly nasty. Part of him wants to grab Brawn by the hair and push his face into the liquid, hearing it fizz, listening to him drowning and choking. Instead, he pulls his fist back and punches Brawn clean in the face, watching him fall to the floor, no arms to stop him, crashing into the concrete with a thud, the screaming instantly over.

He glances down at Maitland again, fighting old loyalties and ingrained suspicions. With Kieran dead, Valdek realizes the rules have just changed. He could stamp on the copper's head, throw him into the bath, see what it did to him. But something tugs at Valdek, something strong and new. Maitland is pulling himself up, surveying Brawn's unconscious form, picking up a small aluminium object shaped like a gun and slotting it into his pocket. He straightens to face him, eyeball to eyeball. The ex-copper looking at him, emotionless and calm. This time, Valdek returns the gaze.

'That address,' Valdek says quietly. 'You remember it?'

Maitland nods. He taps the side of his head with his good hand. 'Up here,' he answers. 'You got a phone?'

'Don't push it,' Valdek answers.

He watches Maitland struggle to get his mobile out of his pocket and make a call, listens to his short description of events, clenches and unclenches his fists, telling himself he is doing the right thing.

When Maitland has finished, Valdek says, 'He won't be there for a while.'

'It's OK. They'll pick him up when he gets back.'

'What about that fucker?' He kicks his leg towards Brawn.

'They're on their way. A couple of ambulances as well. Get that head sorted.' Maitland scowls, supporting his broken arm. 'So, what made you suspect?'

Valdek is quiet. The left side of his vision is closing in around the edges. Fucking coppers. Can't help themselves but ask questions. He chews his teeth, angry, but not knowing what else to do but spit it out. If the copper wants the truth, that's what he's going to get, like it or not.

'It's all been about you, helping Kieran. Giving him ideas, learning the ropes. Without you, he'd have been caught a long time ago.'

'How do you mean?'

'He sees your gloves, your shoe covers, what you look for on a body and where you check. He watches you, talks to you . . . I reckon he learned how not to get caught from you.'

Maitland stares at Valdek, almost sad, as if he already suspects this. 'But what did he actually do that made you think — ' He winces in pain. 'I mean, you beat Ethan de Groot to death.'

'Nathan, not me. Always had a bit of a temper. Kieran called me to come in and clean up. He went crazy at him before you got there. Sent him out to cool off, get his act together.'

Valdek falls silent. The factory as he had seen it that day less than three weeks ago. The Dutchman lying ruined on the floor, Nathan gripping the bar tight, red with someone else's blood, Kieran asking Valdek to tidy up. Nathan. His weights partner and buddy for six years. Calm, popular, well liked. But getting stranger and more erratic. Flying off the handle, pounding fuckers to death, Valdek having to come in and mop up the pieces, dispose of the bodies. Talking about night-time black-outs. The things he let slip, seeing the way he was around women, the interest he took in the Thames Rapist story, the nights he went missing.

'You know, a lot of gym guys do stacking, but Nathan's been taking it even further. Oral and injections. He's been obsessed. And there are side-effects. I don't need to spell it out.'

Maitland nodded. 'Increased desire, decreased performance.' He made eye contact to force his

456

point across. 'And sexual aggressiveness.'

Valdek heard the sirens coming. He was dizzy on his feet, a lot of blood loss, aware that he was rambling slightly, his thoughts coming and going in snatches, but letting it out anyway.

'And see, Nathan's missus, I've only met her a couple of times, she's a bit of a one. Big girl, if you know what I mean. Not averse to giving Nathan a tongue lashing, putting him in his place. I just — '

Valdek stops. Something tells him that he has said enough. The far door opens. There is a sense of relief, of things coming to a head, of difficult decisions being broached, of a bottled suspicion finally out in the open. He glances back at Maitland. Less cuntish than most police, but still . . .

'Look, nothing personal,' he says. 'I just fucking hate coppers.'

A female officer approaches. She is pretty, dressed in jeans and a tight jumper. She ignores him and goes straight to Maitland. Valdek is unsteady on his feet again. He knows he needs treatment. The back of an ambulance, some stitches, maybe a couple of units of blood. He thinks again of Nathan and Kieran. One about to be put away, the other dead. Valdek stumbles towards a medic who is running into the factory, and wonders where the hell his life goes from here.

26

Three hours in casualty, in the sister hospital to the one Joshua was in. At least there had been gas and air. So much, in fact, that he had almost begun to hallucinate, his voice coming out in a deep echo, the pain not so much eradicated as floating away somewhere just out of reach. But Sarah had sat with him the whole time, sometimes quiet, other times pressing him for information. And then the phone call had come through, Nathan Bardsmore returning home, and Sarah had left in a hurry. there had been an anxious look in her eye as she walked away, glancing back over her shoulder. As Reuben waited for someone to examine his X-ray, he had allowed himself to imagine that the concern was for him.

Later, after the bones had been set under general anaesthetic, Sarah had returned. A small part of Reuben enjoyed the quiet, coming round from the operation, lying in a pastel-coloured room, surrounded not by gangsters, minders or policemen but by slowly convalescing people leafing through magazines and waiting for relatives. Reuben had been told he could leave when he felt up to it, the plaster on his arm shielding the damage beneath, but he was in no hurry. For the first time in as long as he could remember, everyone around ignored him, wanted nothing from him. The anonymous health service. There was no substitute.

Judith had come then, quickly followed by Moray. They felt like his family, the closest thing he had, aside from Aaron and Joshua. Judith was quiet and reticent, Moray talking too loudly, asking about the food, wondering if Reuben wanted a bottle of something smuggling in. And then Judith finally said it, softly and without fanfare.

'I'm pregnant. Five or six weeks, early days. If it's a boy we're going to call it . . . '

She stared down at Reuben's face.

'What?' he asked.

'Anything but Reuben. We want him to have a quiet life.'

The old Judith was breaking through, and Reuben sensed that given time she would recover from the attack.

'Are you sleeping any better?'

'A little. In a funny way it's a comfort knowing it wasn't just a random attack. Nathan knew I had a swab and was going to DNA-test him for exclusion, because of the photo of Kieran Hobbs they found on Ethan de Groot.'

'And then he panicked that you might make a connection to the case?'

'A psycho is a psycho. But that's my best guess at why he chose me to . . . ' Judith smiled sadly. 'Well, you know.'

Reuben held her hand for a moment. 'I know,' he said.

When Sarah arrived again, she was grinning, a warm, toothy smile that normally spelled danger. Now, however, Reuben didn't care. He was officially an invalid for the time being, and no good to anyone.

'Charlie's fuming,' she said as she perched herself on the bed. 'You should see him. The oldest trick in the book, and he fell for it. I mean, did he not think, I'm about to arrest a man whose twin brother is in the same room, I should be slightly careful?'

Reuben allowed himself a grunt of laughter. 'Good old Aaron. Quickest haircut he's ever had. And without him — '

'You'd be fucked. Wormwood Scrubs and no way out. Disappearing for a long time.'

'But what is it with Charlie?'

'You should try working with him.'

'I mean, do you think Charlie and Abner were in collusion?'

Sarah put her index finger to her lips and shushed him. 'I don't think anything.' She glanced in the direction of the bedside cabinet. 'No one send you a card? Flowers? Nothing? For helping me catch the Thames Rapist?'

'Mail me an invite to your promotion,' he muttered.

'I'll see what I can do.'

Reuben sat up.

'So, how did it pan out?'

'Fairly routine, in the end. We spent a couple of hours staking out his flat, waited for him to finally turn up and go in, then we were straight through the door. Heavy back-up, you know, some of the larger boys from CID, and a lot of them. I was expecting a fight, and he's a big man.'

'And there wasn't?'

'Not at the beginning. He just stood there, staring at us, grinding his teeth. We got him cuffed and out. Ankle restraints as well, just in case. Then I heard he kicked off in the van, went mental and butted a couple of the arresting officers, put them both in hospital. But with his limbs tied, even a man like Nathan Bardsmore is up against it in a van full of coppers.'

Reuben tried to picture the scene. Nathan raging, unstable and erratic, twenty stone of muscle fighting right to the end.

Sarah waggled her mobile phone, sweeping a strand of blonde hair from her eyes. 'You know, I've had some interesting calls today.'

'Oh yeah?'

'I wondered if you could help me sort a few things out.' The coldness was back, the smile gone, almost as if it had never existed. 'Abner's dead. Hobbs is dead. Probably, Michael Brawn got shot by Abner but was wearing a bullet-proof vest. Right so far?'

Reuben shrugged, patting his pillows and propping himself up in bed. Really, he should be out and about, but he was enjoying the rest too much.

'Which means you've got a lot of explaining to do.'

'If you've got the time, I've got the explanations,' he replied.

'I'm all ears.'

Reuben scratched at his stubble and sighed. 'Abner made sure I was fired over the Shaun Graves case by leaking the details to the press.

461

Then, when he was supposed to be fixing GeneCrime, he used his position to get Michael Brawn inserted into Pentonville, to erase the only witnesses to his past.' Reuben slid open a bedside drawer and pulled out the pheno-fit and the folded yellow Post-It note. 'Using the DNA from Judith's attack I performed predictive phenotyping on the Thames Rapist. Only the pheno-fit wasn't immediately apparent. Bits of it were. When I bent it, though, it suddenly began to click. Widening of the face. Altered musculature. Years of steroid abuse. Classic coarsening of the features. And then I began to think. What does excess testosterone do?'

'Make you drive like an idiot?'

'I'm being serious.'

'So am I.'

'Come on, basic biology. Reproduction 101. Negative feedback. It switches off your sex hormones FSH and LH. Stops testicular function. Makes you impotent. The great irony of becoming more masculine is you actually head the opposite way.'

'Sex after death?'

'That's what I began to think. All that desire, but a profound lack of performance.'

'We just interviewed Nathan Bardsmore's wife. They've been having what she will only describe as marital problems.'

'So he's impotent, can't perform, his wife doesn't understand, maybe mocks him. He's stacking steroids, oral and injections, brain all over the place — '

'But why each victim? Joanne Harringdon, for

462

example, or Judith?'

'Judith had recently swabbed Nathan for exclusion. Long story, probably not for the ears of a DCI. But he must have guessed there was a chance that Judith could have run his sample through the national database. As for the GP, presumably he had some medical contact with her at some stage . . . The others are down to you guys to clear up now.' Large gaping holes had been ripped in families that would never heal, daughters or mothers or sisters destroyed and violated.

'Believe me, we're working on it.'

Reuben fingered the Post-It note. 'Anyway, I had Michael Brawn's phone number and last known address from his police record.'

'Ian Cowley's?'

'Whichever. Realized he might not actually be dead. Judith and Moray had found no evidence of a body and when I looked closely I couldn't see any blood residue at all in the lab. Tried his number, and guess what? The evil fucker answered.' Reuben frowned, biting his lip. He wasn't proud of what he had done. It had been impulsive, the kind of fighting you do when your back is against the wall, and when all other options are gone. 'I saw a way of straightening things out. For him, for me, for everyone. And then I was going to hand his details over to you guys so you could arrest him. Only things didn't quite work out that way. And when this all shakes out, you didn't get any of this from me, OK?'

Sarah's face hardened, taking it all in but

463

struggling to understand exactly what Reuben had done.

'Look, how did you do all this?' she asked. 'We're still trying to work out where everything fits. Dead gangsters, police commanders, acid baths, psychos with dislocated arms. What exactly was your role?'

'Maybe I should call my brief.'

'You wouldn't be concealing something, would you?'

'That depends.' Reuben sighed, and scratched a fingernail along the blue surface of his lightweight cast, vainly attempting to address the underlying itch. 'Look, Sarah, you're either on my side or you're not. You either arrest me or you don't. Let's say we stop beating around the bush we've beaten around all these years.'

Sarah ran a finger along the delicate curve of her eyebrow.

'Are you propositioning a senior Metropolitan officer?' she asked.

'Are you with me or against me?'

'Let's say I'm with you. Then what?'

'My son is alive. Everything else is just icing.'

Sarah stared long and hard into Reuben's face.

'And me?'

Reuben took it all in. The light blue irises with the deep blue borders. The pale face with colour leaking into its cheeks. The pink unpainted lips, pouting slightly, a hint of concern. Sarah Hirst, feelings emerging from hibernation, revealing themselves just for a second, maybe about to run away and hide again for ever. Years of building to this one single moment, a short question, two small words saying more than a decade of working together ever had.

'Maybe,' he said, slow and unhurried, revelling in the moment, 'you could be the candles.'

'You know, I might just have you arrested after all,' she smiled. 'Prison seems to have done you some good.'

Reuben closed his eyes. In a while, when he had the strength, he would walk out of the ward in his stockinged feet, through the hallway, up the stairs, along a link corridor, across an internal walkway which traversed a road outside, through another passageway, into a lobby, past the reception area and into the heart of the other hospital. He would smile at his ex-wife, raise his eyebrows at Shaun Graves, bend down and hold his son, his own flesh, blood and DNA.

We do hope that you have enjoyed reading this large print book.

Did you know that all of our titles are available for purchase?

We publish a wide range of high quality large print books including:
Romances, Mysteries, Classics
General Fiction
Non Fiction and Westerns

Special interest titles available in large print are:
The Little Oxford Dictionary
Music Book
Song Book
Hymn Book
Service Book

Also available from us courtesy of Oxford University Press:
Young Readers' Dictionary
(large print edition)
Young Readers' Thesaurus
(large print edition)

For further information or a free brochure, please contact us at:
Ulverscroft Large Print Books Ltd.,
The Green, Bradgate Road, Anstey,
Leicester, LE7 7FU, England.
Tel: (00 44) 0116 236 4325
Fax: (00 44) 0116 234 0205

Other titles published by
The House of Ulverscroft:

CRY FOR HELP

Steve Mosby

Dave Lewis is a man with a history. Haunted by his brother's murder when they were children, and drowning his sorrows over his lost love, Tori, he tries to leave the past behind. Dave had made a promise to Tori, which got him into trouble before, but he won't let that happen again. Detective Sam Currie is a man with a past. A shadow of grief lies over his marriage and his career. He's directed his hatred towards the man he sees as responsible, but he has other priorities right now. A killer is stalking the city, abducting girls and sending texts and emails to their families before he kills them. When Dave Lewis appears to connect both investigations, it's an opportunity Currie can't resist . . .

RITUAL

Mo Hayder

Nine feet under water, police diver Flea
Marley closes her gloved fingers around a
human hand. Disturbingly, there is no body
attached. Even more disturbing is the
discovery, a day later, of the matching hand
. . . Seconded to the Major Crime Investigation Unit in Bristol, is DI Jack Caffery. He is
looking for a man recently released from
prison, who sleeps rough and walks the
country roads as he relives the memories of a
terrifying crime. Caffery and Flea soon
establish that the hands belong to a boy who
has recently disappeared. Their investigation
leads them into the darkest recesses of
Bristol's underworld, where drug addiction is
rife, and where an ancient evil lurks: an evil
that feeds off the blood — and flesh — of
others . . .

WHITE NIGHTS

Ann Cleeves

Midsummer in Shetland, the time of year when the birds sing at midnight and the sun never sets . . . When an unknown Englishman turns up in tears at an art exhibition hosted by Bella Sinclair at the remote Herring House gallery and claims not to know why he is there or even his own identity, the evening ends in farce and confusion. The next day he is found dead, hanging from a rafter in a boathouse, a sinister clown mask on his face. When a local musician is also found murdered, Detective Jimmy Perez becomes convinced that the killer is local. But are his personal relationships clouding his judgement? Or is it just this unsettling time of year, the time of the white nights?

COLD IN HAND

John Harvey

Valentine's day. A dispute between rival gangs results in one teenage girl left dead, another injured, and a police officer caught in the crossfire. Detective Inspector Charlie Resnick is recalled to the front line. But the dead girl's father seeks to lay the blame on DI Lynn Kellogg, his colleague and partner, and for Resnick the line between personal and professional is dangerously blurred. Meanwhile, a murder case in which Kellogg is the chief investigating officer has stalled. A witness is threatened, and another is missing. But then SOCA — the Serious and Organised Crime Agency — becomes involved, suspecting links to international gunrunning and people trafficking. Lynn Kellogg is drawn into a web of deceit and betrayal that puts both her and Resnick in mortal danger . . .

THE PRICE OF DARKNESS

Graham Hurley

DC Paul Winter is working undercover to infiltrate the inner circle of the city's premier drug baron, Bazza Mackenzie. Adrift in a brutal world of hard-won respect and easy money, Winter appears to be in his element. Worryingly so . . . But headquarters' concerns about Winter become supplanted by two high profile Portsmouth murders: a visiting property developer is shot dead with clinical efficiency, and a government minister visiting the city is assassinated by two helmeted motorcyclists. DI Faraday, Winter's erstwhile boss, is involved in both enquiries and finds that there is evidence which implicates the beleaguered Paul Winter. The relationship between the two men has never been easy, but now the time has come to bury their differences . . .

CITY OF FIRE

Robert Ellis

A businessman arrives home to find his wife in bed, carved from belly to throat with a sharp knife . . . Detective Lena Gamble, from the Robbery-Homicide Division of the LAPD, prepares for her first major case with her new department. The murder is one of a series of brutal crimes against women, and the killer is dubbed 'Romeo' by the Hollywood media. Lena is wary of the public eye after her experience with it on the night of her rock-star brother's unsolved murder five years ago. And now she risks a far more dangerous fame as a cloud of conspiracy descends on her investigation and she edges into Romeo's deadly line of sight. Lena must catch this psychopath before she becomes his next glamorous victim . . .